CINDERELLA AND THE SURGEON

SCARLET WILSON

MIRACLE BABY FOR THE MIDWIFE

TINA BECKETT

MILLS & BOON

First Published in Great Britain 2020
by Mills & Boon, an imprint of HarperCollins*Publishers*
1 London Bridge Street, London, SE1 9GF

Cinderella and the Surgeon © 2020 by Scarlet Wilson

Miracle Baby for the Midwife © 2020 by Tina Beckett

ISBN: 978-0-263-27959-7

MIX
Paper from
responsible sources
FSC® C007454

Printed and bound in Spain
by CPI, Barcelona

CINDERELLA AND THE SURGEON

SCARLET WILSON

MILLS & BOON

This book is dedicated to my lifelong friend Julie Clark.
When she reads it, she will understand why!

And to my fabulous editor Carly Byrne, for giving me
a helping hand when I needed it most.

CHAPTER ONE

ESTHER MCDONALD RUBBED her eyes for the twentieth time as she made her way to work. She'd hoped the walk along the footpath next to the Thames would have woken her up a little, but it clearly wasn't working.

She'd pulled an extra shift last night working until midnight at another hospital in London. Anything to help pull in some extra cash. She already planned to text the agency again today to see if they had anything else for her.

It wasn't that her own job wasn't well paid. It was and she loved working in the neonatal ICU at the Queen Victoria. But right now she needed every penny she could get. So that meant working every shift available.

She was lucky. Because she was dual-trained she could work as a nurse or a midwife, which meant she had multiple opportunities for extra shifts. Usually she could pick up shifts at short notice for the A&E department in the Queen Victoria on her scheduled days off. But the duty manager had noticed how often she'd been working and had passed comment more than once. So, Esther had registered with an agency as well.

She filed through the main doors of the hospital along with a whole host of other staff heading for the early shift. She was worried about a tiny preemie she'd been looking after for the last few days in ICU. Billy, the twenty-four-weeker with a heart defect, had seemed even more fragile than normal yesterday afternoon when she'd left. His young mother hadn't left his side since he'd been born a few days earlier and was looking sicker and sicker herself. Esther just hoped the 'wonder' doc they'd all been talking about had finally managed to turn up to assess the little guy. Billy needed surgery that only a few neonatal cardiac surgeons could do. Trouble was, this guy had been over in France operating on another baby, so Billy had been left waiting.

She tugged her pale blue scrubs over her head and pulled her hair back into a ponytail, catching a quick glance of herself in the changing room mirror. Ugh. She looked awful. The quick sweep of make-up she'd stuck on her face this morning couldn't hide the dark circles under her eyes.

As she headed to the stairs her stomach grumbled loudly. She'd been so tired she hadn't had time to make breakfast this morning. She'd have to try and sweet-talk her colleagues into letting her take first break. One of the Queen Victoria's freshly baked scones would easily fill the huge gap in her stomach. She smiled at the thought of it.

'Morning,' she said in her best bright voice as she entered the NICU, stowing her bag and washing her hands. She got a little buzz every time she walked through the door. It was everything, the lighting, the sounds, the staff and patients—even the smell. She'd done her nurse training in Edinburgh and came down to London to also complete her midwifery training. Only a few specialist centres offered the shortened eighteen-month training these days and she'd been delighted to join the programme at the Queen Victoria, joining in with an already partly trained direct entry midwifery programme. She'd made some of the best friends she'd ever had—and even though some of them had gone to other parts of the world now, they were all still in touch.

The midwifery training had been a revelation for her. Esther had always imagined she'd end up as a community midwife, but from the first second she'd set foot in the NICU, she'd known that's where her heart lay. There was something about the vulnerability of these tiny babies. The role of often being their safe-guarder in the first few days of their lives. The little bits of progress she could see every day.

Of course, there could often be heartbreak. Her job was as much to take care of the families as it was to take care of the babies. But there was something so special about helping a preterm baby latch on to their mother for the first time. Or watching them become more aware of the world around them. Or seeing their reactions to lights or voices. Now she was here, she couldn't imagine working any place else.

One of the other midwives stood up and put her bag over her shoulder.

Esther glanced at the chart. 'How's Billy doing?' She checked the whiteboard, making sure she'd been assigned her favourite patient again today. Yip. Perfect. Billy, and a thirty-six-weeker in the next crib who'd been born to a diabetic mother in the early hours of the morning. That little one was likely just being monitored for a few hours to keep an eye on blood sugars.

Ruth, the other midwife, sighed. 'You look tired.'

'I am. Weird. Extra shifts never usually bother me.' Esther stretched out her back. 'You know how things are. Win the lottery and give me a share and I promise I won't work an extra shift again. Until then, I'll take all I can get.'

Ruth shot her a look and started the handover. 'Billy hasn't had a good night. His sats dropped, his feeding tube dislodged and X-ray haven't been able to get back up to ensure the new one is in the correct place. Hence, his feeds haven't started again.'

Esther shook her head. She knew exactly how important it was to ensure the nasogastric feeding tube had gone into the stomach and not a baby's lungs. No feeding could commence until it was confirmed.

'I'll call them again. If Callum's working I'm sure he can get someone up here now.'

Ruth smiled. 'Perfect. He always listens to you.'

She scanned the rest of the charts. 'Anything else?'

Ruth nodded. 'Billy's cardiac surgeon is supposed to arrive today. No idea when, but all his tests have been completed, so hopefully the surgeon will just be able to check them all, listen to his chest and schedule the surgery.'

Esther nodded. *Please let it be today.*

'By the way,' said Ruth as she handed Esther another chart. 'He's supposed to be a duke or something.'

Esther had already started scanning the other chart. The other baby was Laura, thirty-six weeks, born via emergency caesarean section to a Type 1 diabetic mother. Laura's blood sugar levels had been erratic for a few hours after delivery. That could happen with babies born to diabetic mothers, and it wasn't unusual for a baby to have close monitoring for just a few hours. Laura's levels had stabilised in the last hour, so Esther would just do a few more checks, then get her back to her mother's bedside.

She looked up and wrinkled her nose. 'What did you just say?'

Ruth laughed. 'I said the new surgeon. He's a prince or a duke or something.'

Esther shrugged. 'And what difference does that make? Is that why he's late? He's too busy with his—' she held up her fingers '—other duties.' She frowned as she picked up some nearby equipment. 'Better not be why he's keeping my baby waiting.'

Ruth shook her head as she picked up her bag to leave. 'Lighten up. Maybe this new guy is single.' Ruth sighed and gave Esther a look that made her want to run a million miles away. Pity. Esther hated that. She hated anyone feeling sorry for the poor little Scots girl. 'All I'm saying is that maybe there's more to life than work, that's all.' Ruth gave a shrug and walked over to the door. Then she turned back with a smile and wagged her finger at Esther. 'And make sure you're on your best behaviour. Don't have our new guest surgeon meeting Crabbie Rabbie instead of super midwife Esther.'

Esther looked around for something to throw but Ruth had ducked out the door too early. She shook her head as she walked over to do her checks on her babies and parents.

She'd earned the nickname within a few months of

getting here as a student midwife. Because she'd already been qualified as a nurse, she'd caught a few shifts in the wards while completing her midwifery course. Truth was, Esther was never at her best on night shift. That whole 'turn your life upside down for a few days' thing just messed with her body and brain and tended to make her a little cranky—or crabbit as they called it in Scotland.

She'd clashed with one of the junior doctors one night on the ward when he'd continually tried to re-site an IV on an elderly patient, rather than come and ask for help. Once she'd realised he'd had four attempts he hadn't fared well.

The whole ward had heard him getting a dressing-down, her Scottish accent getting thicker by the minute as she got angrier and angrier.

It had been 25 January. Robert Burns Day in Scotland—named after their national poet. This doctor had known that and had walked away muttering, 'Oh, calm down, Crabbie Rabbie,' much to her fury, and the rest of the staff's delight.

She'd never managed to shake it off—even though she mostly kept her temper in check these days.

One of the other staff on shift wandered over. 'Problems?'

She shook her head. 'All stable. I've chased up the x-ray for Billy, just waiting for them to appear. I'm going to take Laura back along to the maternity ward. Her blood sugars are fine and she's starting to grizzle. Must be due a feed.'

'Okay, do that, and then go for first break. You look as if you need it. I'll keep an eye on Billy.'

She laughed and put one hand on her hip. 'I must be looking bad if you're sending me on first break.'

'Go before I change my mind.'

Esther rechecked Billy's obs and chatted with his mum for a few minutes, making sure everything was meticulously recorded and phoning down to Callum again to chase up the x-ray. Then she gathered what she needed for Laura and threw her bag over her shoulder. Ten minutes later, Laura was back at her mother's bedside and happily feeding.

Esther stretched out her back as she headed to the canteen. It didn't normally bother her but today it was aching. Maybe all the extra shifts were taking a toll on her. The smell of freshly baked scones hit her as soon as she walked through the canteen doors. Two minutes later she had a large coffee and an even larger scone with butter and jam before her.

She glanced around the canteen. She couldn't spot Carly or Chloe, the friends that she normally sat with. There was a group of other nurses that she knew, but a seat in the far corner of the room was practically crying out her name. She was too tired to be sociable.

She moved quickly and slid into the seat before anyone else claimed it. Most of the seats were hard-backed and sat around the circular tables in the canteen. But there were a few, slightly more comfortable chairs a little further away—obviously left over from a ward refurb a few years ago.

The scone was gone in minutes and as she sipped her coffee she closed her eyes for just a moment. The door nearest her opened with a bang and a large crowd of people walked in, all talking and laughing at the tops of their voices.

She gritted her teeth. Just five minutes of peace. That's all she wanted. She shifted uncomfortably on the chair, pulling her scrub top from her skin. It seemed unusually warm in here.

The noise continued. Esther watched through half-shut eyes. There was a guy at the centre of it all. Handsome, in a TV doctor kind of way. Tall, broad-shouldered, with dark rumpled hair. The rest of the people around him seemed to be hanging on his every word, occasionally throwing in a word of their own as if they hoped to garner some approval. Maybe he *was* some kind of TV doc?

'This place is a hospital, not a blooming circus,' she muttered.

She checked the clock on the canteen wall. Five minutes. She had another five minutes left of break time. Esther usually never bothered with timings. Most days she grabbed some food, bolted it down and went straight back to the NICU. But she couldn't believe how tired she felt—it was unusual for her, she did extra shifts frequently and never felt like this—so, for once, she settled back into the chair. For once, she would take her full break.

'Esther, Esther!'

The voice came out of nowhere. Esther jerked awake. Liz, the admin assistant from NICU, was shaking her shoulder. 'Wake up.'

Esther sprang from her seat, knocking the still-full coffee cup that had been balanced on the edge of her chair, splashing coffee up the legs of her scrubs and sending Liz jumping backwards.

'Oh no,' she groaned. She gave herself a shake and glanced at the clock on the wall. She was more than fifteen minutes late.

Liz pulled a face. 'Abi told me to come and find you. The surgeon's arrived. He's reviewing Billy right now.'

Esther stared down at the rapidly spreading stain on the lino beneath her feet. 'Leave it,' Liz said, waving her hand. 'I'll get it. You just go.'

Esther put her hand on Liz's arm. 'Thanks, Liz. I'm so sorry. I'll make it up to you.'

She dashed back down the corridor towards NICU, crashing through the doors and heading straight to the sink to wash her hands. Abi was standing in the middle of a crowd of strangers that must include the new surgeon; she raised her eyebrows and said in a louder than normal voice, 'Oh, good, Billy's midwife is here. She'll be able to update you.'

Esther dried her hands and moved over quickly, making her way through the crowd. 'Hi there, I'm Esther McDonald.' She looked around trying to decide which one of the many bodies wearing white coats must belong to the surgeon. All she knew was he was male. Abi handed over Billy's chart and Esther could see from a glance that he'd had his chest x-ray and his tube feeding had restarted while she'd been gone. She breathed a sigh of relief.

'You're the midwife?'

The deep voice was practically at her ear and she jumped, stumbling over her own feet.

She spun around. Mr Imposing was standing in her

personal space, his arms folded across his chest, looking her up and down in a disapproving manner. Okay, so the NICU probably wasn't big enough for all these people, which could explain the space thing. And the massive splatter of coffee all over her scrub trousers probably wasn't helping her appearance.

But right now she could smell his clean aftershave and see into those toffee-coloured eyes.

'Weren't you the nurse who was sleeping in the canteen?'

She could feel the blood rush to her face and all the hairs on her body prickle in indignation. Who did this guy think he was, sweeping in here with his giant entourage?

Nope. No way.

'I'm sure you know that we limit visitors to NICU. Maybe other NICUs relax rules for you and your entourage, but the Queen Victoria doesn't.'

She started to count in her head just how many people were in his little gang. She'd reached twelve when his deep voice sounded right in front of her again.

'Isn't this a teaching hospital? Famous the world over for its training programmes?' There was a mocking tone in his voice.

Esther had been around long enough to recognise an arrogant doctor. As a nurse, and a midwife, she'd met more than her fair share—both male and female.

She hated anyone being dismissive with her. And she didn't stand for it. More than once she'd used her Scottish accent to the best of her ability to give someone short shrift.

There was something about her accent that generally

made people take a step back—particularly when she was angry. If this guy didn't watch out, he'd soon find out exactly who Esther McDonald was. She'd barely had a chance to look this guy up. All she knew was he was one of a few specialist surgeons who could do the procedure that Billy needed.

She mirrored his stance and folded her arms, tilting her chin towards him as she put a fake smile on her face. 'Maybe you'd like to introduce yourself and let me know why you think your needs are more important than the needs of the very special babies we have in here?'

She could do sarcasm too.

He inhaled deeply, almost like he wanted to show her just how broad his chest was. But Esther had never been easily intimidated by anyone. 'I'm Harry Beaumont. I'm here to do the surgery on your patient.'

She raised her eyebrows and nodded. 'Ah, so *you're* here to do the surgery on Billy.' She pointed one finger at him. 'In that case, *you* can stay. Everyone else can wait outside. Unless you've brought your own anaesthetist with you.' She shrugged. 'If you have, then he, or she, can stay too.'

Eleven other faces exchanged anxious glances, so Esther turned her head a few times as she spoke. 'The babies in here are just too susceptible to infection to have this many people around. Visitors are strictly limited, for good reason.' She looked at them all. 'As I don't know who any of you are—and to be honest, I'm a bit funny about letting people I don't know into my NICU too—I'm just going to assume that you're all either medical professionals or trainees, therefore I don't need to explain the principles of infection control to you, so you'll all completely understand that this amount of people is overkill—' she turned her head back towards Harry '—even for a surgeon.'

She'd spoken quite a lot, but knew entirely that all the emphasis was on the things she hadn't said, but had left implied.

There was a tic at the side of Harry's jaw. He was mad. She didn't care. She wanted to tug at her scrub top again. NICUs were always really warm, but this amount of people in close proximity was making her sweat. But tugging at the top would mean she'd have to unfold her arms and that would be a sign of weakness. So not happening.

It was the longest pause. Harry gave the tiniest nod of his head. 'Francesca, will you stay with me, please? The rest of you, if you wait outside we'll find a teaching area where I can explain things in due course.'

Francesca was a petite redhead who was grinning conspiratorially at Esther. She let the rest of the entourage leave, then asked, 'Can I see Billy's films? I'd like to review them before we examine him.'

'Of course,' said Esther, gesturing for both of them to follow her to the nearest computer screen. 'Have you been assigned temporary log-in credentials?'

'I have,' said Harry, moving over next to her and tapping his details in.

It only took a few moments for a scowl to come over his face. 'I sent a list of tests to be completed for Billy before I got here. Some are missing.'

'They are?' Esther moved closer, checking the screen. She'd checked before she'd gone off shift yesterday when there were just a few still to be completed. Ruth had said the rest had been done. What was missing?

She turned to Harry. 'What is it that you're looking for?'

'His bloods. From this morning.'

Of course. 'I'm sure they were done—they've probably not been reported on yet. Don't worry, I can phone the lab and put a rush on them.'

Harry straightened and gave her an incredulous glance. 'What do you mean you're "sure they were done"? You mean you don't actually know? And why wasn't there already a rush put on them?'

She stiffened. He was speaking to her as if she was incompetent. Of course she should know if Billy's bloods had been done or not. But the specialist phlebotomist would have been here while Esther was on her break. If she hadn't been late back, she might have had a chance to check...

She kept her face blank. Her back was aching. 'The orders for the bloods were put in last night. At that point, you hadn't told us when you were coming, or let us know if you'd secured theatre time for Billy. If you had, there would have been a rush put on his bloods.'

She moved over to the desk to pick up the phone. Every word he'd said had annoyed her. But what irked most was that they felt true.

What was wrong with her? She prided herself on being meticulous at work. It wasn't like she'd made any kind of mistake but...in her brain it *almost* felt like that. Double-checking things was second nature to her.

'I'm used to working with professionals. I guess the standards here are not what I'm used to.'

'Excuse me?' She couldn't help herself. There was no way she going to let anyone accuse her of being unprofessional. It was the biggest slight that someone could say to a nurse or midwife.

But it seemed that Harry was off on a rant. He kept his voice low, so that no one else in the unit could hear. 'Why does Billy still have a feeding tube in situ? In order for Francesca to anaesthetise him, she needs to ensure his stomach is empty. His feeding should have stopped a few hours ago.'

Now Esther wanted to shout at him, but just at that moment a voice answered at the end of the phone. 'Lab,' came the weary response.

Something inside Esther panged. Whoever was working there was obviously every bit as tired as she was. 'It's Esther from NICU. Can I chase bloods for a baby that's going to Theatre?'

There was a sigh and murmur of consent. She replaced the receiver and turned to face Francesca, completely ignoring Mr Entourage. She wasn't even prepared to use his name right now.

'If you refresh the screen in around five minutes Billy's bloods will be available. One of the machines was down for a few hours this morning but it's back up and running now. Billy's bloods had already been in the system. They're just waiting for his clotting factor.'

Francesca gave a nod. 'Perfect.'

Esther looked at Harry's screen. He was looking at the cardiac echo that had been taken yesterday. Billy needed his surgery, badly.

She moved alongside Harry. 'I have many skills, Mr Beaumont, but mind reading isn't one of them. Like I said earlier, if you'd given us notice of Billy's procedure, then we'd have made sure his feeds were stopped in good time. As it was, his tube dislodged last night and had to be replaced. Billy already had a few hours without sustenance, while his tube was re-sited and then checked. His feed only started again in the last hour.' She braced herself and turned her head towards him. 'And for me, unprofessional is a surgeon sweeping into a NICU with an entourage of twelve people with no regard for the patients or parents who are already in a stressful environment. For a surgeon with your apparent experience, I'd expect better.'

Harry was trying his absolute best to keep his temper in check, but this midwife was trying his patience in every possible way. It didn't help that she had a cheek to be angry at him, or that when she was clearly annoyed she spoke so quickly he had to concentrate to make out a single word that she said. Her Scottish accent was fierce. A bit like she was.

By rights she should probably have fiery red hair to match. But she didn't. She had dark hair that was up in a ponytail, and her skin looked as though it had once been tanned but was now strangely pale. He couldn't possibly ignore the dark circles under her blue eyes, or the dirty scrubs she was wearing. He wasn't quite sure what all this meant—apart from the fact she was looking after the baby he was due to take to Theatre.

Harry had spent his life in and out of NICUs across the world due to his surgical speciality. There weren't many people that wanted to work on such tiny hearts and veins—particularly when the tissues were so fragile and these little lives could literally be on a knife edge.

What the staff in the NICU at the Queen Victoria clearly didn't know was that he was the new visiting surgeon, which meant that, where possible, babies with heart conditions would be brought here for him to operate on. For those who were too sick to travel any distance, he would still go to them. But having a semi-permanent base with a team around him would be good. He'd hoped to find professional colleagues he could trust and rely on. But first impressions of this midwife weren't exactly good.

There was no way he wanted her watching Billy postsurgery.

But what annoyed him most of all was the way she'd quickly and determinedly told him to get his staff out of 'her' NICU.

And she'd been right. They always tried to reduce the amount of close contacts that prem babies had. It was important. Their immune systems were often not fully developed, and most humans were walking petri dishes.

People could be carrying bugs for days without any signs or symptoms. Something that caused a mere sniffle in an adult could be deadly to a premature baby. It might be a teaching hospital but even he wouldn't expect any NICU to let in that many students and trainees. He'd been in such a hurry to get in here and see his patient, and been so swept away by the enthusiasm of the staff at his side, that he hadn't stopped to think. And Harry didn't make mistakes like that. So being called on it was embarrassing.

'You must have known Billy was going to Theatre today,' he said briskly to the midwife.

She gave him a weary look that told him she was getting very bored by all this. 'I *hoped* you might show your face today. I hoped that Billy wouldn't have to wait another day for surgery. I was told that you were *supposed* to turn up today, but no one knew when. I look after both baby and mum, and if you'd communicated a little better, there was also the chance I could have prepared mum more for his surgery today.'

She put her hands at the back of both hips, leaned backwards and winced as if she'd touched something painful.

'Blood results are in,' said Francesca in a manner that could only be described as deliberately distracting. It was clear she was trying to break the tension between them. 'His blood gases are a little lower than I would have liked. But not anything I wouldn't have expected.' Francesca gave a little sigh and Harry felt a rush of sympathy for her. They'd worked together for a long time. She was a great anaesthetist. It took great skill to manage these tiny babies in Theatre and he depended on her completely. Francesca's chair scraped on the ground as she stood up. 'I need to sound his chest. Let me wash up first.'

He followed her over to the sink in the treatment room, completely sidestepping Esther and washing his hands too. He needed to prioritise this baby, not the midwife who looked as if she could currently fall asleep on her feet.

As he stepped back his arm brushed against hers and

she jerked away. But not before he noticed how hot she was. 'Do you have some kind of infection?'

She looked shocked. 'What?'

'You're burning up. What's your temperature?' His arm swept out across all the cribs in the NICU. 'If you have anything respiratory you're putting the lives of all these babies at risk.'

'I don't have anything respiratory,' she snapped. 'My chest is clear as a bell.'

For one strange second he realised that her words had made him look exactly at her breasts hidden under her scrubs. He turned back to Francesca. 'We should see this baby on our own.'

Esther stepped into his path. 'No, you won't. I know Jill, his mum, best. She needs support. She trusts me.'

Harry glared at her and she held up her hands. 'Okay, I won't touch Billy, right now. I'll run down to A&E when you're done and get a clean bill of health. But you don't see him without me.'

Harry pressed his lips together, stopping himself from just getting into a pointless argument. 'Only speak to mum, then,' he reiterated.

She gave an exasperated nod and held out her hand. 'This way.'

Harry and Francesca followed her over to the left-hand side of the unit to where a young woman sat staring at her baby lying in the crib and rocking backwards and forward in the nursing chair. Harry had dealt with lots of anxious parents. NICUs were the most intimidating places on earth. Parents frequently felt everything was out of their control, and he was used to comforting and supporting parents who were overwhelmed with helplessness and focused on every word that was said to them. This mother was young. Her lank hair was pulled back from her face. It looked as if it hadn't been washed for a while and from first appearance he actually wondered when she'd last eaten. Now he understood just why Esther was being so protective of Billy's mum. It was clear she didn't have many support systems in place.

'Jill, this is Harry Beaumont. He's the surgeon that's going to do the surgery on Billy.'

Harry crouched down so he was level with Jill. She'd sat forward but hadn't stood up. He gave her a broad smile. 'It's a pleasure to meet you, Jill. I'm here to take a look at Billy. I'm hoping we'll be able to take him for surgery later today. Do you mind if I examine him?'

Jill paused for a few moments as her eyes filled with tears, then she gave a tiny nod. 'Of course.'

She was terrified. He got that. Harry used some of the NICU hand sanitiser before opening the crib to examine Billy, while Francesca introduced herself as Billy's anaesthetist. He could tell straight away that Esther completely understood, and after a few moments, he could see the tension in Jill's shoulders start to dissolve as he spoke to Billy in a calm, quiet voice as he examined him.

'Hi, Billy, I'm here to see how you're doing. Let's have a little listen to your heart and lungs.' He took his time, listening carefully, then checking his oxygen sats, his feeding tube and his colour. Babies this small frequently had skin that was almost translucent. Their circulatory systems—and particularly Billy's—weren't functioning quite right, and they often couldn't regulate their temperatures. Operating and anaesthetising these babies carried huge risks. He gave Francesca a nod as he moved his stethoscope back to Billy's chest. 'Want to take a listen?'

She nodded and moved alongside him. There was no point her touching Billy too when she really just needed to listen to his heart and lungs. So, she listened through Harry's stethoscope, nudging him to move it on occasion.

Harry could sense Esther watching them curiously. She wouldn't know they'd done this a dozen times before. As Francesca finished her examination it struck him how similar Esther and Jill looked. Exhausted and tired. He could understand it for the mother. But for a member of staff—it wasn't good enough.

Francesca gave him a nod and he removed his stethoscope and pulled a chair over next to Jill and spent the next few minutes explaining Billy's surgery to her in simple terms. He brought out some notes that he'd prepared earlier. He always gave the parents of the babies he operated on some clear notes that they could refer to later. Experience had taught him that although parents listened, anxiety meant that they didn't always remember or understand what they'd been told.

He could feel Esther's eyes on him the whole time. He would expect the midwife assigned to this child to listen to his explanation. It would mean that she could reiterate anything to the mum at a later date. But somehow, today, it irked him. And he couldn't quite understand why.

'Do you have any questions?' he checked with Jill. She shook her head and he gave her a small nod. 'If you think of anything later I'll still be available to answer any questions. I'm going to organise some theatre time now. I hope to take Billy later this afternoon. We'll stop his feeding for the next few hours, and I'd expect the surgery to last around six hours. You can come down to Theatre if you want while Billy goes to sleep, and I'll come and find you as soon as we're finished to update on how things have gone. Okay?'

Jill gave a nod.

'I'm just going to have a chat with your midwife, and then I'll talk to you in a while and get you to sign the consent forms.'

He smiled and walked back over to the nurses' station with Francesca and Esther. Francesca sat down and started making some notes. Esther turned to look at him. 'You aren't doing the consent form now?'

He shook his head. 'No. I've given her a lot to process. I want to give her a bit of time to think about everything I've told her before I get her to sign the consent form. She might have more questions later.'

Esther gave a brief nod.

He narrowed his gaze. Was she actually listening? He glanced at the board he'd noticed yesterday. It was a shift rota for staff.

The next few days would be vital for Billy. It was important that whoever was looking after him was at the top of their game. Esther's name was on the rota for tomorrow. He couldn't let that go.

'You're tired. No, scrap that, you're exhausted. And I think you're sick. I don't think you should be at work and I certainly don't think you should be assigned to Billy. For the next few days he's going to need someone who's alert and on their game.' He paused for the briefest second, because he knew what he was about to say wasn't exactly nice. 'And to be honest, I'm not convinced that's you. I want another midwife assigned to Billy.'

'What?' Well, that had certainly gotten her attention.

'I'm sorry. But I can't take the risk of performing this surgery and having his postoperative care compromised.'

'How dare you!' she hissed at him. She glanced down. 'What? Because I have a little coffee spilled on my scrubs and I haven't had a chance to get changed yet, and because I dared to close my eyes in the hospital canteen, you've decided I'm not fit to do my job? Just who do you think you are?'

He cringed. He hadn't exactly said those words but it was certainly how he'd felt. 'I think you're sick,' he said quickly. 'I think you might need to be checked over, and have a few days' rest.' He could see a couple of other staff members looking their way—as if they'd picked up that something was wrong. The last thing he wanted when he was taking up a position here was to cause a ruckus with the staff.

'My priority is my patient,' he said quietly but firmly.

'And mine isn't?' He could tell she was mad.

That wasn't what he meant, even though he'd clearly just implied it. But then again, did he really want this midwife looking after his patient if she wasn't at the top of her game?

Francesca glared at him from over her computer. Oh no. That didn't usually happen. Francesca normally had his back.

He took a deep breath. 'Esther, I have to call things the way I see it. I think you're running a temp and maybe need to take some time off. You agreed you'd go down to A&E and get checked over. Why don't you do that and we'll take it from there.' It was a compromise. But it was the best he could do right now.

She kept her face entirely straight and pulled up a few things on the computer and grabbed the chart from the base of Billy's crib.

'Here, Mr Beaumont. I'd like you to check my work. Here's all the orders I made for Billy on my shifts for the last few days. Here's all my nursing notes. Here's every temp, blood pressure, pulse and respiratory rate. Here's his medications I've administered, and his feeding. Here's his skin care chart. Here's his colour chart. Here's how many times I've sounded his chest to ensure that it remains clear. Here is exactly how many times he's had a wet or dirty nappy.' She pulled up a final chart. 'And here's how many times I've had to chase doctors, other departments, test results—all to ensure Billy's care is up to my standards.' She held herself very still, but there was the tiniest tremble in her voice. 'I want you to take the time to look at what I've done. Because I record everything, *meticulously*.' She emphasized the word, then gave a wave of her hand. 'And once you've done that, I can pull up all the same information for his mother, and you can check my recordings for Jill too.' She paused for a few seconds as he glanced over what she'd handed him. 'Unfortunately I'm not on shift twenty-four hours a day, so I've only given you what I've done for Billy. Hospitals have emergencies, as I'm sure you're aware. Blood machines break down. Feeding tubes dislodge and can't be safely used again until there's been an x-ray that's been checked by a physician. I'm not responsible for other people's time constraints.'

He was checking. She was right. He couldn't deny it. Her recording was meticulous. Some of the best he'd ever seen, and he'd been in a *lot* of NICU units.

She'd felt warm to the touch earlier, but as she'd moved closer as she spoke to him he couldn't hear any sign of a wheeze or rasp in her breathing. Every person was different. Maybe she didn't have an infection. Maybe he was overreacting. It could be that her body temperature just ran at the top end of normal. It happened.

What was clear was he couldn't tell her why he'd overreacted. He couldn't tell her that deep down there was an underlying paranoia about his patients and their welfare.

Before he could blink she'd stepped right up in front of him, her accent thick but perfectly legible. 'You know, Harry, I'm actually glad that you're here. Because even though you're an insufferably arrogant fool, I know how much Billy needs this surgery. And I put him first. Always. But I'm only going to say this once. Don't *ever* talk to me like that again and don't *ever* question my professionalism or my competency at work.' She put both hands on her hips. 'I wish you luck with Billy's surgery today, but after that, I hope I never have to see your sorry ass in here again.' And with that, she turned on her heel and walked away, leaving Harry feeling about as welcome as a thorn in a space suit.

Francesca tutted and gave him a sarcastic smile. 'Well done, Harry. First day on a new job and you've made friends.' She picked up her bag. 'And to be honest,' she said in a low voice as she walked past. 'Against her? I don't fancy your chances at all.'

CHAPTER TWO

THE SIGNS HAD been there but she'd been too busy to pick them up—looking after Jill, worrying about her mum. Esther cursed herself all the way down the stairs towards A&E. She hated the fact that it took that pompous prince, duke or whatever he claimed to be to point them out before the penny had finally dropped for her.

Abi had told her to go on down for the check while she took care of Billy but Esther already knew exactly what was wrong with her. She'd ducked into the treatment room and took her own temperature. Yip. She was burning up. She grabbed some paracetamol from her handbag. She had to start somewhere.

Rob, one of the advanced nurse practitioners, was at the nurses' station in the middle of the A&E department. He took one look. 'You okay?'

She shook her head. 'I think I've got an upper UTI. Can I borrow you for five minutes?'

He nodded. 'Sure.' Then he smiled and handed her a specimen bottle. 'Let's get you sorted.'

It took a little more than five minutes because Rob liked to be thorough. Once he heard her past history of having kidney problems as a child, leaving her prone to upper urinary tract infections, he gave a little nod, dipsticked her urine, rechecked her temp and listened to her symptoms of fatigue and an aching lower back.

'You couldn't come down earlier?'

She sighed. 'I'd felt a bit tired but my back only started aching this morning and the new neonatal cardiac surgeon arrived today so I've been flat out dealing with him too.'

He gave her a nod and scribbled some notes. 'What normally works best?'

She told him the name of the antibiotic that normally resolved her infections and he scribbled a prescription, then went to one of the cupboards and pulled out a bottle, signing a form to record it. 'Okay, so I won't make you trek to the pharmacy. But I'm still sending your sample away to make sure you're on the right antibiotic. Results should be on the system tomorrow. I'm working then—will I give you a call?'

Esther gave a grateful nod. The computer system in the Queen Victoria meant that no staff could access their own records or results—no matter how tempting it was. 'Perfect. Thanks, Rob.'

'Any time. Not many perks to being in the NHS. We've got to look after our own. Are you going to take some time off?'

'Me?' She smiled and shook her head. 'As soon as I start taking these, they usually work fast. This time tomorrow I'll start to feel better. I'll just take some paracetamol until then.'

He gave a nod. 'Fine, but let me know if there's anything else you need.'

'An assassination attempt on a visiting surgeon, maybe?'

Rob looked up in surprise. 'He's annoyed Crabbie Rabbie? Wow, he's brave.'

She waved her hand. 'Don't worry. I've told him how much I love him already. Hopefully he'll do his surgery, fix my baby and leave.'

She gave Rob a nod and disappeared out the cubicle and back along the corridor. In a way she was happy. This had obviously been working on her for the last few days. At least now she knew why she was so unnaturally tired. It was sort of a relief to know that after a few days of antibiotics she'd be back to herself again.

As she pushed open the door, the manager of the A&E department was heading towards her. Shirley had her hands full, so Esther held the door for her.

She gave her a grin. 'Lifesaver, thanks.'

'No probs.'

Something flitted across Shirley's face. 'Hey, don't suppose you could cover a shift on Thursday?'

Esther glanced at the pill bottle she'd just pushed into the pocket of her uniform. Thursday. Three days away. It was her next scheduled day off and she was bound to be feeling better by then. 'Sure.' She nodded.

'Great,' Shirley shouted over her shoulder as she continued to speed down the corridor.

Harry was doing his absolute best not to try and cause trouble. Only because Francesca had torn a few strips off him.

'You were way out of line yesterday,' she said quietly as they met the next morning.

'How was I out of line? I don't want some flaky member of staff caring for my baby.'

'Your baby?' Francesca raised her eyebrows.

He sighed. 'You know what I mean. If I operate on them, they're all my babies.'

'Don't try the mushy stuff with me. You're being harsh. So, she spilt coffee and didn't have time to change. Who hasn't? Half the times I was called to a cardiac arrest, I went with half my lunch down me.'

'Did you sleep in the hospital canteen too?'

Francesca shrugged. 'Sometimes. If I'd been up all night on call, I might grab five minutes when I had to. Can you really say that you've never done that?'

He took in a deep breath and gave a conciliatory shrug too. 'Okay, I might have.'

Francesca gave him a hard stare. 'I'm just saying. This is the first time you've operated here. I'd try not to get on the wrong side of everyone you might come across if you're going to be a visiting surgeon.'

'Now who's being harsh?'

Francesca started pulling up some results on a nearby computer. 'Anyway. I would tread carefully. I've heard she's got a nickname.'

'A nickname?'

Francesca nodded and smiled. 'Yep. Crabbie Rabbie.'

'What?' Harry frowned.

'Something to do with Scotland's national bard?'

'I know who Rabbie Burns is.'

'Well, apparently she got the nickname just after she arrived. Something to do with her strong accent and the fact she takes no prisoners with people she thinks are annoying.'

'Are you trying to tell me something?'

'Just that I think you've clearly just put yourself into the annoying category.'

He shook his head. 'Oh, thanks for that.' The door to the NICU opened and the day staff filed in, Esther among them.

Her dark hair was swept up in an elaborate plait. She still looked tired but maybe she'd put a little more make-up on, because there was more colour in her cheeks than there had been yesterday. She was wearing a different colour of scrubs today. Bright pink. He'd noticed the staff in the NICU wore different colours—sometimes even with child-friendly designs. The brighter colour made her not look quite so washed out.

It was odd. On any other day—with any other member of staff—he might actually have admitted that he thought she was quite attractive. But he didn't have time for that. Harry didn't usually date anyone from work. Too many complications. And he and Esther hadn't exactly got off to a good start.

He wanted to ask if she was fit to work. He wanted to ask if she still had a temperature. He knew he wasn't entitled to. Staff in NICUs were extremely familiar with the dangers of exposing babies to potential infections. He shouldn't second-guess anyone.

Francesca tapped his arm. 'Okay, I'm off to see another baby.' She shot him another look. 'Now, behave. Play nicely.'

He shook his head as she walked out the door.

* * *

Esther had raged last night as she'd tried to get to sleep. It was ridiculous. All day all she'd wanted to do was sleep, but actually put her in comfy pyjamas and give her her own bed and she lay there blinking and plotting horrible futures for that annoying surgeon. The man had even stolen her sleep from her.

She ignored the fact it was noisy outside, the pipes creaked, the radiators hissed and upstairs seemed to be having a party again. Her back might have ached a little too, and she'd needed to pee on numerous occasions. It was funny how when you finally got a diagnosis your body practically slapped you on the face with it. But no, it was none of those things that prevented her from sleeping; it was definitely smug Harry Beaumont with his entourage and unflattering words.

She burned from a few of the things he'd said to her. But most of all was his threat to ask for another mid-wife to be assigned to Billy. She was pretty sure that the charge nurse for the unit would give him short shrift. Oona was from Northern Ireland, and was much more like Esther in temperament than she cared to admit. She wouldn't take kindly to some visiting surgeon dictating what happened in her NICU.

But as Esther walked through the door of NICU she could see Harry sitting at the nurses' station. It was 6:50 in the morning and clearly her worst day in the world was just about to start.

It didn't help that he was looking like Dr Delicious in his pale blue shirt that was a little damp around the collar. He'd obviously just showered and was currently charming the few staff around him; they were laughing and joking.

She braced herself, waiting for someone to tell her she couldn't look after the little boy she'd spent the last few days tending to. Her eyes hesitantly went to the board. Esther McDonald was written next to Billy Rudd and Akshita Patel. She let out a sigh of relief and went straight over to hear the report.

Somehow she just knew that every single step of the way Harry's eyes were watching. What was he waiting for?

She pointedly ignored him. Billy's surgery had apparently gone well, which was a relief. She hurried over to his crib to get a look at him for herself, making sure she gave Jill a hug first.

His colour was different—straight away. Some people might not have found it obvious, but Esther was an experienced NICU member of staff and had always noticed the slight dusky tinge to Billy's skin. Today, it was gone. His skin still had the translucence of a premature baby, but the colour had definitely improved.

She breathed and caught a scent. She tensed. She recognised it from yesterday, some kind of woody undertones. Harry. She was determined not to turn around.

Jill had got up and gone into the small kitchen in NICU to make herself a cup of tea.

'Things went well?' she asked Harry in an even tone. They might have got off to a bad start but there was no point in being uncivil.

'Yes, and no,' he said in a low voice.

'What do you mean?'

'I mean, things took a little longer than expected. We

ran into some problems. The surgery ended up taking about eight hours.'

Esther turned to face him in shock. She knew how long the surgery should have taken. 'But…'

He shook his head. 'It's all under control. The surgery was successful. Billy will need regular reviews and be carefully monitored for the next few days, but—' he paused and gave a slow nod of his head before his dark eyes met hers '—the next few days will be the most crucial.'

Her skin prickled. He wasn't saying anything out loud. But it felt like he was accusing her of something.

'Experience with these babies tells me that if something is going to go wrong, it generally happens in the first forty-eight hours after surgery.'

The time when she was part of the team watching Billy.

She tilted her chin, part of her felt defiant, and part of her felt distinctly annoyed by his unsaid implication.

She glanced at the clock on the wall. She knew when surgery had started yesterday. If it had taken eight hours, it couldn't have finished until well after midnight. Harry had already been here when she'd come in for her shift. She knew she hadn't slept last night, but had he?

'Are you staying close by? You've had a quick turnaround.'

She wasn't even sure where the observation came from, and the instant it came out her mouth she wasn't entirely comfortable with how it sounded.

But Harry didn't seem to notice. 'I'm only a few

miles away in Belgravia, but I stayed here last night to keep an eye on Billy.'

'Oh.' She nodded. Belgravia. Of course. He was supposed to be some kind of royalty, wasn't he? Of course that's where he'd stay. Not like herself, who had to travel nearly an hour each day to get to work.

He pulled something from his pocket, then cleared his throat. 'I left a note for the NICU nurse last night about all the things I wanted monitored in Billy.'

She glanced at the piece of paper in his hand. 'I do know how to do postoperative care, Harry. This isn't my first rodeo, you know.' There was no way she was touching that list. Her eyes quickly ran down it. It was what they would do for every baby postsurgery, with the exception of one test that could easily be ordered with the rest of the blood work.

She pressed her lips together and tried not to snap. Everything about this guy just seemed to annoy her. Even the way his aftershave seemed to linger in the air between them. 'I guess when you move around a lot you don't know what's normal in each NICU. But you don't need to worry about the Queen Victoria. We have a reputation of excellence because we've earned it.'

Was that too pointed? She didn't think so. It seemed more factual to her.

He wasn't wearing a typical doctor white coat and her eyes were drawn to the muscles beneath the pale blue shirt he wore. The shirt was clearly tailored, defining all the parts of him it should. It had short sleeves— just like all doctors were supposed to wear in clinical areas, but the short sleeves drew her attention to his biceps. Some place she definitely didn't need to look.

'Point taken,' said Harry frostily. 'But I'd still like my post-op instructions followed. I don't think that's unreasonable.'

He was still holding the piece of paper towards her. It was like a standoff. She didn't want to take it. She didn't. But Jill came out of the kitchen and started walking towards them. The last thing she needed was for Billy's mum to think there was any kind of issue between the staff looking after her child. Esther reached out and grabbed the paper, stuffing it in her pocket.

'Fine.'

One of his eyebrows quirked upwards. 'Fine,' he agreed before turning and walking away.

She moved quickly, doing her routine checks on Billy, followed by routine checks on the little girl she was taking care of too.

She'd hoped that Harry would take the cue to leave the NICU. Surely he must be tired? Or at the very least have other work to do. But apparently not. He settled in and made himself comfortable in a corner of the NICU, opening up a laptop and sitting next to one of the phones.

The phone calls were brisk. He seemed to consult on a whole host of cases, some in the UK, and some in Europe.

Not that she was listening to what he was doing. Of course not. She just kept hoping that one of those calls would give him an incentive to actually leave the NICU.

Every time she turned around she felt as if she could feel his eyes on her. At first she told herself it was her imagination. But on the few occasions she looked up, they definitely locked gazes, making heat rush into her cheeks.

She chewed the inside of her cheek as she logged in to one of the patient monitoring systems to update her nursing notes on Billy.

There was a little pink flash in the bottom right-hand corner. Someone else was in these notes. That wasn't too unusual. The lab could be uploading results. Or someone else could be viewing x-rays or ultrasounds. But then the little flash turned blue, and Esther's temperature turned red.

Now, someone was looking at the nursing notes. *Her nursing notes.* The ones she hadn't even written yet. And all of sudden she didn't have a single doubt who it was.

This guy was checking up on her, and that made her mad. She couldn't even remember being supervised this much as a student nurse. When she'd come to the Queen Victoria to do her additional midwifery training it had only taken a few shifts for the staff she worked with to realise she was already trained as a nurse and was clearly competent. Of course, labour and deliveries were supervised. But when she was giving out regular medicines and writing up notes, the staff didn't need to double-check as she already had a professional registration. So this definitely felt like being under the microscope. And she didn't like it—not one bit.

The temptation to write *Get Lost* in the electronic system was overwhelming. It would appear to him in live time. Unfortunately this system was designed to keep a permanent log of everything recorded. So, if she typed it once—even if she deleted it a few seconds later—it could always be pulled up on a previous search.

It was designed to stop users changing records at a later date, but had actually proved a fail-safe for one midwife who'd accidentally recorded notes in the wrong patient record, deleted them, then had to deal with an emergency. The timing had meant she'd totally forgotten to go back and add the notes into the correct patient record. When questions had been asked later, the system could prove the record had been made, just not in the right place.

The midwife still got into trouble, just not as much as she could have.

Esther ignored Harry. She had to. Instead, she quickly typed Billy's latest observations and results, along with a few thoughts of her own. Then she flipped into the records for Jill and made a few notes too. Jill was also still under observation and Esther had a few concerns.

An hour later, Harry was back by her side. He didn't speak, but his shoes came into her line of vision. Italian handmade leather shoes. Something she'd only ever seen on movie stars before. Even his shoes annoyed her.

Was she maybe being irrational?

She waited until he'd sounded Billy's chest again. 'Why were you checking my notes?'

His hands flinched. 'I wasn't specifically checking your notes, Esther.'

'You were. I can tell when someone is looking at the page I'm on.'

He gave her a sideways glance. 'I was reviewing all of Billy's records. From his delivery, to his first films, his consecutive test results and *all* of his medical and nursing notes. I like to be cautious. I like to take a big-picture look at my patients.' He turned to face her. He gave her a reluctant kind of look. 'I often think that the observations of the midwives or nurses that care for the patients are the most important. They might notice things that other people miss.' He paused and ran one hand through his thick rumpled hair. There was something about that motion. The look on his face as he did it that made her breath catch somewhere at the back of her throat. Sorrow. Pain. Regret.

'I've found over the years when we've had to do significant adverse event reviews, or even child death reviews, that often in case notes we can pick up tiny comments that might not seem like much to begin with, but when you stop—' he held up his hands and swept them around '—and look at the whole picture, they all prove to be part of the jigsaw puzzle. The one that we often don't put together until it's far too late.' He bit his bottom lip... There was something about this; she could tell he was keeping his emotions in check, and it made her stop feeling quite so angry at him. He took a deep breath. 'So, I've learned to pay attention. To read all the notes—by everybody involved—and keep everything in mind.' His toffee eyes locked on hers. 'Because what's the point in doing all these reviews if we don't actually learn anything from them?'

Her mouth had gone dry. There was so much more to this story. Yes, she felt under the spotlight by him. Yes, she felt as if his words yesterday had been unjustified. But now he was telling her exactly why he was being meticulous, and her previously irritated brain could absolutely understand it.

He worked around a variety of hospitals. It was doubtful that he could remember anyone's name. Everyone knew that some hospital units were better run than others. Esther could write a list right now of places she would never apply for a permanent position. Was it any wonder he didn't think twice about handing over written instructions postsurgery for a patient?

Maybe she was letting her annoyance with him yesterday colour her judgement.

He was still standing there. Just a few steps away from her. She could see the rise and fall of his chest under his tailored shirt. The shirt that probably cost more than any outfit in her closet at home.

It was hard not to see the differences between them both. His cut-glass accent both annoyed and intrigued her. What was it really like to be a member of the upper classes? She was pretty sure she'd never met anyone before who would fall into that category. Had Harry been guaranteed a place at one of the best medical schools as part of his birthright? Or was all that outdated nonsense? She really had no clue.

What she was sure about was that he hadn't had to juggle school work with two part-time jobs at school, and study into the late hours to make the grades he needed. Esther wasn't some natural genius. She'd worked hard to get what she needed to get into university in Scotland. Doing the conversion course to midwifery in London had only been possible because of a grant from a Scottish millionaire who stayed in her area and invited Scots people to apply. Scotland was one of the few places on the planet where university tuition was free for their kids. But if a Scots kid wanted to do a course that was only offered in England? Then, like everyone else, they had to pay. She'd only been able to get to the Queen Victoria through getting the grant to fund her fees. It had also covered her rent during her training, so she was much luckier than most. But somehow she knew that Harry Beaumont had never had to worry about tuition fees or accommodation in his life.

Her mind drifted. Wondering if he'd ever been to Buckingham Palace or knew anyone there. Maybe he'd been best friends with one of the younger princes? He'd be around the same age.

Esther's eyes fixated on his arms again. The muscles made her wonder if he was a rower. That would be it. He'd probably been part of either Oxford or Cambridge's row teams.

There was a soft cough to her left and she jerked, turning to see Jill watching her with a strange expression on her face.

'Everything okay?'

Jill looked between them both. 'That's just what I was about to ask you. You both seem to have been here awhile. Is there something wrong with Billy?'

Harry automatically stepped backwards. 'No, no, everything is fine. I'm very pleased with Billy's progress.'

He seemed to rethink his words. 'Of course, we're still going to keep monitoring him closely for the next few days. But, so far, he's making a good recovery.'

Esther felt a tiny flash of something. The way he'd retreated from his initial words. It was almost like he didn't want to seem too confident that Billy was out of the woods. Not to give Jill too many reassurances that could lead her to think that nothing else could go wrong.

She wondered if Jill had even noticed. But it didn't really matter because Esther had. She put her hands on her hips and gave a little stretch backwards. It was odd. She was still having to take paracetamol for her temperature and she had still had that odd heavy feeling. Usually by this point the antibiotics would have started to kick in, and the tiredness at least would have begun to lift.

But not yet.

Her appetite hadn't quite returned either. Yesterday she'd ate that scone, and then hadn't eaten until later at night—and that had just been a bowl of soup. This morning she hadn't even eaten breakfast, just made do with a caramel latte. That had been on the way into work, and funny thing was, she still wasn't hungry.

She gave Jill a smile. 'How you doing? I'll be going to the canteen later for some food. Want to come with me?'

It didn't matter whether she was hungry or not. Some of the other staff had noted that Jill hadn't been eating much. Hospital meals were always supplied for parents in the NICU, but Jill hadn't been touching hers. She did occasionally leave the NICU and say she was going to buy something—usually from a vending machine—but Esther wasn't convinced. Maybe it was time to try another tack.

Jill shot a glance at the crib. 'But if you're with me, who will watch Billy?' There was genuine apprehension in her voice.

'I will,' came the deep reply without hesitation. 'I intend to be around most of the day, so let me know when you both want to go, and I'll make myself a coffee, and take up post in the most comfortable chair in the place.'

He pointed to the reclining chair that Jill had next to Billy's crib and she let out a laugh. Not all of the chairs in the unit could tip back the way Jill's did and she was the envy of some of the other parents. 'You promise you won't leave him?' She looked over at Esther, then turned back to Harry. 'I know all the staff are good, but I trust Esther the most. I only ever leave Billy for more than a few minutes if she's here.'

He held up his hands, laughing. 'So what am I? The sloppy second?'

Colour rushed into Jill's cheeks but Esther quickly took a step towards Harry and nudged him. 'That's what I like. A surgeon that knows his place.' She couldn't hide the glint in her eye.

They'd definitely started off on the wrong foot together, but she was beginning to understand him just a little more. He might not be quite as arrogant as she'd first thought. As if right on cue her stomach gave a grumble.

'Oh,' said Jill. 'Shall we go now? Let me grab my bag.'

Esther put her hands to her stomach and let out an embarrassed laugh. 'Oops.'

'Better make my coffee, then,' said Harry quickly as he ducked into the NICU kitchen.

Esther went to check with one of her other colleagues that it was fine to leave. 'Harry's apparently watching Billy,' she told her.

Danielle raised her eyebrows. 'The surgeon? How on earth did you manage that one?'

'I didn't,' she said, feeling a little uncomfortable. It was unusual. She couldn't remember a surgeon ever offering to keep watch on a baby. Not to cover a break at least. 'He offered.' She paused for a second, then added, 'I think he's concerned about mum. I offered to take Jill down to the canteen but she was reluctant to go and leave Billy.'

'Ah. That makes sense. Try and get her a bit of fresh air too. She needs it.' It was almost like Danielle had instantly forgotten the first part of the conversation. She stuck her hand in her pocket and pulled out some coins. 'Here, get me something sweet. This diet I've been on is killing me. I need a chocolate fix.'

Esther smiled and nodded. 'No probs. See you soon.'

She checked back at the crib. Harry had settled into the seat and had pulled the flap down on the crib and was talking in a quiet voice to Billy. As she walked over he pretended not to notice. 'Watch out, Billy. Here comes Crabbie Rabbie. We've got to behave around her or we'll both get into trouble.'

Esther's mouth hung open. 'Who on earth told you that?' She'd always known her nickname. Her colleagues frequently used it with affection, but she hadn't expected some visiting surgeon to come out with it. People had clearly been talking.

'What?' Now it was his turn to have the glint in his eyes. He glanced over each shoulder as if someone was standing behind him. 'Did I say something?'

She leaned at the edge of the crib and looked down

at Billy. 'Billy, don't you listen to these bad influences. You know who the favourite is.'

She touched Harry's shoulder on the way past. 'And you're right. You do have to behave. Don't forget it.'

Jill hurried over with her bag on her shoulder. 'Are we good to go?'

Harry smiled. 'Absolutely, your boy is in safe hands. Now take your time. I'll be right here waiting.'

He shot Esther a quick glance. A silent message passing between them. Their joking was pushed aside again. Jill was the priority here. There was so much evidence about healthy mum, healthy baby. Esther took it completely seriously, and it seemed like Harry did too.

Esther held open the door for Jill, taking one final glance backwards as something warm spread through her. Most surgeons she met were quite insular. Only interested in moving on to their next surgery once the job was done. Harry seemed to be taking a much wider view. It was nice.

His head was dipped close to Billy and he was chatting away, his cup on the table next to him. She watched as he used some gel nearby before stretching his hand inside and letting Billy grasp his finger.

A smile lit up Harry's face.

And that was the moment she knew he was trouble.

CHAPTER THREE

SHE DIDN'T SLEEP too well that night. She might as well have covered the night shift the amount of times she was back and forth to the toilet.

By the time she took the route along the Thames she'd reached that strange point where sleep now seemed like an optional extra, so she bought the biggest coffee she could from one of the street vendors with two extra shots to try and give herself the oomph that felt missing.

It was a huge relief when she walked into the NICU and Harry wasn't there. Last thing she wanted was him calling her on how tired she looked. Apparently he'd gone back to France to see the baby he'd operated on previously.

He'd been so scrupulous about Billy's monitoring— almost as much as she was—and she'd heard him on the phone to France yesterday on a few occasions. It was clear he kept a close eye on any baby he'd operated on.

Yesterday they seemed to have reached an uneasy truce. There hadn't been a single word about her expertise or competence. She'd spent most of the day looking after both Billy and his mother, but Harry had constantly stayed around. Lingering doubts had hovered in her head and part of her wondered if he was keeping an eye on Billy, or if he was really keeping an eye on her. The more she'd thought about it last night, the more it seemed to amplify in her mind. Could he have hung around yesterday to assess her competence?

Once the seed was planted there she just couldn't shake it off. She'd re-examined every conversation they'd had. The fact he'd offered to sit with Billy to let her take Jill to the canteen. The truth was Jill hadn't eaten much at all.

But for the first time Jill had agreed to leave Billy's bedside and have a few hours' sleep in an actual bed. The NICU had two small rooms—just big cupboards, really—where parents could actually lie down and sleep, then have a shower if they wished. If Harry was examining her care, surely he could see how important it was to take care of mum too?

Billy's post-op care had been unremarkable, but when she'd read the theatre notes Esther realised just how touch and go it had been for him. Even if she'd initially detested him Harry Beaumont was a skilled surgeon, and looking at the neat clean scar line on Billy's tiny chest and the way his lungs filled with air every few moments, the scare in Theatre seemed a lifetime away.

Esther's stomach had churned as she'd made her way to the unit that day. She'd washed her hair and made sure her scrubs were immaculate. Even applying a little more make-up to her still slightly pale face. And that annoyed her too, because she'd always been immaculate at work. So why did it seem even more important that day? In a way she'd almost been annoyed when she realised Harry Beaumont wasn't there after all. But the annoyance had quickly given way to relief. On a day like today she wanted to be comfortable at work. All her concentration had to be on Billy and his mother. Not on some random, tall, dark and handsome arrogant fool with toffee-coloured eyes.

Heat rushed into her cheeks as she finished another set of Billy's checks. Where had that thought come from?

Abi nudged her elbow. 'So, anyway, I was telling you. We've found out what branch of royalty our new surgeon has.' She smiled brightly as if she thought Esther might actually be interested. 'He's from your neck of the woods. He's a duke. From Scotland. The Duke of Montrose.'

Esther wrinkled her nose. 'There's nothing Scottish about him. Have you heard that cut-glass accent?'

Abi laughed. 'What—you don't have posh people in Scotland?'

Esther had to smile too. 'Sure we do. But not in my neck of the woods. Anyhow, when these people get titles, it doesn't mean it relates to where they stay, or where they're from. The Prince of Wales wasn't born and brought up in Wales, was he?'

Abi frowned for a second. 'I guess not.' She waved her hand as she started to walk away. 'Anyway, just thought you'd want to know.'

Esther was surprised. 'Why on earth did you think I'd want to know?'

Abi's eyebrows rose. 'Just in case you were plotting a murder. Thought you'd want to know who he is before you kill him.' She was grinning as she left, but Esther pressed her lips together.

Okay. Abi hadn't mentioned anything about the day before. But people were clearly talking. At some point she'd expect Harry to appear again and review Billy. If she were lucky, somebody else would be on duty. If not, it was really important that she didn't give off *those* vibes. The ones that said, *If I was a superhero and had powers, I'd strike you down with my laser vision.*

She had to maintain her professional composure. It didn't matter they'd had a few fallouts. The patients were the most important thing in NICU. It was important that an easy ambience was kept in place. She could be civil. She might not smile, but she could certainly be civil.

'Hey, Esther, can you take a call from Harry Beaumont? He wants a report on Billy.'

She stiffened and picked up Billy's chart. 'Sure.'

It seemed like she'd have to start right now. She picked up the phone from where it was lying on the nurses' station and did actually smile as she kept things deliberately formal. 'This is Esther McDonald, Billy's midwife, can I help you?'

There was a pause at the end of the line. 'This is Harry Beaumont, the neonatal cardiac surgeon who carried out Billy's surgery yesterday. Can you give me an update on how he's doing, please?'

Oh. It seemed that two could play that game.

The smile stayed on her face. She gave Harry a quick rundown on all of Billy's obs, new blood results, his colour and then…she did what she always did. She told him how she felt. There was something to be said about the instinct of a health professional. She always believed it should never be ignored. Sometimes, even though there was not a single piece of scientific fact, a health professional just seemed to know if a patient was going to go 'off.' So many times, their instincts had been correct. Studies had even been done on the phenomenon.

So she went with her gut. 'Billy's good. Everything is going well. I think he's on the road to recovery.'

'That's your professional opinion?' There was something in his tone. She wasn't quite sure if he was mocking her, or if he actually got it.

'I have a good feeling,' she replied.

'Okay.' His voice was thoughtful. He paused for a few seconds. 'Thanks for the update. I should be back by tomorrow. I'll review him in person then. How's his mum doing?'

Once again, Esther was a little surprised. The surgeons she'd worked with before generally didn't take the time to consider the parents. 'Sleeping,' she said. 'For the first time in days. She's taken a shower and washed her hair too. When she wakes up, I'm going to send her down to the hospital canteen with one of my colleagues to make sure she eats.'

'Does she really have no supports? Does no one else come to visit Billy?'

Esther's curiosity was piqued. Not only was he interested, he actually sounded concerned. 'Not the whole time I've been here,' she said.

'Hmm…' She could tell he was thinking. Her brain was whirring. Maybe he wasn't quite as bad as she'd first thought.

'Esther, can I just check? Your temperature yesterday, it's resolved?'

And there it was. Just when she'd finally had a reasonable thought about this man it was like he'd just pulled the rug from under her feet.

In a way she understood the question. His issue was protecting the baby he'd operated on. But the question was intensely personal. Just as well she didn't have anything to hide.

'My temperature is resolved.'

'The reason?'

She bristled. It seemed to be her permanent state when she had any contact with this man. She couldn't remember the last time she'd felt like this about anyone. He was checking up on her—again.

She decided to put all her cards on the table. 'Don't worry. I don't have a respiratory infection.' If she had, she knew she'd have to have bailed out of the NICU for a few days. There were strict rules adhered to by all the members of staff in the NICU. 'I have a UTI,' she added. 'Long-term history, and I've got antibiotics.'

It was too much information. But she wanted this guy off her back. As a health care professional she wasn't embarrassed to talk about medical conditions. She really didn't think she had anything to hide.

There was a few moments' silence at the end of the phone, then his voice sounded deep and husky. 'I hope you feel better soon, Esther.'

She licked her lips as she put down the phone, a strange buzz going up her arm. She was feeling a little warm again. Maybe it was time for some more paracetamol?

CHAPTER FOUR

HER PHONE BUZZED and she checked it as she walked into A&E. 'Hi, Mum, everything okay?'

She listened for a few minutes as her mum filled her in on the last few days. Her heart always twisted in her chest when her mum's name came up on her phone. It always made her wonder if it was going to be something she didn't want to hear.

Her mum had fought cancer a few years ago, the worst part being she'd initially kept it a secret from Esther because she didn't want to distract her from her studies. Esther had been absolutely devastated when she'd found out—particularly when she'd realised her mum had gone through the diagnosis and some of her treatment on her own. Guilt had overwhelmed her, that her mother had put her first in her own biggest time of need. They'd always been so close and the treatment had left her mother unable to work any more. Hence, why Esther worked every shift she could. She had to pay rent in London, which was always extortionate, plus the mortgage payment on her mum's home in Edinburgh. But there was only two years left on the mortgage. She could do it. She just had to keep up with the extra shifts.

'I'm glad you're doing okay,' said Esther, her shoulders going down a little in relief.

'Please don't work too hard, honey,' came the reply. 'I'm so sorry about all this.' This conversation happened in every call. Her mum felt massively guilty that her daughter was helping support her now.

But what else could she do? Her dad had died a few years earlier. He'd been wonderful, if a little harum-scarum. He'd drifted from job to job. Her mother had always really been the breadwinner in the household. Her father's jobs had always revolved around his passions. He'd been an extra for film companies, a body-double, had a go at training as a stunt man, then he'd taken jobs everywhere as a tour guide. He'd always seemed to like jumping from place to place, before coming home to his girls with a whole host of wonderful stories to tell.

Although they'd both loved and adored him, his attitude to work had put a strain on things for her mum, who'd counted every penny. It had ingrained in Esther the fact that security and a steady job were one of the most important things in life.

'It's fine, Mum, please don't worry. You paid the first twenty-three years, let me pay off the rest.' She spoke for another few minutes, then ended the call.

The board in A&E was full. It was going to be a busy night.

She walked down to where the shift handover normally happened. The first person she saw was Rob, the ANP. He groaned and grabbed her elbow. 'I called yesterday—didn't you get the message to call me back?'

She shook her head. He walked into one of the consulting rooms and took out a key to open a locked drawer. 'The lab work showed that the antibiotic you're on won't work this time. You need something different.'

He handed over a prescription bottle with her name on it.

She nodded. 'I wondered why I wasn't feeling better so quickly. Okay, I'll swap them over.' She opened the bottle and swallowed the first tablet with some water. 'All good.' She smiled at him.

'Are you sure?'

'Yes, now let's get to the handover.'

Thursdays were a strange day in A&E. Everyone always expected weekends to be busy, but Thursdays liked to keep staff hanging, wondering if it was going to be a lull before the storm, or a full-on tornado.

Today, the waiting room was packed.

'Where do you want me?' asked Esther.

'Can you cover cubicles?' asked the charge nurse as he tried to assign everyone to their spot.

'No trouble.' She picked up the charts for the cubicles nearby and scanned them. Stitches. A fractured wrist. A patient waiting for a bed in Respiratory. Another patient needing a catheter inserted due to urinary strictures, and a confused elderly patient that had been found wandering near one of the parks and was bordering on hypothermic. More than enough to keep her busy.

Six hours later she still hadn't had a break. Esther knew she really needed to grab some more paracetamol and another dose of her new antibiotics but she literally hadn't had a minute.

'Where's the nurse who works in NICU?' she heard a harassed voice say. 'And someone call the paed doctor?'

Esther stuck her head from behind the cubicle curtains where she'd just finished stitching up a laceration. 'I'm here. Need a hand?'

The doctor she didn't know that well nodded. 'Please, I've got a newborn who doesn't look great.'

Esther nodded. 'Absolutely.' She snapped off the gloves she was wearing and grabbed a new pair, striding quickly alongside the doctor. She could sense his panic. And she understood it. He was new to the department and relatively junior. Dealing with babies could be scary. Paediatrics wasn't everyone's bag.

She stepped into the cubicle and saw the baby still clutched in its mother's arms. She sat down in the chair next to her. 'Hi there. I'm Esther, a midwife and a nurse. Can you tell me what happened today?'

The mother was trembling. She knew it was important to get a good history from the mother, and to try and keep things calm.

She caught a waft of something and sensed someone had come in at her back. But she kept her concentration on the baby. She really needed to get a look at either he or she.

'I h-had a home delivery last week. Everything was fine. But...he's just gone downhill fast. He's not feeding well, he keeps being sick. His colour is bad, and he gasps when he's breathing.'

Esther nodded and held out her arms towards the mother. 'Okay, sounds like I need to take a little look at him. What's his name?'

'Jude.'

She smiled and kept her hands outstretched. 'Do you mind if I take a look at Jude?'

The woman hesitated and then finally handed over

the little baby. Esther moved slowly and laid the little boy down on the A&E trolley.

She knew instantly that the person on her shoulder was Harry, and after one look at this baby, for once, she wasn't too sorry he was there.

He'd walked into the cubicle just a few steps behind Esther. Paeds had received three panicked calls from A&E. He couldn't quite understand why Esther was working down here, but he gave her space to talk to what was clearly a very anxious mother. She handled the situation well and he waited until she'd moved the baby to the trolley before moving to the other side. He gave a nod to the mother and opened his mouth to speak but Esther got there first.

'Was Jude full term when he was born?'

The mum shook her head. 'Thirty-eight weeks but the midwife said there was nothing to worry about.'

Harry took his stethoscope from his neck and smiled at the mum. 'I'm Harry, I'm one of the paediatric doctors. I'm just going to check Jude over if that's okay with you.'

The woman gave an anxious nod and Harry waited patiently as Esther unwound a finger probe from the paed monitor and attached it to Jude's tiny finger.

Harry had learned not to introduce himself as a paediatric surgeon; it had a tendency to freak people out. Truth was, the paed doctor who was on call was dealing with a meningitis case in one of the wards upstairs. When Harry had heard there was a baby with potential breathing difficulties, he'd offered to cover the call.

And he was glad he had.

This little guy was using all his accessory muscles to breathe. It only took a few seconds to show that he was bradycardic, and his oxygen saturation was lower than he would have hoped for.

Esther didn't say a word, just reached for the oxygen and handed him the chart. She was efficient, he'd give her that.

She slid the nasal prongs into place and picked up an ear thermometer. Harry listened carefully to Jude's chest, hearing exactly what he expected to.

There was a definite heart defect. One he'd need to diagnose after a few more investigations. In the meantime he pulled over the sonogram without waiting for a sonographer and had a quick look for himself.

Esther was talking in a low voice to little Jude. He was responding, blinking and kicking his arms and legs. His skin was a little dusky, but not enough to cause huge concerns for Harry. He suspected this was something he could solve with surgery in the next few days. It wasn't uncommon for heart defects not to be obvious in babies straight away. The most severe were normally picked up at prenatal scans. But the less severe could be missed.

He moved around and sat in the chair next to the mum, then paused, realising he didn't know her name.

It was like Esther read his mind. She glanced at the chart he'd left sitting on the other side of the trolley and gave a casual smile. 'Claire, Harry our doctor is going to explain what he thinks is going on with Jude right now.'

Harry gave her a grateful nod. 'Is there anyone else here with you?'

Claire shook her head, her eyes bright with tears. 'I just panicked and brought him in. I tried to phone my husband and my mum-in-law but neither of them answered. I left messages.'

Esther nodded. 'How about I have a quick check in the waiting room to see if either of them have arrived?'

Two minutes later she returned with a breathless man and an older-looking woman with her bag clutched to her chest. Both of them immediately crowded over Jude. Harry waited for them to ease their panic. The guy came and put his arm around his wife. 'What's going on?'

'He went a funny colour when he was feeding and it just didn't get better.'

The older woman was stroking Jude's head and whispering to him. It was clear Claire had supports in place that Jill in the NICU could badly do with. Harry introduced himself and shook hands, then took some time explaining what was wrong with Jude's heart, drew a diagram for them explaining how surgery would fix things.

It was clear they were horrified, but Esther was smooth, finding tissues for tears, then a chair for gran, whose legs seemed to fold once she found out her precious first grandson needed surgery.

'But who can do it?'

'I'll do it.'

'You do surgery on babies' hearts? Doesn't that need to be a specialist?'

'I am a specialist. I'm a visiting surgeon at the Queen Victoria. Cardiac surgery in babies is my speciality.'

Esther's eyes locked with his, and she gave the slightest nod of her head, as if she approved of how he was talking to the mum.

'How many times have you done this operation?'

Harry counted in his head. 'This will be number twenty-seven.'

There was an audible sigh of relief. He understood that. Esther made a few notes and stepped outside the cubicle while he kept talking to the family.

When she came back in he had just finished explaining that they'd transfer Jude upstairs and make arrangements for admission.

'Done,' said Esther, handing him the paperwork. 'Porter is just coming. Francesca will review Jude on the ward.'

Harry raised his eyebrows. 'You don't waste time.'

She gave him a tight smile. 'Some people call me efficient.'

He shifted on his feet. Was she mad at him again? He thought they'd sorted things. The porter arrived quickly and Harry decided to head up to the ward with the family

He booked the theatre time for the next day and spoke to Francesca before heading back down to A&E. It only took him a few minutes to find Esther again. She was clearing up a tray of bloody swabs.

'Whoa.'

She looked up. "Gunshot wound. Thankfully it was just a graze.'

'Do midwives normally treat gunshot wounds?'

She blinked. 'I'm a nurse too. That's why I get to work in A&E.' She paused for a second and then added, 'How's your baby in France?'

He pulled a face. 'Post-op complications. He developed a pulmonary embolism. Probably not much bigger than the head of pin. But in a twenty-five-weeker...'

He looked up and realised she was holding her breath. 'Oh, everything's good now. We're back to a "wait and see."'

'How come you were down covering?'

'I'd just got back from France and came in to check on Billy. I'd gone along to the ward and saw the messages about the A&E referral. The doc in Paeds was dealing with a meningitis case so I offered to cover.'

'That was nice of you.' Her eyebrows were raised.

'What? You don't think I can be nice?'

She tilted her head to the side. 'To be honest, I don't know what I think of you, Harry Beaumont, or should I call you the Duke of Montrose?'

He winced. His title followed him everywhere. Not that he ever really used it. Only at family occasions when he had to.

Her hand went to her mouth to cover a yawn, and he was instantly suspicious.

'Excuse me,' she said as she dug her hand into her pocket and pulled out some antibiotics, tipping one out and swallowing it.

'You're still not feeling better?' They were under the bright lights of the treatment room and it struck him that she pretty much looked like when he'd seen her on that first day.

She gave a half-hearted shrug. 'They've changed my antibiotics. I was resistant to the first lot and I didn't get the message until today.'

'So, you still have a temp and feel knackered?'

She spun towards him in surprise. 'Since when did you get all Scottish?' She let out a little laugh. 'Have you any idea how that word sounds in an accent like yours?'

He grinned at her. 'Does it sound any better when I say Crabbie Rabbie?'

She crossed her arms in front of her chest. 'Right, that's it. It's official. You're banned from saying that. In fact—' she headed to the door of the treatment room '—you're banned from any Scottish words.' She shot him a teasing glance. 'I'm not buying the Duke of Montrose title. You're about as Scottish as the London subway.'

He opened his mouth in pretend horror. 'Esther McDonald, are you mocking me?'

She gave a shake of her head. 'Oh, Harry, I haven't even started yet.'

She started to walk away, 'Sorry, got to run. Busy.'

Things just got crazier. And Esther got more and more tired by the second. Could there be a chance the second set of antibiotics weren't right for her either? That would definitely be unusual. Plus it would start to freak her out that she might have an infection that was multiresistant. That had never happened to her before, and she knew they could be serious.

The more tired she got, the more patients crowded through the door. She spent time with a young woman who came in with symptoms of pregnancy that she clearly was ignoring. She kept refusing to accept she was pregnant and her behaviour got more and more erratic. Eventually Esther realised she needed someone other than the A&E docs to assess this young lady. She called one of the psychiatric liaison nurses who was able to discover that their patient had a pre-existing mental-health condition and had in fact realised she was pregnant, and had stopped her regular medication in case it caused harm to her baby. Now, her condition was spiralling and she needed some help.

Next up was an elderly lady who'd fallen and broken her hip, lying on the ground for a few hours before she was found. Hypothermia was setting in, and Esther had to try and get her warmed up in the first instance before she could even be assessed for potential surgery.

As the evening progressed Esther started to develop an unconscious itch. She couldn't understand it. It started on her back, then moved to her abdomen. She was monitoring her lady's temperature for the fifth time when Harry caught her standing on one of the corners of the department using the wall edge to scratch her back.

He stopped walking and looked at her. 'Esther, have you looked in the mirror lately?'

'Do I look as if I've had time to look in a mirror lately?' It was snappier than she meant it to be.

He put his hands firmly on her shoulders and walked her across the corridor to the accessible toilet that had a large mirror on the wall. He flicked on the light and she gasped.

Red blotches stared at her, climbing all the way up her neck. 'Oh my...' Propriety was out the window. She pulled up her scrub top and looked at her abdomen. Yip. Covered, along with a whole host of scratch marks. She lifted her scrub top at the back. 'Can you check my back?'

She wasn't the least embarrassed to ask. He was a doctor, and he was right there.

He bent down and took a look, just in time for one of the other A&E members of staff to walk by and raise their eyebrows. Thankfully Harry didn't notice as he stood up and shook his head. 'You're covered.' His finger touched the top of her arm where her scrub top ended. 'Look, they're starting to appear on your arms too.'

She looked down; sure enough, a red, angry-looking blotch was only half hidden by the sleeve of her scrub top.

'No wonder I've been so itchy.' She sighed. She'd been so busy she hadn't had time to stop and think about it.

'New body lotion? New washing powder?' he asked.

She shook her head. 'No, nothing.' Then something lined up in her brain. 'Oh, darn it.' She reached into her scrub top and pulled out her pill bottle. 'These antibiotics. I've never had these before. It must be them.'

Before she had a chance to say anything else Harry reached over and wrapped his hand around her wrist. She didn't get a chance to object as he led her down the corridor to the treatment room. He stuck his head back out. 'Rob!' His shout was loud and commanding, and a few seconds later Rob the ANP appeared.

'Do you have the key for the medicine trolley?' Harry asked as Esther let out a few coughs.

Rob frowned, glancing from Harry to Esther, his eyes narrowing as he looked at her. He pulled the keys from his pocket. 'Yes.'

Harry held out his hand. 'I think she's having an allergic reaction to those new antibiotics. I'm going to give her some antihistamines.'

Rob moved over, touching her face and turning it from side to side to check either side of her neck. 'Any wheezing? Difficulty breathing?'

She shook her head but let out another cough.

'How bad is the rash?' he asked. She sighed and partly lifted her scrub top again, letting Rob bend down to have a quick check.

'Darn it,' he said. 'I'm going to record this in your notes and get you something else.'

Harry named another antibiotic. 'Try that one,' he said to Rob as he opened a bottle of tablets and tipped two into Esther's hand.

Esther turned on the tap and swallowed the antihistamines with a little water in a medicine cup. This rash was getting itchier by the second.

Okay, she'd been itchy earlier. But she knew this was psychological. Now she'd seen it and realised it was there, she just wanted to claw at herself. Lovely.

Harry had a worried look on his face, and she wasn't sure whether to feel grateful, or a bit annoyed. She put her hand on the worktop in the treatment room for a second as a wave of tiredness hit her.

She calculated in her head how many days she'd been fighting this infection now. The tiredness had still been there but she'd tried her best to ignore it, believing as soon as the antibiotics kicked in, it would just lift. That's what had always happened in the past.

'I have to go back and check obs on my woman,' she said to Harry. 'Thanks for the help. I guess I'll see you later.'

'You can't go out there looking like that. And wait until Rob comes back with some new antibiotics. I think you should sit down for a while.'

Her face went automatically into a frown and he held up both hands. 'Not trying to tell you what to do.'

His mouth started to form other words and she thought for a second he was going to use her nickname, but he smiled, must have thought better of it and stopped. 'But have you had a break today?'

She shook her head. 'Then what about a coffee? Even in the staff room for five minutes? Let Rob write up his paperwork and come back with something.'

The thought of sitting down for five minutes was tempting. 'But what about my patient?'

'Cubicle five?'

She nodded.

'Let me tell the charge nurse you need a five-minute break and ask if someone else can check on your lady.' Harry pulled a face. 'I hate to break it to you, Esther, but you are actually having an allergic reaction to antibiotics. It's quite severe. Let's just be sure it doesn't progress. Let's be safe.'

It was the way he said those words. She was so much of the 'drag yourself into work no matter what' mentality—one that a lot of nurses had—that she never really stopped and took time for herself. The truth was, with the extra hours she'd been doing, she hadn't had any time. Would five minutes really matter? She should have been sent for a break a few hours ago.

'Okay,' she said reluctantly.

Harry nodded and walked down the corridor in long strides. Esther made her way to the staff room and flicked the switch on the kettle.

There was a huge box of cupcakes and doughnuts in the middle of the table from a bakery that was quite exclusive. Anything left in the staff room was pretty much a free-for-all and she was surprised there were any left.

As she took down a couple of cups Harry came back through the door. 'All sorted. I told Rob where we are and he's just finished the paperwork.'

Where *we* are. She wasn't quite sure how she felt about that phrase.

She turned back. 'Does that mean you're planning on hanging around?'

He nodded. 'I'm monitoring your reaction.'

As soon as he said those words she scratched again.

'Whilst eating cakes,' he added.

She spooned coffee into two cups and filled them with boiling water. It would be rude not to, but she didn't plan on being too hospitable. 'Milk's in the fridge if you want it,' she said as she handed over the cup.

He stood quickly to get some. 'Don't you want some?' he asked as he added milk to his cup.

She smiled. 'No, not here. I never trust milk dates when I'm in the hospital. I always drink my coffee black in here.'

He stared suspiciously into his cup as he sat back down. 'Yeah, thanks for that.' He pushed the box towards her. 'Eat something.'

'I wonder where these came from?' she asked as a strawberry cupcake seemed to shout her name.

'Me,' he said.

'You brought cakes to A&E? You didn't even know you'd be down here.'

He gave her a calculating smile. 'I brought multiple boxes. I left one in NICU, one in Paeds and one down here.'

'Trying to win people around because occasionally you can be a bit brusque?'

He lifted a chocolate doughnut and met her gaze. There was something quite electric about those eyes. She was glad she was sitting, because the look would likely have stopped her in her tracks. 'Has anyone ever told you that you speak your mind?'

She laughed. 'No. Why would anyone ever tell me that?' She nibbled at the cupcake. 'But let me warn you, you think I'm bad? Try meeting Oona our charge nurse. If you think I was smart about the entourage, she would have chewed you up and spat you out.'

'Nice.' He nodded. 'Okay, then, if this is a teaching hospital, exactly how many am I allowed to bring in to NICU?'

'Students?'

He nodded.

'Two. And they better follow the infection control procedures. To the letter.'

He leaned over and gently slapped her hand. 'Stop scratching.'

He was right. She was clawing away at her neck again and hadn't even noticed. 'When are these antihistamines going to start to kick in?' She let out a long, exhausted breath.

Harry glanced at his watch. 'Probably not for another hour at least.'

Now she'd sat down, tiredness was really starting to overwhelm her, and it didn't matter how nice Harry had been to her today, because of their altercation a few days before, the last thing she wanted to do was show him just how tired she was at work. Not when she had patients to see, and other staff relying on her.

But Harry was being nice to her. She couldn't pretend anything else. Today, he'd given her space to deal with the mother and baby. Not all doctors were like that. Some would just have barged in and taken over.

The truth was, she was slightly curious about him. He must have worked hard to gain his position as a neonatal cardiac surgeon. As for the duke stuff? He certainly hadn't told anyone his title, but information like that was quick to follow a person.

She was suddenly conscious they were the only people in the room, and even though she was at the other side of the coffee table, his fresh scent was drifting over towards her. When she was feeling as tired and woozy as this, it was kind of hypnotic. She felt as if she had to get out of here.

She pushed herself up. 'I better get back. I have another hour before I'm off shift. You've seen it out there, it's chaos. I can't stay here eating cakes.'

She'd made it to the door by then, but Harry was right alongside her, his fingers brushing her arm. 'Even if you're sick?'

She licked her lips. She couldn't pretend she felt one hundred per cent. She was feeling hot again, and she wanted to find Rob and get started on the third set of antibiotics. No wonder her body felt so tired from constantly fighting an infection.

She gave him a tight smile. 'You know how the health service is.' She ducked out the door before Harry had a chance to say anything else, his fingers burning an imprint on her skin.

She didn't finish her shift an hour later. Harry knew, because after reviewing Billy in NICU, and making arrangements for the new baby's surgery, his feet just seemed to automatically take him back downstairs to A&E to check on her.

It was crazy. He didn't even understand it himself. But there was something about this occasionally angry Scottish midwife that was just pulling him in.

He was quite sure she didn't want him there. But even though they'd had a bad start, he'd watched her interactions with others, with patients, and the respect she had from other staff, and all of it intrigued him.

So he stood in the corridor as he watched her dash back and forward between cubicles. Rob came and stood alongside him, folding his arms and leaning against the wall like Harry, mirroring his stance.

'Are you doing what I think you're doing?'

'Her rash seems to have died down a bit, but shouldn't she have gone home by now?' He turned towards Rob. 'Shouldn't you have gone home too?'

Rob shrugged. 'You know how it is.' His eyes went to Esther, who hadn't noticed either of them as she stopped for a second in the corridor and put her hand on the wall. She looked absolutely exhausted.

They shot each other a glance and walked over to her. 'Okay,' Rob said quickly. 'Esther, I'm officially sending you home. I should have done it earlier, but to be truthful I thought you would have responded much quicker to the antihistamines. I'm sorry.'

'But my patients…'

Rob interrupted her. 'They'll be reassigned.'

She sagged a little as relief clearly flooded over her. 'Great.'

He tilted his head and looked at her again. 'Is there someone at home with you?'

She scowled. 'No. Why?'

Rob bit his bottom lip. 'I actually wonder if I should make you stay overnight in the combined assessment unit—you know, for observation?'

He was glancing at Harry again.

She shook her head fiercely. 'No way. Not a chance.'

'Esther, I'm not sure I should let you go home. What if something happens in the middle of the night? What if you feel unwell? How will you get back in?'

Esther gave Harry a look of panic. The dark circles under her eyes pulled at something inside him.

No member of NHS staff wanted to see a colleague look like this.

Harry stood for a few moments next to her, not wanting to leave. It was a strange sensation for him. A few days ago he'd been ready to do battle with this midwife, questioning her competence. But here she was, working in A&E as well as NICU. There had to be a story there, and he was curious what it was. Now he'd seen her working, he knew she was dedicated. He just didn't know why she was taking on so many shifts to the detriment of her own health. He might not be an expert, he might not even know her that well, but from what little he'd seen, Esther was on the verge of burnout.

She gave a soft smile, and shook her head again. He could tell she was going to try and persuade Rob to let her go. She gave an unconscious scratch of her neck and gave Harry a sad kind of smile. 'Thanks for looking out for me earlier.'

'Of course.' He meant it. He'd look out for any member of staff that was clearly unwell at work.

He held up his hand. 'Stay here. Both of you. Don't move.'

There was a phone on the nearby wall and he picked it up, calling up to first NICU, then the paed ward. Everything appeared to be under control. The other doc on call was more than competent. 'Head home, Harry. Anything happens with your own patients I've got your mobile and I'll give you a call. But you can trust me, you know?' he added in a jokey tone.

'Okay.' Harry hung up the phone. He had to get better at that. Trusting others with his patients. Maybe it was because he'd spent so long being the visiting expert surgeon. It meant he couldn't form relationships long enough with people to feel assured about their competencies.

Or maybe it was because of the way he'd been brought up. No child asked to be born to parents who weren't the least bit interested in them. A child had been a necessity for the duke and duchess. Someone to carry on the family name. But that's all he'd been. It had taken him a long time to realise that the relationship he had with his parents wasn't entirely normal. Most kids who boarded did actually get to spend some time at home. But not Harry. It made forming relationships hard for him. He'd spent most of his childhood thinking he didn't deserve love, and most of his wild teenage years looking for love wherever he could find it. Medicine had been his blessing. His focus. Surgery his ultimate goal. He'd managed to keep everything right on track until the death of his father had derailed one of his first surgeries.

He'd had to leave. It was unheard of for a son not to attend his father's funeral. The gossip columns would have loved it. His mother had died years previously, so he was the only family left to make the arrangements. So, only two days after his first neonatal cardiac surgery, he'd had to travel home for the funeral.

He'd had to leave the tiny baby he'd wanted to watch like a hawk. And it had happened. The death. While he wasn't there. His first experience of a child death review with his name as the surgeon. It was devastating for him, and had almost derailed his career. He would never know if something else could have been done to save that baby. None of them would. But it had left an indelible mark on Harry. One he couldn't ever shake off, or forget.

These babies were his responsibility and he could never forget that. Working with a hundred different teams across a variety of continents was difficult for him. Being a visiting surgeon was hard.

Some weeks he didn't even get to sleep in his own bed. Constantly moving from place to place—sometimes from country to country to perform his specialist kind of surgery. At first he'd liked it. Enjoyed it even.

But constantly working with different staff was wearing. He'd never considered it before, but the thought of having his own team—a team that he would train by himself and he could trust—had started to play on his mind.

He could also get to know all the staff who worked in NICU and Paeds and perhaps even have a little confidence in the people around him. He could actually start to get a life again—or even get to spend some time in his own bed, in his own home. Now that would really be a miracle.

He walked back over, the decision already made in his head. 'Okay, Esther. You're coming home with me.'

'What?' She looked entirely stunned.

He shrugged. 'This is easy. You have two choices. You let Rob admit you, or you let me take you home and keep an eye on you overnight.'

She opened her mouth to speak but he kept talking.

'I know what's happened. I know the history. I'm not going to tell anyone else, and you don't need to tell anyone you stayed with me. If you're unwell during the night I can bring you back in.'

The stunned look hadn't changed. Harry's conscience was tugging at heartstrings he didn't even know he had. But every cell in his body told him this was the right thing to do.

Rob shot him a glance and a nod. He folded his arms across his chest. 'Sounds good to me, but it's entirely your choice, Esther. I think you need supervision for at least the next eight hours. Where you spend them is up to you.'

She shot them both a look of complete exasperation. 'Fine, fine.' She threw up her hands. 'Just let me go and get changed.'

She turned and walked off to the female changing room. Harry went into the other changing room and stowed his white coat and pulled out his jacket. He was still waiting to be allocated an office. Hospital space was always tight, so until then, he was happy to have somewhere safe to leave his things.

As he pulled his car keys from his trouser pocket he saw Esther standing at the exit to A&E. Her head was turning from side to side as if she were contemplating the option to run. The weather had turned and rain was bucketing down.

He moved outside, his shoulder brushing against hers. The sun was setting in the sky, sending purple streaks above them.

Harry didn't hesitate. 'Your place or mine?'

He could see something flit across her face. 'Why are you doing this?' Her voice was quiet, almost a whisper.

He'd asked himself the same question. 'Because I should,' he said simply. 'It's the right thing to do.'

There was a long pause, then Esther's shoulders sagged a little, just like they had earlier, as if she'd accepted that answer. 'It will take too long to get to mine. You must be tired. I'm sure you stay closer.' She was saying the words but he could see something else in her eyes. Maybe she didn't want him to see where she lived?

'You're sure about this?' she repeated, her hand gripping tightly to the handle of her bag.

'I'm sure. Come on.' He started walking across the car park, pressing the buttons on his remote to open the doors. 'Relax,' he laughed over his shoulder. 'You're acting like I'm kidnapping you. Rob knows I've taken you home. If you're never seen again, he'll send the police after me.'

'Oh, reassure me, why don't you,' she quipped back.

As they reached the car she stopped walking and

looked at him, eyebrow slightly arched, as the rain thudded around them. 'Really?'

He shrugged. 'What? Excessive?'

She opened the door to the dark blue Aston Martin and climbed in. As he slid in beside her she shook her head. 'No, excessive would have been a royal carriage. And at this point in the day, I'd go home in anything.'

She leaned back into the seat. 'Should I call you James Bond, instead of Duke?'

He smiled at her teasing. 'Harry will be fine, thanks.' He started the engine. 'I think I told you before I'm not far from here. Where do you live?'

'Dagenham, not the same as you in Belgravia.' The edges of her lips curled upwards.

He gave a nod and pulled out of the car park. No wonder she was tired. The tube between the Queen Victoria and Dagenham would add almost an hour each way onto her journey every day.

He waited until they were in the traffic before he glanced towards her. 'So, how come you work so much?'

Her eyes were already halfway closed. She let out a sigh. 'My mum needs some help back home. She's had cancer and although she's in remission the chemo and radiotherapy meant she's never got back to full fitness and can't get back to work.' She turned her head. 'I need to cover the mortgage. It's only got a couple of years left. I can do it.'

The words came out in a stream and he knew if she hadn't been half as exhausted she probably wouldn't have told him any of this.

His head was immediately filled with a barrage of questions that it wasn't good manners to ask. At least now he understood. She had a real reason to work every hour there was. She obviously felt responsible for her mum.

Something twisted in his gut. Even those few words let him know that Esther and her mother had a real bond, a real connection. He shifted in his seat uncomfortably. He'd never known what that felt like. His parents had always been like distant ornaments sitting on a grand mantelpiece.

He'd spent more happy years at boarding school, and at university, than he ever had being back in their grand estate. Taking ownership of the Belgravia town house had felt like a huge sigh of relief that he wouldn't be expected to be under the same roof as them for any length of time.

Esther's eyes were fully closed and her breathing steady. She was fast asleep and they'd barely been in the car a few minutes.

Her dark hair was coming loose from its braid and for a few moments his eyes fixated on her long dark lashes. How had he not really noticed them before?

The car behind him beeped and he moved the Aston Martin quickly through the traffic, letting some quiet music play in the background as they drove.

Esther remained fast asleep. He could still see the edge of some of the rash at the bottom of her neck. The steroids should have kicked in a few hours before. Her reaction had obviously been a bit more serious than any one of them had realised.

By the time he'd pulled into the parking for his town house, his initial confidence had waned a little. He switched off the engine and walked around to her side of the car. The lift in the converted basement could take him right up to the top floor of the town house, where the bedrooms were.

He opened the door, and paused again to see if she would wake. Nothing. 'Esther,' he said gently. 'I'm just going to pick you up.'

She murmured something in reply. It didn't sound like a no, so he slid his arms under her and picked her up, grabbing her bag and closing the car door with his hip.

The lift took them upstairs in seconds and he flicked on a light with his elbow, and walked down the corridor towards one of the empty bedrooms in his house.

They were all beautifully decorated, fresh and light. He laid her down on top of one of the beds, then slid off her shoes. He didn't want her to panic if she woke up, so when he closed the heavy curtains, he turned the bedside light on, setting it to dim.

The en suite bathroom was stocked with supplies. She could find anything she might need in here. Her jacket pocket jangled as he slid it from her shoulders. Of course. Her new antibiotics. He couldn't let her go without them.

He sat the antibiotics on the table and saw that Rob had added in a couple of extra antihistamines. Harry grabbed her a glass of water from the bathroom and sat out the pills she needed to take.

He spoke as gently as he could. 'Esther, you need to take your antibiotics, and another antihistamine. You still have a bit of a reaction going on. Can you take these for me?' He pressed them into one hand and held the glass in his other.

Something must have clicked in her brain. She didn't open her eyes, but put the tablets in her mouth. Harry closed her hand around the glass of water and her body acted automatically, lifting the glass to her mouth and swallowing. The second it was done she hunkered back down into the bed, lying on her side.

Harry pulled a pale yellow blanket up from the bottom of the bed. She wasn't actually under the duvet, as putting her there seemed intrusive, so he refilled her glass of water and tucked the blanket around her.

At the last moment, he scribbled a note on the pad next to her bed before he walked out and closed the door.

He'd check on her again in a few hours.

He smiled, remembering words he'd heard her say to someone else earlier that day. Something about having their head in their hands to play with if they didn't do what they were told.

It seemed highly likely that tomorrow that person would be him.

But Harry wasn't scared. In fact, he liked it.

CHAPTER FIVE

SHE HADN'T FELT this rested and comfortable in a long time. There was the warmest feeling around her, almost as if she were sleeping in some kind of luxury cocoon.

She sniffed. And that little action woke her up. A slight hint of lemon. Her flat did not smell of lemon. No matter how many air fresheners she bought. Her flat always had an underlying odour of damp.

She sat bolt upright, eyes widening at the pale yellow walls, unfamiliar furniture and the space in the room. She felt like Dorothy, waking up in a place that certainly wasn't Kansas.

There. At the bottom of the bed was a tray, with a large teapot, a slight trail of steam coming from the spout. A china cup and saucer sat next to it, along with a milk jug and small plate containing slices of lemon. That's where the smell was coming from.

Her mouth felt yucky. And she swung her legs off the bed as she tried to make sense of things in her head. She should be shouting. She should be screaming. But she had the oddest sensation of not being gripped by panic. It was just as if her brain was playing catch up.

There, sitting on the bedside table, was her bottle of

antibiotics along with a glass of water. She took one automatically and walked through to the bathroom. Her reflection in the mirror wasn't pleasant. But the accessories sitting around the white sink and vanity unit were strangely welcoming.

Her head was starting to unfog. The shift last night in A&E. How busy it was. She unconsciously scratched at her skin. She walked back and picked up the antibiotics again. Of course. These were new.

She patted herself. She still had on all her clothes. The only things removed were her jacket and her shoes, and even from here she could see these sitting clearly on a high-backed chair in the room.

Realisation struck. Harry. She'd agreed to go home with Harry. They'd got in the car together but she had absolutely no memory at all of getting here. She let out a groan. She'd fallen asleep, hadn't she?

Heat rushed into her cheeks. He must have carried her up the stairs. Just how strong was Duke Harry?

She licked her lips and poured herself some tea. She wasn't exactly in a rush to go and find him. One glance at her watch showed her how early it was. She had time to shower, and use some of the products in the bathroom to tidy herself up. She walked over to the window and pulled back the heavy drapes.

Wow. Her fingers caught on the obviously expensive material. She ran her fingers over it a few times before hauling the curtains backwards. The road outside was peaceful; she peered downwards through the checker-paned windows at the luxury cars parked in the street outside. The house seemed to be in some kind of square.

She gave a shudder, not even wanting to take a guess at what a place like this cost.

She sipped at the tea, and turned on the shower, slipping out of her clothes and putting on the cosy white dressing gown that was hanging handily behind the bathroom door. With her hair tied up on top of her head it only took a few moments for her to start waking up once she'd stepped in the steaming hot shower. Once she'd scrubbed herself dry and used the rose-scented toiletries she felt a little better. The ugly rash from last night had all but vanished. She brushed her teeth and walked back through to pull her clothes back on. But something made her hesitate. Pulling on yesterday's clothes seemed a little unpleasant. Her hand hovered next to the door. The guy had carried her upstairs and put her to bed. Would it really be so wrong to ask for a T-shirt?

As soon as she opened the door she could smell food cooking.

Her feet took her down a plush-carpeted corridor, a small set of stairs and into a white shiny kitchen. The kind normally found in a new show home that looked untouched.

Harry was in the middle of this kitchen with fresh toast, and mixing up some scrambled eggs. 'Oh, Esther, are you okay? How are you feeling?'

She moved over towards the island in the kitchen, perching on one of the stools as she watched him cook. He seemed pretty relaxed. He obviously didn't feel awkward about last night and she was thankful. This could have been a really uncomfortable morning.

She leaned her head on one hand. 'I'm sorry. I must have zonked out on you last night.'

He gave her a wary glance as he tipped the scrambled eggs onto two plates. 'That's okay. How are you feeling this morning?'

'Okay, I think. I don't have the intense itch that I remember from last night. But there is something else.'

'Yeah? What?' His eyebrows rose as he looked at her quizzically.

She smiled. 'I'm just waiting to see if you're going to sue me for back injuries.'

He laughed and pushed the toast across the counter towards her. 'Here. Eat up. You must be starving.'

She nodded in agreement. 'Yip. I am. I missed out on the beans I was going home to last night.' She buttered her toast and took a spoonful of scrambled eggs. 'Wow. You can actually cook.'

He sat down opposite her and picked up a cafetière of coffee. 'Want some of this?'

She nodded as he poured. 'Why are you being so nice to me?'

'I am?' He fixed his dark eyes on her. It was clear he'd not long showered. The tips of his ruffled hair were still damp. When he smiled he had little crinkles around his eyes. Ones that were still there when he stopped. Obviously Harry usually smiled a lot, just not generally around her.

'Yes.' She nodded. 'You are.'

Something flashed into her brain. Something she'd told him last night. She automatically straightened in her seat. 'You felt sorry for me.'

He looked up from stirring his coffee. 'What?'

'Last night. I told you something I shouldn't have. You felt sorry for me.' She wanted to stand up and walk away. Every cell of her body was in defence mode right now.

His spoon paused just as he went to set it down. 'I didn't do this because I felt sorry for you, Esther. I did it because you were a colleague, and I was worried about you. You were clearly—' his lips turned into a smile '—knackered. And you'd had a reaction to your antibiotic. I was just looking out for you. Not—' he shook his head '—feeling sorry for you.'

She couldn't help but smile back at his use of one of her frequently used words.

She wriggled her shoulders a bit—almost as if she were trying to shake off some of her anxieties.

'How's your rash?'

She raised her eyebrows. 'Oh, so we're getting personal now?'

He wrinkled his nose in amusement. 'Well, I've seen part of your body now anyway. Is it gone?'

She shook her head at him. 'Seems to be.'

'So, no reaction to the new set of antibiotics, then?'

'Thankfully not. Don't want to end up Ms Antiresistant. That would be a disaster.'

'You said you were prone to these infections?'

She nodded. Some might find the question intrusive. But Esther wasn't like that.

'Yeah. Kidney issues as a kid means that if I'm ever a bit run-down I tend to get a flare-up. Usually I notice the symptoms quickly and get things sorted out. But I was late to notice this time around. I've been too busy working and I've never had a reaction to antibiotics before.'

'Any idea what could have caused it? Anything changed? Medical condition?' She could tell he was running through a whole host of things in his head. His eyes met hers. 'Pregnancy?'

She laughed. 'That would require a partner,' she said bluntly. 'So, not a possibility.' Her skin tingled. Had Harry actually meant to ask that question?

'So, no other half?'

Yip. He obviously had. If she didn't know better she'd say there had just been an explosion of butterflies in her stomach.

'Maybe I'm just too crabbie?' she said, half joking.

'Or maybe you're just picky,' he said, giving her an easy get-out clause.

'Don't you have a duchess stashed away somewhere?' she asked. 'Should I expect some lady in satin to walk down the corridor any second now?'

She hated how much she really didn't want that to happen. Up until this point she hadn't thought to ask the question. Now she really, really wanted to know the answer.

A slow smile spread across Harry's face. As if he could see into her curious mind right now. He waved a hand ever so casually. 'There's no duchess. No other half. Quite frankly, I haven't had the time. I'm never in one place for any length of time to even form a friendship, let alone a relationship.'

Something flitted across his face as he said that, and she immediately knew there was a whole load more to that story.

'So, as our new visiting surgeon…' She let the words trail off for a moment.

He took a sip of his coffee. His eyes stayed steadily fixed on hers. 'Yes?'

'How long you going to be visiting?' She knew her tone was teasing.

He smiled. 'Depends how nice the staff are.'

Esther put down her knife and fork. The scrambled eggs had been delicious, but they were gone now. One of her fingers twiddled with a loose piece of her hair. 'So, in my experience, what generally happens when you start working at a new place is you come in and introduce yourself to the staff and be nice to people.'

'I wasn't?' He'd raised his eyebrows. His tone was teasing too.

Esther shook her head. 'You were a rat bag and you know it.'

He laughed out loud.

'Maybe I should call you Flash Harry. In and out of the unit, after you bandy about your title and wreak havoc.'

He rolled his eyes. 'Flash Harry, like I've never heard that before.' Then he grinned. 'I like Crabbie Rabbie better.'

She shook her head. 'Will you do many surgeries at the Queen Victoria?'

She was probing. She knew she was. But the truth was, she did actually want to know how often Harry was likely to be around.

Some might say he was being mildly flirtatious with her. She wanted to know if she should be flirtatious back. She wasn't interested in anything permanent. She didn't have time for that. She couldn't even remember the last time she'd been on a date or had any down-time because she spent so much time doing extra shifts. Maybe it was time to open herself to the possibility of a little bit of fun?

Harry was watching her carefully. 'I might do a few. The theatre equipment at the Queen Victoria is brand new. I've been guaranteed theatre time for any baby affected across four counties.' He wrinkled his nose. 'If I was guessing, I'd imagine that could be around six babies a year for me.'

She gave a little smile. An occasional guest. That's how she could term him. Not around enough to inter-fere with her life. But maybe a familiar enough face to have a little fun with.

He licked his lips. 'It just so happens that for the next little while I'll have a few babies scheduled for surgery in the Queen Victoria. It always happens like that. So, I might be around for the next few weeks.'

The next few weeks. It could almost be music to her ears.

He closed his eyes for a second. Then he opened one and squinted at her. 'You might need to get used to me. If you'd known that at first, would we still have fought?'

She gave a thoughtful nod. 'Oh, I think so,' she said slowly, her lips curling up in a smile. She said her words with an even more teasing tone than before. 'That just seemed inevitable.'

His hand reached across the table, as if he were ac-tually going to touch her fingers. But then it stopped midway, as if his brain had thought better of it.

His voice was low, continuing with the mutual teasing. It was like they were scoping each other out. 'Some people say that opposites attract.' The words sounded like a question.

What had seemed like an explosion of butterflies in her stomach now turned into a firework explosion in her brain.

But not in a good way. Not the way it should.

He knew they were opposites. He'd asked where she lived and she'd told him. As a man who'd probably lived in London all his life, she imagined he knew exactly what her home area was like in comparison to his. But was that what Harry was talking about? Was he talking wealth and prestige? Meaning that Esther was obviously poverty-stricken and not from an upper-class family like his?

That burned somewhere deep inside. And not in any way she liked.

'Those kind of things generally don't work out,' she said flatly. She pushed herself up from the chair. All of a sudden she wanted to get of here. She didn't need to see this luxury town house with furnishings and decor she could only dream about. There were probably paintings or chairs in this place that were worth more than the value of the flat she was currently renting.

She realised she might be being rude. It didn't matter that for a few moments she could have sworn there was some electricity in the air between them, and the fact it seemed to have disappeared in a flash was leaving a heavy feeling in the pit of her stomach.

'Thanks for looking after me last night,' she said quickly. 'But I should go now.' She looked down for a second and remembered she didn't have anything clean to put on. Would second-day clothes really be so bad?

But her second-day clothes were things that she'd slept in all night. Underwear she'd been wearing since yesterday morning.

'Don't suppose I could borrow something to put on?'

Harry's face had fallen a little as she'd spoken a few moments ago and her new words made him perk up. 'You want my clothes?'

She gave a shrug. 'Why not? I've never worn a Bond Street tailored shirt. I'm not entirely sure I'd suit it.' She let out a little laugh. 'But if you had a T-shirt and some joggies I'd be delighted. I promise to wash them and give them back. I won't hold them hostage.'

He stood up. 'Come with me, then.'

She followed him up the stairs and back along the corridor before she realised he was actually taking her to his bedroom. As they stepped inside she held in the gasp. The room was enormous. Pale green, but bright and sunny.

Whilst the decor was pleasant, her eyes went immediately to the bed that seemed bigger than any she'd seen before. It was made, which was a revelation. Most of the male friends she knew climbed out of a bed in the morning, and back into a bed at night, without doing the stuff in between. The straightening and smoothing down of the sheets and duvet.

He opened the biggest walk-in wardrobe she'd ever seen. She couldn't help but mutter, 'It's actually criminal that a guy should have this.'

He laughed and glanced over his shoulder. 'Esther McDonald, are you being sexist?'

'Of course not.' She wandered up and down. There was surprisingly a small amount of clothes in here. She could see a number of impeccable suits hanging up, polished shoes on a rack on the wall and tailored shirts lined up by colour. But the whole space was maybe only a quarter full.

'Tell me you do own some T-shirts,' she said, glancing around.

He nodded and pulled open a drawer. There they were, all neatly lined up.

She sighed. 'Harry, do you actually do all this yourself?'

He shook his head. 'Of course I don't. I spend so many hours flying between hospitals and consulting on cases I couldn't even tell you how to work the washing machine. Let alone have time to stack everything neatly.'

She folded her arms across her chest and leaned against the wall. 'Oh, how the other half live.' She said it in joking terms, but it felt like yet another divide for her. Showing just how far apart they were.

He pulled out a pair of grey joggers and a white T-shirt. 'What about these?'

'Perfect,' she said as she reached out to grab them. The soft feel of the T-shirt made her want to quickly look at the label. But she resisted the temptation.

Harry stopped above another drawer and hesitated. 'This could be a bad question.'

'Could it?' Her brow wrinkled. What was he going to ask? She shook her head. 'We've already done the falling-out part, so just ask away.'

'Do you want some socks and some underwear?'

She burst out laughing, and once she'd started she couldn't really stop.

Harry looked a bit panicked. 'Okay, was it a bad question?'

She shook her head and wiped her eyes. 'No, but I'm so wishing the shoe was on the other foot right now, and it was me, asking you, if you wanted a loan of underwear.'

He started laughing too. 'Now that *would* be interesting. I love to think what you'd offer me.'

'Don't get too excited. You might be sadly disappointed.'

There was a twinkle in his eyes. 'Oh, I doubt it.'

There it was again. The buzz she thought she might have imagined earlier. Nope. She definitely wasn't imagining this.

His phone rang and he pulled it from his pocket. She leaned against the wall and listened while he rattled out the biggest list of instructions ever for a baby that was in another unit somewhere. Something flashed in her brain and she remembered hearing Harry speak to someone a few days ago about the same baby. His face was serious, almost twisted, while he spoke, and she hated the deep furrows that had formed on his brow. She'd been offended by the way he'd spoken to her previously— even though she might not have made the best impression by sleeping in the canteen. Now, she was realising that this was how he spoke to everyone looking after the babies he termed as 'his.' She folded her arms and shook her head as he finished the call and put the phone back in his pocket.

He saw her glance and attempted to change his demeanour. 'Where were we?'

She shook her head. 'No, Harry. No, you don't.'

'Don't what?'

She licked her lips. 'You don't get to brush me off.'

There was a flicker at the edge of his eye. 'What do you mean?'

She gestured with one hand and sighed. 'Why? Why do you do that?'

'Do what?'

'Speak to staff like that. Do you even realise that you do it? Micromanaging people. Have you any idea how that makes someone feel? It's almost like you don't trust them to do their job.' She shook her head. 'Not good for staff morale.'

'It's not about staff morale. It's about competent care for the babies that I've operated on.' The words just seemed to snap out of his mouth.

'Why, Harry? We all want these babies to do well. We all want them to survive. We all want to give them the best possible start in life. It's why we do those jobs.' She stepped forward and put a hand on his arm. 'But why do you act the way you do?'

Confusion flooded his face for a few seconds. As if it were taking him a few moments to process her words.

He opened his mouth to speak, and then paused. It was like his shoulders deflated, and some of the air seemed to go out of his body.

He looked at her. He *really* looked at her. And she saw something flicker in his eyes. A decision. It was like he let down a shield—a barrier. The face that he always kept in place for people.

'Something happened just after my very first neonatal cardiac surgery. Something that meant I had to leave for a few days. I'd left strict instructions for the post-op care.' He took a deep breath. 'While I was away. The baby—Joe—became very sick. He threw off a pulmonary embolism. There was nothing anyone could do and by the time I got back he was dead.' Harry twisted his hands together. 'I wished I hadn't gone. It was a family matter. Something no one else could deal with.' He faltered for a second. 'I hadn't even wanted to go in the first place.' He closed his eyes for a second, 'And when I realised what had happened to Joe, I was angry. I was beyond angry. I was sure, if I stayed there in the NICU, I might have picked up on things earlier and been able to stop what happened.'

Esther breathed. It was like little pieces of the puzzle slotting into place in her brain. 'That's why you're so pedantic about instructions?'

He nodded. 'Some people would just call me paranoid. But when you've had one neonatal death that you think you could have prevented, you don't ever want there to be another.'

She pressed her lips together for a moment, reaching across and putting one hand on his. 'But I've been in NICU a long time now, Harry. You must know that with the best will in the world, and even a sixth sense, we can't predict everything.'

He gave a slow nod. She knew he understood. 'I know that.' His voice broke a little and as she looked up into his eyes she could see how affected by this he'd been. 'But it doesn't mean that I'll ever stop trying.' He closed his other hand over hers. The warmth flooded through her. He'd been nice to her yesterday. He'd reached out. And now she wanted to reach out to him.

'So that's why you deal with staff like that? You're afraid?'

For a moment he said nothing, and then he gave a small, hesitant nod. She kept their hands together. 'You have a good team at the Queen Victoria. You can trust us, Harry. You can trust us with your babies. You might not know that yet, but you have to give us a chance. You have to let us show you that we can do the job you want us to.'

They were so close right now. All she could feel was the heat emanating between their bodies. He'd finally revealed a tiny part of himself, but it felt like just scratching the surface.

She shouldn't ask. She knew she shouldn't. But she couldn't help herself.

'Why did you have to leave, Harry?'

His eyes locked on to hers and her breath caught in her throat, wondering if she'd just pushed him too far.

'My father died,' he said bluntly. 'I had to leave to organise the funeral. There was no one else.' He shook his head, a sheen across his eyes.

'Oh, Harry,' she sighed, and naturally reached up one hand to the side of his face.

He squeezed his eyes closed and his jaw tightened. 'Don't,' he breathed. 'Don't feel sorry for me. We weren't close. We'd never been close. I didn't have a traditional happy family life.' He let out a hollow laugh and stepped back. 'Part of this is all caught up in my anger. I almost blamed my father for dying and ruining the outcome of my first surgery. How bad is that? What kind of a person does that make me?'

Her stomach twisted. There was real hurt in those words. She had no idea what had happened between Harry and his father. The animosity was real, but so was the regret—even if he couldn't see it for himself. Pain practically exuded from his pores.

But now she knew. Now she knew why he acted that way. And she had understood. He had to learn to trust his colleagues, her included.

He looked at her again and she could sense the change in atmosphere from them both. They'd both revealed a tiny part of themselves. Like Harry, she didn't want him to feel sorry for her, but now at least they understood each other's reasons—his, for being pedantic about instructions, and hers, for wanting to work so hard.

If she lit a match in here right now she was sure the place would go up in flames.

She licked her lips. His eyes were watching her every move, and she could feel the tiny little hairs on her body standing to attention underneath the thick robe.

If he just took a few steps forward...

She blinked and breathed in. She was being ridiculous. She knew she was. But the prickles on her skin told her differently. And the way that Harry was looking at her...

'I'd like to take you up on that offer,' she said, her voice coming out much more throatily than she'd expected.

There was a moment of confusion. 'What offer?'

She gave him a slow smile. 'The underwear.'

For a second he didn't move—as if he were processing her words and seeing all the things that lay underneath them. All the sparks she could feel in the air.

He broke their gaze and pulled open the drawer,
grabbing a pair of soft jersey boxer shorts and black
socks. He held them out to her and as she reached to
take them her hand trembled.

His skin brushed against hers. Fingers to fingers.

And before she knew it, his half-full hand closed
around her wrist and pulled her towards him.

It wasn't so much a pull. As soon as they'd connected
she'd been ready to close the space between them. She
didn't wait for him to put his lips on hers. She moved
first, going up on tiptoes and letting her hands slide
around his neck.

Harry responded easily, his hands anchoring on her
hips and his lips locking with hers. This was no slow
easy kiss. This was rapid and passionate with a whole
host of pent-up frustration.

Her body signalled for her to do more. But she was
conscious of the fact she was naked under the robe and
Harry was fully dressed. Esther didn't like inequalities.
If there was going to be a repeat of this, they would be
on even ground.

His hand moved from one hip and tangled in her hair
that was still caught in the make-do knot she'd used in
the shower. As she kissed him, she inhaled. Catching
the clean fresh smell of his shower gel and finding the
still-damp hair at the nape of his neck.

Their kiss slowed. Both of them conscious of what
could happen next. Esther wasn't ready for that. This
was a guy she'd hated a few days ago. Now, she was

semi-naked and kissing him in his walk-in wardrobe after he'd revealed a tiny part of himself. Honestly, she couldn't make this up. Her head still didn't quite believe it.

Their lips parted and he rested his forehead against hers for a few seconds. She liked that. A little moment together with both of them catching their breath. There was no embarrassment. No jumping back as if they'd done something wrong. They were two consenting adults. And it had been a long, long time since anyone had kissed her like that. A kiss that left her breathless and panting and listening to the pitter-patter of her heart against her chest.

Harry smiled. 'Well, that was unexpected.'

She gave a small nod. 'Indeed.'

It was a word she didn't use often. But she was feeling kind of speechless.

She stepped back and picked up the underwear and socks that had landed on the floor. 'I better get dressed,' she said quickly.

Harry blinked as if he'd gone somewhere else for a moment. 'Oh, yeah. I have surgery. I'd better get to the hospital.'

As she stepped outside the wardrobe he caught her arm. 'But I'll take you home first.'

She shook her head. 'No way. What time is it anyway? You're usually at the hospital early. They'll be looking for you. Driving me across town will just hold you up.'

He shrugged. 'That's okay. And I don't think you realise just how early it is. It's just after six. My surgery isn't until 1:00 p.m. I have plenty of time to drop you back home.'

She knew she should say no again. She knew exactly what the traffic would be like across London—even more so when he was battling to get back to the Queen Victoria. But somehow the words wouldn't come out of her mouth.

She loved her job. She didn't mind working hard. But it left so little time for anything else. She *liked* the fact that someone had actually taken the time and trouble to take care of her for once. Her mum was back home in Scotland. Apart from the handful of friends she'd trained with here, she didn't really have any deep friendships. Lots of casual acquaintances from work, but nothing else.

So, even though good manners meant she should probably insist she say no to Harry, the problem was, she just didn't want to.

'Give me five minutes,' she said, turning to leave and trying her best not to look at the giant bed in front of her. She swallowed and shook her head. One kiss. That's all she'd had and she was already starting to have crazy thoughts.

She walked down his corridor, seeing his wealth everywhere. This guy was a duke, why on earth would he be interested in a midwife from a wee place in Scotland? She wasn't exactly his type. And he wasn't exactly hers.

It was beyond odd that she'd gone in a few days from wanting to plot a guy's murder to thinking about his lips.

She reached her own room, pulled on the clothes and stuffed her own inside her large handbag. There was something intensely personal about slipping her legs into Harry's jersey shorts. They were big for her, and it just made her consider how snugly they fitted him. Esther let out a groan and shook her head. 'Get a grip,' she muttered to herself.

The clothes were miles too big so she cuffed the joggers so they didn't swallow her so much. Then hung the robe back up on the bathroom door. She had a quick check to make sure she hadn't left anything behind, then slipped on her shoes and jacket.

Harry was waiting for her in the middle of the hall and pressed a button revealing a lift.

She blinked and shook her head. 'Your house has a lift?'

He nodded. 'Of course. The car is in the basement downstairs. I think I've used the front door only a handful of times since I moved in.'

She sighed as she stepped in. 'And here was me thinking you must have carried me up legions of stairs. It's not quite so gallant knowing you just shoved me in a lift and pressed a button.'

He grinned. 'I can assure you, I didn't shove you anywhere. But—' he let out a laugh '—but the lift did help.'

She nudged him. 'If only you'd strained something.'

He turned to her, that gleam back in his eyes again as the door slid open to a dark basement. 'Oh, I think we can definitely agree that I strained something.'

She couldn't wipe the smile off her face as he opened the car door for her and she slid inside, quickly giving him the postcode for her address.

The journey across London was easy, and they chatted all the way. Sometimes about patients, sometimes about other members of staff, and Harry asked a few questions about Esther's mum. There was little point in trying to keep things secret. She'd already told him about her mum's illness and her keeping the family afloat, so nothing seemed intrusive. She kept quiet about her own father. She loved him, she'd adored him, but telling more about him would mean she would have to admit he'd been a dreamer and a drifter. It was why a stable life and stable job were so important now.

But she was curious about him. She wanted to ask more about his relationship with his parents. He'd only said a few sentences. But the resentment he'd had towards his father was very real. She wondered what kind of life he must have had to make him feel like that.

It was a little odd. But she didn't feel as if she could pry. She was acutely aware that one kiss didn't give her the right to ask for a full family history.

They drove into Dagenham and her stomach gave a little flip. She wasn't ashamed of where she stayed, but it was certainly different from his town house in Belgravia. Her basement flat was dark, with cracked windows and a few broken lamp posts nearby. Her whole flat could probably fit into his large bedroom and walk-in wardrobe and she hated the thought he might judge her because of it. Rents were high in London and it was the best she could afford.

As they pulled up outside her flat her phone beeped. She couldn't believe it actually still had any charge left. As she pulled it from her bag it beeped again and she smiled and shook her head. Harry's eyes were still on the road as he manoeuvred to park. 'Something wrong?'

She shook her head. 'Just my friends. Chloe—you might have met her. She works in A&E and covers the air ambulance service too. She's just come on duty and heard I was unwell last night. She's texting to see how I am.'

'She texted twice?'

Esther smiled and shook her head. 'Oh no. The second text is from Carly. She's a community midwife. Chloe will have asked her if she's heard from me, and now Carly is texting too. I bet if I check my emails I'll have one from Isabella too. She trained with us but is in New Zealand right now.'

'They're checking up on you?'

A warm feeling spread across her stomach. She should have known the girls would all contact her as soon as they heard she wasn't well.

Sometimes London felt a bit overwhelming. It didn't matter they all worked in different places. She knew if she picked up the phone to any one of these girls at any point, they would be there for her.

They all understood why she had to work so hard. Chloe frequently told her about extra shifts in A&E.

'They're my friends. We check up on each other.'

Harry gave an approving nod as the car came completely to a halt. She turned her head to the side and caught her breath. She looked at her flat every day. But coming from his plush town house to her basement flat with the row of run-down shops next door didn't make her feel proud.

Before she had a chance to say anything he was out of his seat and holding open the door for her. She climbed out and gave him a smile. Goodbyes could be awkward. 'Trying to get rid of me?' she joked.

'Nope,' he said, his hands going to her hips. 'Just making sure you don't run inside without kissing me goodbye.'

His lips were on hers in an instant. And she didn't resist. She wrapped her hands around his neck again as her body pressed against his. This was brand new, but it felt more comfortable than it should. Although her brain was telling her they lived different lives and had absolutely nothing in common, her body was telling her something different.

Harry wasn't permanent. This could be a passing thing. She could still commit to her work without getting too involved. She might actually have five minutes of fun. It had been so long she'd almost forgotten what it felt like. Hopefully he would be on the same wavelength.

They were in the middle of the street, so after a few moments she pulled reluctantly away, her lips already feeling swollen. 'Rest up and I'll see you at work,' he said.

She watched as he walked back around his car, slid behind the wheel of the Aston Martin and gave a wave as he drove away.

She wasn't quite sure whether to feel happy or sad. He hadn't asked for her number. He hadn't made any kind of promise or intention.

She took a few deep breaths. Her eyes caught a familiar face walking down the other side of the road. One of the orderlies from the hospital. He gave her the briefest nod and headed on down towards the train station.

Her cheeks flamed. Perfect. So much for keeping things low profile.

As she headed down the steps to her flat, part of her was still frothy and light. It didn't matter how much she wanted to pretend otherwise, Harry Beaumont had definitely gotten under her skin.

CHAPTER SIX

SHE'D SPENT THE day lying on the sofa, eating bite-sized chocolates and drinking tea. It was the first day off she'd had in a month.

By the time she got up the next morning she was feeling much better. It was clear the antibiotics had finally kicked in, and any sign of the previous reaction was completely gone.

There was a definite spring in her step as she walked along the Thames that morning. The NICU was quiet when she entered, which was usually a good sign. It meant things had been fine overnight.

The handover went smoothly and she was pleased to see Billy again. His charts showed he was starting to gain a tiny bit of weight and his wound was clean.

Her phone buzzed in her pocket and she checked. Carly. Take second break. Need to meet you in canteen.

She frowned. Was something wrong? By the time she reached the canteen, Chloe and Carly were already sitting at a table waiting for her, coffee steaming from mugs and a plate of scones in front of them. As a community midwife Carly didn't spend quite so much time in the hospital so Esther was immediately suspicious.

She pulled her chair out warily, looking from one face to the other. 'What's going on? Does one of you have something to tell me?'

Chloe tilted her head just a fraction to the side. 'Why, that's just what we were about to ask you.'

'Okay, so what does that mean?' asked Esther as she pulled one of the coffee cups towards her.

Carly had mischief written all over her face. 'Should we curtsey?'

Esther leaned her head on one hand. 'You got me. I have no idea what you're talking about.'

Chloe pulled a face. 'Don't forget where I work.'

'I know exactly where you work.' Recognition started to dawn. 'Oh, is this about me being not well?'

Carly drummed her fingers on the table. She obviously wanted to get to the point. 'More about who looked after you when you weren't well.' Cutting right to the chase.

Chloe sliced open one of the scones. 'Viktor came in this morning and took great delight in telling everyone you were in a lip lock with Harry Beaumont early yesterday morning and it was clear he was dropping you off.'

Esther's mouth fell open. She put her head on the table. 'Oh no.' Viktor. The orderly. Of course.

'Oh yes,' said Carly with glee in her voice. 'Now spill, girl. I want to know all the details.'

Esther stayed quiet for a few moments. These were her friends. At least they'd warned her she was the latest piece of hospital gossip.

She pulled her head back up. 'I'm the talk of the steamie, aren't I?'

'Yep,' said Chloe, nodding her head. 'But I want facts, not fiction.' She grinned as she looked at Esther. 'So did you, or did you not, spend the night with Harry Beaumont—our resident duke?'

There it was again—the rush of heat to her cheeks when she thought about Harry. It was getting to be normal for her.

She bit her bottom lip and tried to think of how to put this. These guys were her friends, they weren't going to judge her.

'I was working in A&E and had a bit of reaction to the antibiotics I was on. I'd been feeling tired for days and finally worked out it was due to an infection. The first set didn't work, the second set gave me hives and Harry got me some steroids and checked me over.'

Chloe's eyebrows shot up. 'Checked you over, did he?' Her voice was like a cartoon character.

Esther gave her a nudge. 'Stop it. Because I'd had a reaction they said I could only be discharged if I had supervision. Harry offered to be the supervision. I think he just felt sorry for me, because we'd had a fight a few days before. He took me home that night and I fell asleep in the car. When I woke I was in his town house.'

'Where's his town house?' asked Carly quickly.

'Belgravia.'

Both of her friends gave a little sigh. 'Well, he is a duke,' said Chloe.

'So, you slept all night, *alone*?' asked Carly.

'Yes.' Esther nodded determinedly. 'Alone.'

'So what about the love fest outside your flat, then?' Chloe was smothering her scone with jam.

Esther reached up and grabbed a strand of her hair from her ponytail and started twirling it around her finger. 'Yeah, that.'

'Yeah, *that*,' repeated Carly. 'Get to the real story, we're on a time limit here.'

Esther started stalling, wondering how she could tell the story without a whole heap of mixed emotions swirling around in her head. She buttered her scone ever so slowly.

Chloe let out a big sigh. 'Any time this year, Esther.'

For some reason she couldn't quite meet any of their inquisitive gazes. It was so much easier to stare at the scone, even though her appetite wasn't quite what it should be. Normally the Queen Victoria scones lasted around thirty seconds on her plate.

'Well…' she started slowly. 'He made me breakfast that morning.'

'In bed?' asked Carly.

Esther shook her head. 'No, not in bed, in the kitchen. I'd had a shower and asked him for some spare clothes to change into. He took me into his walk-in wardrobe and while we were in there…'

'While you were in there, what?' Carly pressed.

Chloe laughed and waved her hand. 'Sorry, I stopped paying attention once you said the words "walk-in wardrobe."'

Esther sighed. 'While he passed me some clothes, our hands touched and, well, it was just like…something.'

'Something?' Both girls spoke in unison and leaned forward.

She couldn't tell them the rest. She couldn't tell them what he'd revealed. It was private. Just like her story about her mum.

'Yeah, something. You know how it is when you meet someone and then all of a sudden there's just this feeling and…then he kissed me.'

'And?' asked Carly.

'And I might have kissed him back,' she admitted.

'Wait a minute,' said Chloe. 'So this guy, who three days ago you texted me and said he was an arrogant git and you hated him, now he's kissing you and you're kissing him back?'

When she said it like that it seemed ridiculous, and Esther cringed. 'Yeah, maybe.'

'And then he dropped you back home and kissed you all over again outside your flat?' said Carly.

Esther nodded. She took a bite of her scone in the hope they might stop asking her questions.

Chloe was grinning, giving Carly a conspiratorial nod across the table. 'Sounds like quite a turnaround.'

'It does.' Carly grinned too and folded her arms across her chest. 'So, like I said, should we start curtseying around you?'

'Oh, stop it, you two.' Esther shook her head and gave a wistful sigh. 'I have no idea what happens next, if anything. He's just passing through. We didn't make plans. He didn't ask for my number. He just said he'd see me at work.' Her stomach gave a squeeze. Saying those words out loud made her feel as if she'd been entirely led on.

For the first time there was silence at the table.

Eventually Chloe spoke up, her voice artificially bright. 'Well, that doesn't mean anything. Maybe he's waiting to see how you react. Maybe he doesn't want to come on too strong.'

'Yeah, that's it,' agreed Carly quickly. 'He's waiting for your lead.'

'Or he's clearly not that interested,' said Esther flatly.

The people at the table next to them stood up and Esther checked her watch. 'Gotta go, time's up.'

Chloe gave her arm a little squeeze. 'This could be a good thing. You might get to have a little fun.'

Esther picked up her bag and gave her a weak smile. 'Let's just wait and see.' It made her feel a bit stupid. Half the hospital would now know she'd locked lips with Harry Beaumont, as gossip spread quicker in the hospital than an infectious disease.

She gave the girls a wave and hurried up the stairs. For the next few days she'd keep her head down. She could only hope that the gossip about her and Harry would pass quickly and move on to someone else.

CHAPTER SEVEN

HARRY NOTICED THE strange atmosphere as soon as he walked in the NICU. Billy was progressing well, and baby Jude had been operated on successfully two days before. He'd had half a mind to ask the sister this morning to allocate both babies to Esther. Working with one midwife was easier than working with two, but that might have seemed a bit presumptuous. Oona didn't strike him as a woman who liked someone else to try and influence her staffing.

There seemed to be lots of strange sideways glances, and he moved over to where Francesca was reviewing a new baby for surgery tomorrow. 'What's going on?' he whispered.

She let out a low laugh. 'Haven't you heard? You and a—' she glanced across the unit to where Esther was standing '—certain midwife are current persons of interest. I hear you got a little friendly with our feisty midwife.'

Harry let out a groan. 'Oh no, where did that come from?' He hated being gossiped about at work and had learned over the years never to do anything that put him in that position. It seemed he hadn't paid attention to his own advice. That tiny flicker of fire that had flashed through his brain on the drive to work about having a little fun was quickly dying down to an ember.

'Someone down in A&E told me,' Francesca said. 'So I take it that it's true, then?'

He kept his gaze elsewhere. 'Might be,' he said non-committally. The grin on Francesca's face got wider. She touched his arm. 'Connections, Harry. That's good.'

He felt himself bristle as he moved over towards Esther to check on Billy.

He started to talk to her but she raised her hand. 'Give me a minute.'

He was startled by her apparent brush-off and stood next to Billy's crib as she walked swiftly away. She knocked on a door just away from him. 'Jill, are you okay in there?'

When there was no answer she tried again. Heads started to turn in the unit. Esther's voice wasn't low.

She pulled a coin from her pocket and used it to turn the lock from the outside—a common trick in a hospital. She stuck her head around the door, then pulled it back out. 'Put out an emergency call,' she yelled as she squeezed through the gap in the door.

All the staff moved in unison, Harry included.

He ran straight over, grabbing an emergency trolley behind him. He stuck his head through the gap to see Esther already on the floor, pulling Jill towards her. Jill was collapsed just behind the door, blood pooling on the floor. Esther looked up at Harry. 'I need a trolley.'

'Possible PPH,' he shouted to the staff. 'Can someone find us a trolley?'

Once Esther had pulled Jill over, he slid behind the

door after grabbing a few things from the trolley. That was the funny thing about hospital bathrooms—they always seemed a reasonable size until there was an emergency in one of them.

'Does she have a pulse?' he asked.

It didn't matter that Harry's speciality was tiny babies. All tiny babies had a mother and he'd dealt with more than his fair share of obstetric emergencies.

A loud buzzer sounded. The emergency call had gone out.

Esther looked up at him, her face pale. 'Barely,' she said, lowering her head to watch for the rise and fall of Jill's chest. It was clear she was well versed in the protocols. Her fingers remained at Jill's neck.

He ignored the blood on the floor. The volume was great, and he could see a large amount of clots. Jill had clearly come to use the bathroom when she'd collapsed.

'How did you know?' he asked Esther.

'My gut,' she replied. 'I thought she looked off when she said she was going to the bathroom.'

In the few seconds it had taken her to say those words Harry had already inserted a cannula into one of Jill's veins. When someone had lost so much blood it was important to try and replace body fluids as soon as possible.

They didn't need to talk. Esther had already started running the gelofusine through the giving set.

Francesca appeared at the door, took one glance and handed in the bag and mask, which Harry started using. Jill was still breathing, but not nearly enough.

A few seconds later Esther shouted, 'Connected,' as

she stood with the IV set, letting it drip through Jill's vein rapidly.

One of the other midwives managed to get part way through the door and connect a BP cuff and monitor to try and get some reading from Jill. Two seconds later, Francesca was back, throwing some gloves towards Esther and Harry.

Harry snapped them on, knowing his trousers were already covered, as were Esther's scrubs. It was impossible to miss the blood while they were kneeling on the floor.

'Trolley,' came another shout.

Robin, one of the hospital porters, slid through the gap in the door. The space in the toilet seemed smaller by the second. Someone had thought ahead. Robin was covered in a temporary theatre gown and a pair of gloves. He was slight, which was the reason he got through the gap, but before Harry could position himself differently to help, Robin bent down and picked Jill up in his arms. He stood back against the wall, allowing Esther to pull the door inwards and put it against the wall, letting him place Jill on the waiting trolley. At least seven other staff were poised outside, ready to spring into action. One of the midwives grabbed the IV bag from Esther's hands and Francesca took over with the bag and mask, standing on the end of the trolley so she moved with it when it was dashed away.

Harry blinked and looked down. The thing about blood was, even a little could look like a lot when spilled on the floor. Oona appeared in front of them both. 'I'll call Housekeeping. Go clean up, you two. In fact—' she looked Harry up and down '—stay there a sec. I'll bring you both clean scrubs to change into, then hit the showers and change again. You can't walk down the corridors looking like that.'

A few moments later Oona handed the scrubs in, along with a plastic laundry bag. Her mouth gave an almost smile. 'I'm sure you'll both cope with changing in front of each other.'

She knew. Rumours always spread fast in a hospital. Her voice carried as she started to walk away. 'And, Esther, I'll cover your patients. I know you'll want to go and check on Jill.'

They stared at each other in stunned silence for a few seconds after the shocking event. Then Esther's eyes started to fill. 'Oh no...' she said. He moved over and wrapped his arms around her. Every part of her body was trembling. His was too. He couldn't pretend that what happened hadn't shocked him. Of course it had.

Emergencies always occurred. But that didn't mean that they didn't impact on the staff.

Jill would be in better hands than his. He wasn't an obstetrician. He was a neonatal surgeon. He wouldn't be surprised if Jill was headed directly to Theatre.

Harry stayed exactly where he was. Oona appeared at the door with one of the housekeepers following behind her with a trolley laden with equipment, but Harry just shook his head wordlessly at her, and Oona gave a nod and retreated.

It was five minutes before Esther stopped crying, her breathing steadying. They were still chest to chest and her breathing fell into unison with his. She stepped back and wiped her face. 'Sorry,' she whispered. 'I can't bear the thought of something happening to Jill.' She pointed to the door. 'You've seen out there. She's got no one. Billy's got no one apart from her.' The last few words broke her. Her hands still trembled. 'Why didn't anyone notice anything? Why didn't *I* notice anything?'

He put his hand on her arm. 'Jill might just have been a mother who had no symptoms, or maybe she had symptoms but didn't want to tell us in case we told her she'd have to leave Billy's side.'

There was a flicker of recognition in Esther's eyes. It was clear she knew that was likely to be the truth.

She stared down at the bottom half of her scrubs, moving over to where the clean sets were sitting. She didn't even look at him as she pulled her top over her head, replacing it with a clean one, then peeling the scrubs trousers from her legs. She ran some paper towels under the tap and wiped her legs before pulling on the clean set. Harry mirrored her moves, replacing his shirt and trousers with scrubs, and shaking his head at his shoes before dumping them in a plastic bag. They'd have to go in the disposal. He had spare shoes in his locker.

They stepped outside the bathroom. The NICU was silent, only the noise of a few monitors in the background. The housekeeper was standing to the side and disappeared silently into the messy bathroom behind them. Esther's feet led her straight to Billy's crib. She placed one hand on the plastic and leaned over, looking down on him. 'Oh, honey,' she whispered. 'I'm going to go and find your mummy. I'll make sure she's okay.'

It was the look on her face that did it for him. He didn't care that every set of eyes on the unit were currently on him. He would never leave a colleague who was upset like this at work.

Often in health care they recognised trauma for their staff and offered counselling or debrief sessions at a later date. But that would be for later, not for now.

He put his arm around her shoulders and guided her away. 'Let's get cleaned up properly. I'll meet you outside the changing rooms once we've showered and changed and we'll check on Jill.'

Esther didn't speak on their long walk down the corridor and he noticed a few heads turn in their direction. He didn't move his arm from her shoulders. He didn't really care what people had to say. It was nobody's business but theirs.

She turned to face him at the changing room door, her blue eyes meeting his. 'Thank you,' she said in a croaky voice, before lowering her head again.

'No, thank *you*,' he said, putting his fingers under her chin and tilting her head towards his. 'You just knew. And you acted. Thank goodness. Jill could have been in the bathroom for much longer. She could have bled out completely. You acting on instinct made all the difference.'

He pressed his forehead down against hers. 'Have faith, Esther. We got her in time.'

As they stood together her hands reached over and squeezed his. It was unexpected. Every move had been his. But this felt just right.

After a moment he reluctantly stepped back. 'Meet you in ten,' he said.

'Meet you in ten,' she repeated as she backed in through the changing room door.

* * *

Everything felt like her fault. Her head had been in the clouds, full of daises and unicorns, when her mind should have been firmly on the job.

Jill's postnatal checks had been routinely carried out every afternoon since Billy's admission, and she hadn't complained of pain or discomfort that morning, so Esther had no reason to change the routine. Her bleeding had been within the normal range, and she'd displayed no obvious temperature. Her notes all said that her uterus was contracting as expected. But none of these things mattered to Esther. What mattered was that Jill had taken unwell while she'd been on shift. She wasn't quite sure what it was that had triggered her bad feeling.

Had Jill pulled a face just as she'd closed the bathroom door? It had to have been something. Something that told her to go and check. And thank goodness that instinct had been there.

Stories of nurse, midwife and health visitor instinct were often described as old wives' tales—similar to a mother's instinct. But Esther didn't believe that for a second. She'd witnessed too many incidents. Too many times there had been no explanation for a health care professional, or a mother, to check in on a patient or child only for them to discover something amiss, for there not to be some kind of explanation for it. One day she'd love to do a scientific study on it. But today was not that day.

She scrubbed her skin in the staff showers, watching the water turn from pale pink to clear. She rarely used these, preferring to shower at home. The hospital towels were always rough and slightly scratchy, so she dried quickly and redressed in yet another set of scrubs.

Harry had been so good to her. So nice. So supportive. It didn't help that everyone had already been looking at them. It didn't matter what the truth was; it was clear that others were assuming that more had happened between Esther and Harry than was true. She wasn't quite sure whether to feel happy or sad about that.

Taking things fast in a relationship had never been Esther's style.

She wasn't even sure that Harry wanted any kind of relationship. She couldn't even sort out her own feelings about it. They were from such opposite ends of the social spectrum. So much about him made her secretly a little mad. Money made life easy for people. And the ease of money just seemed to emanate from him. The voice, his stance, his clothes, even his attitude.

Esther was proud of herself, and her upbringing. Did she really want to associate with someone who, through no fault of his own, could make her feel less of a person? She didn't need that. She didn't want that.

But as she opened the door to the changing room she found Harry leaning on the wall opposite, answering a text on his phone. His white coat was back in place, along with new shoes and clean scrubs. Her heart gave a strange little flip. Making its feeling clear.

'She's in Theatre Five,' Harry said quickly. 'Come on.'

They waited nearly an hour before Jill's obstetrician came out, her face serious. She stuck out her hand straight away. 'Thank you, guys. My girl is only here because you both acted so quickly.'

Esther made a strange little sound at the back of her throat she was so relieved. She knew Dr Gillespie, the obstetrician, well but hadn't been able to read her face at all as she'd walked towards them.

'What happened?' she asked.

Dr Gillespie pulled her theatre hat from her head. 'Part of her placenta was retained. I've no idea why she hadn't reported symptoms. Once we got her into Theatre I thought I was going to have to do a hysterectomy.'

'Did you?' asked Esther.

Dr Gillespie shook her head. 'No, thank goodness. But I suspect she'll need careful observation in any future pregnancies.'

Even though the news was still serious, Esther couldn't help but smile. Jill was alive. She was safe. Billy still had a mum.

Dr Gillespie gave them both another nod, then headed back down the theatre corridor.

'I need to go and tell the staff in NICU,' said Esther.

Harry nodded. 'Of course. Go ahead.'

A smile broke across her face. She stood up on tiptoes and kissed Harry on the cheek. 'Thank you.' She smiled. There was a little cough from someone who walked past.

Harry smiled too. 'Let's give them something to talk about,' he said as he pulled her towards him.

CHAPTER EIGHT

ESTHER STARED AT the smooth envelope pushed through her door. She'd been talking to her mum on the phone and making some toast when she'd noticed the unusual post.

Even running her fingers over it made a little shiver run down her spine. This was expensive stationery.

It must be a mistake, but as she turned it over it was definitely her name that was on the front.

But there was no address. Just her name, in fine script. *Ms Esther McDonald.*

She couldn't help but be intrigued. She slid the envelope open. Inside was a stiff card invitation. She pulled it out and stared at it.

Lord and Lady Brackenridge invite the Duke of Montrose and guest to the Avistock Charity Ball at Eglinton Hall.

There was a cute dinosaur sticky note stuck to the invitation in writing she recognised from the NICU as Harry's. *Will you come with me? They hold this event for a kids' charity every year and I don't want to let them down by being a no-show. Harry x.*

Esther staggered back onto the sofa, laughter bursting out of her. A ball? Her? Was Harry crazy?

She turned the invite over in her hands. He'd obviously driven to her house and posted it through the door last night. Why hadn't he knocked? Why hadn't he mentioned it at the hospital?

She wasn't quite sure where they were. Harry would be moving on soon. It seemed like the whole hospital were now assuming they were dating and sleeping together. Neither of which were true. She'd never dated anyone she'd worked with before. This was all new territory for her and she wasn't quite sure how to navigate it.

She ran her fingers over the thick card. A ball. Since when did a girl from one of the worst areas of deprivation in Scotland get invited to attend a ball with a duke?

The smile across her face felt infectious. She didn't care how ridiculous it was. She didn't actually care if it just brought home to her how different she and Harry were. For one day it might feel nice to live the life of someone else. To walk in a different set of shoes. Yes, she could worry about a dress, because she knew straight away that there was nothing suitable in her wardrobe, and she certainly couldn't spare the funds to buy something appropriate. But that's what friends were for. Before she even gave herself time to think about it she shot off a text to Carly and Chloe.

OK, girls, I've been invited to a ball. You've seen my wardrobe. The Princess Leia costume and gold hot pants are not going to cut it. Anyone got something I can wear?

Instantly she could see little dots appear on her phone.

Chloe sent a row of laughing emojis followed by a line of question marks.

Carly's reply made her heart jump. I've got just the thing. Dark navy ball gown with a little bit of sparkle. Will leave it in NICU for you later today.

Esther tried not to let out a squeal. They were roughly the same size so she knew it would fit fine.

Perfect. Now she knew she had something to wear she just had to worry about everything else. Like how it would feel to be Cinderella at the ball...

Harry wasn't quite sure he was playing this right. And those thoughts were strange to him, because he'd never really been in a relationship where he'd worried about things like that.

The issue was, the whole hospital assumed that he and Esther were a 'thing.' And to be honest, that didn't bother him at all. Because he was only passing through.

Sure, he'd heard all the things about not mixing business with pleasure. But over the years he'd known lots of colleagues who'd had relationships with workmates. Some good, some bad.

As soon as he'd received that invitation he'd thought immediately about Esther. He'd driven over to her house, stuck a little note on it and put it through her door. She'd smiled at him the next day in NICU and said she'd be glad to come.

And that had been the point he'd realised he hadn't *really* been thinking about Esther. He hadn't thought that going to a charity ball with him might mean turning down an extra shift she could do, or that she would have to conjure up something suitable to wear. Part of him had wanted to go back and offer to buy her something. But somehow he knew Esther would find that completely insulting.

So, here he was, sitting outside her door, waiting to pick her up. He pulled at the sleeves of his jacket as he stepped outside the car and walked down the dark steps to her front door. She opened it on the first knock, a broad smile across her face.

A scent of orange blossom floated towards him and he wasn't quite sure if it was coming from her, or the flat.

The room behind her was compact but immaculate. There was a large squishy red sofa, with a coffee table in front, perched on a colourful rug. The floor was the laminate that lots of people had now, and in the back of the room he could see a neat white kitchen.

Photos were everywhere. Adorning her mantelpiece, walls and tables. All of family, and even from here he could see that most of the photos had people with their arms wrapped around each other, laughing.

Something twisted deep inside. He couldn't ever recall a moment in his life where he'd been at an event with his parents that resembled anything like this. The moment, the warmth, the adoration.

Never. His life had never replicated anything like that. For a split second all he could feel was envy. Envy for her simpler, and yet immensely fuller, life. He pushed those thoughts away.

His eyes went automatically back to Esther. 'Wow,' was the only word he could form.

She was wearing a long navy gown. The shoulders

and cap sleeves of the dress were part-sheer, with sequins scattered across the top, then the middle was
ruched, emphasizing her waist, then the sheer navy fabric fell in layers to the floor, making a light swishing
sound whenever she moved. Her dark hair was piled on
top of her head with a few tendrils escaping at the sides,
accentuating her sparkling blue eyes, which were fixed
directly on him. The effect was dazzling.

Esther beamed. Literally beamed—it was like a glow
was coming off her. One that she clearly didn't see herself.

'Wow yourself,' she said lightly. 'It's not every day
I see you in a tux.'

He paused for a few seconds, taking in the full view
of her.

Hospitals were odd places. He saw the same faces in
virtually the same clothes. There were so many other
things going on there that it frequently didn't give anyone time to stop and really look at the people around
them.

Now he could see it all. The shine of her hair, the
bounce, even though it was tied up in some elaborate
way on her head. The swoosh of her long skirts. The
cinch of the fabric on her curves. He was looking at her
with new eyes, just like the way she was looking at him.

He tugged at his collar, instantly self-conscious. 'I
definitely don't wear this every day. But today is a special occasion.'

'Yeah, it is,' she whispered. His mouth was dry. For
a second he wanted the world to stop. He wanted to stay
and look at Esther the way she was looking at him. He
wanted to forget about the ball. And forget about any-

thing else. He wanted to close the door behind them and kiss her right now.

There was something about being in her company. Tonight was about tradition. About being a duke. Nothing in his life to do with his title had ever felt like fun. But tonight, going to the ball with Esther, was the first time he'd actually really, really looked forward to doing something. After a shaky start, she was beginning to become that person for him. The one he actually enjoyed spending time with. This part of his life—the duke stuff—had always been separate. His stomach coiled for him in an unusual way. She didn't even know it, but she was opening up other doors in his mind. Places that had been closed for so long.

Esther blinked. Breaking the spell he was casting in his head.

She gave a thoughtful nod as he gestured to the stairs. "Ready to go? Your carriage awaits.'

They were in the car a few minutes later, crossing London towards Eglinton Hall.

'Tell me about Lord and Lady Brackenridge,' she said as she settled into the seat, 'and tell me more about this charity ball.'

Harry gave a nod. It was only fair that he gave her some background to the event they were about to attend. It was one of the few things he'd continued to go to since the death of his father.

'I've known them since I was a child. Their two daughters are just a few years younger than me. They had a son—Gavin—who died from neuroblastoma when we were all teenagers. It's still rare, but even less was known about it then. They had their first charity ball a few years after Gavin died. They choose a different children's charity to support every year, and I've always gone along.' He paused, taking a breath for a moment. 'Originally the invite was for my parents, but for the last ten years it's come to me.'

'You don't have any siblings?'

Harry shook his head. 'Nope. Just me. I think I was enough of an inconvenience to them.'

Esther's head spun around in surprise. 'What do you mean by that?'

He bristled, not quite sure how to answer the question. But it was his own fault. He shouldn't have made that comment.

But it was too late. There was no point lying about it. 'I don't think they were really the parenting type.'

He could tell that Esther found that statement surprising. 'Why's that?' she asked.

He gave a shrug. 'It was probably more of a duty thing.'

There was a few moments' silence. 'Okay, I have to admit, I don't get it. What do you mean?'

He snaked his way through the traffic, his hands gripping the steering wheel probably a lot harder than he needed to. 'Duty,' he sighed. 'The duke title is inherited—passed down to the male heir. I'm quite sure they had me to ensure the title passed on.'

From the corner of his eye he could see Esther wrinkling her nose. 'But what if they'd had a girl?'

He let out a low laugh. 'She probably would have been treated as if she was worthless and they would have kept trying for a boy. Thankfully for everyone, that didn't happen. My mother only had to go through a pregnancy once, and when I was born she made it very clear to everyone she had no intention of ever doing it again.'

'Wow,' said Esther softly. 'It sounds kind of medieval.'

Harry nodded. 'Yeah, that's about the size of it. Children should be seen and not heard was very much the mantra in my family. I had a nanny until I was five. Then I spent the rest of my time at boarding school—often during the holidays too—and then at university.'

Esther's head shook. 'I just can't imagine a life like that.' Then her hand shot up to her mouth as she realised how that might sound. 'Oh no, I—'

He stopped her by putting his hand on her leg. 'It's fine, Esther. It is what it is. I had a roof over my head, food in my stomach at all times. I know plenty of kids who had a far worse upbringing than me. These people tonight, Lord and Lady Brackenridge? They were probably the only adults I met who showed any warmth towards me.' He pulled a face. 'Of course, I didn't realise at the time they were trying to match me to one of their daughters.'

Esther let out a gasp. 'This is like a blooming TV show.'

He shot her a glance. 'Yeah, but am I the hero, or the villain?'

Her hand threaded over the top of his, which was still on her leg. 'Oh, I think we can safely say you're the hero.' Her eyes glinted. 'But I'll let you know if you slip.'

He couldn't help but laugh. 'Don't worry. These people are actually fine. They realised pretty quickly that I wasn't a good match for either Penelope or Priscilla.'

'Penelope and Priscilla? That's really their names?' He could hear the disbelief in her voice.

'Oh yes. That's their names. They used to be part of a larger group of friends but I haven't seen either of them in a while. Priscilla is a barrister and last I heard she was dating some millionaire businessman. Penelope has had three engagements—maybe four—each ring bigger than the last. I think she's dating some actor now.'

Esther looked a little stunned. 'Hmm, how the other half lives,' she said quietly.

All of a sudden he realised she might be a bit intimidated by all this. He squeezed her thigh. 'Don't worry,' he said. 'Tonight should be fun.' He wasn't sure if he was trying to reassure her, or himself.

'Hmm…' Esther fixed her eyes on the view outside. He could tell she was thinking. Had he read all this wrong?

He'd wanted to take her out. He'd wanted to take her somewhere special. Of course he did. And this invitation had given him the perfect excuse. Didn't people like balls?

The girl he'd first met as a crabby midwife was sitting next to him looking like perfection, but he could see her knotting her hands in her lap. He hadn't meant to make her uncomfortable. Or maybe it wasn't the ball. Maybe it was the fact he'd just revealed a bit more about himself and his difficult relationship with his parents. He knew that she adored her mother, and maybe she hadn't liked the fact he'd been so up front about how things had been totally different in his household.

He'd tried his best to forget about that part of his life. His heritage was always there. The title a daily reminder. But Harry actively chose not to use it on a regular basis. He introduced himself to everyone as Harry Beaumont, neonatal surgeon. Not as Harry Beaumont, Duke of Montrose.

As he pulled his car up the long, winding drive of Eglinton Hall, he'd already made up his mind. They'd only stay as long as they had to. If he had to, he could use a patient as an excuse for leaving. But the truth was, Billy, his mother and baby Jude were all doing well. He had four more surgeries scheduled in the next few days, with two babies being transferred from other hospitals, and two mothers whose babies had cardiac issues delivering in the Queen Victoria especially so their babies could go straight for surgery with Harry.

This was practically his only night off for a while, so he intended to use it well.

'Busy place,' murmured Esther as they joined the line of cars filing up to the main doors with liveried staff opening the doors, then whisking the cars away again.

Harry gave her a worried smile as they pulled up next. Waiting as she walked around the car and holding out his arm for her as they climbed the steps.

This night would be good. He'd make sure of it.

Cinderella had arrived in a horse-drawn carriage, and Esther arrived in an Aston Martin. She wasn't sure which one was better.

Carly's dress was a dream. She gathered the skirts

in her hand as they climbed the stairs and stepped into the biggest reception hall she'd ever seen.

This whole place was magnificent. From the impressive sand-coloured stone building, the elegant windows and the four towers at each corner of the house. Except it wasn't a house. Not in the normal sense. It was one of those gorgeous mansions owned by the rich, the very rich and the very, very rich. The size and scale reminded her of Kelvingrove Museum in Glasgow that she'd visited as a school kid when it housed Egyptian relics and dinosaur bones.

Who actually lived in a place like this?

The huge reception hall had tiny white and black tiles on the floor that looked like marble. The walls were covered in dark wood panels but the whole place felt light and airy, brightly illuminated by the biggest chandelier she'd ever seen.

Staff stood with silver trays of long-stemmed glasses at the entrance way to a room on the right. Harry nodded at a few people casually. He wasn't stunned by these surroundings at all. He seemed quite at home as he led her through to the next room. Voices were low as people chatted and sipped their champagne.

Thank goodness for Carly. Although Esther was quite sure the dress she was wearing had probably cost a lot less than most of the other female guests' gowns, she didn't feel out of place at all. Most wore full-length gowns. Some beautiful. Some daring. And some just a little...strange.

But Esther's felt fine in comparison. Nearly every gentleman wore a tux like Harry's. She shot him a sideways glance. But every gentleman didn't look half as good as Harry did. She could see him getting admiring glances from other women. But his arm had slid around her waist as they'd entered this room, and there it firmly remained. It made her heart flutter in a way she wasn't ready to acknowledge.

'Harry!' came a deep voice near to them. A tall man came over, arm outstretched, and shook Harry's hand enthusiastically, gripping his arm with his own hand. 'I'm so glad you're here.' He leaned over conspiratorially. 'You can always help me hide when it gets too much.'

Harry's smile was broad and genuine. 'Lord Breckenridge—David—I'd like you to meet my good friend Esther McDonald.'

The older man turned towards her, shaking her hand just as enthusiastically as he'd shook Harry's. 'It's a real pleasure—any friend of Harry's is always welcome.' He turned and waved over to a woman behind them. 'Sabrina, Harry's here.'

The woman was dressed in black satin, her grey hair pinned elegantly back. She didn't walk; instead, she seemed to glide over to meet them, encompassing Harry in a hug. He kissed both of the woman's cheeks. 'So nice to see you.'

After his comments in the car she'd wondered what to expect. But his affection for this pair was obvious, and Esther was secretly relieved. What must it have been like to grow up with parents who treated you as if you were merely part of the furniture?

The woman wasn't only elegant, she had an old-world charm about her. She spoke to Esther, asking her questions about her job, and seemed genuinely interested in her answers.

For the first time, the initial fear of fitting in, in a place like this, finally started to leave Esther.

'It's so nice to see Harry bring a friend,' Lady Brackenridge said in her ear.

'Thank you for having me.' Esther smiled. 'Harry told me you have the ball every year in memory of your son. I was so sorry to hear about him.'

Lady Brackenridge put her hand on Esther's arm and gave it a little squeeze. 'It was a long time ago. But I still miss him every day. Just like I should.' She put her hand up to her heart. 'Harry and Gavin were such good friends. I've always looked out for him.'

There was genuine affection in her eyes and Esther spoke carefully. 'He seems so comfortable around you both—and comfortable here too. That's nice. He told me about his difficult relationship with his father.'

'He did?' Lady Breckenridge's eyes went wide. She glanced at Harry and her head gave a little nod. Her lips gave a hint of a smile and she shot Esther an approving look. 'I'm glad. Harry is nothing like his father—or his mother for that matter. I always hoped that Harry and his father would make up before the duke died. But it wasn't to be. Old age didn't suit the duke. It just made him more ill-tempered and irrational than before, and poor Harry always bore the brunt of it.' She leaned towards Esther and cupped her cheek. 'You, my girl, might just be the joy that Harry has always been looking for.'

Esther jerked a little at the unexpected affectionate movement. It made her stomach flutter, partly with warmth, and partly with the fear of the expectation that seemed to have just descended on her. Lady Bracken-ridge spun around as someone came up behind her, greeting her loudly.

There was a loud announcement at a door just ahead. 'Guests, you are kindly invited to take your seats for the Avistock Charity Ball.'

Harry appeared out of thin air and held out his elbow for Esther again. She was still digesting what Lady Brackenridge had said, a tiny swell of panic in her chest. This was temporary. This was just supposed to be fun. She slipped her arm through his and followed the crowds through the double doors.

The ballroom was opulent, decorated in gold and white. Large round tables, covered in white linen with twenty seats at each, covered the expanse of the room. Harry gave their names and they were given a table number. As they sat down, Esther picked up the little card in front of them.

It was a programme for the auction and her stomach muscles tightened. Of course. A charity auction. Realisation flooded over her as other guests took their seats at the table.

Of course. A charity auction with a programme of items up for bids. A shopping trip at one of London's most exclusive stores. Four seats at an extremely popular football cup final. Four seats and travel to an even more popular European football cup final. A box at a show in New York that had a years-long waiting list for tickets. VIP tickets to a gig by one of the biggest pop stars.

Esther's hand went automatically to her champagne glass, which she instantly downed—her mouth had never felt quite so dry. One of the staff placed some plates of hors d'oeuvres on the table. Esther hid her smile. The food was actually so small it could hardly be seen.

Harry leaned closer, his cheek brushing against hers. 'What are you smiling at?'

She looked up at him. He was so close she could see every eyelash and the pale gold flecks in those toffee eyes. She kept her voice low. 'I'm just thinking that if you served those in a pub in Scotland you'd have your head in your hands to play with.'

He let out a low laugh and shook his head. 'I love your crazy expressions.'

'Oh, I have lots more where those came from.' She blinked.

'And I want to hear them all,' he whispered, moving closer.

'Harry!' The voice came from directly behind them and they jumped apart.

He cleared his throat a little awkwardly. 'Penelope! How nice to see you.'

A woman with blond hair wound over one shoulder and an enviable figure slid into the chair on the other side of Harry. She was wearing a bright cerise pink dress that clung to every curve. She flung her arms around Harry and kissed him on both cheeks—just a little too close to his lips—leaving her bright red lipstick on him like some kind of marker. Esther stiffened in her seat.

A waft of expensive perfume floated across the table towards her. Harry returned the hug, a little less enthusiastically, before sitting back in his chair and allowing Esther an even better view of a woman who could simply be described as perfection.

'Penelope, I want you to meet my good friend Esther McDonald, who has accompanied me tonight.'

Penelope didn't seem at all perturbed. She slid her arm across Harry's body, showing a set of immaculate pointed nails, exactly the same colour as her dress, inviting Esther to shake her hand. 'Pleasure to meet you, Esther.' She beamed.

Esther gulped and shook the hand far more limply than she intended to. Wicked thoughts immediately dashed through her mind. Like how Penelope could easily whip a man's testicles off with one swipe of her nails. She could see Penelope having a quick glance at Esther's short blunt nails. Just the way a nurse's should be. But Esther couldn't help wishing she had put on a quick coat of nail varnish before she'd left the house tonight.

Penelope slid forward, one arm draping conspiratorially around Harry's neck. 'So, how did you two meet?'

It was the voice. It was delicious. Like syrup. All accented, immaculate sounds. Esther knew her own accent was thick. She liked it that way. A few times she'd purposely spoken much quicker than usual in order to put another person firmly in their place. A Scots accent could do that—particularly when dealing with a drunk in A&E. There was a real no-nonsense attitude about a thick Scottish accent that Esther relished.

But tonight? It just made her feel uncouth.

She tried to speak properly, dulling her accent and finishing every word. 'We met at work,' she said, ignoring the look that Harry shot her. 'I'm a midwife in NICU.'

Penelope blinked. 'What's NICU?'

'Prem babies,' said Esther quickly.

Penelope slapped her other hand on Harry's chest—and left it there. 'Oh, of course. Silly me.'

Her eyes went between them both, her smile getting wider. 'So, you met at work. That's kind of cute.'

Harry shifted in his seat. Esther was suddenly intensely aware that on both times Harry had introduced her—first to Penelope's parents, and then to Penelope—he'd described her as a 'good friend.' What did that mean exactly? It was sort of bland. Sort of nothing. Or at least nothing important.

Was that what they were? They hadn't even had that conversation yet. And Esther didn't like the way that burned inside.

She was also trying really, really hard not to bristle at the way Penelope had draped herself possessively around Harry. The girl wasn't giving off vibes. The kind of 'I was here first' thing you sometimes got with exes. Instead, she was showing how comfortable she was around Harry.

Penelope waved her hand for some more wine and a waiter appeared immediately. He lowered his head to Penelope's. 'My usual,' she said easily. 'Harry's too, and—' she leaned forward '—pick your poison, Esther.'

Esther didn't miss a heartbeat. She named a tonic wine that was commonly known in Scotland. Something she was entirely sure a posh place like this wouldn't have in a million years. She wasn't quite sure why she did it.

Was it because she already knew she didn't fit in and wanted to send a message that she had no intention of conforming? She didn't even like that tonic wine, and hadn't touched it since she was a teenager. But it was like all her spiny prickles were coming out at once.

Penelope blinked and smiled. 'Never heard of that one.' She repeated it to the waiter, who quickly disappeared.

A tuxedo-suited man stepped up to the podium at the end of the room, announcing the start of the auction. Penelope shot Esther an excited glance. 'Which one do you want to bid on?'

Every cell in Esther's body prickled. She was almost sure that Penelope didn't mean to make her uncomfortable. The woman had a generally welcoming nature. Maybe she just believed the rest of this room was just as rich as she was. But Esther had already told her that she and Harry worked together. Did she honestly expect a NHS worker to have funds to spend on the charity auction?

Within a few minutes Esther realised that the bidding here wasn't for the faint-hearted. Her knuckles were turning white holding the programme as the bids climbed and climbed.

The room felt oppressive, as if the heat were closing in around her. The waiter appeared back with the drinks. He shot Esther a grin as he lowered her familiar drink next to her. 'None of the monk's wine,' he said, revealing his Scots accent. She started. Only someone who'd been brought up in Scotland would know that the traditional tonic wine was made by monks. The man's eyes gleamed as he sat down a tall glass in front of her. 'So I brought you our other favourite.'

Esther laughed out loud as she looked at the bright blue liquid topped by ruby red, a memory of home shooting through her. She hadn't even been much of a drinker as a teenager, but this definitely reminded her of stale village halls and sitting in the park on a summer's day.

Harry leaned closer. 'What on earth is that?'

'A bit of my past.' She grinned, taking a sip and grimacing.

'What's in it?' he asked.

'Vodka and port.' She pushed it towards him. 'Try it.'

He took a tentative sip and wrinkled his nose. 'It tastes like…' He paused, clearly trying to place it.

Esther named a popular fruity carbonated drink.

'That's it,' he said, throwing his hands up.

'Harry Beaumont, thank you for your bid.'

Esther felt the colour drain from her as Penelope let out a shriek of laughter. Her hand landed on Harry's arm again. 'Oh, you clown. Do you know what you just bid on?'

He sat back in his chair, looking relaxed, if a little stunned. Esther couldn't breathe. She felt sick. This was her fault.

Penelope opened her programme and pointed to something. 'Here. You've just bid on a two-day break in a cottage in Scotland.'

Harry shrugged. 'How much did I bid?'

'Twenty thousand,' said Penelope, as if she'd just mentioned a sum of money that bought a chocolate bar.

'Oh, okay,' said Harry, barely blinking.

'Okay?' All heads at the table turned to Esther's incredulous voice. Inside she felt like she was dying. Harry had just spent twenty thousand pounds by mistake and he didn't seem the least bit bothered. Just how rich was this guy?

That thought alone made her immensely uncomfortable.

Penelope leaned in front of Harry and gave Esther a comforting grin. 'Don't worry. That's spare change to this guy.'

Esther just couldn't find words. She sat back in her chair and watched the spots form in front of her eyes. She'd never felt more like Cinderella in her life. This must be some kind of warped fairy tale.

The auction continued and she sat in a blur. Every cell in her body told her she should be apologising to Harry for being part of the mistake, but she could see he honestly wasn't the least bit bothered and that worried her much more than a blazing argument over whose fault the errant bid was.

Money meant everything to her. In a horrible, materialistic, never-admit-to kind of way. She counted every single penny. She had to, in order to help her mum. Five days out of seven she would pack her lunch. She only allowed herself a coffee from the cart on the Thames twice a week. She couldn't remember the last time she'd bought herself something new to wear. Why buy more clothes when she had perfectly reasonable ones in her cupboard?

A thought of her own life back in Scotland shot into her head. How different it was. This place was all smoke and mirrors. The words Lady Brackenridge had spoken were stuck in her mind. Harry hadn't experienced the same love that she had. Would she have swapped her parents and small house in Scotland for a life like this? Never.

She kept her face perfectly calm as she took some long slow breaths in and out. Harry's hand had crept over to hers and his fingers intertwined with hers. Tingles shot up her arm. Tingles that she really liked.

But this was wrong. Nothing about her and Harry was a match.

She watched as he chatted easily to Penelope. The girl was gorgeous. She seemed genuinely nice and every now and then tried to include Esther in the conversation. But they were talking about friends and casual acquaintances—people that had never, and would never, move in the same circles as Esther.

The more she watched, the more she felt a distance grow between her and Harry. Penelope was a good match for him. She was beautiful. She was intelligent. She fitted easily into his life.

Not like Esther, with her extra shifts and shabby flat.

Even though she was sitting here in Carly's beautiful gown, her previous confidence was ebbing away little by little.

Then all of a sudden the auction was over. The guests all stood as the tables were removed and a band was spirited in through another door. The music began as waiters started to circulate with drink-filled trays again.

Harry gestured towards one and Esther shook her head. 'No thanks. Want to keep a clear head for tomorrow.'

'You're working again?'

She nodded. 'Just my normal shift in NICU. I'm looking forward to it. I want to see my babies, and I want to see Jill.'

Harry gave a nod as the music changed. He held out one hand towards her. 'How's your dancing?'

'Rave or highland?' she asked cheekily.

He gave a surprised jerk at the spectrum. 'I was kind of thinking of something slower,' he said. Her hand was now in his and he pulled her closer and slid his hand around her waist.

It didn't matter how much her brain had been screaming at her. Telling her that she and Harry weren't a match in any sense. Her heart wasn't listening at all. It was beating wildly at the feel of his body against hers.

His hand slid up to the bare skin at her neck and brushed some of her fine hairs that escaped from the top of her head. The touch was like butterflies on her skin, their wings flapping in a tickly sort of way.

His face broke into a smile, one that only seemed for her. 'You okay?' he asked.

She wanted to spill out a whole lot of answers. But she remembered him in the car, talking about his parents. The expression on his face. It was the first time she'd seen Harry looking vulnerable and less than confident.

She couldn't offload onto him. It didn't seem right. She licked her lips. 'I guess I'm just seeing how the other half live.'

A frown creased his brow as he moved her smoothly around the floor in time to the music. 'You're not happy? Do you want to leave?'

For a second she saw his eyes scan the room, looking back to the bar where Penelope was sipping wine and talking to someone.

She stiffened. She couldn't help it. Maybe he was embarrassed by her, tired of her, and would prefer to spend time in the company of his peers. 'Do you want me to?'

He stopped dancing and looked down at her. 'No. Why on earth would you think that?'

Esther's heart felt as if it were fluttering against her chest wall. 'I... I just...' The words stuck somewhere in her throat. She was making a mess of this.

His hand came down and slid through her hair, resting at the back of her neck. His mouth only inches from her face. 'Esther, I'm sorry if I've made you uncomfortable. I thought you might like it tonight. Maybe I wasn't thinking...maybe I should have—'

She put her finger up to his lips and shook her head. 'I don't think this is about you, Harry. I think we're just different. Different lives, different backgrounds.'

'Opposites attract.' He looked her straight in the eye.

Part of her heart ached for him when she thought about what Lady Brackenridge had said earlier. But this close up to Harry, she could feel her pulse rate rising.

She couldn't help but smile. 'I might know a guy who told me that.'

He leaned forward and kissed her. 'Then trust him. I think I know that guy too. He's okay—in fact, I think he wants to take you to dinner.'

Every part of her wanted to wrap her hands around his neck and keep kissing him. But they were in the middle of a ballroom with five hundred other people; it was hardly appropriate. She leaned back. 'He does?'

'He absolutely does.' Harry grabbed her hand and led

her straight across the dance floor, dodging the other people and not stopping to speak to anyone. He pulled his phone from his pocket and made a one-minute call. His car pulled up moments later and he held the door open for her.

She clicked her seat belt. 'Harry, what are you doing?'

'Taking you to the place I should have done earlier.'

She twisted her head at the rapidly vanishing hall behind them. 'But what about your friends?'

He shook his head, his dark eyes meeting hers, and he halted at the bottom of the driveway. 'I'm not interested in them. I'm interested in you.'

'Oh.' It was the only answer she could find. The traffic was much lighter now and they crossed London easily, pulling up and parking on a street she was unfamiliar with.

He came around and opened her door again, then bent down and lifted the hem of her dress just an inch. 'What are you doing?' She let out a high-pitched kind of squeal.

'Checking your shoes. How do you think they'll do on cobbles—want me to carry you?'

She'd only had a few seconds to consider the question before he swept her up into his arms and started striding down a street just around the corner.

'Hey!' She let out a laugh as he covered the street easily, stopping outside a red wooden door and setting her down gently.

He knocked on the door and Esther leaned back to see the front of the building. She could see a small sign in French, along with a sign for the famous stars that were awarded to restaurants around the globe.

The door opened and a short man with a broad smile greeted them. 'Don't say I'm not good to you.' He nodded to Harry.

Harry took Esther's hand again and led her up a flight of stairs. The restaurant he led her into was small and welcoming, and completely empty.

She spun around. 'Where is everybody?'

He held out his hands. 'It's ours, for the night.'

The short guy appeared again behind them and held out his hand to Esther. 'Armand.' He nodded his head towards Harry. 'It seems I'm your personal chef for the night.'

Esther's eyes widened. 'What? No way.'

Armand gave a casual shrug. 'What can I say? I owe him. He asks for the restaurant for the night, he gets it.'

Armand waved his hand and started to walk to the kitchen, then paused, his hand on the door. 'Any allergies?'

Esther shook her head.

'Anything you absolutely won't eat?'

She shook her head again.

'Oh good, then let me go and create for you something wonderful. Help yourself to wine, Harry,' he shouted over his shoulder as he disappeared into the kitchen.

Esther shook her head and held out her hands. 'How on earth do you get a starred restaurant for the night?'

Harry held out a chair for her. 'The place officially closed last night for refurbishment. So I knew it would be empty tonight. The work doesn't start until next week.'

'And Armand is a friend of yours?'

He grinned as he selected a bottle of wine. 'Armand actually did his first two years of med school with me. But he had a change of heart. His dream was being a chef, not a doctor, and he followed his heart.'

She watched as he poured the wine into the glasses on the table. This all seemed so surreal. She took a small sip. 'So, how does he owe you?'

Harry made an awkward kind of sound as he sat opposite her. 'I gave him the backing to start his first restaurant.'

'Oh.' She wasn't quite sure how to reply to that one. She had no idea what that amount of money would have been, but she was sure enough to know it wouldn't have been insubstantial.

'He's paid it all back.' Harry gave a smile. 'So he doesn't really owe me. It's just a figure of speech.'

Esther sipped the wine again and tried to ignore the little tight coil currently in her stomach It had eased a bit since they had left Eglinton Hall.

She rested her head on one hand. 'I can't believe you did this.'

Harry looked surprised. 'Why not? Don't you think you're worth it?'

All she could do was blink, because those words hit a whole bunch of nerves she didn't even realise she had. It was like a chilly breeze over her skin. She didn't lack confidence as a person. She knew she was good at her job. And she was comfortable in her own skin. But to-night, in a place that had practically smelled of money, she been distinctly *uncomfortable*. And Esther didn't like feeling like that. Every cell in her body had prac-tically told her to leave.

But there was more than that. It was something much deeper, much more fundamental. *Being worth it.* Those words mattered so much. When her father had flitted from one job to the next, leaving the financial security to her mother, she'd seen how much his every decision hurt her mother. She'd seen her mother's confidence slowly and surely ebb away. They'd both still loved him. He didn't realise how his actions hurt the women in his life. But him, constantly choosing to move on to another job—none of which had been close to home— had always left Esther with a feeling of not being worth staying for.

She never talked about it. Never discussed it. Because then she would have to admit the rose-tinted memories she kept of her father weren't perfect. That he'd hurt them both. But Harry's words had struck a chord. Much deeper than she'd expected.

'Because I think you are,' Harry added. He'd been watching her for the last few seconds, as if he was giving her space to think.

Her phone beeped and she automatically pulled it from her bag—glad of the temporary distraction. She took a breath as she tried to straighten out her thoughts. 'My mum, just let me reply.'

Something flashed across Harry's face. An expression she hadn't really seen before from him. Was that regret? She tapped the keys on her phone quickly and pressed Send, pushing the phone to her side.

Armand appeared a moment later and set two plates down. The aromas instantly drifted up around her. 'Just as well you gave me that warning call,' he said to Harry. 'Enjoy!' He waved his hand and darted back to the kitchen.

Esther laughed. 'How on earth does he move so quickly?' Her hands had automatically picked up her knife and fork. When something smelt this good she didn't want to wait.

'It's one of his many talents,' said Harry as he picked up his cutlery too. 'Dig in. I'm hoping you'll love it.'

And she did. All eight courses that Armand supplied. The food was delicious, the portion sizes just right. She stuck with the one glass of wine, sipping it slowly between courses.

There was something about having the place to themselves. Both of them seemed to relax more. The anxieties of earlier slipped away.

'Have you settled in at the Queen Victoria?' Esther asked as they finished their puddings.

'I think so. We've agreed protocols between hospitals for transfers.'

'So, you'll be at the Queen Victoria more than before?'

He nodded. 'I'm still just a visiting surgeon. It just gives me a base when I get referrals from other counties.'

'Will you still do surgeries in other countries?'

He sighed. 'Of course. I go where the babies are. Staying in random hotel rooms around the world is what I do best.' He paused for a second. 'But I have to admit the facilities that the Queen Victoria have for parents are far superior than any others I've come across.'

Esther nodded in agreement. They didn't just have the parent beds in NICU. The Queen Victoria also had a series of apartments where whole families could stay if their children required long-term care. She wasn't quite sure why she'd started questioning him so much about his job. Or why some of his answers disappointed her. It was ridiculous. Nothing had changed. He was a visiting surgeon. He would come. He would go. She'd known that right from the start. So why did that make her stomach twist and turn?

'Don't you wish you could be somewhere more permanent? Have your own team? Stay in your house instead of random hotel rooms?'

She watched as his shoulders tensed. The far-off expression on his face made her want to reach out and hug him.

'Home? What does that even mean?' He didn't even try to hide the huskiness in his voice.

Her heart squeezed in her chest. Did Harry really not have a sense of home? How must that feel? How did a child grow up when they never had the sense of warmth and love that she'd experienced?

She clasped her hands in front of her. 'Home is the place you can be yourself. The place you're most comfortable, and the people you're most comfortable with. Where you don't need any masks, or faces. Where you can be exactly who you want to be.'

She was remembering the expression on Lady Brackenridge's face. Remembering some of the things that she'd said—and wondered if she'd said too much.

She almost jumped as Harry stood up, the chair scraping on the floor behind her. He held out his hand towards her.

'Esther, will you come home with me tonight?'

She held her breath. He didn't need to say anything else out loud. He wasn't just asking her back to Belgravia. He wasn't just asking her back to the pristine town house that didn't really look as if anyone lived there.

She knew exactly what he was asking. She licked her lips and swallowed. All the fears and uncertainties she'd had back at Eglinton Hall threatened to swamp her.

She was with Harry. The guy she'd initially hated, but now was slowly but surely stealing little parts of her heart. They'd only kissed up until this point. But she couldn't ignore the attraction that flared in her body every time she glimpsed him. Every time she caught a waft of his aftershave. Every time his skin came into contact with hers.

For the last few hours she'd let herself be swamped by all the differences in wealth between them—but was that fair to Harry?

Neither of them had asked to be born into the life that they had. They were just two people whose lives had suddenly become intertwined.

She knew this wasn't destined to last forever. Harry was only here temporarily. But did she really want to ignore the spark between them? She'd gotten so used to only concentrating on work that she'd forgotten what it actually felt like to have a real connection with another human being. Someone to share with. Someone to have fun with.

And now? Now, she had one question to answer.

They were a million miles apart. But she'd never felt so close to someone in her life. She didn't need forever. She didn't need her perfect match.

But the electricity in the air was telling her what she needed, right here, right now.

She reached out her hand towards his. 'Yes,' she said clearly.

And as his hand closed over hers and pulled her towards him, the moment couldn't have been more perfect.

CHAPTER NINE

ALL OF A sudden he became part of the couple that the hospital had already believed existed.

It was amazing what quickly became normal.

He picked her up and took her back to his house. The immaculate town house became a little more rumpled.

A toothbrush appeared in the bathroom, along with shampoo, deodorant and a pink hairdryer.

Jeans were left over a chair in the bedroom. A small bag sat on the same chair filled with underwear.

Lemon marmalade and a certain brand of biscuits emerged in his kitchen cupboards. His long-ignored coffee machine took on a whole new lease of life. He'd lost the instruction manual ages ago, and could never remember all the functions that it took Esther less than five minutes to figure out.

He started to look for her constantly. In the canteen at work. In A&E. Every time he pushed open the doors to NICU—even when he knew she wasn't on shift.

No matter how many times he tried to persuade her otherwise, she wouldn't stop doing the occasional extra shift. She was proud, and needed the money for her family. It didn't matter that Harry could write her a cheque in seconds. It didn't matter that he wouldn't even miss the money from his bank account.

What mattered was that any conversation that went down that road could hurt Esther. Even when he bought her things—perfume, flowers, a book she wanted, a top she'd admired in a shop window—her first reaction was to bristle. Her second reaction was to tell him not to spend money on her.

For a woman who counted every penny and saved as much as she could, Esther was the least materialistic person he'd ever encountered.

He'd met his fair share of females in the past who knew exactly how wealthy he was, and were more than happy to accept gifts, holidays, even cars. The most forthright had left a catalogue from an exclusive jeweller's with a few items circled. The most expensive being an engagement ring that could take a baby's eye out with its sharp edges.

Esther was the opposite. She didn't want things. She didn't place value on things. She was happier with a written note, a card, a chocolate bar hidden under her pillow.

He had a sneaking feeling she resented his wealth a little. But it was a conversation they'd never had. It was like she'd drawn a line under it, accepted it, but was determined not to let it affect what happened between them.

Part of him was glad no one could ever label Esther as a potential gold-digger—that was a particular tabloid favourite. But part of him was sorry that she would be reluctant to accept any financial help that he might want to offer her. He tried to play it carefully because he respected her, and their relationship was still developing.

She'd even met a few of his friends. Penelope had drifted back into the background after sending him a few playful texts saying how much she liked Esther and she wanted to know when to buy a hat. Most of the friends he spent time with now were fellow surgeons, and Esther could more than match any of them.

It had taken a little pushing to get an introduction to Carly and Chloe, two fellow midwives she trusted. There was a third member of the quartet, Isabella, but she was apparently in New Zealand right now. He'd liked them both. Chloe had a cute kid that he'd entertained for more than an hour while the girls gossiped, but he'd liked that. He liked that Esther hadn't felt as if she constantly had to drag him into the conversation. She'd treated him like she expected him to be around for a long time, and this was something he should get used to. That sent a warm kind of glow around him that he hadn't expected.

Once they'd reached home they'd chatted as he made omelettes. Her phone had buzzed again. 'Your mum?' he asked.

She shook her head. 'Shirley, the A&E manager with an offer of shifts next week.'

'Don't,' he said, quicker than he meant to.

Her brow creased. 'What do you mean don't?'

It was too late to pull it back, but now was the time to say something that had been on his mind. 'You work every single day. We hardly ever get to spend time together. You know—like a normal couple. How about we have a day off together—a night off together where one, or both of us, doesn't have to get up at five in the morning to go into work.' He gave a sad kind of smile. 'Believe it or not, I actually like waking up next to you. How about we try and do it at least once a week?'

Her mouth was open, but she wasn't actually speaking. He had no idea what was currently spinning around in her mind. All he knew was his stomach was churning in case he'd just played this entirely wrong.

But Esther's eyes were on his, and the only thing he could see in them was warmth. 'A night falling asleep in each other's arms, and waking up the same way, could be kind of nice,' she said.

He moved around the counter towards her. 'It could,' he agreed.

She slipped her arm around his waist and smartly pulled his phone from his back pocket. 'Let me check your shifts. There's no point in me turning down these if you're already scheduled to work.'

He held his breath while she checked. She bit her bottom lip, then looked up at him. 'Okay, next Saturday. We'll have our first official day—and night—off together.'

He punched a fist into air. 'At last.'

Esther wasn't quite sure what came over her. She'd been so used to working seven days every week that the shock of taking one day off a week to spend with Harry felt like a permanent holiday.

She dined in some gorgeous restaurants; they attended the theatre together, went for long walks around some of the parks in London and enjoyed a private ride on the London Eye at night.

She tried hard to stop thinking about money all the time. That was her issue, not his.

But the best times were the ones where they just curled up on his sofa and watched TV. She was hardly spending any time in her own flat now. It seemed easier to stay at Harry's. A few of her possessions had taken up residence in his town house—her favourite cookbook, a framed photo with her mum and most of her clothes. Life felt like a fairy tale.

She'd gotten used to the stares at work, and the quiet whisperings. Hospitals were always the same. Next week, somebody else would be hospital news and she and Harry would just fade into the background.

In the meantime she was happy living a life that felt like part of a fairy tale.

She rubbed her eyes as she headed to the cash machine. Night shifts were never her favourite time. Every cell in her body protested to the wrench of its natural flow. She slid her card and blinked as she saw her balance. That couldn't be right.

She pressed a few other buttons. But the figure didn't change.

Her mouth went dry. There was a standard amount of money she always sent her mother and that would still be covered, but for the last few months, she'd managed to send an extra few hundred pounds because of all the shifts she covered. Her mother had never asked her for more. But Esther liked to do it.

This month, the money wasn't there. And she knew why.

Harry.

She leaned against the wall for a few minutes. She'd

been turning down shifts on a regular basis. She still did one extra every week. But all of a sudden it didn't seem like enough.

Her stomach growled loudly and she walked to the vending machine to buy a sandwich, and stopped. She could do without. It wasn't like she'd fade away to nothing.

Her skin prickled. Her spending habits had changed in the last few weeks too. She'd stopped being so thrifty. She'd started heading to the canteen a few times a week instead of bagging her lunch. She didn't want him to pay for everything while they were out—even though he tried to insist. But those casual purchases of pop-corn and coffee were all adding up. None of this was Harry's fault, but somehow, being around him had made her forget her priorities.

It was time she had a rethink.

She pulled her phone from her pocket, returning a text Shirley had sent earlier offering shifts in A&E. She said yes to them all.

Then she texted the agency too. There was still one day this month where she could squeeze in an extra shift.

Her eyes caught sight of a text from earlier. Harry. Wishing you were here with me tonight. See you in the morning. She smiled and stuck the phone back in her pocket. She'd need to talk to him at some point.

Harry would be fine. He'd understand.

He was already sleeping when his phone rang.

His eyes narrowed at the name on the screen. 'Pe-nelope?'

'Hey, Harry, sorry if I've woken you.' Her voice

sounded a little shaky, not the self-assured way it normally was. Harry sat upright in bed.

'What's wrong?'

He heard her take a few slow breaths. 'Penelope?'

'I'm sorry, this was silly. I'll be fine. I shouldn't have called.'

All of his senses were on alert. 'Penelope. Tell me what's wrong.'

He suddenly realised that whilst her voice was low—as if she were whispering into the phone—there was also a slight echo around it. 'Where are you?'

She named a well-known venue in London. 'I came here with Lance Derby.'

Harry rolled his eyes. Lance wasn't his favourite. A banker who was arrogant and opinionated. 'And?'

'He's had a bit too much to drink—we both have, really—and...'

Her voice tailed off. Harry swung his legs out of bed. 'And what?'

'He's been more than a bit forward with me.'

'What do you mean?' Harry was already on his feet, looking for his clothes.

Penelope let out a noise that sounded like a sob.

Her voice cracked. 'I'm sorry, Harry. I feel like some kind of teenager. I shouldn't be calling you.'

'Whereabouts are you at the club?' he asked as he pulled his T-shirt over his head.

'In the bathroom,' came the whisper.

He stopped. 'You're in the bathroom?'

'It's the only place I feel safe,' she admitted. 'I know he's waiting outside the door. I've heard him shouting at a few people. He wants to take me home, and I just don't want to go back out there. Not when he's drunk like this. I… I'm not sure what he thinks taking me home means.'

Harry's mind had already been made up a few minutes ago. 'I'll be there as soon as I can.'

There was an audible breath of relief, then Penelope added, 'But, Harry, I'm not sure they'll let you in. It was an invite-only event tonight.'

Something clicked in Harry's brain. He walked to his dresser and rummaged through the mail lying on top. 'I think I had one of those. Give me a sec.' He pulled an envelope out from the stack. 'Yes, I've got it.'

He glanced at his reflection in the mirror and realised that joggers and a T-shirt wouldn't gain him entry to the exclusive members club. 'Okay, don't move. I'm changing and I'll be with you shortly. If you feel safe in the ladies', then stay there. Don't move.'

He changed into a suit, shirt and tie in record time and jumped into his car. Thankfully the streets of London were much quieter at this time of night and it didn't take him long to reach the venue.

He waved his invitation and stepped inside. Sure enough, Lance Derby was pacing outside the ladies' bathrooms. Harry did his best not to grit his teeth but the sensations were pretty much overwhelming. Lance wasn't just drunk, he was very drunk, loud and obnoxious.

He walked towards Lance, who'd started to talk loudly to another male guest, telling him exactly what he was waiting for.

Harry didn't hesitate. He grabbed Lance by the scruff of the neck and the seat of his pants, practically lifting him from the floor as he marched him back to the front door. One of the members of staff visibly gulped, panic on her face.

Lance started to try and wrestle his way from Harry's grip, but his drunken moves were uncoordinated and his shouts slurred.

'Get off me, get off me.' He turned his head and caught a glimpse of Harry. 'Oh, it's you,' he said in a mocking voice. 'The white knight. Well, get lost, Harry. You had your chance. Penelope's coming home with me.'

He was still trying to struggle as Harry nodded to one of the staff to open the front door. Several people had come to some of the doors of the club and were watching every movement. This could be dangerous. Harry had spotted a few paparazzi at the end of the street. There were obviously a few events going on in the same area of London tonight. He paused at the entrance way. 'Is there a cab outside?'

The doorman took a quick glance and waved his arm. 'Just a moment, sir.'

Lance kept wrestling, but Harry's grip was strong.

The doorman gave a nod. 'Can you open the door for me?' asked Harry.

A few seconds later there was a shout from outside. 'Ready!'

Harry bundled Lance down the steps and straight into the empty cab, thrusting some money towards the driver and rattling off Lance's address. He'd known him long enough to know exactly where he lived.

He waited a few moments as the cab drove off, then straightened his suit and walked back inside.

He knocked on the door of the ladies' and waited a few moments before gently pushing it open.

'Pen? Are you here? It's Harry. Lance is gone. I've put him in a cab and sent him home.'

The door to one of the panelled wooden stalls opened and Penelope walked unsteadily out, her face streaked with tears. She collapsed into Harry's arms. 'I'm so sorry to phone you. Say sorry to Esther too. It's the middle of the night.'

Harry shook his head. 'It's fine, and Esther's working. Even if she hadn't been, she would have been fine with me coming for you.'

He took a deep breath. 'Did he touch you? Did he do anything to you?'

Penelope shook her head. She didn't meet Harry's eyes. 'It didn't get that far. He just got drunker and drunker and told me exactly what he expected later. That was enough. I thought I could just duck away, but when I came to the bathroom, he started hanging around outside.' Her voice was trembling. 'And I wasn't sure who would have my back if I'd gone outside again.'

Harry trembled as he kept his rage buttoned up inside. He put his hands ever so gently on Penelope's face. 'No one should ever make you feel like that. No one should ever make you feel unsafe. I'll always have your back, Pen. Know that. Know that always. Any time, day or night, that you don't feel safe, you can call me. That's what friends are for.'

Her eyes finally met his and he could feel her whole body sag in relief. She put her hand over his. 'I'm just glad you were able to come and get me.' She took a long, slow breath. 'Would you mind taking me home?'

'Of course not.'

She nodded, then turned to the mirror. 'Give me a second.'

She cleaned up her face and combed her hair, rapidly looking more like the polished Penelope the world normally viewed. He gave her a few moments while she put her hands on either side of the sink and did some deep breathing.

'Ready,' said Penelope, sounding a little more like normal. 'Thank you,' she said again. 'I'm sorry to phone in the middle of the night. But I just knew I needed some help—and you were the first person I knew I could count on.'

He gave her a thoughtful nod. 'Any time, Penelope. Any time you need help, just pick up the phone.'

She slid her hand into Harry's arm as they walked outside towards Harry's car.

'Duke, Penelope,' came a shout nearby.

They turned automatically as a camera flashed. Harry shook his head as he opened the car door for her. 'Sorry about that. I'd seen them, but thought they were at the club down the street.'

'No probs,' said Penelope as she fastened her seat belt. 'Just get me home. I can't wait for this night to be over.'

Esther's phone rang, sending a jolt through the staff who were currently sitting at the nursing station in NICU. Her heart missed a few beats when she saw the name on the screen. *Mum.*

She automatically stood up, stepping away from

her colleagues towards the back wall of NICU. 'Mum, what's wrong? Is everything all right?'

She froze. The voice at the end of the phone wasn't her mother's. It was one of the neighbours.

'Esther, I'm so sorry to phone you at this time. It's Gladys. There's been a bit of an issue here.'

'Where's my mum? Is she okay?'

There was a long intake of breath. 'Yes, yes, I think so. They've just taken her away in the ambulance. A bit of smoke inhalation, but they think she'll be okay. I'm just going to follow the ambulance but she wanted me to phone you first.'

'Smoke inhalation? What's happened?' She couldn't keep her voice quiet right now. All heads in the unit turned towards her.

'I'm so sorry, honey, but the house…it's gone up in flames. The fire brigade are here now. They have no idea how things started and they think they have the blaze under control, but—to be honest, Esther—your mum can't go back there. The roof is damaged, the kitchen…' She let her voice tail off.

Esther sagged back against the wall just for a second as she blinked back tears.

'I'm coming. I'm on my way.' She brushed the tears from her face. 'Tell her I'll be there as soon as I can.'

She finished the call as her colleagues surrounded her, instantly asking if they could help.

'I'll cover your patients.'

'We can arrange some emergency leave.'

'Do you want me to go online and book the first flight for you?'

She nodded as she tried to collect her thoughts. 'Harry,' she said in a low voice. 'I should phone Harry.'

Two of her colleagues exchanged glances. 'Maybe not,' said the one that was usually more bolshie.

Esther shook her head. 'Why?'

There was an awkward pause, then one of them took her phone from her pocket and pulled up the Twitter feed for one of the daily rags. *Has the Duke Found His Bride?* was the headline of just over an hour ago.

The picture that accompanied it was of Harry, dressed in a suit with his arm around Penelope, looking her usual glamorous self. Harry looked worried—was that because he knew his picture was being taken? But Penelope didn't look worried at all. She had her hand on the front of Harry's chest and was looking at him like Harry was some kind of saviour. Esther's stomach twisted into a knot.

Harry had texted earlier and said he was in bed. Alone.

The text from earlier must have been a lie and that made her stomach clench in anger and humiliation.

Because this picture showed something entirely different. And the way that Penelope was looking at him... made her wonder if she'd missed something completely. Could that be love? Adoration?

Whatever it was it made her want to be sick all over her shoes and punch a wall.

Nothing like being humiliated in front of the world.

'I'm sorry, honey,' said Caroline, one of her older colleagues. 'But you've enough to deal with right now. Concentrate on your mum. Anything else can wait.'

It was clear she could tell that the tears forming in Esther's eyes were a mixture of things.

Esther trusted Caroline. She'd never steered her wrong in the past. Caroline put her arm around her shoulders. 'Get your things. I'll walk you down and see if we can get you a cab.'

Esther's mind was swirling. She didn't know what to think. Anger was racing through her veins. What she really wanted to do was dial his number and scream and shout. But grabbing some things and getting to the airport was so much more important right now.

And even though she knew that, it didn't stop the horrible aching of her heart, or the hurt at the apparent betrayal.

But there was something else. Even if this hadn't happened. Part of her knew that depending what she found when she got back to Scotland, she might never come back here. She had to put her mum's needs first— because she was all she had.

She tilted her chin upwards defiantly. Maybe this was all for the best. The end for the two of them was inevitable. It had just happened sooner than she'd expected. She'd been too trusting. She'd had her head in the clouds.

She'd lived the Cinderella fairy tale for too long.

And everyone knew that fairy tales weren't real.

CHAPTER TEN

HARRY WOKE EARLY—even though he'd had very little sleep.

Penelope had managed to gather herself by the time he'd taken her home. She was starting to get angry, and he didn't blame her.

He was glad she'd called. Glad he'd been able to help her out. He knew he would do it again in a heartbeat.

But coming home to an empty bed made him feel odd. He'd gotten so used to having Esther here that now it seemed off when she wasn't. He loved the heat from her body and the way her skin seemed to mould against his.

Waking up now made the town house just feel... empty.

He froze.

Empty had been pretty much how his life had felt for a long time. It wasn't just that he didn't form relationships with other people; it was just that he had been brought up that way. It wasn't the norm for him.

He'd never opened up to another person the way he had with Esther. He'd never shared with someone else the way he had with Esther. Of course he had friends, colleagues and a scattered extended family.

But who was really there to think about him? To consider him?

He thought back to the night he'd received the call about his father. Regret swamped him. He couldn't pretend he hadn't almost hated his father. But, as an adult, he regretted the opportunity that he'd missed to have one final talk. His father had collapsed and died quickly. He hadn't had some painful disease. There had been no suffering. Harry had thought the old man might actually have lived until he was a hundred.

But the last few weeks, seeing the strong relationship Esther had with her mother filled him with regret. His father might have always remained an opinionated, self-centred, hateful man. Or maybe, if he'd been ill or sick, there might have been some regrets.

And that's what left Harry with a hole in his heart. There was no sense of closure. He wished he'd driven down to the country estate at least one time in the five years before his father had died. Even if it had resulted in yet another fight, it might have made him feel a little more sure about his complete avoidance of his father in the last few years of his life.

Maybe it was just his own idea of a fairy tale—that his father would have lived to regret the wasted years between them. The way he'd treated Harry, the way he'd ignored him. That there could have been some last-minute kind of reconciliation. He'd spent his life feeling so isolated. So alone.

Being around Esther had broken down a whole host of barriers he'd spent his life reinforcing. She challenged him. She excited him. She celebrated and commiserated with him. When he sat on the sofa at night now, he didn't feel comfortable unless she was perched alongside him.

It hadn't even been that long, and maybe he was crazy, but it felt like his life had changed immeasurably.

She was helping him fill out the little parts of himself that had always felt as if they were missing. The parts that his parents had stolen from him, and he'd never had a chance to steal back.

Seeing her relationship with her mother had taught him it was all right to have regrets about how things had turned out with his father. There had never been a good relationship between him and his father in the first place. But that didn't mean he hadn't secretly wished for it. He would have loved to have the kind of relationship with his dad that Esther had with her mum. The love, the mutual respect—even the genuine interest in each other—was something he'd spent most of life yearning for, just not letting himself admit to. He'd never allowed himself to feel that way before. He could now wish things had been different—even if it was much too late. It didn't make him weak. It just made him human.

She would be finishing at work soon. If he got ready and left now, he could meet her with her favourite coffee before she left for home—his home.

Their home.

He swallowed. He hadn't asked her yet.

He'd been letting the idea float around his brain for a few days while he got comfortable with it.

No, actually, that was a lie. He was comfortable with

it as soon as it first got there. But what he didn't want to do was scare her off and send her running for the hills.

Was it normal to ask someone if they wanted to move in permanently after a few short weeks?

For the first time in his life Harry had found something he wanted to keep hold of. Found something he wanted to build and nurture. Last thing he wanted to do was ask the question and watch her squirm as she struggled to find a way to say no.

He also had a secret to tell her that could help their budding relationship.

His brain played with the thoughts all the way to the Queen Victoria. He noticed his hand was trembling as he paid for the coffee and it made him smile.

He liked these nerves. They felt like good nerves. Maybe asking Esther to move in with him after a night shift wasn't the best idea on the planet—he could probably time it better, arrange a more romantic setting than the hospital entrance—but all he knew was he didn't want to wait.

He wanted to ask her now. Ask her while things felt so good between them, so right.

He glanced at his watch. The shift handover was taking longer than normal. He'd just go on up to NICU. He had patients to check on anyway.

He swung the doors open with a cheery 'Good morning,' only to be met by silence.

He strode across the entrance way and sat the coffee cups down on the desk. 'Where's Esther?' he asked. He knew who she'd been working with last night and the rest of the staff was still there.

One of the older midwives closest to him sucked in

her breath through her teeth. Another midwife shot him a dagger-like glare. Two others just pointedly ignored him as if he hadn't spoken at all.

He turned to the woman beside him. 'Caroline, what's going on—is Esther okay?'

Caroline pressed her lips together for a few seconds as panic started to grip at his chest. He could tell she was considering what to tell him. She kept her voice low. 'She got a call last night from her mother. It was an emergency. There was a fire at her mother's house and she had to go back to Scotland.'

'What?' He nearly dropped the coffee that he'd picked back up. He yanked his phone from his pocket. 'But she would have called, she would have texted.' He stared at the blank screen.

Another voice cut in behind him. 'Hey, you, Mr Flighty, my office, now.' The thick Irish accent was curt.

He turned around to face Oona, shaking his head. 'No, I can't. I need to talk to Esther.'

The small, burly woman stepped closer, barely an inch from his face. 'It wasn't a request.'

Harry was taken aback, his fingers already pressing the buttons on his phone to dial Esther, but he followed her into her office, watching in bewilderment as she closed the door with a kick.

Oona folded her arms across her chest. 'Don't bet on Esther answering your calls.'

'What?' He looked up from his phone screen.

'After your shenanigans last night, I doubt she'll talk to you again.'

He frowned as a text beeped on his phone. Penelope. He could see the first line of the text. *Oh no.*

He shook his head as he tried to work out what on earth was going on. 'What…shenanigans?' He didn't even like saying the word. *Harry* and *shenanigans* had never been in the same sentence before.

Oona waved one hand. 'Had a good night, did you?'

He wrinkled his brow. 'What?'

She gave him a hard stare. 'You're looking remarkably fresh for someone who was out until two in the morning.'

Something prickled at the back of his brain—and it wasn't good.

'How do you know that?'

She gave him a look of disgust. 'The whole world knows that, Harry. If you're going to play away, have the decency not to be so public about it.'

He took a deep breath. 'I have no idea what you're talking about.' He resisted the temptation to pull up the rest of Penelope's message.

Oona's look of disgust stayed firmly in place. 'I'd like to use words that would be deemed "unprofessional," so I won't. But this is my unit, my NICU, Harry, and I expect my staff to be treated with respect. Maybe no one warned you about mixing business with pleasure, but when things get messy like this, the atmosphere can affect everyone who is in here. Staff, patients and relatives. Humiliating a member of my staff in public is hardly going to result in an atmosphere for babies that's conducive to healing, is it?'

He was beginning to get mad. Esther's phone was just ringing out. Perhaps she was on the plane?

'Why don't you explain exactly what you think I've done, Oona, and stop speaking in riddles.'

She gritted her teeth and pulled her phone from her tunic, turning it to face him. 'You—and your apparent potential bride—are all over social media since the early hours, after falling out of some club together. And yes. Esther's seen it. Which is why I doubt very much she'll answer any of your calls.' Oona shook her head. 'You really couldn't have timed this any worse.'

Dread swept over him. The headline above the photo of him and Penelope was bad enough. *Will Penelope Brackenridge Be the New Duchess of Montrose?*

But the photo certainly didn't help. It looked...kind of compromising, even from his gaze. It didn't matter that he knew what had happened. It didn't matter that he knew there was absolutely nothing in it. He knew exactly what the press were like. And his heart sunk at the thought of Esther being confronted with this last night in the midst of the bad news from back home.

He straightened his back and looked Oona straight in the eye. 'That picture is not what you think. Penelope is my friend, has been since we were five. She phoned me last night when she felt threatened. I picked her up and took her home.' Anger was rising in him. He didn't need to give Oona an explanation of his behaviour, but he wanted to—for Esther's sake. At least Oona had been up front with him; now he knew exactly what was going on and why Esther hadn't answered his calls. He turned to walk away. He had things to sort; he needed to find cover for today, and probably tomorrow too. Then he'd need to try and find a flight.

His hand was on the doorknob when he turned back

around. It was like every little light had taken fire in his brain at once. He could explain this to Esther, of course he could. But more than that, he wanted to be by her side. She'd be devastated over what had happened back in Scotland and he didn't want her to go through that alone. She shouldn't have to, and she didn't need to.

He turned back to Oona. 'Just so you know, I would do it again—in a heartbeat—for any friend, male or female, who told me they felt unsafe.' Then his expression softened. 'And why on earth would anyone think that I'd cheat on Esther—the woman that I love?'

He watched as Oona's eyes widened as he stepped out of the office and picked up the phone. He had no surgeries scheduled in the next few days, but a couple of babies who would require surgery when delivered. He made sure his contact details were available for the responsible hospitals as he knew that even with the best-laid plans, babies sometimes had ideas of their own.

Francesca appeared at his side. 'You okay?'

'No,' he said honestly. 'But I will be.'

She didn't ask questions, just gave his arm a squeeze. 'You know you can leave any instructions with me.'

He pulled his notes from a pad. 'And I was just doing that.' He gave her a hug. 'Thank you for this, and phone me if there's anything at all.'

She nodded slowly and pressed her lips together. 'I'll try my best not to.'

He wasn't worried about the hushed atmosphere around him now. Oona would spread the news in his absence, and gossip like this would fly through the hospital like a firework.

He'd just declared his love for Esther.

He hadn't even known until that second that he was going to say those words.

But right now, he needed to tell them to the person who mattered most.

And that was exactly what he planned to do.

CHAPTER ELEVEN

SHE COULD ALMOST swear that her heart hadn't stopped racing in her chest until that moment that she finally saw her mother lying in the hospital bed and rushed over to wrap her arms around her.

Finally, she could breathe.

She was here. She was alive.

It didn't matter that her mother was lying in a hospital bed with crisp white sheets, or that she was wearing a pale blue hospital gown. As Esther encompassed her in a hug, all she could smell was the smoke. It clung to her mother's hair and skin, with even a smudge of something on her cheek.

Esther tried to hold back her tears. It wouldn't do for her mum to see her so upset. She sat at the edge of the bed—ignoring all the rules that said she shouldn't—and took both of her mum's hands.

'I am so glad you're safe. What happened?'

Her mum didn't speak for a few moments. 'I'm not sure. I was in bed. I think it might have been the washing machine. That's what the fire officer said. One minute I was sleeping, and the next the place was full of smoke.' Her voice was trembling now. 'I just grabbed my slippers and dressing gown and ran down the stairs.' She shook her head. 'My bag was sitting on the table near the front door so I grabbed it too on my way out.' Her eyes were filled with tears. 'I couldn't even go near the sitting room.' She shivered. 'The heat coming out of there was too much.'

Esther couldn't hide the fact that she was shaking too. She'd seen too much in A&E, saw the impact of house fires. Helped when trying to resuscitate adults and children who'd been overcome by smoke. Knowing that one of those people could have been her mother was just too much.

She hugged her again tightly. 'Oh, I'm so glad you woke up. I'm so glad you ran.'

Her mother bowed her head, holding on tight to her. Esther knew her mum was just as glad to see her. She must have got such a fright last night. 'You didn't need to come all this way,' her mum whispered. 'I'm so sorry. You're so busy. And you've got so much to do. You shouldn't need to worry about me.'

Esther put her hand on her mother's cheek. 'I'll *always* worry about you. You're my number one priority.'

Her mother's voice stayed low. 'But you shouldn't be doing that. You should be out living your own life, having fun.'

Something twisted inside Esther. She didn't like the way this conversation was going. She knew her mother too well.

When she was stressed about something, she tried to find a way to say words without actually having to say them. Just like she was doing now.

She'd already told her mum that she was dating

someone—she just hadn't filled in all the blanks. But it didn't feel like this was where this was going.

'What is it, Mum? Just tell me.'

Her mum's eyes brimmed with tears. 'I don't think you'll be able to stay in the house. There'll be too much damage. Gladys says you can stay with her tonight.'

'Don't worry about me. Let me sort things out. I'll arrange to get the house cleaned up, and the place assessed. I'll contact the insurers. Just you rest. Worry about getting better. Let me worry about everything else.'

Harry had only been standing outside the small fire-damaged house for a few minutes when one of the neighbours approached. 'Are you looking for Mrs Mc-Donald?' she asked.

He nodded. 'And Esther—I'm looking for her daughter too.'

The woman glanced back at the house and shuddered. 'Come with me. Esther will be staying at mine tonight. I'm sure she'll be back once she's done with visiting at the hospital. Let me make you some tea.'

He'd barely blinked before a large teapot appeared, along with an eclectic array of mugs and a plate of biscuits and thick wedges of fruit loaf.

'I'm Gladys,' the woman said, sitting at the other side of the table. She gave Harry the eye, in the way that a woman of a certain age only could. 'Are you Esther's young man?'

He wasn't quite sure how to answer that one. He wanted to be. He wanted to be more than her young man, but until he'd spoken to Esther it didn't seem fair to introduce himself that way.

He stretched his hand across the table. 'I'm Harry, Esther's friend. We work together.'

Gladys's eyebrows lifted. 'From what I hear, that's the only way to see Esther these days.'

He nodded in agreement. 'She works very hard.'

Gladys opened her mouth as if she were about to say something else, then stopped, giving a simple nod. 'She does.'

The doorbell rang and Esther walked through the door. 'Harry.' She stood frozen in shock. She looked tired out, her skin pale and her eyes dark.

Her gaze flitted between Harry and Gladys. 'How...?'

'Here.' Gladys jumped up. 'Have some tea. You look like you need it. I need to pop to the corner shop. So now that you're back, I'll leave you and Harry for five minutes.'

Within a few seconds Gladys was gone but Esther still stood frozen on the spot. Harry stood up and stepped over. He tentatively lifted an arm to put around her shoulders but stopped as she flinched.

'Don't touch me.' She thudded her bag down on the table. 'And what on earth are you doing here?' Angry tears were flooding her eyes and he hated that this was his fault.

'Nothing happened. You must know that, Esther.'

'Really? All I know is that you told me you were spending the night in bed when you were actually falling out of a club in London with Penelope!' Her words cut in before he had a chance to add anything.

Her hands were on the table, her body leaning over towards him, and he could see her whole body was shaking.

'How's your mum?'

'What?' She seemed taken aback by his question. Then she stopped and took a breath. 'My mum is okay. Smoke inhalation. Because of her frailty, they've kept her in. She'll get reassessed tomorrow.'

She sagged down onto the chair behind her and he poured her some tea. There was so much he wanted to say, so much he wanted to rush in with, but this wasn't about him. It was about her.

Her hands were still trembling as she picked up the mug. 'Tea.' She grimaced.

'I didn't like to ask Gladys if she had any coffee,' he added, but his light-hearted tone seemed off.

She didn't even look at him. Just closed her eyes and leaned her head on one hand. 'I can't even see the house until later when the fire chief comes back. I don't even know if anything is salvageable—if the house is even salvageable.'

Every part of him ached for her. He took a breath, knowing how these words might sound. 'It's only a house, Esther. You've still got your mum and she's doing okay.'

She sobbed into her hand. 'I know that. I know that. When I got to the hospital I just remembered every patient I've ever treated who'd been involved in a house fire. I couldn't even breathe just thinking about it.'

He winced. He knew exactly what she meant. The way that smoke lingered in the air of the department after they'd been treated. The horrible charcoal-like smell of burning skin. It was one of the hardest things to deal with, and for Esther to think that might have been her mum...

He stood back up and walked around the table, this time not giving her opportunity to flinch. This time just pulling her up to him and hugging her to his chest.

She didn't fight it. She just slowly wrapped her arms around his waist and stayed there. He wasn't sure how long they stood. Much longer than the five minutes that Gladys said she'd be.

When she finally pulled her face back from his chest she just shook her head. 'What are you doing here, Harry? Why did you come?'

The furrows in her brow were deep and her eyes littered with confusion.

'Why do you think I came? I came because I love you, Esther, and I didn't want you to be alone.'

Her muscles tensed and she stepped back, holding out her hands.

'But that picture. The lies you told me...'

'No. I told you the truth. I was in my bed. But Penelope phoned and she was in trouble. She'd gone out with someone who'd made her feel threatened. She was drunk and asked if I'd come and get her.'

Esther blinked, no words coming out. 'What?' It was barely a whisper.

He bent down towards her. 'You know there's nothing between Penelope and me. It's just not like that. I love her like a sister, and in a way, I wish she was, at least then I'd have a family that was worth caring about.'

She stepped back and sat back down. When she

looked at him again with those big blue eyes he sensed something from her. It was time for truths.

She put her hands on the table. 'Are you going to tell me about your father? Your parents?'

He spoke honestly. It was the only way he could do this. 'I was part of a family that my sole purpose was to be the heir. There was really no other requirement. Neither of my parents was interested in having a child. They just saw it as their duty.'

Esther just looked confused. 'Who looked after you at home? What about school holidays? Surely you spent some time with them? They spent all your time ignoring you?' She was shaking her head as if she really couldn't get her head around it.

He stayed patient for a moment. Then took a deep breath. 'Esther, you seem like a girl who spent her childhood surrounded by love. It was normal for you. It wasn't normal for me.' He put his hand to his chest. 'I thought what I had was normal. I thought it was normal to have parents who didn't look at you when you entered the room. Who didn't care how you were, or how you felt. I spent my life being brought up by an ever-changing rota of nannies. Most of them left before I ever really got to know them. There was one maid who worked in my parents' house for seven years—she was the only person who ever laughed and joked with me. I went to boarding school. I rarely saw other kids interact with their parents, so I thought that what I had was entirely normal.' He felt his own voice start to break, so he stopped talking.

Esther sat with her eyes wide. As if she were taking everything in and processing it.

Harry breathed again. He was here to tell her that he loved her. He wanted her to move in with him. To take a chance on him. He had to let her know exactly what she was getting.

He tightened his grip on her hand. 'But I'm not crazy. I know that is ridiculous. But everything about my relationship with them—my parents—coloured every part of my life. It's hard to learn to love, to share with someone, when you've never had an example of that to learn from. I didn't see it every day. That's why you're so important to me, Esther.' He looked over and met her blue gaze. 'You're the first person I've met that I've found it easy to love.'

Her mug clattered against the table. He'd said it three times now. Once to Oona, and twice to Esther. She seemed to be listening, but was she hearing?

Her fingers tightened around the mug. 'Why?'

He gave a slow nod. She wanted to know it all. 'Because you never asked me for anything. You didn't want me for anything.' He gave a gentle smile. 'You didn't even like me to begin with. Then I started being around you. I could see the relationship you had with your patients and their families. I could see how you worked hard in amongst your colleagues. And you could adapt, you could work anywhere—' his gaze met hers '—because you felt you had to.'

'And that makes me easy to love?'

'Sure it does. Because it's all about how big your heart is, and how much you love. Your only agenda is looking after your mum. Making sure she's okay.' He paused for a second, wondering if he should actually say these words out loud.

'And the worst part is that even though I know they ignored me, I spent years witnessing it. Deep down, I still wanted them to love me. When my father dropped dead, I realised that was it. It was all over. There would never be any kind of shot at redemption. I'd never get to sit at the side of my dying father's bed and listen to him apologise for how he'd treated me, and tell me that he did actually love me. I shut all those thoughts and possibilities out.'

'Oh, Harry, why?' She sounded incredulous.

'Because I wanted to be loved. I wanted to feel worthy of being loved. I wanted parents who would be proud of me. Just like your parents did. People look at me and think, *He's rich, he's got everything.* But I never had an iota of what you had. I've spent my life keeping my distance from people. Not letting my guard down. Because letting your guard down means you can get hurt.' His voice broke a little. 'And you're the only person I've felt able to do that with. I love watching what you have with your mum. The two of you are as close as can be. You talk all the time. You have pictures of your mum, and dad, all around your flat. And in those pictures? You're all in each other's arms, wrapped around each other.' He paused again, his voice hoarse. 'You've no idea how much I wish I'd had the same normal as you. And up until now, I've never admitted that. Not to anyone. Not even to myself.'

She blinked, her eyes wet, and as soon as he saw that he immediately wanted to take back all the parts of himself he'd exposed.

He straightened in his chair. 'I was never abused. I was never cold, never hungry. I didn't want for anything, really, apart from love and somebody to show some interest in me.'

'That doesn't make it right,' she said bluntly. 'We see the worst of some families in the health service. Being fed, clothed and having a roof over your head doesn't mean you didn't suffer from neglect. That sounds exactly like what happened.' She moved from her chair at the other side of the table over next to him. Her gentle floral scent following her across the room. It was all he could do not to breathe in and inhale it strongly.

'You swept me up in a fairy tale,' she said, the edges of her voice a little sad. 'I wasn't looking for a prince, or a duke, but I found one anyway.'

His hands moved to her waist. 'And is that good, or bad?'

'Both,' she said without qualm as she sat down in his lap. 'You know, you're making assumptions. I have an almost great relationship with my mother, but it's not perfect. Not the way you think. Do you know she didn't tell me straight away about the cancer?'

'What?' Harry was surprised.

She shook her head sadly. 'She didn't tell me straight away because she didn't want me to worry, about her, and the fact she couldn't manage to work any more. She didn't want to put the responsibility on to me. I was really hurt when I found out.' She stopped for a second and swallowed. 'But I understood she did it out of love.'

She took another breath. 'And my dad wasn't perfect. I admit, I loved and adored him. But as a child I didn't realise how his flyaway behaviour put extra pressure on my mum to be the foundation of the family. To try and hold down more than one job.' She put her hand to her chest. 'It's affected me more than I've ever realised.'

She took a few moments to speak, and when she looked at him again her eyes were filled with sorrow. 'But how can I leave now I've come back to find this? I can't walk away from my mum when everything is in such a state.'

It was like someone switching a light on in his brain. Even though she'd been mad at him for the photo— even though she hadn't really understood the context— it hadn't been the most important thing to her.

He'd seen how damaged the house was. It could take months to fix—if it could be fixed. Esther had already made up her mind that she needed to stay to support her mother. She had no intention of coming back to London.

He looked at her as his breath caught halfway up his throat. He hadn't even considered this—and to anyone that knew Esther, this was obvious.

'We can find a way to work things out,' he said determinedly.

'How? You in London, me up here?' She shook her head. 'That's crazy. We both know it is.'

There was a loud knock at the door and Gladys came back in, a shopping bag clasped in one hand, and a large man at her shoulder.

'Esther,' she said apologetically. 'The fire guy is here. He said he can let you collect a few things from the house.'

'Let me help,' said Harry as he grabbed his jacket.

For a second he thought she might refuse, but then she gave a little nod of her head. 'Okay.'

Her voice was cracking again; as she headed out in front of him, Harry hoped it wouldn't be the last word he would hear from her.

Five minutes later Esther had a hard hat on her head and some strict instructions from the fire guy. They'd had a quick chat about things she would really like to retrieve from the house and where they might be. Part of the roof was dangerous and was a complete no-go area, along with the kitchen.

'Brace yourself,' the guy said. 'The inside of the sitting room is completely smoke-damaged.'

Harry's face had remained steady. He put his hand on her shoulder as they went through the front door and she was glad to have it there.

The acrid smell of smoke burned her throat as she stepped inside. It seemed that even though many of the items of furniture in her mother's house met with the newer fire regulations, there had still been a few older pieces that had burned to a crisp. Amazingly, her mother's old heavy curtains were entirely intact, even though they were blackened by the fumes.

Harry moved quickly, picking up the photos she'd asked him to from the mantelpiece and the walls. Esther pulled open a cupboard under the stairs and retrieved the box with all the documentation they would need with her mother's bank details and different policies. Next were some photo albums, and a few more sentimental pieces.

'What about upstairs?' she asked.

'Which side of the house?' asked the fire officer.

Esther pointed. He nodded. 'Okay, I'll send one of

my team up. That side is unaffected but I'd still rather it wasn't you. Tell me what you need.'

A few minutes later she had most of her mother's clothes and shoes in boxes. The majority of the items had very little obvious smoke damage as they'd been sealed inside an old-fashioned wardrobe. It was likely, with a quick laundry, her mother's clothes would be fine.

Esther gave a sigh of relief. 'I think that should be everything for now.'

The fire officer nodded. 'We need to make the house secure in the meantime until repairs are done. You might not get back in here for a while.'

She gave a tearful nod. This was the house where she'd grown up, created all the memories that Harry was so envious of. But that's all they were. Memories. She still had her mum, and she needed to make sure she got things sorted out. As she picked up the last few things she wanted to take with her she was over-whelmed with sadness.

Of course she was going to do this for her mother. But part of her heart ached in sadness over Harry. He'd kept a stoic look in place as she'd told him that she couldn't come back to London, and she would never ask him to give up anything for her. She had to. Of course she had to.

When he'd told her exactly how things had been for him as a child all she'd wanted to do was run over and wrap him in her arms. But what would that achieve? Twice she'd heard him use the words that made her heart want to swell with joy. She couldn't let herself respond. She couldn't tell him that he'd completely and utterly stolen her heart too. Not when she had to tell him she wasn't coming home.

The word was like an arrow through her heart.

Home. That's what Harry's house felt like. Not her own flat back in London—it had never felt like home. But the town house? It felt like home because Harry was there. Every association she had with that place revolved around him. Him lying in the bed beside her. Her slumping in his arms on the sofa. Him cooking eggs and pancakes in the kitchen, sometimes for breakfast, sometimes late at night. If she stood in the town house and breathed in, she could smell him, because Harry smelled like home to her now.

'Hey? Okay?' He'd walked over and slipped an arm around her shoulders, obviously thinking she was upset about the house, and not the person who was standing next to her.

She blinked back the tears. She had to. Her heart was still aching for him. She wanted to tell him that she loved him too. But how could she do that when she couldn't see any way for them to be together now? She'd have to start looking for jobs. Anything would do. There was a nursing home nearby; she could try them first. It wouldn't be the same salary she'd be getting in London, but it was somewhere to start.

She shook the hand of the fire officer. 'Thank you.' Right now, as much as she loved this place in the past, she couldn't wait to get back outside.

She walked quickly back down to Gladys's house. Harry put a hand on her shoulder. 'How about I go and find us some coffee?'

She nodded and pressed her lips together. It was almost like he knew she needed a few moments alone.

She started going through the box of documents. The sooner she started to deal with things, the better. But the first phone call to the insurance company made her stomach plummet.

'What? What do you mean?' She listened, thinking that the woman at the end of the phone was clearly from another planet. 'Not paid. When? That can't be right?'

Her mother's bank statements were neatly filed in a little folder. Esther started to flick rapidly through them, finding all the direct debits and swallowing as she saw the bank balance, and that some had been refused.

This couldn't be happening. Please no. Not now.

She listened for a few more moments. The woman at the end of the phone was being lovely, but quite clear. As soon as the payments had defaulted, letters had been sent. There was a thirty-day window to make good on the payment, and then the policy was void.

She replaced the receiver in shock.

'What is it?' Gladys asked.

Esther glanced at the clock. The conversation had lasted more than an hour, but it felt as if it had gone by in the blink of an eye.

'Sh-she has no insurance.' Esther's voice came out choked and half audible.

To her surprise, Gladys just gave a little nod of her head and sat down opposite her.

'But I was sending her money. The last few weeks I hadn't managed to work quite as many shifts, but I still sent her the same amount she'd always needed. I just couldn't add any extra.'

Gladys's face was sympathetic but tight. 'Costs go up, Esther. The shopping, the gas, the electricity. The council tax went up here a couple of months ago.'

'What? She didn't tell me that.'

Gladys met her gaze. 'She didn't want to. She thought you were putting too much on yourself already. She didn't want you to make yourself unwell.' Gladys sighed. 'She also thought you weren't giving yourself any chance of a life.' She shot Esther a sympathetic glance. 'You know, Esther, she told you often enough. You just don't like to listen.'

Esther flinched. She'd no idea her mother had told Gladys quite so much. Tears swilled in her eyes. Not only had her father let her mother down, now she had too.

'But she's defaulted on her payments now! She's going to lose everything.'

She was already upset but now she was completely and utterly overwhelmed. She didn't know how they could possibly find any way out of this. The repairs to the house would require another mortgage—and could you even get a re-mortgage on a house that was fire damaged?

As for the contents—the entire kitchen would need to replaced, and the roof. That was before they even thought about the decor. Esther put her head in her hands. She had no idea what to do next. This was so much worse than she'd first imagined.

'Who's going to lose everything?' Harry's voice came from the doorway and both heads snapped around to his.

'Maybe I should leave you both alone,' said Gladys quickly, standing up to leave.

'No,' said Harry as he crossed the room and held his hand out to Esther. 'You've been so good already.' He looked down at Esther. 'Why don't we get some fresh air?'

Esther's head was swimming. She couldn't even begin to think about what all this meant. But Harry was right. She'd imposed on Gladys long enough. She didn't want to have a complete breakdown in front of the poor woman. Fresh air wouldn't help, but it would give her a bit of space.

She gave a reluctant nod and stood up, putting her hand in Harry's. 'We'll walk to the hospital. It will be visiting time soon and I want to see how she's doing.' She glanced back to Gladys. 'Please don't tell anyone about this. Let me see if there's anything else I can do.'

Gladys gave a thoughtful nod and left them to walk outside.

Esther was trying her best to hold it together. She got as far as the end of the street, where Harry seemed to know to lead her over to the empty children's swing park.

He sat her down on one of the swings and put his hands on her shoulders. 'Tell me what's happened.'

She couldn't stop crying. 'I didn't send her enough money. She missed her insurance payments. She had no insurance. I have no idea how we can fix the house.' By the end her words barely came out at all and Harry just pulled her towards him, letting her sob. 'This is all my fault.'

Part of him twisted inside. When he'd first met Esther she'd worked every hour on the planet. He'd been the one to encourage her to take some time off. He'd been the one to persuade her to spend one day a week with him. The nights just hadn't been enough for him. He'd wanted more. He'd wanted every day. Look what his actions had caused. A horrible sick feeling rose in his stomach. He couldn't let her think this was her fault. Not for a second.

He bent down and pushed back the hair that had stuck to her face. 'Esther, we can sort this.'

'How?' Her eyes were bright with tears.

He pulled a set of keys from his pocket. 'I didn't go for coffee. I called a letting agency and picked up some keys to a house, a few streets over. Your mum can move in straight away until things get sorted.'

She stared at the silver keys in amazement. 'You did what? But you didn't know anything.'

'But I'd seen the house. I knew she couldn't go back there tonight. And I know that if she's anything like her daughter, she won't want to stay with someone else and impose.'

Esther took a few deep breaths. Her brain had been whirling so much she hadn't even considered tonight. 'But—'

'We can all stay there. The letting agent was in the area and was able to show me around. It's clean, tidy and furnished. We can go and get some bedsheets and some towels before we collect your mum from the hospital.'

'But… I need to pay you… How much was this?'

'Nothing,' came the quick reply.

'No.' She shook her head firmly. 'No way.'

But Harry turned to her with an equally determined

look. 'Esther, if you hadn't been with me, if I hadn't *persuaded* you to take some time off, you would still have been able to send the money to your mother that she needed.' He put his hand on his chest. 'This is my fault. Not yours. And I'm so, so sorry.'

Her nose wrinkled. 'How can you think this is your fault?'

He held out his hands. 'Because I wanted you. I wanted all of you. I wanted all your time and all your attention. Being around you has been special for me. You've opened my eyes to so many things. You've brought fun into my life—something I never really thought I might deserve.' He paused for a second. 'And the relationship you have with your mum? Made me ask myself questions about how things turned out with my dad. Ones that I hadn't wanted to give myself the time to examine, because I wouldn't like the answers.'

She shook her head. 'But I've let her down, Harry. I've painted you a rosy picture of my life. And I do have a great relationship with my mum. I love her. I'd do anything for her. But my dad…' She let her voice trail for a second. 'Things weren't perfect. He was a drifter. A dreamer. And every time he jumped from one job to the next, he made life harder for my mum. He let her down. And I think I've done that too.'

'What?'

She sniffed and took a deep breath to stop the words from getting stuck in her throat. 'She kept telling me not to work too hard. She kept telling me to get the work/ life balance right. But I kept being single-minded. I kept wanting to work too hard, even though my body was telling me to stop.' Her eyes locked with his. 'Then I met you, Harry. I started to realise what fun was. And I kept telling myself this was a fling. A temporary thing. That it would go nowhere. But deep down, my heart wasn't listening. It was jumping in, feet first. Even though my brain knows I can't do this to myself. I can't fall for a guy who isn't around. I've already been hurt by that man. My father.' She whispered, 'I'm sorry, Harry. I should have stopped this before it started.'

His eyes went wide. She half expected him to argue back with her, to fight with her. But he surprised her by taking a deep breath and sitting down on the swing next to her, interlocking his fingers with hers. It took him a few minutes to start speaking. 'I thought when I came up here today, I just had to explain about the photo. I thought once you realised there was nothing in it, we could be fine.'

Esther froze. 'And now you think we can't?'

It didn't matter that she'd realised inside that she had to stay in Scotland. That it was likely there was no way to keep their relationship afloat. Now that he might be saying it back, every part of her body wanted to protest. To grab him and hold him tight again. To tell him that there had to be a way.

'We're so different,' he said sadly.

'You're right, we are so different,' she agreed. 'And if I was feeling really brave I would tell you that fairy tales aren't real. Not for people like me.'

He looked over at her with wounded eyes. 'So, why does it feel like—no matter what else has gone on— the only thing that really matters to me is you?' He ran his other hand through his hair and shook his head. 'I don't even deserve you, Esther. I'm not good enough for you. You've got a big heart. You're easy to love, and I can't promise you that I can be the same.'

'Why on earth would you think you're not good enough for me?'

His head fell. 'Because you know how to live life. Love. You've lived it every day of your life. You embrace it. You and your mum wouldn't know any other way to be.' He shook his head. 'My experience of love has been very different to yours. Non-existent even. How can I ever be what you need me to be?'

She could almost feel something tear at her heart muscles. She loved this guy. She loved him so much it could physically hurt if she let it. And here he was, thinking he wasn't good enough for her. Thinking he didn't have enough love to offer because of the messages he'd been left with by his mum and dad.

She tilted her head to the side. 'But everyone's got to start somewhere, Harry. Nature, or nurture? We could argue for both. I would say that every day of your life you've learned to love something. Whether it was a person, or a thing, a pet, a food, a moment.' She held up her hands. 'A sight, a sound, a taste. All of them build the person that you are, and from where I'm sitting—' she gave him a half-smile '—you don't look too bad.'

He smiled and shook his head, his voice barely a whisper. 'I'm going to tell you something I've never told anyone. When I heard that my father was dead, part of me was relieved to be free of the storm clouds that felt as if they constantly hung over my head. But part of me—' his voice trembled a little '—was still that five-year-old little kid, wondering what on earth he could do to make his mum and dad love him the way that other families did. It seemed like something was wrong with me. And I wanted to be... I wanted to be enough.' He reached over and touched her cheek. 'You were the first person that made me think I might be good enough. Good enough to love. You don't care about the duke stuff. You don't care about the surgeon stuff. And I too thought this would just be fun. Just be a fling. But, Esther—' he put his hand to his chest '—I can't be that person. I can't be the person that moves around. I've spent so long looking for love that now that I've found it, I don't ever want to let it go. I want to be enough. I want to be more than enough for you. I've never wanted anything more. I don't want to live this life without you.'

He was looking right at her, and she could feel the question in the air.

Her hand was trembling as she reached up and ran her fingers through his hair. 'Harry, what you told me about your father? That you'd never told anyone else? It makes my heart break for that five-year-old boy. It takes a lot to admit that you still wanted that connection—after everything that happened. That no matter how much he'd hurt you, you still wished for something different.'

He shook his head and closed his eyes. 'Five minutes. A five-minute conversation to see if he would ever have changed his mind. Regretted how things had been. But it wasn't to be. And I'll always have to wonder.'

She pressed her hands on either side of his head. 'But you don't have to wonder. Because I can tell you. You're worthy of love, Harry. I love you so much I think my heart might burst. I have never, ever loved anyone the way that I love you, and I never, ever will. Because you have my heart, Harry Beaumont. You have all of it.'

Now she saw tears swimming in his eyes as he bent his head towards hers.

She held her breath. 'Everything's such a mix-up right now. I have so much work to do here. To help my mum, to get back on our feet.'

'Is that a no?' he asked in a quiet voice.

'No. It's not.' She said it so quickly it surprised even herself. It was completely instinctual and straight from the heart.

He stood up and pulled her towards him. 'Tell me what you want, Esther. Tell me what you need.'

Here it was. Everything she'd ever wanted.

That was the laugh. She'd never even known she wanted this. She'd never even dared to dream she would be the Cinderella girl. It hadn't even occurred to her—not for a second. Her dreams had always been about earning money and living independently, and part of her was still that girl.

'I need some time,' she breathed. 'I need some time to sort things out.' The keys were clenched in her hand. 'These are a godsend. Thank you. It means my mum can have a roof over her head until I try and see if I can sort the insurance out.'

'Or you could let me sort the insurance out.'

She pressed her lips together and looked up at him with her blue eyes. Her heart was swelling in her chest as if it would burst. 'If I said yes, I wouldn't be me. And my heart would be sad forever.'

His face broke into a wide smile and he slid his fingers through her hair. 'I wouldn't love you any other way.' He closed his eyes for a second and gave a slow nod. 'How about, if you didn't say yes. How about, if something just happened that allowed your mother to rebuild her house?'

Her hands were on his arms now. He was treading so carefully, respecting her space, but still trying to help.

She let out a half-laugh. 'What on earth could happen?'

'A lottery ticket. A windfall. A forgotten pension of your father's. An old insurance policy that everyone had misplaced and now secretly pays out.'

She held her breath. He knew her pride would never let her accept direct money from him. He guessed her mother would be exactly the same. Now, he was giving her a get-out clause. A way that she could sort things for her mother, with a little help from Harry.

'Where did I find you?' she whispered, her hand reaching up to thread through his hair.

He was doing this for her. To let her save face. To let her pride stay intact. To stop her feeling as if everything was outside of her control, and that everything was hopeless.

He leaned forward and murmured in her ear. 'You found me in a scary place with tiny babies. It's where I'm most at home—and where I think that you're most at home too.'

Tears brimmed in her eyes. She'd started this day thinking the man she loved had betrayed her, and she'd have to pack up and leave the job she loved in London to help out her mum.

Now, he was right by her side and offering her an opportunity to stay, with both him and the job she loved.

'I have something else to tell you,' he said quietly. 'And I hope it's what you want to hear.' He tightened his arms a little around her. 'I've said yes to something else.'

'What?'

He breathed slowly. 'I've said yes to a permanent position at the Queen Victoria with my own team. I said yes because I've found the place I want to be home for me. And that's with you. I'll help you sort things with your mum. Because you don't need to do this on your own. You don't need to carry the load on your own. I'm right here, Esther. And I plan on staying.'

She leaned back but stayed in his arms. 'Harry?'

He put a gentle finger to her lips. 'I know there are a hundred questions. Maybe even a thousand what-ifs. But let's start with the most important one. I love you, Esther. Whether things are good or bad, I want to be by your side. I can't imagine loving anyone else the way that I love you.'

Nerves made her interrupt. 'Is that a question?'

He smiled. 'I know it's soon. I know you might think I'm crazy, but I guess now I've found somebody to love, I want to tell the world.' His words were soft, quiet and straight from the heart. 'So, after we've sorted everything for your mum, how do you feel about making things more permanent between us? Will you move in with me, Esther?' His gaze fixed on hers. 'Will you marry me?'

Every part of her body rejoiced. 'You want to get married?' She laughed.

'Yes.' He nodded. Then he looked at her. 'Wait, why are you laughing?'

Esther didn't stop. 'You think someone like me should be the Duchess of Montrose?'

He picked her up and spun her around. 'I think someone like you should be *exactly* the Duchess of Montrose.' He lowered her slowly to the ground, letting their bodies brush against one another. 'What can I say? Scottish.' He smiled. 'At least you'll be the genuine article.'

She wound her arms around his neck. 'Oh, so was it me you wanted, or was it any old Scottish girl?'

His lips lowered towards hers. 'Don't doubt for a second, it was definitely you.' Then he stopped, as if he'd just realised something. 'Hey? Was that a yes?'

She nodded. 'That was definitely a yes,' she murmured as her lips touched his.

CHAPTER TWELVE

'HE'S SUCH A nice young man,' sighed Esther's mum from her prime position on the sofa. She hadn't taken her eyes off him since they'd been introduced in the hospital and Harry had put all the arrangements in place to get her back to her new temporary home.

She ran her hand along the yellow sofa. 'This place is so nice. It was lucky you were able to get it at such short notice.' She lifted her chin and looked out of the window. From here she could see right along the coastline to Leith. 'I've never had a sea view,' she murmured.

'Do you like it?' asked Esther curiously.

'Of course I like it.' Her mother smiled. 'It's my dream house.'

Harry walked up behind Esther with some papers in his hand. 'Then it's lucky you don't have to move out.'

Esther blinked. 'What?'

Harry gave her a quick glance, then smiled at her mother. 'This house was up for rent, with the chance to buy. With the insurance money to fix your home, once that's done, you could sell your other place and move permanently here if you like.'

Esther reached behind her and grabbed his hand.

She knew exactly what he was doing. There was no insurance money, but they'd both agreed not to tell her mother that.

'But isn't this place much more expensive than my house?'

Of course it was. But Harry spoke smoothly. 'This is a flat. Not a house. Esther can take care of things regarding the sale and purchase, but if you like this place best, there's no reason you couldn't have it.' He bent down next to her head and glanced out the window. 'You're right, the sea view is nice.'

Now he was bending things a little further. Letting her mum feel as if all of this was being done within her own budget.

Her mum pulled the blanket up to her chest and gave Esther a nervous glance. 'You know, I wouldn't need to worry about the garden, and there's a security entrance here, and a lift.' She ran her hand back along the sofa. 'And everything is just so new.' Esther could almost see her mum's heart jump. 'And there's room enough for you and Harry to stay too when you visit.'

Oh dear. For about the tenth time in twenty-four hours, tears threatened to spill. But these were happy tears. Esther sat on the sofa next to her mum and gave her a giant hug. The lines on her face didn't seem quite so deep, and she had a little colour back in her cheeks. 'Leave it with me, and Harry,' she added as she shot him a smile. 'We'll take care of everything for you.'

He gave a nod and knelt down in front of them. 'There is one final thing,' he said, reaching into his back pocket.

Esther caught her breath at the sight of the small

black velvet box. When on earth had he had time to go shopping for that?

It flipped open, showing one of the biggest emeralds she'd ever seen, with a diamond set on either side. 'Family heirloom,' he said. 'It belonged to the last duchess who had Scottish blood in her veins, my great-great-grandmother, so I thought it might be fitting.'

He pulled it from the box. 'Esther McDonald. You've brought light and life and joy into my life and I hope to do the same to yours. Now, and always. Will you do me the pleasure of becoming my wife?'

She couldn't speak at first, just gave a nod as she held out a trembling hand and let Harry slip the giant ring on her finger.

Her mother let out a squeal and started clapping as Harry picked her up and spun her round and round and round.

As he set her back down he whispered in her ear. 'So, Duchess of Montrose, what will be your first wish?'

Her eyes gleamed. 'That? Oh, that's definitely for later, and for just you, and me,' she said as she kissed him once again.

* * * * *

MIRACLE BABY
FOR THE MIDWIFE

TINA BECKETT

MILLS & BOON

To my husband...as always

PROLOGUE

ADEM KEPLER REMEMBERED the car ride like it was yesterday. The rough blanket from his bed had rubbed his cheek raw as he tried to brace himself against the bumps on the dirt road he'd once called home.

His dad's breathless call had set the wheels in motion, the flashing lights of the plane that had sent them on a flight to a new country. A new home. He hadn't realized at the time just how sick his younger brother was until he was several years older.

But at fifteen, all he really knew was that his mother's tears seemed endless and his dad had a white pinched look around his mouth that said his family's whole world was about to change. Looking back, he could see it was a blessing in disguise and the flight into the night had saved Basir's life.

He'd had no idea of any of that at the time.

But he did now. Brain tumors knew no nationality. No financial status. No gender. All he remembered was the powerlessness and anger he'd felt as he left all of his friends behind.

The first years had been hard. Learning a new language. A new culture. But slowly, the angry teenager became a man who understood the sacrifice his parents had made, even though he'd hated it at the time. Where the seriousness of Basir's condition should have brought the family together, it had taken an already strained marriage and turned it into a battleground. They were too proud to seek outside help, so the arguments and fights had morphed into silence and resentment. His dad had lost himself in the restaurant he'd opened, spending more and more time away from the house.

Many of Adem's decisions had been the product of his childhood, even his decision to go into neurosurgery. And it was also why he'd petitioned the administrator of London's Queen Victoria Hospital to open a clinic in one of the city's poorest neighborhoods. When asked if he'd head up the project and run with it he'd jumped at the chance, becoming the clinic's director.

He could make a difference for people like Basir. He believed that. If he had anything to do with it, this new clinic would minister to those in crisis, whether it be illnesses, family relations or pregnancy. It was where his heart was. He might not have been able to fix his parents' problems—or the fallout from it in his own life—but maybe he could help others avoid some of those pitfalls.

If Adem could change one person's life for the better—just one—it would be worth it.

It had been his mantra as he settled into medical school, as he'd done his training and as he managed the clinic.

And he would allow nothing to come between him and that goal.

Ever.

CHAPTER ONE

Five years later

CARLY ELISTON WALKED through the halls of the NICU of the Queen Victoria Hospital holding a clothes hanger in one hand, while draping the bottom portion of a long slinky dress over the other arm. Navy blue with a scattering of sequins across the bodice, it had been an impulse buy—something for herself—after wearing three different bridesmaids' dresses. Four years later, that blue gown still had the tags on it when she'd loaned it to her friend. She'd told Esther she didn't need to return the dress, but her friend had insisted. It wasn't like Carly would need it any time soon. And evidently it had made a bigger hit than her friend had expected, since she and Harry Beaumont were in love and headed toward marriage.

Maybe the dress was enchanted. If so, Carly should wear it herself. She shook her head. No, she didn't need a man in her life right now. One failed relationship was more than enough. Fortunately her ex-fiancé had moved on to another hospital and a new love. Rumor had it that he was now happily married with a child of his own on the way. It was what he'd said he wanted most: a family...children.

For Carly, scarring and one lost ovary made the proposition of that ever happening iffy, although Kyle swore that wasn't the reason for the breakup. She'd gotten the old "It's not you, it's me" explanation. Maybe he just hadn't realized how hard it would be for her to get pregnant. They'd tried. For over a year. The harder things got, the more rigid and regimented her life became in an effort to somehow force her body to comply—to will that remaining ovary to function. And each time her period came, she became more desperate. Until Kyle finally...

Ugh! Old news, Carly. Get moving.

The feeling that she needed to shake her life up—to make a change—had never been so strong as it was right now.

When Carly leaned against the door and tried to juggle the dress so she could reach the latch, it suddenly swung outward, causing her to career into someone on the other side.

A man.

Landing hard against his chest, she gave a quick glance up. Adem Kepler. Perfect. The doctor in charge of Victoria Clinic where she normally worked. Adem had kind of a playboy reputation—one which made her avoid him whenever she could. His relationships were "all fluff and no substance" according to reports. If there was anyone she wanted this dress to work its magic on, it was certainly not him. Despite the way her crazy pulse sped up whenever he was near.

And when he flashed that sardonic grin at her—

the one that had just now kicked up the left side of his mouth—she was a goner.

"Going somewhere?"

She planted her feet back under her and hefted herself off his chest in a hurry, trying not to be distracted by that smile or the slight accent that peppered his speech. After all, her American accent was still fairly noticeable, even after living in the UK for over ten years. "Sorry. I didn't expect the door… I was just trying to…" She took a deep breath to calm her nerves, which were spinning in circles. This was not quite the "change" she'd envisioned a few moments earlier. "I was taking this to my car before heading to work."

Adem fingered the fabric of her dress. "Nice. But this is not your normal style, is it? And the hospital fundraiser isn't until next year."

"Hospital…?" Oh, he thought *she* was borrowing this for a party. She swallowed, trying to push down her disappointment. There was no shame in borrowing a dress from someone; after all, she'd thought nothing of loaning it to Esther. It was more the fact that he assumed that wearing a dress like this would be out of character for her.

Wasn't it? At least for the Carly who'd been consumed with thoughts of babies during the last year of her engagement.

She'd bought the dress a week before Kyle announced his decision to leave, hoping to shake things up. Instead, the gown had hung in her closet, price tags still attached, until she'd loaned it to Esther.

Her face burned with embarrassment. "I know when the fundraiser is. And this dress is very much my style.

I bought it, after all." She certainly didn't need to tell him why she'd purchased it, though.

Up went dark brows in…disbelief?

Oh, no, he didn't.

Her fiancé used to tease her about her lack of a social life too. Maybe that was another part of why he'd dumped her. If anything, she owed some of her seriousness to her mom, who'd raised her all by herself after Carly's dad died, working hard to make sure her daughter had everything she needed. It was something she didn't take for granted.

But that didn't mean Carly didn't know how to have fun. She tipped her chin up. Hadn't she said she wanted to shake things up? Well, maybe now was the time. She could start doing things differently.

"Just because *you* haven't been lucky enough to see me in the dress doesn't mean I haven't worn it."

You haven't, Carly.

"I never said you haven't worn it. But you're right in that I wasn't lucky enough to see you in it."

Oh, perfect. Now she'd come across as conceited. "Maybe some other time. Now if you'll excuse me…"

She waited for a moment, but he didn't move. He wasn't exactly blocking her path, but since the door behind her had already swung closed she would need to sidestep to make it around him.

"Do you have a few minutes? I was actually going to try to catch you at the clinic. I'd like to discuss some changes for the community midwife program we're putting into place."

Accent or no accent, she found herself bristling.

"The women in that community need access to what we can—"

"Relax. I'm not taking anything away. I was here at the main hospital asking for additional funding for the program. It was approved. We're adding two mobile ultrasound machines. But we'll either need additional technicians or a few midwives at the clinic to be certified in their use."

Her heart stuttered in her chest. She'd put in a request last year for portable machines, but never dreamed…

She took a careful breath. Then another. Trying not to let her thoughts run away with her, although that was almost impossible with him standing so close. Looking so devastatingly handsome. She did her best to force back those thoughts. "I would like to be in on that training."

"I thought you might. So I hoped we might talk over tea. Does the request seem more attractive now?"

Yes. And it wasn't just the request that looked more attractive. How did he do that? No wonder he had a reputation.

"Okay. Can I meet you in the canteen after I take my dress to the car?"

"Of course. I'll see you there."

Five minutes later, her shaky hands free of everything except for her purse, she headed toward the canteen. She wished she felt a little more centered—a little more in control of her emotions. Crashing into him must have shaken her more than she realized, because as soon as he was out of sight, muscles that she hadn't realized were balled up tight went limp. So much so that she'd had to stop and lean against a wall for a few seconds to steady her legs.

But portable ultrasounds. He had no idea how much she'd wanted them—how much they would help everyone involved with the program. Or maybe he did, since he'd requested the funds.

They would no longer have to ask patients with issues to come into the clinic to have the imaging done. Some of her patients didn't trust government institutions, even hospitals, and were wary of such requests.

Reaching the canteen, she quickly spotted him at a table in the corner and took a deep breath, before giving him a cheerful wave and heading up to get some coffee. When she was stressed or nervous, her American roots came out, and she opted for that dark bitter brew her mom drank. Dumping a measure of powdered creamer into the coffee, she went to join Adem.

As soon as she dropped into the chair, he poured something from a little silver pot into a teacup. It was very black, almost thick looking. There were no tea bags anywhere. "Is that coffee?"

He glanced up. "Yes. Turkish style. I grind the beans at home and normally brew it in my office. Today, I had to make do with an electric kettle. I see you're not drinking English tea either."

No, and she didn't really want to go into the reasons why. "I guess my heritage comes through sometimes too."

"Your mum teaches music at the International University?"

She hesitated and wasn't sure why. "Yes, she does. It's how I came to be in London years ago. When it came time to choose whether to continue my education here or in the States, I decided to stay near my mom."

"Same here. My parents moved to the central part of Hackney when I was in high school. My father owns a restaurant not too far from the clinic." Adem smiled. "I think he wanted me to take it over when I grew up. Luckily my brother showed a lot more promise in that area than I did."

"No sisters?"

"Nope, just me and my brother." His voice tightened slightly. "You?"

"Only child. Just me and my mom actually." She glanced at him. "My dad was an archaeologist, but he died while on a dig when I was ten."

"That must have been tough."

She smiled, her nerves finally beginning to settle a bit. "It was. But I have good memories of him." She'd been a tomboy growing up and had loved digging around in the garden pretending to find old bones and carefully cleaning them with a brush.

"You didn't want to become an archaeologist?"

"No. I thought about it, but my mom had complications during a pregnancy when I was young and lost the baby. She was never able to have another one. So, I guess it awoke an interest in prenatal health and delivery." That interest had become bittersweet as she wrestled with her own fertility issues.

"I'm sorry. About your mum, not your interest in babies."

Babies.

The way he'd said that word sent a shiver through her. She hadn't said she was interested in children. But

he obviously hadn't meant it the way she'd taken it.
There was no way he could know about her struggles.
She decided to clarify, just in case.

"I'm interested in the moms *and* their babies."

He took a sip of his coffee, regarding her over the
rim of the cup for a few seconds with those dark-lashed
eyes of his. "That is what I meant, of course."

This time, the ripple of awareness had nothing to do
with children and everything to do with the man himself. Oh, Lord, what was wrong with her?

"Of course." She decided to change the subject to
something less sticky. "So we're getting portable ultrasounds. What's the certification process?"

"I looked into it when I put in the request. If I understood correctly, if you have a nursing degree—which
you're listed as having—you'll need to do a year-long
course. For midwives without that, it would probably
take two years. Another option is to schedule the use
of one of the machines in the field and request that a
tech accompany you to the appointment."

That would work. "Will we have enough techs to
go around?"

"That's where having extra staff would help."

"Frieda is a tech here at the hospital. We're friends.
She might even donate an extra hour or two a week like
some of us who already work at the clinic."

Adem set down his cup, hands resting on the table.
His head tilted. "You're donating hours?"

Uh-oh. He didn't sound happy about that. "Is that
a problem?"

"I'm just not sure why you would."

She was right. He wasn't thrilled. "The Queen Victoria uses volunteers for a wide range of services. Besides, I don't want to strain the funding more than necessary. After all, we may not have gotten those portable ultrasound machines if we demanded to be paid for every single second we're at the clinic. I know I'm entitled to be paid for rest breaks, but I like to donate hours where I can, just to help out."

"Understood, Carly."

The low gruff way he said her name made her insides quiver in a way that was too delicious for words. And that made her take a mental step back. Yes, he was a doctor, but he was also a man—and one she'd had trouble maintaining her cool around. She really didn't want to get into another problematic situation with a colleague, the way she had with Kyle. And actually Adem was practically her boss. It was okay to fantasize about the man. But it was absolutely *not* okay for him to know about those fantasies.

"Seriously, it's not a problem, right? I don't always have something planned every night, and it's not like I'm putting in a hundred hours a week."

She'd gotten some ribbing recently from a couple of her friends who'd tried to get her to go out with them on a few double dates. But once burned... She really didn't want to jump into another relationship. And working extra hours gave her a ready excuse to turn down those offers.

I know you've been hurt, but there's such a thing as being too cautious. Wasn't that what Frieda had said?

But her relationship with Kyle had left a sour taste in her mouth. And if he really had left her because of her inability to have his baby... She didn't want to explain her issues to anyone else.

One side of his mouth kicked up again. "If we were talking about a hundred hours a week, that might be a problem. Since we're not, then no."

It took her a second to realize he was responding to her earlier comment. "I'm not. But I want to make a difference."

"Oh, you are. More than you know." There was a darkness to his gaze that hadn't been there at the beginning of their conversation.

She gulped down the last sip of her coffee, which was now tepid, and decided it was time to get out before her straying thoughts gave her away. "Speaking of differences, I'd better get myself over to the clinic and start my shift. Thanks for letting me know about the ultrasound machines. Any idea of their arrival time?"

"Not yet. But you'll be one of the first to know. In the meantime, I'll confirm the certification requirements and put them on the board in the staff lounge at the clinic."

"That would be great. Thanks." She nodded at the silver teapot and, before she could stop herself, added, "Someday I'd like to try Turkish coffee."

His eyes focused in on her. "Someday, Carly, I will make some for you."

And just like that, the reactions that had been percolating in the background were suddenly right there for all to see—nipples tightening, breathing growing almost frantic.

Do not get caught up in the man's charms.

"Thanks. See you later."

"I'm sure you will."

With a hard swallow, she forced herself to carry her cup and spoon up to the front of the canteen and deposit them on the conveyor belt. And then she pushed through the door and reentered the real world. A place where Adem was just an ordinary doctor and not someone who hit some of the buttons she'd done her best to deactivate. Evidently a few of them had decided to come back online of their own volition.

And that was the last thing she needed to happen with this particular man.

Today. Or any other day.

Adem sat back in his chair after Carly left the canteen and realized how little he knew about her. There was something reserved in her mannerism. Seeing her carrying that dress had surprised him, and he'd very nearly insulted her by blurting out the first thing that had come into his head.

The woman had a private life. At least she said she did. One where she wore dresses like that for parties he knew nothing about.

He'd heard about a broken engagement, but never bothered much with gossip, so he didn't know the circumstances. Not that it was any of his business. It wasn't like he had a stellar track record in the relationship arena. He'd left that to his brother, who was now married and hoping for children of his own. It seemed that Adem's attempts to shield him from his parents' fights might have paid off.

The image of Carly in a slinky blue dress that he

knew would play up that fair skin and red hair swam in his head. Damn.

It wasn't like the dress had just made him aware how attractive she was.

He'd already realized. And noticed. More than once. And was now wishing like hell that he hadn't.

Carly hung the dress next to the three bridesmaids' dresses. She was really glad it had worked for Esther. She and Harry made a great couple. And it wasn't like Carly was jonesing for a white dress with frothy layers. Not anymore. Thank God she'd never gotten around to actually purchasing her own during her engagement. She'd been too busy structuring her life around getting pregnant.

No, she was happy that some of her childhood and university friends were finding the love of their lives.

Did Kyle's exit from her life mean there was no one special for her? Her heart twinged, but nothing stronger than that, which was good after all that had happened. Maybe she'd been more in love with the idea of marriage and a family than in love with him, which in retrospect made her realize that marrying him would have probably been a huge mistake.

She had a full life. Maybe Carly was more like her mom—who'd worked hard to raise her after her father's untimely death—than she realized. Her mother had never remarried and seemed to find her fulfillment in her work. She was independent to a fault.

Like Carly? Probably. But it served her well now. She didn't need anyone else's company. At least not permanently. For the first time since the breakup, she realized she was free. Free to do what she wanted with her life, with no interference from anyone. Free to make her own choices about who to sleep with and when.

She glanced at the blue dress, once again seeing the surprise that had splashed across Adem's face when he'd realized it was hers. Oh, how she wished he really could see her in it.

Not going to happen, Carly.

She closed the door with a firm click. If all went well with Esther, it looked like Carly might be adding another dress to her collection before too long. And her other friends from university? The ones who still weren't attached?

She and Izzy Nicholson had met at the international school, along with Raphael Dubois, who was one of the hospital's obstetricians, while she knew Esther McDonald and Chloe Larson from the midwife track at university. Life had sure given all of them some twists and turns. Chloe had a three-year-old daughter now. School had cemented their bond, and they'd all remained close over the years.

It made her glad of the decision to remain in the UK and build her life here.

Her mind swung back to Adem. They had at least two things in common. They were both in England because of their parents. And they'd both decided to stay here as adults.

So did lots of people. She'd worked at the clinic for a year now—ever since her breakup—and Adem had been there ever since Victoria Clinic opened five years ago. He'd done her interview, in fact.

Ha! That interview process had been kind of agonizing

actually. His dark good looks had made it hard to think, even as he asked questions about her experience, her right foot doing a little dance as he'd detailed the job requirements. She'd had to uncross her legs to make it stop. At the time, she'd chalked it up to the stress of having her relationship implode in her face.

But it happened again. Several times, and when he followed her into her dreams one night, she decided maybe she'd better actively avoid him. Which had been almost impossible.

Well, she could no longer blame her reaction on her breakup, because at the meeting in the canteen, her foot had done its twitchy little best to keep pace with her heart. She'd uncrossed her legs again, planting both of her feet on the ground under the table. Her pulse hadn't been quite as easy to control.

And to find out he found her too dull—or unadventurous—to pull off a sexy dress…

Well, if the chance ever presented itself, maybe she would have to prove him wrong.

Lord! This was ridiculous. She needed to either get past this or figure out what to do about it. Doing nothing wasn't an option. One thing her father had taught her at an early age was to pursue something until you figured it out. It was what she needed to do now.

But how was she supposed to do that when there were these weird itchy emotions popping to the surface one after the other?

She wasn't sure. But she'd controlled what she now called the Adem Twinges for the last year, so whatever was happening, she could just push those suckers back down until they got the hint and disappeared for good.

Her cell phone buzzed on her dresser, making her jump. She swallowed as she walked toward it.

It's not him. He has no reason to call you at home.

She picked it up, and then frowned. Naomi Silver, one of her patients. Naomi was almost nine months pregnant and so far had had a normal pregnancy—even if the events leading up to it hadn't been. Like Carly, Naomi had had her own fertility problems. She'd had adhesions that had kept her from getting pregnant for the last five years. She and her husband had even adopted a daughter, thinking they'd never have a biological one. And then, out of the blue, she'd gotten pregnant.

Her phone buzzed again. Naomi never called her at home, so her belly tightened.

She pressed talk. "Hello?"

There was no sound, except some kind of weird snuffling sound.

"Naomi? Are you okay?"

"I—I'm so scared."

Fear struck her heart. "What's going on? Where are you?"

"I'm home." A broken sob hit. "But my head hurts so much. I'm... Could I be having a stroke?"

Oh, God. A million possible diagnoses went through her head. Migraine. Preeclampsia. Eclampsia. Fetal demise. Her speech didn't sound slurred, but Carly wasn't willing to take any chances.

"Can you get to the hospital?"

"The clinic?"

She ran through the possibilities. The clinic could do C-sections in a pinch, but it wasn't set up with an MRI or other of the more expensive diagnostic equipment. "No. The Queen Victoria."

"Yes, I think so. My husband can bring me."

"Good. I'll meet you there."

The second she got off the phone, she tore out of her yoga pants and nightshirt and dragged on a black skirt and blouse, shoving her feet into low wedged heels that she normally wore when she was at the main hospital campus. Then she gritted her teeth and did the one thing she wasn't thrilled about doing. She called the man she'd just been trying to forget. It went to voice mail, but she left a quick message asking if there was any way he could meet her at the hospital.

And if he was with some woman?

She swallowed. Images she couldn't banish swept through her mind.

Dammit. Now was not the time.

She glanced at her watch. It was only seven o'clock. If he didn't get her message, there would either be a neurosurgeon present at the hospital or on call. She dialed the hospital number as she scooped up her car keys. Before she got an answer, her phone buzzed.

Adem.

She hung up on the hospital and answered his call. "Hey, I'm sorry to disturb you, but I have a patient coming into the Queen Victoria with some troubling symptoms."

"Like what?"

He didn't ask why she was calling him—a neurosurgeon for a pregnancy issue. For that she was grateful.

"She has a terrible headache, and she's really scared. And Naomi isn't one to panic without a good reason.

Any chance you can ask someone to meet us there? I'm on my way in."

"I'm five minutes out. Headed back now. See you soon."

The line went dead. And if Naomi's problem turned out to be a simple migraine?

She grimaced. Simple migraine. That was an oxymoron if she ever heard one. It could be that a change in blood pressure had set one in motion. Except that many migraine sufferers experienced a lessening of symptoms during pregnancy due to the change in estrogen levels.

Well, she could hope that's all it was. And since Adem had volunteered to come without her specifically asking him to, it wasn't like he was changing plans just for her.

She hoped, anyway.

But he could have passed her off to a colleague, if that were the case.

It took her a little longer to make it to the hospital, since she had to come across town. By the time she arrived, Adem was in the A&E waiting area. He was in jeans and a white button-down shirt, the mixture between ultracasual and business attire a stunning combination that made her mouth go dry. She did her best to shake off her familiar reaction to him.

"Sorry to ask you to come."

"You didn't."

She frowned. "Sorry?"

"You didn't ask me to come, so don't apologize. It was my choice."

He was right. It was. But she still felt guilty. "I appreciate it."

"Were you on your way out?"

"Out?"

"You're dressed up."

She glanced down. Ah, she normally had a lab coat on over her blouse when she was working, and at the clinic she dressed a lot more casually, so maybe she did look different. "No. I tend to wear a skirt when I come in here, since the atmosphere is different from the clinic."

"I should have figured."

"What's that supposed to mean?"

Before he had a chance to respond, Carly spotted her patient walking up the path, one arm wrapped protectively around her belly, while her husband gripped her other hand, their daughter, Tessa, perched on his hip.

God. Naomi would be devastated if something happened to this baby. "That's her."

Grabbing a wheelchair, she rushed out the doors, not waiting for Adem. She had Naomi sitting in a flash.

"What's happening to her?"

Her husband Douglas's eyes were full of concern. Although they were from a deprived area of the city, they did their best to provide for their daughter and unborn baby. "I'm not sure, but—"

Adem went down on his haunches, a penlight in his hands. "I'm Mr. Kepler. I hear you have quite the headache."

"Yes. It's horrible. I called Douglas home from work. I never, ever do that."

Adem glanced up at the other man. "I'm glad you came. We'll get you inside in a minute. Can you follow the light?" He flicked on his penlight and took her through a set of commands right there outside of the hospital.

"Your pupils look good," he said. "Let's put you in an exam room. Douglas, you and…"

"Tessa."

Adem smiled. "You and Tessa can come in with her, if you'd like."

"Yes, please."

"Carly, can you get them in and registered? I'm going to check on something. I'll be right back."

Without another word, he walked back into the hospital. Had he found something troubling, despite his comment about her pupils?

Douglas wanted to wheel his wife inside, so Carly took Tessa in her arms, talking to the child as they made their way to the admissions desk. She went up to the window and explained the situation.

"Go on to exam room three. It's a slow night. We'll come in and get her information in a minute. I'll let Mr. Kepler know where to find you."

So Adem had stopped at the desk? There was no sign of him right now. Maybe he really was canceling plans. He was dressed to go out to a restaurant. Her heart plummeted.

Well, so what? Hadn't he asked her why she was so dressed up?

None of your business, Carly.

Maybe not, but she was suddenly glad he thought that some man might want to take her out for a night on the town. She could have shown the neurosurgeon a thing or two, if it had been him. Especially after his reaction to her blue dress.

Really? Because you haven't shown a man a thing or two in, like...well...ever. Even her relationship with Kyle had been...sedate. Even as they tried for a baby.

Maybe Frieda was right. Maybe she really didn't know how to have fun.

Why the hell did she keep thinking about that?

She found the exam room and took Naomi and her husband inside. "Do you think you can get on the exam table? I want to listen to the baby's heart." Thankfully she'd remembered to wind her stethoscope and shove it into the pocket of her skirt before coming over.

Handing the baby back to her father and feeling a little twinge of emotion as he enfolded the child in his arms, she took out her stethoscope. "I'm just going to ease your slacks down."

Naomi was wearing the very type of stretchy wear that Carly had changed out of, so rolling down the waistband was a simple affair. A quick kick from the baby, visible through the skin of the woman's belly, assured her that it was alive. She breathed a word of thanks, warming the scope against her chest before placing it against Naomi's abdomen. She listened, moving the instrument to a couple of different spots before finding what she was looking for.

There. The baby's heart was strong. She counted the beats. Perfect. Not too fast. Not too slow. "I hear your baby." She stood and looked down at her patient. "Other than your headache, does anything else seem out of the ordinary? Any bleeding? Signs that your water has broken?"

"No. I was doing the dishes and a pain hit right at

the back of my head. I had to grab the counter to keep from falling, it was that bad."

Adem came back into the room. "I've arranged for an MRI. They're just finishing up with another patient." He moved over to the bed. "Where is the pain exactly?"

She pointed an area just above the base of her skull.

Carly's gut tightened. Not a good place. It was near the brain stem, the part of the brain that controlled autonomic functions such as heart rate and respiration.

"And how long ago did the headache start?"

Naomi shrugged. "About two hours ago. I called Carly when it didn't go away."

He shot her a look she couldn't decipher. If he dared lecture her on giving out her phone number, she was going to give him a piece of her mind. It was what midwives did. Babies came on their own schedule. She'd delivered many in the middle of the night.

Yes, she could let another midwife go out on some of those calls, but Carly was fiercely protective of her patients and tried to follow them all the way through to delivery and beyond whenever possible. Yes, there were sometimes instances when she couldn't—for example if two women started laboring at the same time, but that didn't happen that often.

Naomi moaned and arched her neck. "It's back. It comes in waves."

Without him asking, Carly grabbed the cart that contained the blood pressure equipment, wrapped the cuff around the patient's upper arm and pumped it tight, waiting as the tick of the needle bottomed out. "One twenty over sixty."

"Within the normal range."

A nurse came in and asked Douglas to accompany her outside to get some information. Things between the clinic and the hospital were shared, so they should also be able to pull up Naomi's file with a few clicks of computer keys. Adem glanced at the husband. "If we're not here when you come back, it's because they've called us up for the MRI. The nurse can tell you how to find us, but one of us will try to catch you as we're leaving."

With that the pair were out of the room, leaving Adem and Carly to continue working to find the cause of their patient's headache.

Adem's phone buzzed. He glanced at it and then at her. "They're ready for us."

He was back to his businesslike self. Whatever she'd sensed in the canteen that day was gone. It had probably never been there in the first place. Just like that crazy dream she'd had. All just drummed up by her subconscious.

They helped Naomi back into the wheelchair. Fortunately her symptoms hadn't progressed to numbness or weakness. Just her massive headache, which was still worrying due to the location. Carly ran to tell Douglas and then met up with Adem and Naomi again at the elevator. As the doors opened, all Carly could do was hope for the best and pray that everything turned out well for both Naomi and her baby.

CHAPTER TWO

NAOMI WAS ON the sliding table of the MRI machine as Adem discussed what they were going to do. "We're actually going to do what's called an MRA or Magnetic Resonance Angiogram, which looks specifically at the blood vessels in your brain. We want to see if what you're feeling is caused by a problem with a vessel."

Her hands slid over her belly. "And if there is?"

"Let's cross that bridge if and when we come to it. Our on-call obstetrician is on her way in to check on you as well."

"I want Carly to deliver the baby."

Carly gripped her hand. "Let's take this one step at a time, okay? The most important thing is to keep you and your baby healthy. I don't want to jeopardize that in any way, and I know you don't either."

He appreciated her willingness to hand her patient off to someone else when necessary. She was definitely an asset to the clinic.

But damn, had his stomach knotted when he'd seen her name come up on his phone earlier. He'd been so shocked that he'd stared at it until his phone stopped ringing. He'd dialed her back immediately, though.

Her voice had been breathless in a way that had made him think…

How wrong he'd been. He should have realized that the cool and calm midwife wouldn't call him for personal reasons.

And that was exactly why he needed to get his mind back on his job and off Carly.

Naomi's medical history included the fact that her mother had died of a brain bleed during the birth of her fifth child, and that fact alone warranted being very sure that there wasn't an aneurysm hiding somewhere in the young woman's gray matter. There were sometimes genetic components at play.

"No, I don't want to do anything that would hurt him or her. Okay, let's go ahead. Are Douglas and Tessa here?"

"Yes, they're in the waiting room. This should only take about twenty minutes. You'll be back with them before you know it."

And if it was an aneurysm as he suspected? Then they'd have to decide whether to deliver the baby via C-section first and address the defect afterward. Or if they needed to treat the aneurysm first.

They'd already inserted the IV into Naomi's vein and they injected the contrast through a port in the tubing.

The tech then finished getting the machine set up, handing Naomi a set of earbuds that could pipe music through as well as allow communication between the tech and patient. "Are you feeling okay?"

"Yes. Just nervous about the procedure."

"That's perfectly normal. Are you claustrophobic? We'll need you to lie perfectly still for a period of time.

You'll hear a lot of clicking and clacking from the machine, but that's normal as well."

"I'm not claustrophobic that I know of."

"Good. If you start feeling that way, the best thing to do is close your eyes. Blocking out your surroundings can help in a lot of cases. But if you start to panic, just let me know." He handed her a remote with a switch on it. "You can press this. And there are also speakers in the tube."

"Okay."

The tech helped her put the earpieces in and then they all went into the observation area. "I'm going to slide you inside the machine now, Naomi. Try to hold as still as you can."

The table moved forward until her head and shoulders were inside the tube. He pressed a button. "I'm going to start up the machine. I'll pipe some music in to help keep you occupied."

They'd asked her preferences in music and found that she liked orchestral selections, so Carly had suggested the London Orchestra. Trevor, their technician, had scrolled through the selections until he found one.

Adem turned toward her. "You like the orchestra?"

"My mom plays cello for them. So yes, I've heard orchestral music almost my entire life. I'd better like it or my mom might disown me."

He studied her for a moment, processing this new bit of information, before turning his attention back to the screen where images were flipping through at a rate that never ceased to amaze him. Carly sat next to him, crossing her knees, one foot wiggling back and forth as if having trouble sitting completely still. He seemed to remember her doing that nervous gesture a couple of other times. He touched her arm. "Hey. We're going to figure this out."

He wasn't sure why he said it. Maybe because Carly was emotionally invested in her patient. It was a no-no, but was almost inevitable in certain cases. It was probably harder in the case of a midwife, who got to know her patients over the course of nine long months.

Interestingly enough, he'd known Carly for a year and felt like he knew very little about her still.

"I hope so. Naomi is the nicest person you'll ever meet. She had a very difficult childhood, but her family means the world to her. She told me that being a mom is her calling in life. She works as part of the cleaning staff at one of the larger hotels but is now on maternity leave for a few months." She paused, a shadow appearing in her eyes. "She had a hard time getting pregnant, so I'm sure this is especially scary."

"This is her first pregnancy?"

"Yes. Tessa is adopted."

"I see. I was surprised you came back to the hospital to meet her."

Her foot went still. "Naomi needed me."

So did a lot of people, judging from the tired smudges around her eyes. "I wasn't trying to lecture you."

"I'm sorry, I guess I'm just worried. In the same way that Naomi's family is her calling. She's mine." She paused. "Well, not Naomi specifically, but women like her. Those who have fertility issues."

Fertility issues? Because of her mother's problems?

The tech turned. "We're getting close to the end. So far I haven't seen… Wait a minute. What's that?"

Adem got up and leaned over the screen, scanning it with trained eyes. *"Kahretsin."*

The swear word rolled off his tongue before he realized it. But at least it was in his native language, not something either of the two people in the room would understand.

"What's wrong?" Her voice came from behind him.

"She has an aneurysm. Posterior inferior cerebellar artery."

"I'm guessing that means in the back of the head. In the area she's having the pain. Is it bleeding?"

"Not yet. But it's large. If it does…" He didn't finish the sentence. Didn't need to. "I'm glad she didn't wait for it to go away. And she's actually very lucky she felt anything. A lot of aneurysms go undetected until something sets them off."

"Like childbirth." Carly came to stand beside him, her voice very soft. "This is exactly what happened to her mom. Only it wasn't caught. What happens now?"

"I want to examine the scans and consult with some of the other specialists, since there's a pregnancy involved. We'll have to put together a plan as a team. But I'll ask that she be admitted at least for the night so we can monitor her. You seemed okay with handing her off to an obstetrician."

"I am, absolutely. I'm only interested in her well-being." She glanced at him. "Adem, this might be the only baby she can have."

"We're talking about her life here. But I understand what you're saying. Let me make a couple of phone calls while they take her to a room, and then I'll come talk to her."

He wanted the best outcome, for both Naomi and her baby, surely Carly knew that.

"I'd like to sit with her and her husband. I won't tell them any specifics, just that you're going over the scans and will be there shortly."

"That sounds good." He glanced at his watch. "Have you eaten yet?"

"No, but I'm okay."

His brows went up. "After putting in a full day at the clinic and then coming back this evening? Have you had anything since our coffee?"

When he'd promised to make her some. A huge mistake, because that thought had burrowed in his head, refusing to leave. What had started off as a polite comment had turned into something else entirely.

She tilted her head. "Have you had anything?"

It was a challenge. One he recognized and found himself responding to. Maybe it was the tiredness of a long day. But somehow he didn't think so. "Nope. Which is why I was hoping to grab something after we're done here."

The smile she turned on came out of nowhere. "Sorry. My mom is very independent. I'm a little too much like her. But I would like to know what the plan is for Naomi. Maybe we could talk about it there."

"That was my thought too. You choose where we go and I'll be down to see our patient as soon as possible."

The treatment plan was in place. Sitting in a restaurant that served Indian cuisine, Adem waited until they'd ordered before going over the results of his conference call. He'd spoken to Raphael Dubois, one of the hospital's obstetricians, and explained the situation. And while Naomi was far enough along to be able to deliver the baby, they both felt like to do so might cause the aneurysm to burst. So, ideally, it would be treated before she delivered. As soon as possible, in fact.

"I think we're going with an endovascular coil, which is less invasive than clipping the vessel would be."

"So no cutting open her skull?" Carly wasn't an expert on neurosurgery, but she knew a little. Clipping involved using a metal clamp to seal off the neck of the swollen blood vessel. But doing so meant having to do brain surgery, whereas the coiling procedure sent a catheter up through the femoral artery until the defect was reached. A thin metal coil was then released into the aneurysm, cutting off its blood supply, just like clamping would do. For Naomi, she could see exactly why they favored the one procedure over the other.

"No, no cutting."

The waiter served their food with a flourish that made her smile. If only she could be more like that. Maybe it really was time to clear away some of the cobwebs that taken up residence in her life. When the server left, she said, "He seems to be enjoying himself."

"Yes. I find that enjoying oneself sometimes means immersing yourself in the moment. In the unexpected."

He said it with a grin that sent her pulse spinning out of control. Frieda's words came back to her: *There's such a thing as being too cautious.*

Was that how others saw her? As cautious? Unable to immerse herself in the moment or to do something unexpected?

Maybe in her race to get pregnant, she really had

lost sight of what made life fun. But she was not about to admit that to this man. "I know how to enjoy myself as much as the next guy. Or girl."

One brow went up, and he leaned back in his chair, crossing his arms over his chest. He didn't believe her. The man knew how to rattle her chain, that was for sure, and from the twitch of his lips, he looked like he knew it too.

Maybe it was time to do something unexpected… so unexpected it would make Adem Kepler's eyes pop from his skull. So here was to immersing herself completely in the moment.

"Just because you haven't *seen* me in that blue dress doesn't mean I don't know how to wear it. I know how to have a good time. More than you can possibly imagine."

She used her sultriest tone on that last phrase. So much so that it made her cringe. And for a second, she was horrified when he had no reaction to her pained attempt at flirting. None. Zilch.

Then a muscle in his jaw popped once. Twice. "Excuse me?"

Now was the time for her to give a bark of laughter and say she'd been joking and that she didn't actually have fun. Not that kind of fun. But her pride wouldn't let her.

"You heard me."

"I heard you. I just don't believe it."

Hell, she was attracted to the man. Had been from the moment they'd met. She'd also said there was nothing she was going to do about it.

Well, why not? Why couldn't she do something? It

wasn't like she wanted anything out of him. But he'd talked about immersing oneself in the moment. Why not this one? Adem was gorgeous. With just the right hint of danger. The likes of which she'd probably never meet again. What would happen if she pressed a little harder?

Doing so would risk a lot more than her pride, though. What if he rejected her outright?

Nothing could be as bad as being rejected by your fiancé. Or being unable to conceive a child. Right?

Maybe she could wipe away that heartache in one fell swoop.

Picking up her glass of wine with a hand that was much steadier than she expected, she took a drawn-out sip of the ruby liquid, then let the tip of her tongue touch the rim of her glass as if capturing a drop that had escaped.

Oh, Lord. What was she doing? Was she crazy?

His eyes tracked the movement and a wash of red marched up his neck. His gaze came back up and caught hers. Tangled for a long, long moment. "Carly..."

Here it was. The moment of truth. Just how brave was she?

Hell, he'd started this, hadn't he? Acting like she couldn't lose herself in the moment, even if she wanted to.

In a burst of courage she didn't know she possessed, she set her glass down and leaned over her plate, her gaze spearing his. At least, she hoped it had. "I seem to remember someone promising to make me Turkish coffee."

"Yes. I did. Do you have a time in mind?"

"How about now? I bet if I asked you to leave our

food untouched and walk out of this restaurant with me, you wouldn't."

"Wouldn't I?"

Acting as if he was either going to wait her out or call her bluff, he stayed put for several painful seconds before pulling out his wallet and throwing a couple of bills on the table. Then he stood with a suddenness that shocked her. Reached out his hand.

He really was. He was calling her bluff.

Their waiter immediately came over to the table. "I'm sorry. Is there a problem, sir?"

"I'm not sure." Adem slid a glance her way. "Is there? Or did you just not believe I would?"

Yep. He'd read her all too well. But she was about to show him how little he knew.

Her chin lifted.

Oh, Lord, she was really going through with it. With her heart pounding in her chest, she stood and placed her hand in his. "There's no problem at all. We've just realized we have somewhere to be."

Adem nodded at the money. "That should more than cover everything."

The man's eyes widened. "Yes…yes, thank you, sir."

Towing her behind him, he made his way through the thinning crowds toward the door. A surreal sense of anticipation began pulsing through her. The likes of which she didn't think she'd ever felt before. Even with Kyle.

Of course, she'd never played games like this. With her ex…or anyone, for that matter.

Even as she thought it, she wondered if things had been leading toward this ever since he'd promised her that coffee. No even before that. When he'd talked about ordering those portable ultrasound machines that she'd wanted so badly. She'd been so thrilled. So happy. Because he knew how much she needed them and it was so thoughtful of him to look out for her department like that. Was going with him a product of that? No, she was pretty sure it wasn't. More likely she'd been determined to show him that she could keep up with him just fine in the romance department.

Ha! Romance. No. This would be a single-use sexual encounter. Something she'd never done before. And would probably never do again.

They went through the door and he glanced back. "Were you hungry?"

Kind of late to be asking her that question, wasn't it? "I'm starved."

She tried her best to give the word a sensual subtext, but wondered if she'd failed miserably for a second, then he responded. "Good. Me too."

He didn't have to work at sounding sexy. That rough gravelly voice of his made everything he said sound like he'd just climbed out of bed after a long night of lovemaking.

She shivered. Would he sound like that after being with her too?

They made it to his car. "Do you want me to drive you to the hospital to pick up your vehicle?"

"Can we do that later? After…coffee?"

A sideways glance made her swallow. "As long as you're okay with it being much later. And the coffee may have to wait for another time."

Her teeth sank into her lower lip. "It wasn't really coffee I wanted."

"I was hoping that was the case."

She was probably setting him up for a huge disappointment. Carly wasn't the girl she was pretending to be. The one who knew all the right moves. But she was a quick learner, when she wanted to be.

And this was something she wanted to learn. With him. Even if she never got to use those skills again in her life.

Sex with Kyle had always been a little tame, even by her standards, even more so when all their thoughts were stuck on pregnancy. There'd been no spontaneity, no desperate need for each other.

Not like the need she felt right now.

He opened the door for her, and she slid into the passenger seat. As she reached around to fumble for the seat belt, he leaned over and kissed her.

And that kiss…

Mouth against mouth, hand buried in her hair, he hinted at things she'd only dreamed of. Her hand curled around the webbing of the seat belt, needing something to hold on to.

God! Tame was one thing this man could never be accused of.

Then he was gone, the door closing as he walked around to the other side of the car.

Somehow she managed to get the restraint buckled, although her hands were now shaking.

Once in the car, he turned to look at her. "Are you sure about this?"

Sure about what? The wisdom of sleeping with him? Or *wanting* to sleep with him? Those were two entirely different subjects. The latter was a resounding yes! The former? Well, she would examine that one later.

"Yes." He didn't kiss her again, but he did drive with an intensity that spoke volumes. "Are we going to your place?"

"Yes. It's close. About five minutes."

She settled back in her seat, his hand on the gearshift doing funny things to her insides. Especially since his thumb was sliding back and forth along it in a way that made her mind conjure up sensations that were becoming very, very real.

Five minutes had never seemed so long. Or so short. Five minutes until her world changed forever.

Well, maybe not changed. But at least rocked on its axis a time or two.

She shook her head. No. She was making too big of a deal about this. This was sex. A man and a woman enjoying spending an hour together. Nothing earth-shattering.

Really? Then why was there a part of her that didn't believe that?

Maybe because she hadn't felt this shuddery awareness before.

She'd played it safe with Kyle. Every time. That cautious nature that had always seemed to raise its ugly head. That had gotten even worse with every failed attempt at getting pregnant. And their last few times together had definitely never felt…special.

This man had left his dinner behind for her. How was that for special?

She shivered. It wasn't like he'd had a fencing match with someone over her.

Unless you counted his empty stomach.

Adem pulled up in front of a block of flats just off the Thames that boasted curved facades and sweeping balconies. Her eyebrows went up. She was used to much simpler accommodations. After all, her mom's university work and orchestral involvement might have caused her classmates to ooh and ahh, but they were not high-paying careers. Not that any of that had mattered.

He pulled into an underground parking area and shut off the car. "Still okay? You've gone quiet over there."

Had she?

She glanced over at him, and the emotions that had started this whole process quickly rose back up. She would probably never spend another night like this in her life. And she found she very much wanted to experience the non-cautious side of life. At least this once. "Oh, yes. Still okay."

They made their way to the elevator, where he pushed the button for the fourth floor. Once the doors closed, he turned to her and tipped her face up, studying it for a second or two. His fingers brushed her temple and traveled down her jawline. "Hell, I want to kiss you. If I wasn't already giving my doorman a hint of what's about to happen, I'd show you exactly how much."

His doorman? Her eyes widened and tracked to a corner of the elevator, where a camera looked like it was pointed right at them. She gave a nervous laugh. "So no acting out a scene from a book?"

"That sounds intriguing." One brow went up, and he leaned forward to whisper against her ear. "I'll keep that in mind for later."

Oh, God. She had no idea what kind of scene he

had in mind, but several possibilities were streaming through her brain, reminding her that she might just be in over her head.

And she kind of liked it.

Playing it safe had always been her MO, so the fact that she was about to do something so outrageously out of character sent another little thrill through her. Her fingers went to his nape as she tugged his head a little lower, giving his earlobe a little nip. "I may hold you to that."

"I'm looking forward to holding *you* in my bed. And in about a thousand other places. Including my plate-glass window."

Her breath hissed in, causing him to chuckle and lift his head. "Don't worry, honey. No one will be able to see you except me."

She wasn't worried. But she was squirming, and certain parts of her were growing uncomfortably needy. "Unless the glass breaks and we tumble out."

"The glass is very, very thick. And very strong." He cupped her face, eyes dark as he stared down at her. "We could do almost anything against it."

She swallowed. She'd meant her words as a joke. But his response sounded almost like a dare.

Well, if this was going to be a night for the history books, she was going to make sure the memory of it would last her for the rest of her life. "That sounds almost too good to be true."

His smile unleashed a barrage of butterflies in her stomach. "I'll have a few survey questions for you after the tour."

"Tour?" The word came out rough-edged, her need for him clearly evident, even to her own ears.

"Carly, didn't you know? I plan to take things one room at a time. One surface at a time. Until neither of us have a drop of strength left."

The doors to the lift opened with a suddenness that shocked her, and it took her a second to get her bearings. He put his arm around her waist and eased her into the foyer, where three doors faced them. Exactly how soundproof were these apartments?

She had a feeling they were about to test that feature.

Spinning her in his arms, he backed her toward the apartment on the right. "Not a single camera out here."

With her back pressed flat against the cool metal surface, his lips covered hers in a kiss that seared her senses. His hands slid behind her, curving over her bottom in a way that tilted her hips fully against him. She had no choice but to twine her arms around his neck and hold on tight.

A tiny portion of her brain hoped there weren't peepholes on the doors of the neighboring flats, but a bigger, less rational part didn't care. After all, she was soon going to be plastered against the glass in his apartment, right?

He pushed against her, leaving no question that he was as affected as she was. If he wasn't careful, they weren't going to make it inside before she came completely undone.

"You have no idea what you did to me back at the restaurant." His hand slid down the outside of her leg until he reached her knee, fingers curling around the back of it. "I could just do this…" He tightened his grip, causing the inside of her thigh to slide along his as her foot left the ground, skirt bunching up.

Was he actually going to do it right here? All he'd have to do was unzip. One tug of her garment would give him access.

Her eyes fluttered closed, not caring, just needing him so badly.

Then he was gone, her foot finding the ground again with a bump. "I need to be inside. Now." The growled words were at odds with the way he'd released her.

So if he needed to be "inside," then why had he...?

He pressed his forehead against hers as if reading her mind. "Inside my flat. So I can be inside of you."

The fact that he'd had to spell that out made her laugh. "Oh! I thought we were going to..."

"Yes. So did I."

He retrieved a key card and swiped it in a slot next to a locked mailbox. A latch softly clicked and the door swung open. They went through, and Adem kicked it shut with the back of his foot. Grabbing her hand, he led her through the living room, the black leather furniture standing out against the white wood floors. He must have a housekeeper. Somehow she couldn't see Adem dust-mopping under the sofa.

The image made her giggle.

The forward momentum on her arm stopped and went slack as he turned to face her once again. "You find something humorous about this?"

"No, I just..." She gulped. "No."

He turned her until she was looking at a huge picture window, out from which jutted one of those balconies she'd noticed earlier.

Suddenly she knew she wanted that. Wanted all of it. Everything he was offering she was going to take. She might be sorry in the morning, but she would worry about that when it came.

Walking her forward, his lips touched the side of her neck, the warmth against her skin sending a shudder through her. It was all she could do to keep her eyes open so she could see where she was going.

And where she was going was to the end of the earth.

A remote part of her brain took in the view and stored it away for later, even as his hands swept aside her hair and continued to kiss her with light feathery touches, his body crowding hers from behind.

She glanced to the side, making sure there were no neighboring windows visible.

"No one can see," he murmured. "I promise."

How did he know that for sure? Had he tried this before?

No. Don't think about that kind of stuff. Just enjoy the moment.

He turned her in his arms and kissed her again, the same defense-shattering melding of mouths, even as she felt his fingers at the first button of her blouse. He slowly worked his way down, cool air rushing in to meet the heated trail his touch left behind.

Her blouse slid off, leaving her in her bra and skirt. His mouth left hers, his hands smoothing over her shoulders, moving down her arms, caressing the curve of her hips, and then he bunched her skirt in his hands, scooping up more and more of the fabric until his fingers touched the bare skin of her thighs. Then he found the upper edge of her lacy undergarment and tunneled beneath the elastic, taking a step back as he eased them all the way down her legs.

"Step out of them."

She did as he asked, and the bikini briefs joined her blouse on the floor. He surprised her by tugging the hem of her skirt back down.

"Are you ready, Carly?" He pulled his wallet out of his slacks and took out a square packet.

She'd been ready ever since they'd left the restaurant. "Yes."

He turned her around to face the window once again. "Then welcome to the first stop on our tour."

Adem wanted her against that window so badly he could taste it. He'd intended on making it their last stop, but doctors never knew when they'd get "that" call. Besides, he really had had to reel himself back in as they stood at the front door. He'd wanted to just find home and take her. But unlike the window, someone could appear out of that elevator or one of the neighboring flats at any moment.

But when he was around her, he had trouble thinking clearly. Even when he'd first offered to make her that pot of coffee, his mind had been heading in this direction.

Her head fell back against his chest when he nipped the cords of her neck. Damn this woman was unlike anyone he'd ever known. So proper and cautious as she did her job. Uptight, even. And here she was squirming under his touch, willing to play a little exhibitionist game with him. He wasn't going to strip her naked, although hell if he wasn't tempted to see how far she was willing to go. And he'd bet she would stand there au natural if he asked her to.

He pressed his cheek tight to hers. *"Seni çok istiyorum... I want you so much."* The words poured out in his native Turkish, telling her each and every thing he wanted to do with her. *To* her.

Hands reached back, her fingers gripping his thighs, edging toward the hard strain of his erection, as she whispered, "Yes, yes, yes..." as if she was having just as much trouble waiting as he was.

It was now or never, and if her hands found what they were looking for, it would be later. Much later. Taking her wrists, he lifted them, flattening her fingers onto the pristine glass surface in front of them.

"Keep them there. You can use them later. On me." He smiled. "On yourself." Yes, he would like to see that. Very much.

Reaching around her rib cage, he found her lace-covered breast, the mound filling his hand as he pressed her to the glass. He caught the nipple between his fingers and gave soft rhythmic squeezes, the moan she gave going straight to his groin. God, he ached. It was all he could do to not to unzip and thrust into her. And he would. Soon enough. His legs splayed apart, trying to assuage the temptation by pressing against the softness of her ass, the slight friction almost driving him over the edge.

He backed off and found the hem of her skirt once again and pulled it up, baring her backside completely.

"Adem..."

His name in that husky accent drove him to unzip and release himself, allowing skin-to-skin contact for a few luscious seconds before tearing open that packet and sheathing himself. His hand skirted her hip, fingers dipping down and finding a moist warmth that made him reel. All that, and he'd barely touched her.

"*Tanri*, Carly."

Then again, she'd barely touched him and here he was fighting for control with every neuron he possessed. Still. He wanted to be sure.

Finding her, he did what he'd done on her breast, trapping her and stroking, squeezing, even as he gripped himself with his other hand and positioned himself. He remained there for several breath-stealing seconds. Then he thrust deep, burying himself and holding completely still. Except for those fingers, which continued to move while he luxuriated in the tightness encasing him.

As if she couldn't take it anymore, Carly pushed against his caressing hand, the movements transmitted to parts of his body that were already struggling. He upped the ante, using his thumb to slide along the small bit of flesh still trapped between his fingers. Her breath hissed in, her movements growing frantic.

The world outside of his window seemed to spiral down into one tight, sexy view: Carly pressed to that glass, squirming against it—against him—her breasts sliding with each movement.

Then with a sharp cry, she rocked his universe, pulsing against him, along him, into him.

It was all over. He drove into her again and again, the pleasure which had been padlocked inside him breaking down the door and pouring through him in a long stream he hoped would never end. He continued to rock to completion, whispering to her, telling her how glad he was that she was here. How he wanted to do more of the same, even as something inside of him began to wave a warning flag at the rush of emotion that was pouring through him.

He ignored it. For now.

Withdrawing, he turned her to face him, and found her biting her lip. He leaned down and kissed it until she stopped. "Okay?"

She opened bright green eyes and regarded him. Then she smiled. "Mmm…can't talk. Don't want to talk. But very glad that glass held."

A laugh bubbled up from somewhere deep inside of him, rolling out and clearing away whatever had been whispering at the edges of his consciousness. He folded her in her arms. "Me too. I have other things we can test for strength, though. Like the bed… The dining room table… The office chair…"

Her eyes widened, but she didn't miss a beat. "I'm ready for the next stop on our tour."

With that he swung her up in his arms and carried her into the bedroom.

CHAPTER THREE

HE WOKE UP to an empty bed. And some kind of note on the side table.

Glancing at the spot where the indent from her head still was, something shifted inside him when his hand reached for it. That same flare of emotion that had rolled through him last night. Instead of letting his fingers trace the pattern, he shook the pillow out and plumped it up until it looked like no one had even been here.

Those warning flags were waving again. Only this time they were flapping under hurricane-force winds, making him sit up and listen. Whatever this strange stirring was, it needed to stop. Now.

His parents had had a less than stellar marriage. Scratch that. Theirs had been that whole commitment-until-dead thing, even when it was so obvious that they were not in love with each other. His dad was a difficult man at times, though. He worked hard, but he didn't play hard. In fact, he rarely ever took any time for himself.

He'd spent much of his teenage years trying to shield his brother from some of what went on, afraid he'd blame himself since it was his illness that brought them to England in the first place. Adem had been angry at first as well, which had added another layer of guilt, although he'd been careful not to let Basir see it. Instead, he'd acted out in other ways, dabbling in things he'd had no business touching.

Fortunately that stage hadn't lasted long. And Basir seemed to be unaware of it—in fact, he seemed to be the only one in their family who'd been able to learn how to love. He'd even gone to work with his dad at the restaurant and was able to brush off his dad's foul-tempered moments.

Because of love, he'd said.

Love.

How on earth had his brother been able to find that emotion? Because he certainly hadn't had an example of it at home. Adem wouldn't know love—the romantic fairy-tale kind of love—if it bit him on the ass. And even if it did, he was almost certain he wanted nothing to do with it.

Hell! Prying himself out of the bed, he showered quickly before remembering the note. He assumed she wasn't simply in the kitchen making breakfast, since he had no sense of her presence.

Not that he would know what that felt like.

Or did he?

Walking into the bedroom clad in a towel, he picked up the paper.

Thanks for the tour. Didn't even realize you had a view of the London Eye until this morning. Headed back to the real world, though. Catching the tube to get my car.

That was it? She "didn't realize he had a view of the

London Eye"? The Ferris wheel was one of the iconic landmarks of London. He guessed he should be glad that she hadn't been staring at it during…

Or maybe she had been.

A day that had started off rough suddenly felt worse. Much worse. Because he sure as hell hadn't been looking at anything but her. The whole night.

He swore.

Somehow what was supposed to be a light, fun frolic—since when had he ever used that word?—had turned into a road that was dark and curvy. And Adem loathed not being able to see what was around the next bend.

So he was going to take the kinks out of whatever this emotion was and set it back on a straight course. Kinks? He grimaced at the term. He'd discovered a few kinks he hadn't realized he had.

He sucked down a deep breath and blew it out, tightening the towel and wandering into the living room. His shift didn't start until nine, and it was barely seven in the morning.

He glanced at his phone and saw that Basir had tried to call him about half an hour ago. Perfect. Maybe that's where some of his thoughts about the past had come from. Some subconscious tickle perhaps alerting him to be on guard?

Nonsense!

But still, he was going to wait and call him back later.

So what time had Carly left? They hadn't even gone to sleep until the early hours. If he were smart he would try to get another hour's worth of shut-eye before he headed to the clinic.

No. Wait. The hospital. He needed to see their aneurysm patient.

Their.

Kahretsin. He'd bet his last pound that Carly was already there, checking on her.

Feeling like a major slacker for even forgetting about the woman, he turned to head back into the bedroom, head tilting as something on the glass window caught his eye. Some kind of mark.

His jaw tightened as he walked closer and realized exactly what those smudges were. Handprints. From their time in front of the window. Images floated around in his skull, bits and pieces of sight, sound and the sensations that went along with them. His body reacted instantly, despite all they'd done last night.

Yes, calling his brother and hearing all about his happy life would definitely have to wait until later. Until after he'd downed a few cups of coffee.

Coffee he'd never had a chance to make for Carly.

Grinding his teeth, he headed for the kitchen and grabbed a bottle of spray cleaner and a couple of paper towels. And in the same way he'd removed the imprint on that pillow, a couple of squirts erased those telltale marks. But not the memories.

He stood back and looked at the glass. There. You'd never know Carly had been here.

Then he saw the London Eye and remembered that note. As sure as the sun was quickly rising in the east, he knew that every time he saw that Ferris wheel, he was going to see her hands pressed against that glass.

He swore louder, letting the anger and frustration wash away whatever softer emotions were fermenting in his gut. Like the fact that he wanted to see her again. Soon.

But like she'd said, it was time to reenter the real world. Before he did something he might really regret.

Like fall for her?

Not going to happen. He was not Basir.

Unlike his brother, Adem had never fallen for anyone in his life. And there was no way a one-night stand was going to change that.

As long as he didn't let himself be put in a situation where it could—like sleeping with her again—there was no reason for that encounter to change anything.

Carly tried concentrating on what Esther was saying, even as she felt him enter the room.

That was ridiculous. You couldn't really feel someone come in.

She glanced back, hoping beyond hope she was right about it not being possible.

Nope. Not right. There stood Adem, looking freshly showered and dressed, while she was still in her clothes from last night—although she had jumped under the spray in the hospital gym to rid herself of his scent. She'd woken up in a panic of not knowing where she was, and that had changed to horror when she remembered what they'd done. She never let herself go like that. Never.

Not that there was anything wrong with it. There wasn't.

Except it had left a deeper imprint than she'd expected. Which was why she hadn't been able to get out of his flat fast enough this morning and had hoped beyond hope that she could get out of the hospital before he arrived. And she knew he would, since Naomi was officially assigned to a team of specialists which he was heading up. Carly had briefed her friend on the situation, and since Esther worked in neonatal intensive care, she'd brought her in to meet Naomi.

Esther's eyes widened slightly when she spotted Adem. Then she turned to Carly. "Have you got this?"

Got what? Adem?

Oh! She was talking about the situation, not her relationship. Not that there was one.

Her friend was trying to politely excuse herself. Did she sense something? "Yep. I know you need to get back to work."

Naomi smiled. "It was nice meeting you."

"You as well. Can't wait to see your little one." Then Esther murmured her goodbyes and slid from the room.

Adem moved in to stand next to her, and her pulse immediately started thrumming in her chest. She took a calming breath, hoping he couldn't see her reaction.

"Did something happen?" He glanced at the closed door, and Carly realized he was wondering why Esther had been in the room. His being here caused everything in her head to turn into a chaotic mess.

"No, everything's fine. Her vitals are still holding steady and the baby's heart rate is perfect."

"Good." He came over to the bedside, laying a hand on the edge of Naomi's mattress. "How's your head feeling?"

"Better. Maybe whatever you thought you saw on the scan turned out to be nothing?" The flash of hope in her voice tugged at Carly's heart. This was the hard part of her job. And no matter how much she lectured herself on not getting emotionally involved, she did. She loved her patients, many of whom had come to her for subsequent pregnancies, keeping her updated with pictures of their kids as they grew and changed.

Carly was the only one who seemed...well, static. Ever since she'd stopped trying to have a baby of her own, she felt stuck in place—her feet planted on an immobile sidewalk while conveyor belts of people whooshed past her into their own happy futures, some never to be seen again. Esther probably would as well. The world was leaving her behind.

Could that be part of the reason she'd jumped at the chance to sleep with Adem? To shake that feeling off? To prove to herself that she was still spinning on this globe called life, just like everyone else?

His voice brought those thoughts to a halt.

"I'll relook at everything, but I don't think there's been a mistake. I'll meet with the team this morning, and we'll come up with a consensus that keeps you and the baby as safe as possible. Okay? You've already met Esther McDonald."

"Yes. And everyone's been so nice." She reached up and gripped her husband's hand. "But I'm actually glad you came to see me. If for some reason you have to choose between me and the baby during surgery, I... I want our baby to come first, so—"

"Hey, stop." Douglas leaned down and kissed her forehead. "You heard him. He wants to keep you *both* safe."

The man glanced at Adem. "When will you make a decision about what to do?"

"Hopefully this morning. I've already called in Dr. Dubois, one of our obstetricians. And of course Carly will be there as well."

She would? She'd asked, but she'd known from the start that there were no guarantees one way or the other. "I want to be there. I have to be at the clinic this morning, though."

Adem turned toward her. "I actually called the clinic and asked them to do some shuffling, if you're okay with that." He smiled at the young couple. "Can I borrow Carly for a few minutes?"

"Oh, of course."

Her stomach dropped to the floor of her abdomen. What on earth could he want? Oh, God, hopefully he wasn't going to rehash last night or warn her that business and pleasure were to remain strictly separate. Not that she was ever going to sleep with him again.

Last night had been too...

Earth-shattering. There was no other word for it.

Plus there was that embarrassing little detail of her forgotten hairbrush. She'd left it on his bathroom counter, dragging it quickly through her hair before she exited the building. She hoped he'd just throw it in the trash bin rather than bring up anything about what had happened.

Feeling like she was trudging through some kind of thick sludge, she made her way to the door and went through it, letting it close behind her.

Adem looked neither happy nor unhappy, although she sensed a wariness in him that hadn't been there last night. Of course, she probably matched him in that department.

And that wasn't the only department in which they matched.

Oh Lord, Carly, knock it off! He says a few words in a different language and you're swooning at his feet.

No, she'd been swooning long before that.

But it stopped right here. Right now.

She jumped in first, not giving him a chance to say anything. "Look, if this is about the…um…London Eye incident—" Could she possibly think of a worse euphemism? "Then don't worry about it. I'm not expecting any more tours or anything else, so don't worry."

One corner of his mouth went up. "That wasn't what I wanted to talk to you about, but now that you've brought it up…" He went over to the nurses' station and picked up a handled paper bag. It was a lot bigger than what would be needed for a hairbrush. And it looked heavier.

"I'm not sure—"

"The restaurant knows me and opted to have our meals put into take-away boxes, which they sent to the apartment building. My doorman had them waiting in the refrigerator this morning. This is yours."

Her face turned to fire. Had the proprietors boxed uneaten meals for him in the past? And worse, they had to have known exactly why they'd skated out of there so fast. "How often do they have to do that for you?"

Adem frowned, the coming together of his brows erasing any trace of that sexy smile. "Never. They assumed one of us was ill."

She'd missed the mark by a mile on that one.

Her eyes closed. "Oh God, Adem, I'm sorry. It's just

been a…" What could she say? A long night? A once in a lifetime event? An event that was never happening again?

"Hey, I understand. You also left something else, but I left the flat in such a hurry I forgot to bring it."

He left in a hurry? Why?

"Not a problem. I have extras at home. I don't need it back."

"How often does that happen?" he mimicked her words, but the frown had faded and the lightness was back in his voice.

She laughed. "Same as you. Never. So are we good?"

"If we can both put this behind us, then I would say yes."

Said as if he'd already done exactly that. It might be a little more difficult for her, but she was sure if she worked hard enough at it, she could forget about last night.

She hoped.

And if she couldn't?

Well, Adem's implication was that if she couldn't, then all would not be good between them. So she would have to make that happen. Somehow.

She took the bag from him and held it between them as if that would somehow magically jump-start the process of forgetting. "So when is the meeting this morning? And will the clinic be able to 'shuffle' things? I'm pretty sure I had two appointments, and if someone goes into labor, I'll have to go."

"If that happens, we can meet later and go over what the team decides. But ideally, you know Naomi better than anyone else on the team. I'm hoping you can let us know if we miss anything important."

"Thank you. I really want to be there for her until the end. And she wants me there. You heard her yesterday."

"Yes. And I want you to be in the operating room with us. I think she'll be reassured if she knows you're close by."

He wanted her there while he performed the surgery? She would have to digest that bit of information later. Her grip tightened on the handles of the bag between them.

Deciding to change the subject, she wiggled the sack. "Do I have time to go home and change?" She'd been planning to swing by her place on her way to the clinic. He might be fresh as a daisy, but even with her shower, she needed some clean clothes. And to do something with her hair.

"The meeting is at ten, so you have about two hours."

Plenty of time. "Okay, I'll be back, or will let you know if there's a problem with one of my patients."

"See you at ten, then."

"Are you going back in there?" She nodded at the door behind her.

"Yes, I want to go over a few things and let her know what to expect, if we go ahead with surgery."

"Great, if you could tell her I'll see her later on today, I'd appreciate it."

"I will."

She waited for him to push through the door, giving him a quick wave as she took her bag and headed for the exit that would take her to where she'd parked her car.

She had two hours before the meeting. Two hours to

change and somehow figure out a way to deal with him on a daily basis without feeling awkward.

And the best way she could do that was eat the food in this bag tonight, so it wouldn't be hanging around her house longer than necessary.

Once that happened, she hoped—*hoped!*—that she and Adem would be able to move back to where they were before this all started. She would retreat like a turtle, going back to the safety of her cautious little life. And next time she was tempted by someone like Adem, hopefully she would be a little wiser about giving in.

Basir and his wife sat in his office. Adem wasn't exactly sure what this meeting was about, but his brother assured him it was important.

It must be for him to leave the restaurant. But something he couldn't tell him over the phone? And why was Adeline here?

His chest tightened as a thought hit him. Had the tumor come back? Adem hadn't asked about the periodic tests his brother had done.

"Is everything okay?"

Basir and Adeline glanced at each other, making the sense of foreboding grow.

Until she giggled. The unexpected sound made him blink, reminding him of the way Carly had laughed in his apartment. But it also served to wash away that sense of impending doom.

"What's going on?" he asked.

Seeing his brother healthy and happy was good for his soul and made him feel he'd done the right thing in taking Basir under his wing all those years ago. Whatever irritation he'd felt the other day faded away.

He should be glad for him. Truly.

"We came to ask you something."

He frowned. "Okay."

"We're looking for a midwife," Basir said.

His heart seized for a minute before realizing they weren't talking about Carly.

"Sorry?"

Adeline spoke up. "A midwife. Someone you'd trust to deliver your niece or nephew, Adem."

A beat went by. Then two. Suddenly it dawned on him what they were getting at. "You two are...?"

Basir's resulting smile stretched from ear to ear. "Yes. We're going to have a baby."

Adem got up from his desk and came around to where his brother had also got up and caught him in a tight hug. "Congratulations." He included Adeline in his smile. "Both of you."

"Thank you. After three years, the time just seemed right, you know?" she said.

He didn't know. Not at all. But for once, he wished he did.

Adem didn't see himself having children any time soon. Or later. While he was happy for his brother, the only emotion that came up when he thought of children was dread. Maybe because in the midst of an unhappy home, he'd taken on so much responsibility at a young age. In some ways he felt like he'd already raised one child. And the weight of doing what was best for his brother had almost crushed him emotionally.

But he wouldn't change it for the world, especially

after seeing the obvious joy on Basir's face. But doing it again?

He didn't think so.

"What does Dad think?" He hoped his father would be happy for them, rather than weigh it in terms of how it would affect his business.

"I haven't told him yet, but I think he'll be happy. Even if he always did think you'd be the first one to give him a grandchild."

Shock rolled up his spine. Why on earth would his father think that? "I don't..."

"You're the oldest, Adem. It's that whole duty thing." His brother said the words as if the reasons were obvious. And maybe they were to Basir, or even his dad, but not to him.

"I'm nowhere near that point." He said the words with a smile he didn't feel. "But I'm happy for you."

"Thank you."

"So back to the midwife question?" Adeline's soft voice came through. "As you know, this is where we come for treatment. Or would we have to go to the Queen Victoria?"

Adem went back around his desk and carefully sat down. Yes, back to the midwife question. "You would come here, of course. And all of the midwives here are..."

Basir shook his head. "We don't need all of them. Just one. Someone who makes you feel cared for and special."

Even though his brother was speaking in general terms and not referring to Adem personally, the same face kept flashing in his mind.

She didn't make him feel special. It hadn't been what he was looking for the other night. He'd needed sex, and she'd offered it.

His jaw tightened. It hadn't been like that at all, and he knew it. But to play it off as anything else was crazy.

And Carly was one of the best midwives at the clinic.

So did he send his brother to someone else to make it more comfortable for himself? Or did he tell Basir the truth? That he'd trust Carly with anyone. Look at Naomi. Someone else might have just told them to go to sleep and see if they felt better in the morning.

Not Carly. She'd met them at the hospital and had taken an interest in her patient every step of the way.

Still he hesitated before taking a deep breath. "Yes, there's a midwife at the clinic who is exceptional."

"What's her name?"

"Carly Eliston." He glanced at Adeline. "How far along are you?"

"Six weeks. We wanted to have it confirmed before saying anything to anyone. And we want to give it a few more weeks before we tell Dad."

Adeline was referring to his and Basir's father, since hers passed away just before their wedding three years ago.

"I can understand that. Let me talk to Carly and see what her schedule looks like. If she can take on another patient, I'll give you her number."

One of Carly's strengths might prove to be a thorn in Adem's side. She took such a personal interest in her patients that it was doubtful that Adem would be able to stand on the sidelines and out of the way.

But he would have to try.

"Is there a chance she'll say no?"

"I don't know. It depends on how many patients she has." Not to mention how she felt about taking on one of his family members. Maybe she wanted nothing to do with him and would say no.

As someone who'd protected his brother for years, that didn't sit well. But he'd have no choice but to accept whatever decision Carly made.

"We can understand that. Maybe if you could contact them in order of skill."

"I'll do that and let you know." Suddenly he wanted them out of his office so he could think.

"What was the name of the person you like the most?"

Hell. Why did he have to put it that way?

"Carly Eliston. And I don't like her the most. Just said that she gave excellent care."

Basir's head tilted and he looked at him funny. As if he'd heard something behind the words. Something Adem had almost certainly not meant.

At least, he hoped he didn't.

"That's what I meant."

Adem stood again, ready to end this impromptu meeting. "Congratulations again. I'll get in touch with Carly and let you know."

In reality he was supposed to see her today, when he did the coiling procedure on Naomi. He could talk to her then.

Or he could lie and ask someone else completely, saying that Carly was busy.

For his own peace of mind?

He already knew he wouldn't do that. When it came to peace of mind, his was normally the one sacrificed for the good of his brother. And he couldn't bring himself to regret it.

Even if the next nine months turned out to the longest he'd ever endured.

Naomi was getting her surgery. Thankfully she'd continued to do well, but since her blood pressure had crept up a bit, the decision had been made to go with Adem's suggestion and place a coil in the bulging vein and cut off its blood supply.

Dressed in surgical gear and paper booties, Carly was already in the surgical suite when Adem swept into the room, hands held up so that a nurse could snap gloves on his freshly scrubbed hands. "Is everyone here?"

He glanced her way with an inscrutable expression, but didn't address her. Something in her chest twinged.

Did he regret asking her to be in the room? She'd held Naomi's hand as they'd administered the anesthesia drugs, the woman's eyes struggling to remain focused on hers, a slight flare of panic appearing before her lids flickered and finally closed. It made her throat clog. Even though Carly had never faced anything like this, she could imagine the things that might fill her mind as she was wheeled into the room: Would she ever see her husband again…would her baby be okay… would she be normal?

Just before Adem had come in, Carly had leaned over the sleeping woman and said, "I'm right here, Naomi. I'm not leaving, no matter what."

And if Adem asked her to?

Why would he? They'd seen each other in passing at the clinic over the last couple of days, but other than being there when the surgical team met, he hadn't gone out of his way to speak to her. If anything, it seemed almost like he was avoiding her.

Or maybe it was that she was avoiding him.

Which she was.

Raphael Dubois was on call at the hospital, if they needed him. And the neonatal ward was ready as well, Esther having told Carly to call her at the first sign of trouble—even before the call officially went to the NICU. They were as prepared as they possibly could be.

Adem moved to the table and gave the go-ahead for the contrast dye and imaging to start. He then made a small incision in Naomi's femoral artery and proceeded to feed the catheter through the opening. The process seemed to take forever as he stared at the screen where the aneurysm was now in sharp focus, a rounded bowl that looked like some kind of strange fruit that was attached to the tree by a stem.

"Preparing to enter the location. I'll need the micro-catheter in a moment."

From what she'd understood from the meeting, he would thread another smaller catheter up through the one he was using now. It contained a thin platinum coil that would fill the aneurysm and cause the blood to clot, effectively cutting off its blood supply and preventing it from rupturing.

"Okay, I'm in place."

The surgical nurse next to him passed him the instrument, and Adem fed it through in the same way he'd done with the original catheter. The process was painstaking and seemed to take forever, even though Carly had been told to expect a couple of hours of standing.

The standing wasn't the problem. It was that with each ticking second, there was the possibility that something could go terribly wrong.

No different than any birth she'd assisted.

That wasn't exactly true. This was dealing with a part of the body that was much harder to fix if a mistake was made.

And yet while there were lines of concentration clearly visible on his face, Adem's hands were remarkably steady and his breathing even and regular. Just like always.

How did she know what his breathing normally looked like?

She closed her eyes for a second to stop that image from forming.

She knew what it looked like. Intimately.

And right now, Adem gave off a vibe of confidence. She could remember times when she'd been worried about a patient's welfare and had had to mask those emotions, wall them off from both the patients and herself—so that she could do her job. Without that ability, she might as well throw in the towel and quit.

It was probably the same with Adem.

"Here we go, people."

She assumed that meant that he was getting ready to put the coils in place. With a flick of his thumb, a hair-thin fiber appeared on the screen and began making a series of what looked like loop-the-loops that quickly filled the defect.

"Giving the electrical charge…now."

The electricity caused the coiling material to separate from the catheter, allowing it to remain in place once the instruments were retracted.

He surprised her by not pulling out immediately after that happened, but remained in place, staring at the screen with narrowed eyes.

Kind of like he'd stared at her, when he strained within her, staying exactly where he was for what seemed like a long, long time.

Oh, God. She put her hand to her throat. Where had that come from?

Very grateful to the mask that shielded most of her face, she swallowed several times, struggling to coil her emotions and shove them back in their container. But unlike the endovascular procedure Adem had almost completed, they weren't cooperating nearly as well.

A couple more deep breaths, though, and she was back in control. And as she glanced at the screen, she saw that the aneurysm seemed less "bright," although she wasn't sure if that was the right word.

Adem must have thought so as well, because he said, "I'm happy with the placement and how it looks. Getting ready to move out."

The process of withdrawing the catheters was a whole lot quicker than the time it had taken to position them. But that made sense, since he'd had to find the perfect path that would take him to the heart of the problem.

And her perfect path? The one that would take her to the heart of the problem with Adem?

Well, she was still trying to find it.

"Placing the closure device."

He must have seen her head tilt, because a few minutes after pressing what looked like a plunger in the area on Naomi's leg, he glanced at her. "I'm closing the incision I made in the artery with a collagen plug. It's faster than manual compression and allows her to become ambulatory more quickly. It dissolves in a few weeks."

Okay, that was interesting.

"Thanks for the explanation."

A nurse assisted in clearing away the tubing from the procedure and Adem nodded at the anesthesiologist. "Let's wake her up."

"Okay. Reversing now."

While a couple of the nurses continued to organize the room, Adem watched Naomi's face. When her eyes flicked open, Carly saw him take a deep breath. Maybe he hadn't been quite as unruffled as he'd seemed. That was good, because she just now realized how tight her own muscles had been.

She'd always thought Adem was a skilled surgeon, but watching him perform that surgery had made her heart swell with admiration. Maybe because Naomi was her patient and she was glad of the outcome. But she had a feeling it was more than that.

The anesthesiologist came around and murmured to the patient and then removed the endotracheal tube. "How are you feeling?"

Naomi's eyes tracked to his face. "Did it work? Baby?"

The croaked words made Carly's chest tighten. She wasn't concerned about her comfort or even attempting to answer the question. Even though she probably wouldn't remember these next moments due to the amnesic effect of the medication, her first semiconscious thoughts were for her child.

Adem put his hand on her shoulder. "It worked per-

fectly, and your baby is fine. We're going to wheel you
back to recovery in a minute and let you get some rest.
I'll let Douglas know how things went, and he can come
see you in just a little bit."

Naomi looked past him and found her. A slight smile
appeared, and she nodded.

Maybe Naomi would remember, after all.

She was so glad she'd stayed. So glad she hadn't
let her personal feelings over what had happened with
Adem deflect her from doing what she thought was
right. And being here with Naomi had been the right
thing to do. One of those cases when, like her patient,
she put her own comfort to the side and worried about
someone other than herself. "I'll go wait with her until
her husband is allowed in."

"Are you sure?"

"Yes. I'll head over to the clinic afterward."

"Okay. I have one more surgery here, and then I'll
be over as well." He smiled. "And I left your missing
item on your cubicle desk. And later, I need to talk to
you when you have a minute."

Her missing item. The hairbrush.

She wasn't sure why he'd felt the need to tell her that,
or why her heart had picked up the pace when he said he
needed to speak to her. She was just going to ignore her
reaction, though, and keep on ignoring it until it became
second nature and that crazy night of Glass Panels, the
London Eye and her Lost Hairbrush faded into the past.
After all, there was nothing she could do to change it.
Any of it. And she wasn't sure she would if she could.

So why not just enjoy the memory for what it was: a
thrilling night that, in the end, changed nothing.

CHAPTER FOUR

"My brother is expecting a baby and needs a midwife."

Carly wasn't sure what words she expected to hear, but those were not them.

She'd gone from elation after Naomi's surgery, to fear that he wanted to rehash what was already over and done with: that night at his flat.

Blinking, she tried to catch up with reality. "Your brother?"

"Yes. I should have said he and his wife haven't been assigned a midwife yet. They're expecting their first child."

"The brother who's working with your dad?"

Adem gave a slight smile. "That's right. He's the only brother I have."

"Oh…yes. I should have remembered that." Being around him again was bringing all those feelings from the other night back to the forefront. Not good. Not good at all. Hadn't she vowed she was going to keep things professional from now on? "You want me to take them on as part of my patient load?"

"I do. They're already patients of the clinic. If you have space, that is."

Suspicion crowded her thoughts. Was it odd that right after she'd spent the night with him, he suddenly wanted her to be his sister-in-law's midwife?

"May I ask why?"

He frowned, leaning against the white wall of the clinic foyer. "Do I need a reason?" His head tilted as if realizing something. "Ah. You think the other night might have had something to do with it. I can assure you it didn't. If anything, it made me think carefully about whether or not to recommend you to them."

And that thought horrified her even more. Had that night been that awful? "I don't really understand what that has to do with anything."

"I don't want to make things any more awkward than they already are. For either of us."

Okay, he had her there, because things had been awkward. For her at least, and a little part of her was glad that it was for him as well. That he hadn't been able just to brush it aside as if it had never happened. "Okay, that's understandable."

"If you don't want to do it, I'll understand."

Since she'd just said she didn't know what that night had to do with anything, she'd be a hypocrite if she suddenly didn't want to have his brother and his wife as patients. "You might, but I wouldn't. Of course I will. I'd like to meet them, if I could. Sooner rather than later. You know I like to follow my patients for as much of the pregnancy as possible."

"I know. Which is why I told them about you."

He had? A warmth infused her that had nothing to do with Adem's future niece or nephew. "I'm flattered."

"Believe me, it has nothing to do with flattery. I just know they'll get excellent care."

"Because of Naomi?"

"Not just her. I've watched you with your patients. While I personally think you might get a little too emotionally involved with them, I also know that it means that nothing will get by you."

"Thank you. I think."

He laughed. "It was a compliment."

She couldn't hold back an answering smile. "I wasn't quite sure."

"I'll have them call you to set up an appointment, if that's okay, in the next couple of days."

"That would be perfect. I look forward to meeting them."

He pushed away from the wall. "Thanks for doing this. I do appreciate it."

"Not a problem."

At least, she hoped it wouldn't be one.

Less than an hour later, her cell phone went off.

"Ms. Eliston? My name is Basir Kepler. My brother heads up the clinic."

She knew exactly who he was. She was just surprised that his brother was calling her so quickly, and that Adem had given them her cell phone number. Maybe he wanted to let her talk to them first before making any firm decisions.

His voice sounded very much like Adem's, with those low gravely tones, but he sounded younger somehow.

Or maybe he was just less cynical.

Did she really think Adem was cynical? Maybe. One thing she did know was that he was very good at keeping his emotions in check. Except for that night in his apartment.

Only that hadn't been emotion. More like lust. Or worse, just biological need.

Except he'd been so sexy. So...focused.

She cleared her throat. "Adem was just talking to me about you." Too late she realized she probably should have used his title rather than talking about him so informally. Hopefully she didn't give Basir any wrong ideas.

Wrong ideas? Like what? She'd slept with the man, for heaven's sake. She sure wasn't calling him Mr. Kepler during that. But she also didn't want Adem's brother to think they had a relationship. Because they didn't. It was one night. And that was all it was ever going to be. She would make sure of it.

To cover up and hopefully divert any personal questions, she asked about him and his wife. "Tell me a little bit more about yourselves and your hopes for the baby?"

"Adeline is on the line with me, so I'll let her do most of the talking."

Soon thoughts of Adem were abandoned—at least on a temporary basis—as they discussed what they knew so far about the pregnancy. It was their first baby, and they wanted to try a home birth, if possible.

The usual excitement grew as it always did when she spoke with a new patient. Maybe she lived vicariously through her patients, allowing their joy of discovery to become her own joy. Or it could be Adeline's bubbly enthusiasm, or maybe just how happy they both sounded. And that's where the difference came in. She sensed a genuine contentment in Basir that seemed to be missing from Adem somehow. Or maybe that was her imagination.

Fifteen minutes later, she'd posted a memo to herself on her phone. She was going to meet Basir and his wife here at the clinic in her cubicle. Later she would go to their home and go through what they needed to have in place for the birth.

"It was nice talking to you, and I look forward to meeting you both."

"Thank you," Adeline said. "Adem speaks very highly of you."

He did? That still left her dumbstruck...that Adem would have wanted her to be personally involved in the case. It also gave her a tiny thrill that warred with the lecture she'd given herself about not getting emotionally involved with him. If that were even possible.

It was. She would make sure of it.

"Well, I'm glad I can help. I'll see you next week."

They said their goodbyes and Carly continued on her way, glancing back as if Adem might have suddenly materialized out of thin air. Thank God he hadn't.

It didn't matter. Because like it or not, Adem was going to be involved in this pregnancy and birth and so would officially be a part of her life. At least until this baby was born and Carly was off the case.

Carly was going to be Adeline's midwife. She'd stopped by yesterday to let him know that they'd met and agreed on the hows and whys. And what had been a lazy current of uneasiness over suggesting her had turned into stiff gusts that were getting stronger by the day. Maybe it didn't have as much to do with Carly as it did with his brother himself.

Of course he deserved to be happy. Adem had bent over backward to make sure that had happened after Basir's surgery and treatment. But could it be that having the evidence of that happiness staring him in the face reminded him of how different he and Basir were?

Not that Adem wanted marriage and babies. And he especially didn't want them just to satisfy his father's idea of birth order. If anything, that just made him even more determined to do things his own way. In his own time.

Besides, he was content with what he had. Which was Work and…

Work.

He blew out a breath, shifting some files on his desk and setting down his pen. Was he becoming his father, who was so obsessed with work that he ignored everything around him, even the things that were slipping away like his wife and kids?

You don't have a wife or kids, Adem.

He didn't, but he'd put his heart and soul into the starting of this clinic to the exclusion of almost everything else in his life. Including relationships.

It was what he wanted, though. And he had his brother to thank for that. If he'd had the option, he would have named the clinic the Basir Kepler Care Centre, but he doubted his brother would have liked having reminders of what he'd been through. He was truly able to put the past behind him.

Maybe they were different in that as well. Adem and his dad had a strained relationship, even now, whereas

Basir worked with their father at the restaurant and would probably own it one day.

Well, no matter. At least he knew Basir would make a wonderful father, judging from what he'd seen of his relationship with Adeline.

The phone on his desk chirped. Glancing at the screen, he put his pen down. Just who he'd been thinking of. It was his brother.

Flicking the button to take the call, he put it to his ear. "Hi. I hear you have a midwife."

"We do and Addy loves her already. We should actually be there in an hour or so to meet with her again and fill out some paperwork. Can you be there? You might think of something we don't."

"I've never had need of a midwife, Basir."

Ha! Actually, he had, but not quite in the way that his brother meant.

"I know, but you know Carly."

Yes, he did. A little better than he had before. The last thing he needed was to sit in and watch her do Adeline's prenatal appointment.

"I don't know. I'm pretty busy."

"Come on, Adem. We're excited and wanted to share it with family. You work right there at the clinic."

"Okay, I'll make it work."

Somehow. He just wasn't sure quite how he was going to face Carly and not see the imprints of her hands against his living room window all over again.

Carly was nervous, and she wasn't sure why. It wasn't the first time family members had sat in on an appointment and it wouldn't be the last. In fact, Basir

and Adeline had requested this meeting after research-
ing birthing options.

But this was Adem.

As much as she tried to tell herself it was because he
was the head of the clinic and that he would be looking
at her through that lens, she knew that wasn't entirely
it. More of it involved having him here while they discussed birth plans. She couldn't stop herself from wondering what kind of birth experience he would choose
for his own child. Would he be involved? Or detached?
Would he want his partner to have a hospital birth or
one at home?

She had a hard time suppressing the tiny pang that
went through her at the fact that she would probably
never know. Nor should she.

And if he got married and asked her to play a role in
his own wife's pregnancy?

It was a completely irrational thought, but one she
couldn't entirely banish. Of course he wouldn't ask.

But if he did?

She wasn't sure she could do it, and she didn't really
understand why.

And that was her cue to get back to the business at
hand.

"We'll have most of our prenatal appointments here
at the clinic until we get closer to your due date. Then
nearer the date, I or one of my team will visit you at
home. We need to have at least one appointment there,
anyway, so we can put everything in place. You mentioned on the phone that you've done some research on
types of home births."

Adeline nodded. "We have and wanted to hear your

opinions, since we're leaning toward a water birth. Since Adem's a neurosurgeon, we thought it would be good to hear his thoughts as well."

Out of the corner of her eye, she saw him stiffen. "I'm sure Carly can guide you through those decisions."

Was he afraid she would be offended that they'd asked him to be here? Nothing could be further from the truth. Glancing over, she said, "I welcome whatever input you might have."

"I am not a birth expert."

Basir spoke up. "No, but you're family. And an expert in your field, and since we've chosen something a little less conventional, we really do want to hear your opinion."

"Water births have been around for a long time," Carly said. They were growing in popularity actually. "We'll need to work out some things, but that is very possible as long as your pregnancy is progressing without complications. We'll do an ultrasound to make sure there's only one baby in there, since we wouldn't want to go that direction with twins either."

"And you've assisted with water births before?" Adeline's voice was soft, her happiness obvious.

"Yes. We even have a birthing pool here at the clinic, which brings me to another question. Where would you get your pool?"

This time Basir answered. "That was part of our research. We found a company we can buy a new one from. We can either keep it for future pregnancies or they'll sell it for us once we're done. They have guidelines set up for how to do it all." He handed her a card.

She glanced at the name. "I've worked with them before. They're very reputable."

"That's a relief."

Basir glanced at his brother. "This is where you come in. What is your take on water births?"

"Are you asking me as a doctor?"

"I am. Since the baby will be born underwater, will there be any problems as far as oxygen? I know everyone says they're perfectly safe, but we just want to make sure."

Carly could have answered that question, but she understood why Basir wanted reassurance from an objective party. Not that Adem was, since he was also family.

"Carly is probably better off answering that question. But if you're worried about oxygen deprivation, there won't be any, since the baby will be still attached by the cord."

"Water birth babies are only submerged for a matter of seconds once they're born, so Adem is right, there's no danger in that regard. But I would hold off on buying an actual birth pool until you're a little further along, just so we can make sure everything is running according to plan."

"How far along?"

"I'm going to say six months. We only want to go that route under optimal conditions, for your sake and the baby's."

Adeline nodded. "I do understand that. And since Adem seems to be in agreement, let's plan on that."

When Carly shot him a look, he was frowning and didn't look very happy. Was he not a fan of water births? Again, it didn't matter, since this wasn't his baby. But as director of the clinic, it might be good to know his stance, since Carly was a proponent of the method.

Fifteen minutes later, they'd finished their discussion and Carly bid them both goodbye. But when Adem looked like he was going to shoot through the door behind them, she asked him to hold up.

When the door of the exam room closed, she got straight to the point. "Do you have a problem with your brother and his wife wanting a water birth?"

"Why do you ask?"

"I'm not sure. You just looked less than pleased once they firmed up their decision."

"It's not my child."

"No, but it is your niece or nephew. And your attitude will make itself known sooner or later. Besides, I would personally like to know what you think."

"Why?"

The way he said that made her hesitate. Then she decided she really did need to know. "Because you're the clinic's director. I'd like to make sure you stand behind our patients who choose to have their baby in a pool."

"Of course. It's just such a different field. I'm a neurosurgeon, so the idea of performing brain surgery in someone's home is unfathomable to me. But it's not brain surgery and obviously some people are more comfortable giving birth in familiar surroundings."

"Yes, that's right. They do. Okay, I just didn't want Basir and Adeline to start down this road only to be sidetracked by some objection you might have."

"Believe me, if I'd had one, you would have known it."

"Well, that's good to know."

His head cocked. "Anything else?"

"No. That was all."

"Okay, so now that we have that out of the way, I'll see you later."

She nodded and watched him walk out of the room, unsure of why she'd gone from nervous to defensive to deflated in less than an hour's time.

That wasn't quite true. She did know why. She just didn't like the reasons for it. Because they involved a man she was afraid was becoming a little too important in her life. He made her pulse soar and her heart trip in her chest. And yet he'd shown no interest in repeating their night together. Or having a relationship of any sort with her.

Lord, she'd already survived one man walking out on her. The last thing she needed to do was set her poor heart on a shelf and wait for it to be knocked down again. Because she had a feeling this time it wouldn't bounce, but would instead shatter into a million pieces.

CHAPTER FIVE

ADEM'S LIFE HAD been so busy he'd barely had time to stop and breathe since the news of Adeline's pregnancy and Basir's question about water births being safe. The question seemed even more poignant this morning as another family faced a horrific choice.

There'd been a string of emergencies related to a terrible pileup on the M1 a week ago. Three fatalities and dozens of injuries, including nine traumatic brain injuries. Adem had either treated or consulted with other hospitals on most of them.

And today he'd had to stand at the bedside of a five-year-old child and listen as her family begged him to find some sign of hope on her EEG readings. But there were none. After the accident, her brain swelled, continuing unabated despite his team's every attempt to stop it, including a craniotomy—removing a piece of her skull to relieve pressure. Nothing worked, and in the early hours, her brain stem had herniated.

At this point the ventilator was the only thing keeping their daughter's body alive. And seeing her mother, also injured in the crash, sit there with a cast on her arm and plead for her daughter's life had wrenched him in a way that he wasn't used to. Unlike Carly, who was deeply involved with her patients for nine months, Adem was able to maintain more emotional distance from his. Whether that had to do with his training or with his upbringing was up for debate.

Whatever it was, he was having a harder time coping today.

The organ donation team was on standby, waiting for a chance to talk to the family. It all seemed so cold-blooded right now, even though he knew he wasn't thinking rationally.

He couldn't imagine being a parent and having to face the death of your child. Hadn't cared about anyone enough to even think of having a family with them. At least until Basir entered the picture with his news. But his brother was happily married. Adem was not, and since there was no one on the horizon, there would be no children in his foreseeable future. He would not make the same mistake his parents had made and bring kids into a less than ideal partnership.

He sighed. Why were those thoughts going through his head today?

Adem had faced other heartbreaking outcomes with patients, but rarely with someone so young. Realizing he'd been staring out of his office window for the last fifteen minutes, he swiveled his chair back toward the front and planted his elbows on his desk. Steepling his hands, he rested his forehead on his fingertips, trying to pull his mind toward other things, even as that child's family was now grappling with the hardest choice a parent would ever have to make.

A knock on his door sounded.

Damn. Here it was. He'd given them his mobile number and asked them to call him, but maybe someone had directed them here. Maybe they wanted to ask him to run more tests. Didn't they know if there was any possibility…the tiniest sliver of hope…? He drew a deep breath and stood, going over to the door and opening it.

Not the family. Or anyone else involved with the case. It was Carly.

He couldn't imagine why she was here. Wait. "Is it Adeline?"

"No. Naomi."

Hell, their aneurism patient. He suddenly couldn't take one more failure. Maybe she saw something in his face, because she put her hand on his arm. "No, she's okay. More than okay. She had her baby this morning. They delivered by C-section and everyone is great. Not a hint of trouble from the aneurysm. The coiling worked."

He blinked. "That's the best news I've heard today. In fact, it's pretty much the only good news I've had."

"The accident?"

"You heard?"

Her head tilted. "It's been all over the news. You were even on television."

He remembered a gaggle of reporters gawking at him last night as he'd left the building, but it was all a blur. All he'd been able to think about was that little girl and the fact that he wasn't going to be able to save her.

"I don't remember talking to anyone."

"No, they just showed a video clip of you walking to your car and saying that your quick thinking had helped save lives at two different hospitals."

"Kahretsin." A dagger speared through his skull. "Not all of them."

An hour. They'd asked for an hour alone with their daughter before making any decisions.

Without being asked, she slid past him and came fully into his office. "What is it?"

He shook his head, throat suddenly too tight to speak.

Carly stared at him for a moment, before shutting the door and taking his hands. "Tell me."

The pain in his chest spread to his jaw, which clenched and unclenched, the muscles in it protesting under the heavy strain. Hell, he was going to break down. Right here in front of her.

Then she let go of his hands and, without saying a word, wrapped her arms around his waist, pressing her cheek to his chest.

They stood there like that for what seemed like an eternity, while he fought to get his emotions under control.

"Adem, it'll be okay."

It wouldn't be. And he wasn't sure it ever would be again. This child was a reminder of what could have happened to Basir during that surgery to remove his tumor all those years ago. Except this wasn't going to end in a child becoming a healthy adult and going on to have a family. Her life stopped right here. Right now.

"I don't think it will. Not this time."

He tipped her face, and even though she had no idea what he was dealing with, those sea-green eyes were moist with unshed tears.

Before he realized what was happening he was kissing her, trying to bury the hideous unfairness of life in the softness of her lips, in the empathy of the arms that still held him.

She kissed him back, hands going to the back of his head and holding him there as if helping him weather the storm that was raging inside of him.

Her feet moved backward, tugging him with her, until she was up against his desk, where the kiss deepened to impossible levels. He wanted her. Right here. Right now. Needed to think about anything else other than what was happening outside his office door.

Lifting her onto the wooden surface, he ignored the sound of his pencil cup falling over, the writing instruments scattering, some of them tumbling off the edge onto the floor.

All he wanted was to feel something. Something that wasn't tragedy. Something that equaled…life.

The life that he felt in her arms. In her touch.

Her hands left his head and went to his belt, undoing it with quick fingers that left him no time to think about anything other than pushing her skirt up around her hips.

And then he was free, and her legs wrapped around the backs of his thighs, dragging him against her, her fingers gripping his already tight flesh.

Just as his tongue speared into her mouth, capturing her moan, she'd somehow connected flesh to flesh with nothing between them.

"Wait." He didn't want to think about anything but her silky skin, the way it felt to be with her, but some tiny rational part of his brain had him digging for his wallet and the tiny packet hidden in there. Especially after that meeting with Basir a week ago.

Then he was sheathed and ready, just as she shifted her body forward. That was all it took. He was inside. Wrapping an arm around her butt, he hauled her against him and buried himself fully.

Ecstasy. That was the only word he could use to describe it. To describe her.

His lips left hers, mouth going to her ear as his breathing roughened. "You're going to send me over, Carly."

Those were the only words he could get out, because her hands pulled him closer, held him tighter. He thrust, the power of the motion scooting her a couple of inches backward. He hauled her against him again, circling his hips to increase the contact between them even as he fought to maintain his own control.

A control that was rapidly slipping.

"Adem…oh! I don't think I can stop…"

A minute later, her body's frantic movements told him all he needed to know. He pulled back, then drove in again, his motions becoming faster, harder, until that emotional release he'd been seeking shot from him, bringing guttural words that made no sense in any language.

And then he was done. Spent. The helplessness and sorrow that had been bottled up inside of him were all washed away. By Carly. It was almost as if she'd sensed his heartbreak and met it in the only way she could.

Gratitude flooded through him, and a strange longing, something he'd never felt before. Just as he started to lean back to smile at her, that little jiggle in the back of his skull turned into an earth-shattering quake. One that could be held back no longer.

He'd done something he'd said he wasn't going to do again. Had sex with her.

"Lanet Olsun!"

He pulled away in a hurry, only to see confusion on her face, which turned to an uneasy frown.

Then her legs snapped together, and she stood, taking a missed step to the side. He caught her just before she fell. He closed his eyes and curved his palms over her shoulders, head tilting sideways so he could look her full in the eyes.

"I didn't mean to… Carly, I'm sorry."

Her eyes widened. "Don't apologize. I'm as much to blame as anyone." She licked her lips. "It just…happened."

Here. In his office. Where anyone could have walked in, including the parents of that child.

But he certainly wouldn't have done what he did if he'd been thinking straight. But he hadn't been. And Carly's empathy a few minutes ago had obliterated his senses and sent him places he had no business being.

No excuse. Absolutely no excuse. Despite Carly's words, it wasn't her fault. It was his.

And those parents were still sitting by their daughter's bedside.

Sex had changed nothing, after all. Certainly not that. And not the emotions that went along with it. It had merely submerged them for a few quick minutes. Now it was back, and a few other worries bobbed alongside it.

"Hell, it's been a very hard day."

Her mouth tightened ominously. "And I just added to it?"

No. She'd tried to comfort him, and he'd turned it

into something else. *He'd* been the one to kiss her. *He'd* been the one to lift her onto that desk. *He'd* been the one who hadn't thought past his own damn needs.

"No, you didn't. But we shouldn't have done this."

"I'm well aware of that." The beginnings of anger appeared in her eyes. "There's no need to keep pounding away at that point."

You'd better zip it, Adem. You're just making things worse.

And if he hadn't got to that condom in time and really screwed things up? Damn, she could have got pregnant.

If she had, would she have told him? Or would she have had an abortion?

The distaste of finding himself with two kids and a loveless union like his parents suddenly fled.

He wouldn't have wanted Carly to have an abortion?

He had no idea. But even condoms sometimes failed.

"Are you on birth control?"

"Um…no. If I remember correctly, you took care of that."

"I did. I just had one screwed-up family growing up. One I wouldn't want to wish on anyone, so I want to make sure that you…that *we* don't—"

"Don't get pregnant? Don't worry, there's absolutely no chance of that." She gave a harsh laugh that cut right through him. "My period is due tomorrow, anyway, so even if we hadn't used something… Well, believe me when I say, I won't get pregnant. I tried once before, but the dice never came up in my favor."

She'd tried to get pregnant?

"I don't understand."

"Neither did I. But it turned out to be for the best."

He touched her hand. "Whatever the reason, I'm sorry."

She stared at him for a long moment. "You have enough on your plate from the sounds of it, without worrying about my problems."

They weren't just her problems, though, they were his. And today his actions, while not exactly reckless, weren't something he was entirely proud of. He'd had impulsive sex, something out of the ordinary for him.

"You'll let me know."

"I'll tell you if something unexpected happens. But I'm sure everything will be fine."

Everything wasn't fine. One day passed, then two. No period. On the third day she woke up with a slight sensation of queasiness that made her frown. There was no way that could be morning sickness. Not with her track record. A year of trying had yielded nothing. Besides, it had only been three days since they'd had sex in Adem's office. Morning sickness took a couple of weeks to develop. At least.

A thought hit her, and she did some quick calculations in her head. Oh, God. What if three days wasn't what she should be worried about? What if three weeks was?

It wasn't three weeks. It had only been two and a half since they'd slept together in his apartment. But they'd used protection all those times.

All those times. There'd been a lot of them.

Think, Carly! There was no possibility that something could have gone wrong? A condom that didn't come off fast enough? Something residual in between times? Something defective?

But how? She and Kyle had tried and tried and nothing had happened. Nothing.

So how was there even the slightest chance that—

Her phone buzzed, making her jump. She glanced at the readout.

Oh, Lord. It was Adem. Probably wondering why she hadn't called to reassure him.

I'm kind of busy right now—trying to reassure myself.

She ignored it, hoping he wouldn't leave her a voice mail. She didn't have an answer for him.

But she could. If she went down and bought a pregnancy test.

Doing so was going to make it pretty plain that she actually was worried about it, when she'd reassured Adem there was nothing to worry about.

And if she was?

How ironic would that be after all this time? She should be thrilled beyond measure. She might still be. She just couldn't wrap her head around it right now.

Her heart stuttered. There was just one catch. Adem did not want a baby. At all. He'd been extremely quick about asking if she was using additional contraception. And about wanting to know if her period started.

Why? So he could pay for an abortion?

No. That might be right for other people, but it wasn't for her. If she was pregnant, she wanted the baby. Especially after the tears and heartache of trying for so long. But she would make it clear that she expected no help—*wanted* no help—from him or anyone.

Her mom had done just fine after her dad had died. It hadn't been easy for either of them, but her teenage years of growing up with a mother who worked very long hours had fostered a sense of independence that she might not otherwise have.

She could do this. She had a career that she loved, and having a child would only enhance her knowledge of what her patients experienced during pregnancy and labor. And she had her mom.

Yes, her mother would be thrilled, marriage or no marriage.

Dammit.

She didn't need to be jumping ahead to cribs and diapers.

Just go and get the test, Carly, and then worry about Adem and all the other stuff later.

An hour later, she had her answer, and despite her earlier thoughts, it wasn't the one she was expecting. It also confirmed when it had happened. Her hormone levels wouldn't be high enough after only three days to register on a home test. But they would after three weeks.

The queasiness grew, helped along by what was quickly becoming panic. Thank God she was off work today. She laid the stick on her bathroom counter and stared at it.

Pregnant.

She was expecting a baby. A baby!

As a midwife, she'd assisted in hundreds of birth. Home births, birthing center births, hospital births, even water births like Basir and Adeline were hoping to have. She'd faced all kinds of situations. But one thing she hadn't had to deal with was a pregnancy of her own.

Looking back, she could honestly say she was glad she hadn't gotten pregnant with Kyle. It might have pushed them into marriage, which probably wouldn't have ended well. No, if she had to do this, she'd much rather do it on her own.

She took her phone and stared at the missed call, which, as she'd suspected, had been from Adem. Her thumb hovered over the name. She'd told him she would let him know if something unexpected happened. Well, this definitely was that. She needed to tell him. It wasn't fair to keep him in the dark. Nor was it possible. She had a feeling her slight nausea wasn't completely caused by nerves, since she'd woken up with it. And Adem was her boss. He saw her at the clinic most days. Kind of hard to hide a growing bump, even under a lab coat.

Call him. Just get it over with.

Except when her thumb mashed a button, it wasn't Adem's phone she was linking to. She was calling the only person she wanted to talk to right now. Her mom.

Three rings later, Madelaine's soothing voice came on the line and her nerves immediately calmed. Her low tones reminded Carly of the cello her mom played so well. She always knew how to talk her off whatever ledge she was on. She would know what to say.

"Hi, Mom. Is there any chance I can meet you for lunch?"

"Of course, honey. Is something wrong?"

Tears sprang to her eyes. She wasn't sure yet if something was "wrong" or if it was just the timing and the partner that was off. All she knew was that she needed some advice from someone that she trusted with her life. She could have called one of her friends from the hospital. Chloe and Esther would both be happy to let her cry all over them. But she didn't want to mar Esther's newfound happiness by sharing her own troubles. And Chloe had been really busy at the hospital lately.

Suddenly she didn't want to wait until they sat in a restaurant to share the news. "I'm pretty sure I'm pregnant."

"Oh, Carolyn, are you sure?" There was a slight pause. "Are you happy about it?"

Her mom only used her full name when she knew Carly was upset about something.

"Yes, I'm sure. And I don't know what I feel just yet. I just found out this morning."

"How far along are you?"

"Only a couple of weeks." There was no way she was going into any more detail than that.

"Why don't you come over to the house. I'll throw together a quiche while you tell me all about it."

"I need to take a quick shower, but then I'll be over." She closed her eyes, and then when she opened them again, a smile formed. "Oh, and, Mom…"

"Yes?"

"Thank you."

"You're welcome. And it's going to be okay."

Her mind clogged with memories. Wasn't that what she'd told Adem that day in his office? Right before she'd welcomed him into herself?

Yes. And as much as she wanted to blame it on that episode, it was pretty obvious her pregnancy had occurred by then. So her words had been a lie. Everything wasn't okay.

Only she hadn't known it at the time.

Well, she needed to shower and drive to her mom's house, which was over by the university where she worked. Hopefully by the time she left there, she would know exactly what she wanted to do. And then she could finally go and confront Adem and tell him the news.

Five hours later, she'd left her mom's house thinking her nerves had finally been put to rest. Her mom was absolutely thrilled. But as soon as Carly got in her car and started driving she found she couldn't stop. Didn't want to go home. She felt prickly and unsettled, and she knew it had something to do with that missed call from this morning. She owed the man the truth.

And if she couldn't screw up the courage to give it to him?

To hell with that. She'd given him her word, and whether she was scared or not, she owed it to him to go in and relieve his mind.

Except she wasn't sure laying something like this on him would constitute relief. At least her nausea was gone. And even though pregnancy tests had given false positives before, she knew in her heart of hearts that this wasn't one of those times.

She would be absolutely devastated if it was actually. After all the railing and tears and pain, she was finally going to get her wish. She was having a baby.

Please don't take this away from me. Please!

She wasn't sure who that question was directed at. Some deity? Or maybe even Adem, who, depending on his reaction, could turn what should be the happiest day of her life into something traumatic.

Well, she was about to traumatize him, wasn't she?

She sighed. It wasn't fair to leave him sitting there wondering. Especially since she'd told him her period was due the day after they were together.

And if he wanted her off Adeline's case for fear it would make things even more complicated?

Complicated for who? Him? Her? He'd said his family relationships were a mess, so there was that. Well, she'd be proactive and offer to step down.

She pulled into a public parking area not far from the university. Taking a deep breath, she went through her missed calls and found Adem's from earlier today. This time she actually dialed his number.

It went to voice mail, and the little bubble of courage popped like a water balloon. Great. She hung up. There was no way she was going to relay this kind of news via voice mail or text. She'd just have to try later. She tossed her phone back into her purse, only to hear it immediately start ringing. She gulped. It was him. It had to be.

She scrabbled in her purse to find the errant phone, pulling it out just as a third ring sounded. She quickly hit the button to answer and put the phone to her ear. "Hello?"

"Carly. Sorry. I left my phone in the office at the clinic to get water to make coffee and it had just finished ringing when I got to it."

She remembered the small silver pot he'd had that day in the cafeteria. That was what had gotten this whole thing started. She'd never even gotten to try it, and after today, it was likely she never would. Once he heard the news, he'd probably want nothing more to do with her, especially if she wasn't open to terminating the pregnancy. Surely he wouldn't even suggest it after what she'd shared with him. Even if he did, there was no way…

She would just make it very clear that she was fine raising this child on her own.

"It's okay. Listen, is there somewhere we can meet?"

There was a long silence on the phone, making her heart cramp. Had he already guessed what this was about? "I take it you're not at the clinic right now. Do you want to come in or meet at my apartment?"

No. She suddenly knew she needed it to be somewhere other than one of those places. Somewhere neutral. She glanced up and saw a sign for Hyde Park. Why not there?

"How long before you finish up at work?"

"Just tying up a few loose ends, then I'm free."

And I'm about to give you a whole lot more loose ends. Ones that can't be tied up in a day or even a few weeks.

Should she ask him about the patient he was so upset about the other day? No. She was pretty sure there had not been a happy ending in sight. There had been a desperation in his kiss that she hadn't recognized. It made what happened a lot more understandable. He'd been distraught, and she'd been a welcome distraction.

A distraction. She was pretty sure that made what she was about to tell him even worse.

Adem had a reputation for keeping his business life strictly separate from whatever life he had outside of the clinic. None of the women there ever claimed to have slept with him or even dated him. So either he didn't date at all, or…

But he'd earned that reputation somehow. And he'd known exactly how thick that glass was.

There were a few other hints that the man didn't live completely like a monk. But she was pretty sure if he'd had a steady relationship, she would have heard about it at some point or other. Not that she'd gone around trumpeting what had happened between them at the clinic.

And a baby? Would the news of who the father was somehow get out?

What a mess.

"Is there any way you could come over to Hyde Park? I'm not far from there now. I can wait."

"Tell me where in the park, and I'll be there."

Carly gave him a spot that she knew could afford them a bit of privacy. She could have suggested one of the nearby restaurants, but she really didn't want anyone to overhear what she had to say. There might be joggers or cyclists in the park, but those folks were normally not interested in anything other than enjoying their surroundings.

She was there within ten minutes, walking down a shaded pathway lined with trees. There weren't as many people here as she expected, but maybe it was the time of day. Coming to the Italian Gardens, where she was supposed to meet Adem, she found a bench facing one of the ponds. Various fountains shot plumes of water into the air, the mists cooling the surrounding area. The portico off to the right featured a Mediterranean-style tile roof and a white stucco finish. All in all, the atmosphere was just what she needed.

She settled back on the bench to wait. Something about the water soothed her senses and maybe even infused a little bit of that lost courage back into her. Calling him had been the worst. And that silence…

She couldn't blame him, and she hated to think about what that drive to Hyde Park was going to be like for him. But telling him was still the right thing to do. And knowing her mom had vowed to help in whatever way she could made her feel…well, not quite so alone, even if Adem wanted nothing to do with the baby.

Stretching her legs out in front of her, she sucked down another cooling breath. If this had happened when she and Kyle were engaged, would it have spurred her into marrying him?

No, and looking back she realized she hadn't been ready for marriage. She still wasn't. She hadn't finished doing the things she wanted to do in life. She enjoyed her freedom, wasn't ready to give that up.

Except a baby would change all of that, anyway, wouldn't it? Yes. In the best possible way. Right now, in this very moment, she was growing a little person inside of her. What she'd thought was impossible had turned out to be very possible. Her hand crept across her belly in wonder, her heart filling with a hope and love she hadn't known existed. How could this possibly be happening?

But it was.

She closed her eyes and concentrated on the light breeze blowing across her body, and the hand on her stomach. No change in the way it felt. Yet. But if things continued to progress, she would soon become aware of it.

Adem hadn't noticed the tiny scars from the laparoscopic surgery she'd had as a teenager, and she hadn't felt the need to tell him the specifics, only that she'd tried to get pregnant and hadn't been able to.

She'd been too caught up in what was happening and in the certainty that the times they'd spent together weren't leading to anything permanent.

Ha! But they had been. Just not the kind of "permanent" she'd been thinking about at the time.

She tilted her head back, trying to enjoy this moment in her life as she listened to the sounds around her. The steady splash of the fountains as water hit water. The twitter of birds in nearby trees. The conversations of people passing her location.

The bench gave a quick lurch as someone sat beside her, and she had to force herself not to jump. It was him. It had to be. Making her movements slow and deliberate, she straightened and opened her eyes, turning to glance at the spot next to her. "Hi."

"Hello, Carly." Adem's dark eyes met hers, the expression in them unreadable. When he glanced at her hand, she realized it was still splayed across her stomach. She quickly moved it back to her side.

So how did she do this? Blurt out the news in the same way you would rip an adhesive dressing off a wound?

The way he was looking at her made her decide against that. She didn't want to add more stress onto whatever else he was dealing with today.

He saved her the trouble. "I take it your period didn't arrive, despite what you said."

Gulping, she shook her head. "No. It didn't. I had a little queasiness, so I decided to go ahead and take a pregnancy test."

"There's no way it could register that quickly."

"You're right. It couldn't. But it could after almost three weeks."

Was it her imagination or was there a quick flash of relief that crossed his face?

"I haven't been with anyone else, if that's what you're wondering."

The look fled in an instant. God. Had he actually thought—hoped—she might be carrying someone else's child?

"I guess I was right worrying about additional protection."

She clasped her hands in her lap. "I really didn't think it was possible. Not with my history."

"Cehennem."

The word rolled off his tongue and passed through her gut with a shivery sense of doom. "I don't know what that means."

Whatever he'd just said was nothing like those sexy words he'd muttered in Turkish during their times together.

"Sorry. I just never wanted… So the test came back positive."

He never wanted what? To have children? Her insides clenched.

"It did."

He blew an audible breath. "I see. What do you want to do?"

"I'm glad you phrased it that way. This is my issue. I don't expect you to do anything. It's my decision, and I want to have this baby. I need to have this baby."

"Why?"

The question was so quick in coming that she didn't have time to formulate a coherent answer. Instead, the truth came tumbling out in a rush. "I told you I tried to have a baby. It was with my fiancé. But it never worked, even after a year. We broke up soon afterward."

"Did you get checked out?"

"No. I already knew the reasons. I had a twisted ovary when I was younger. It had to be removed, so that left me with one. Which should have been enough. But it wasn't. I assumed I would never have a baby." She looked at him. "But here I am."

"Yes. Here you are."

He still hadn't said how he felt about it. "Like I said, I don't expect—"

"This is my baby too. Of course I want to be part of his or her life. I *will* be a part of it. I just can't... I can't do the whole marriage thing."

She turned toward him in an instant, trying to ignore the quick sting of hurt. "I never said *anything* about marriage. I don't *want* to get married. At all. I was engaged once, and it was a disaster. You said you wanted to know...about the other. So I felt you should know."

Evidently he hadn't expected quite that vehement a response because he stopped her with a rueful-looking grin. "Okay, okay. I didn't realize I was that unattractive a catch."

She couldn't hold back a smile of her own, very glad he didn't seem furious that she was keeping the baby. "I didn't realize I was that terrible of a catch either."

He touched her face, one finger sliding down her jawline in a way that made her shiver. "Like I told you, my family is a mess. Believe me, you're a very good catch. For a man who is better than I am. Marriage and permanent relationships just don't seem to be in the cards for me."

"I'm sure if the right person comes along…"

"Doubtful." He gave a half-shrug, dropping his hand as one ankle came to rest on his knee. He looked over the water in the distance. "Anyway, if you're going to have this baby, I intend on being there."

"Like I said, there's no need. My mom is great, so I have a wonderful support system."

"Hmm. That's something I'll have to think about."

She tilted her head in question.

"About how to tell my folks. They're very old-fashioned. I love them, but we don't always see eye to eye about certain things. Basir…well, he seems to have a monopoly on happiness in our family. And I'm very glad for him."

"I'm serious, Adem. You don't have to play any role you don't want to play."

He turned back toward her. "But it wouldn't be a role, like in a play, would it? I am actually going to be a father. And yes. I am going to be part of his or her life. I just need to think through how to go about it."

What did that mean? That he was going to throw money at the baby, without actually spending time with his child? She needed to make something pretty clear to him right up front. "I don't want or need your money. And I also don't want some kind of benign uncle who will slide in and out of the baby's life. I want stability— the kind that I had growing up. Either you're known as his or her father or you can bother not showing up. I'm not going to lie or pretend otherwise."

He touched her arm. "Hey, I didn't mean that at all. I just need some time to sort through the logistics of it. It's going to change a lot. Maybe even our working relationship."

"Why? People have children together all the time."

He dropped his hand back to his side. "Yes, but I'm heading up the clinic. I don't want rumors swirling around about what happened between us. So I need to decide if I have to step down or not before this gets out."

Horror washed through her. She hadn't even thought about that possibility. She'd been worried about the changes to her own life and hadn't even stopped to think that it might change things for him as well. She'd assumed as long as he knew she didn't expect marriage or much of anything from him that life could pretty much go on as usual. "No! I don't want you to do that. There's no reason to."

"I think there might be. You work for the clinic, and I head it up. If the information were twisted in just the right way…"

"I wasn't planning on shouting the baby's parentage from the rooftops. I understand this is a huge deal, but…" She clasped her hands. "You do good work at the clinic, Adem."

"So do you."

"Do you want *me* to resign?" Lord, she didn't want to do that. She loved her job. Loved helping people like Naomi. The stress that she'd released into the universe came crashing back down onto her shoulders.

"No. The fact is, we shouldn't have slept together in the first place. And since there are always consequences for actions, I need to be willing to face them." His eyes dropped to her abdomen for a second before coming back up. "For what it's worth, I'm glad you're keeping the baby. And happy that you were able to get pregnant. Truly. Just give me a few days to process things."

She nodded her agreement, even as her brain tore through the possibilities. He could step down, which would devastate her. He could decide to keep the baby's parentage a secret. Which would also devastate her.

Or he could decide that the reward was worth the risk and parent this child alongside of her.

She already knew which choice she was hoping for. She just wasn't so sure Adem would be willing to walk out on that limb and risk having it breaking off behind him.

CHAPTER SIX

OVER THE NEXT WEEK, Adem vacillated between optimism and dread. He and his brother had grown up in a household filled with tension. What he'd told Carly had been the tip of the iceberg.

Once his brother's health improved, his dad hadn't been around much, needing to spend the time on his fledgling restaurant, and his mum had seemed relieved by his long work hours. And when they were together, the chilly silences were worse than any fight could have been. They smiled and said the right things when they were out in public, but they were both miserable, and because of their deep-rooted belief in duty, they refused to take the obvious way out.

Despite all of that, his knee-jerk response toward the news that Carly might be pregnant was the M word. But because it had kept rushing to the tip of his tongue, even though he knew in his heart of hearts that it would be the wrong thing to do, he carefully and deliberately told Carly that marriage was off the table. He'd seen the instant flash of hurt that went through her eyes before she countered his words by saying that she didn't want to get married either.

He believed her. That kind of vehemence wasn't feigned. She'd said she'd had a failed engagement, maybe that was part of the reason. So at least she could understand what was at stake. But despite all the rational reasons for not getting married, he'd been surprised to find that her words actually did sting. Damn.

The pregnancy was definitely not planned. But, according to Carly, not unwanted.

His younger brother was ecstatic over the fact that he and Adeline were having a baby. Maybe like Carly, he'd wondered if it were even possible because of his tumor. He'd never talked about the fear of it coming back, but he wouldn't be human if it hadn't at least crossed his mind. But despite all of that, Basir had been willing to plunge into those waters and accept the challenges of fatherhood with joy.

Adem was not his brother. And he'd spent a lot of time as a teenager stepping in to provide the things he felt were lacking in their household. And he'd got rid of his own anger as a result.

His brother seemed fairly well-adjusted. Or, maybe as Carly had said, he'd just found the "right" person. The person who could erase childhood wounds.

Adem had no desire to erase them. Or to try to bypass them only to discover he'd been wrong. He wanted no child of his to grow up in the kind of atmosphere that he had. So the kindest thing he could do for this baby was to take a step back and make sure history did not repeat itself.

Hadn't he already wondered if his many hours spent at work didn't mimic his father's blinkered approach to life? Marriage might even make that worse, causing him to retreat to old patterns when things went badly.

Adem didn't even know if he was capable of a healthy relationship.

He got up from his desk and decided to go for a walk to clear his head. As soon as he made it to the front of the clinic, he encountered a couple of familiar faces. Naomi with her husband, daughter and baby in tow were walking across the foyer. Carly came out of a bank of white mini-offices and smiled at them, ushering them toward her cubicle.

Unable to resist, he started toward the group. Carly spotted him first, and the smile that was on her face faded.

He'd caused that. And he hated it. He remembered his dad's unexpected appearances at home doing much the same thing.

Ignoring her look of dismay, he smiled at the couple and Naomi waved, waiting for him to catch up. "How are you, Mr. Kepler?"

"I'm well." He shook their hands, including Tessa's. "How are you? Adjusting to having a newborn?"

He hadn't meant it as a jab, but Carly stiffened almost immediately.

Douglas held his finger below his left eye, tugging down the lower lid. "Does this tell you anything? We adopted Tessa when she was nearly two, so we got to bypass the nighttime feeds and nappy changes."

Despite the bloodshot eyes, the new father seemed ecstatic with their newest family member.

Naomi shifted the bundle in her arms and swatted

at her husband's arm. "You're not the one feeding her in the middle of the night."

"I'm not equipped to do that." He grinned. "But seriously, Doc, you should try it sometime. There's nothing like seeing this little person you helped create look at you for the very first time."

Of their own volition, Adem's eyes went to Carly, whose face looked a little more pink than it normally did.

"I'm sure it's special."

"Yes. It is. And we're so grateful—to both of you—that Naomi is healthy again."

"I'm glad as well. Any other problems? The headaches are gone?"

Naomi nodded. "Completely. I don't know how to thank you."

"Thank Carly. She's the one who asked me to take a look. She could have just told you to take a couple of ibuprofen."

"Naomi might not be around if that had happened. Neither would Charlotta."

Adem smiled. "Is that her name? It's beautiful. Can I see her?"

The baby's face was hidden in a layer of blankets. Naomi carefully peeled them back and revealed a cute week-old baby with a full head of dark hair. She was wide awake, her curious gaze trying to focus on her surroundings.

The couple's other daughter, who clutched her dad's neck, said, "Lotta likes me."

"Yes, she does," Douglas said. "Your baby sister loves you."

"I love her too."

A pang hit Adem as he glanced at Carly. Would she try to have more kids after this one was born? If so, who would she have them with? God help him, he couldn't even picture her with anyone else.

Except him.

That wasn't going to happen.

"I was just going to take them back to an exam room so I could see how Naomi's doing." Carly's tone was a little more brusque than he expected. But then again, they hadn't really talked about what had happened since that day in the park. Oh, they'd exchanged pleasantries, but just in passing. They were eventually going to have to sit down and hammer out some real details and decide what the other's expectations were.

Expectations? Did he even have any?

Damn. He was starting to think he did, and that wasn't good. Maybe that was part of the reason he'd buried himself in work over the last several days.

Double damn.

Yes, they needed to figure this out. Now was obviously not the time. But when?

"I'd like to do a follow-up MRI as well, to make sure that aneurysm is completely sealed off. I'll put in an order for it, if that's all right with you."

"I'm breastfeeding—will it affect that?"

"No. I'll double-check with the pediatrician at the hospital, but I've had a couple of other patients who've needed contrast dye. At the time, the recommendation was that it didn't require an interruption in breastfeeding."

Douglas spoke up. "Then we want it done."

His wife laughed. "Thanks for giving me some input." She glanced at Adem. "Yes, of course. You have no idea how much better I feel after having the procedure. Have you done a lot of them?"

"Quite a few. And yours went very well." He smiled. "I'll let you get back to your appointment. Carly, could I speak to you for just a minute?"

"Of course. Let me just get them in a room." She'd hesitated long enough before answering to let him know she really didn't want to talk to him. Or maybe she just thought it was inappropriate for him to approach her about it at the clinic. Well, he wasn't going to discuss the pregnancy itself right now; he just wanted to set up a time when they actually could talk about it.

She'd acted like she didn't care who knew, that she wasn't going to lie about who the baby's father was. Maybe she'd changed her mind about that.

After she'd closed the door, she nodded toward an area off to the right, where there was an empty office. Since it was later in the day, no one was in any of the chairs. She sat in one, and he sat across from her. "Okay, I'm listening."

"Now that we've both had some time to think, I'd like to discuss things again. Everything is still the same?"

So much for merely suggesting a time and a place.

"Yes. I'm still pregnant, if that's what you're asking. But…" She paused again. "I really don't want this to affect you, Adem. I didn't give you much of a choice, and even if you'd wanted me to terminate, I would have refused. So…now I'm giving you an out."

He blinked. Then frowned. "I think I made it pretty

clear that I didn't want an out. That I was ready to accept the consequences—whatever they are."

"Consequences. That makes it sound like a punishment of some sort."

"I didn't mean it like that."

"I can see how it might seem that way, though. At least to you. So let's just keep things quiet. I'm not going to advertise that I'm pregnant until it becomes pretty obvious. And if someone asks me who the father is, I'll just say he's out of the picture."

Oh, hell, no. Whatever else Adem might have thought, he had no intention of just fading away. Especially not after seeing the joy Charlotta had brought to Douglas's face.

He swallowed, picturing her with an abdomen swollen with child. *His* child.

"And when she runs to me and grabs my legs at the clinic? Will you say the father's out of the picture then?" He leaned in closer. "Because I'm telling you right now, I plan on being very much in the picture."

"Did you say 'she'?"

"He or she. These are all things I'd like to talk about, before people start asking questions."

She nodded. "I agree. It's just hard to know what to do right now. I'll deny you're the father until my dying breath if you say you're going to step down as the director. Victoria Clinic needs you."

"It needs you too, Carly. But no one person is irreplaceable."

"Tell that to your child after it's born."

"Touché. Okay, tell me where you want to meet, and we'll figure this out."

"I don't have a clue, but definitely not here at the clinic. Or at the hospital."

He thought of something. "Listen, my parents have a boat at a marina on the Thames. We could get away, where there's no chance of anyone overhearing us." He paused. "You said you were queasy the last time we spoke. Maybe that would be a problem."

"Actually, I love being out on the water. When I was younger in the States, we used to do these white-water rafting tours."

"I don't think we'll encounter anything like that on the Thames, since there are speed restrictions everywhere. We likely won't get very far. But the boat has a cover, and we could take a lunch with us. Not to pressure you or anything. I just want to work through things while…you…are still in the early stages."

"Okay." She smiled. "That sounds fun. As long as your parents don't mind."

"It's a family boat. My brother and I have both used it before, but I don't see Basir and Adeline wanting to go out with everything else that's going on. But if there's a problem, I'll let you know, okay?"

She stood. "Okay. Let me at least bring the food, since you're providing the boat."

"How about I give you a call in a few days and we can nail that down along with a date." He stood as well.

"Sounds good." Her hand brushed his in a light touch. "And for what it's worth, I don't regret everything that happened."

His lips curved as she walked away from him and said in a voice too low for her to hear, "Neither do I, Carly. Neither do I."

And he realized for the first time since she'd told him the news, he really meant it.

Carly had opted to meet him at the marina, three days later, rather than have him stop by her place to pick her up and she wasn't sure why. Was she afraid to have him over?

Um, that would be a resounding yes. Despite her insistence that what had happened between them was over, there'd been a subtle buzz of anticipation ever since he'd mentioned going out on the boat. If she'd thought Adeline's pregnancy was going to connect her and Adem's lives on a temporary basis, what was having a baby of their own going to mean?

And what about the way she'd reached for his hand and told him she didn't regret what had happened?

Was that true?

Lord help her, yes, it was. As hard as she tried to fight off her feelings for him, they were relentlessly growing. And she wasn't sure how to stop them.

It had to be the baby. Or hormones. Or something other than the fact that the man was eating away at her defenses without even trying.

She still wanted him physically as well, which made it even worse. But Carly did not see herself as a "friends with benefits" kind of person. Were they friends?

She thought they might be heading in that direction…before the pregnancy had happened. And now? She didn't know. What she felt for Adem seemed to blur the boundaries she'd drawn for herself. Well, there was one way to sharpen those lines again.

She could assert her independence and make sure

he knew that, ultimately, she called the shots with this baby.

And when she runs to me and grabs my legs?

As soon as he'd said those words, she'd pictured a little girl with dark pigtails and Adem's smile running toward him, arms opened wide. It was an image she hadn't been able to banish.

It had replayed in her head time and time again, becoming clearer and clearer.

Which made it all the more important to put a cleaver between "want" and what was best. For her. For their child.

And yet here she was, picnic hamper in hand, getting ready to go out on a boat with him. And that anticipation was still there, rumbling in the background, growing stronger by the minute.

It's not a lover's gondola, Carly.

Really? Meat, cheese, grapes—the things she'd brought for their meal? Weren't those the things that were normally eaten in intimate settings?

Not in this case.

Adem appeared on the dock, dark hair ruffling in the breeze, wearing dark brown shorts, those tanned legs sporting the kind of lean muscle that made her mouth water. Her anticipation revved up a couple of notches, becoming the roar of outboard engines.

Independence, Carly, remember?

She suddenly felt self-conscious in a pink sundress that exposed pale calves and white feet. Thinking about it, her leather thong sandals were probably not the best choice of footwear for a boat either. But it was too late now, and like he'd said, they weren't likely to go far with the speed restrictions.

He came up beside her and took the basket. "I'm glad you came."

"I told you I would."

"Yes, you did. I wondered if you actually would, though."

She forced a smile. "You'll find I keep my word."

"So do I."

A reference to when he told her to make no mistake, that he would be a part of his baby's life?

This conversation could get very sticky very quickly. She decided to change the subject to something a little more neutral. "Where's the boat?"

"Halfway down the dock on the right. The *Ankara*."

"Named after the city?"

"It's where my parents were born." He walked beside her as they made their way across the plank walkway where boats bobbed on either side of them. "Where they were married."

"How long have you lived here in the UK?"

"I was fifteen when my dad moved us here."

She didn't know that. But it made sense. "Wow, his restaurant must be fairly successful, since he owns a boat like this."

"Yes. He works very hard. In that he's successful."

But not in other things? He'd said his family was a mess.

Was that why he wanted to be a part of his child's life? To fulfill something that he thought was lacking in his own upbringing? She had no idea, and right now she was afraid to ask. She wanted him to love his child for who he or she was, not because it was a means to an end.

The bubble of anticipation deflated just a bit.

He'd mentioned before that he wasn't sure how he was going to tell his parents, which further supported the idea that things were strained in the family.

The *Ankara* was where he said it would be. All white with sharp black lettering, the boat was immaculate. It wasn't a yacht, but it was bigger than what she'd pictured in her head. With a white canvas cover that stretched from the steering wheel to about halfway back, there were four seats in the shade and four behind that, where passengers could catch some sun.

Adem stepped across onto the boat, set the hamper on one of the seats and then held his hand out to her. She hesitated before gripping his fingers and letting him help her aboard. As the touch continued to linger, she was hyperaware of every inch of his skin against hers.

Lord, hadn't she read that pregnancy could make her crave things? Like what they'd done in his flat? But that wasn't supposed to happen until the second trimester. And in actuality, that craving had been there long before she'd ever become pregnant. If she'd hoped it would magically disappear, she was clearly mistaken.

It was very much alive and well.

She hopped on the boat and let go of him in a hurry, afraid he might somehow guess her thoughts.

"I like your dress."

His smile made her heart trip a time or two. So much for trying to change her train of thought. That evidently wasn't going to happen.

"Thanks. I don't think I've ever seen you in shorts."

His smile turned crooked. "I won't remind you of what you have and haven't seen me in."

God, there was that. She'd seen him in a whole lot of nothing. But reminding her of that fact wasn't going to help either of them. Especially since she was now picturing him without those shorts.

She decided to let that comment pass without a reply.

Picking up the basket, he made his way to the covered area where the steering wheel and controls were, not that she was familiar with nautical terms. "It's turned out to be a really nice day."

"It has. We can unzip the front portion of the cover to let the air blow through, once we stop, otherwise it'll get pretty warm under here."

"I can imagine." She was getting warmer by the minute, in fact.

"Ready to go play?" he asked.

She blinked, suddenly picturing that window in his apartment. *God, Carly, he's talking about getting under way, not playing around on the boat. What is wrong with you?*

"I'm ready to head out whenever you are."

With that, Adem undid the mooring lines that kept the boat tied to the dock, then started the engines. Minutes later, they were out of the marina and moving onto the Thames itself.

There were stairs leading to an area somewhere below deck. Probably sleeping quarters and maybe a galley kitchen. People routinely slept on their boats in the States, where boating was a big business, but she wasn't sure if things were the same here.

She wasn't going to ask for a tour, though, that was

for sure. Because seeing a bed would send her thoughts floating back to another kind of tour. And that was one word she avoided like the plague nowadays.

Instead, she settled in and tried to enjoy the sights on the waterway amid the throb of the engines and the traffic of other boaters. She wasn't sure of their destination, and right now she didn't care.

Adem glanced over. "How are you feeling? I know you said you weren't sick, but I didn't think to ask about seasickness."

"So far, so good." The conditions seemed pretty smooth. If anything, it was exhilarating to be away from the hospital. He'd been right about that. She needed to cut loose and have fun sometimes. She hadn't realized it until she'd spent that night with him. It was one of the few times her mind hadn't been crammed full of thoughts of patients. Maybe that was part and parcel of being a midwife, since one of her patients could go into labor at any minute. Even while she was here on a boat. She glanced down at the screen of her phone, half expecting to see that that had indeed happened, but so far there was nothing there, other than a text from her mom asking if she was free for lunch on Friday. She picked it up and started to reply.

"No work allowed."

Carly crinkled her nose. "I can't exactly schedule when my patients go into labor, you know. And right now my life is free enough that I can easily get away."

"Not right this second, unless you jump overboard."

She laughed. "That's not what I meant, and you know it." She enjoyed this light and easy chatting, felt like she hadn't done this with him in ages, if ever.

"I do. But I also know that soon your life is about to get a lot more complicated."

What? Oh, he meant with her pregnancy. So much for light and easy. But he was right. Things were going to change drastically. Something she didn't want to think about right now. She decided to change the subject. "Where are we going, anyway?"

"There's a little marina I have in mind. It'll take us about an hour to arrive." He nodded toward shore. "Look, the Eye."

She hadn't realized they would pass the London Eye, and it looked bigger somehow from the water. Strangely, she had never been on the iconic Ferris wheel. Maybe because she wasn't really a fan of heights. And then she found herself searching for his apartment building.

Her fear of heights certainly hadn't bothered her that time. Maybe because her mind had been a lot more wrapped up in what he was doing to her.

In more ways than one.

She glanced to her belly, her mouth twisting in a sardonic smile.

What were they going to do?

She had no idea. She was still dwelling on those thoughts when Adem throttled down the engines, pulling into a section of the river where there were all types of boats moored, from large sailboats to vessels much smaller than Adem's family's boat.

Wow, an hour had gone by already. Despite the slow speed, she'd enjoyed puttering down the river.

She got up and, under his direction, helped him secure the boat in one of the berths, tossing some kind of padded bolster things over the side. "What are these called?"

"Fenders."

She leaned over and felt one of them. "I would have guessed bumpers."

"Well, they serve the same purpose. Thanks for the help."

She hated to admit it, but it was fun. There was a weird camaraderie between them that she'd never really experienced before. Not even with Kyle.

She realized she'd been on the defensive with Adem more often than not in most of their earlier dealings. When had that started changing? Maybe with Naomi and her aneurism?

She wasn't sure. But something had definitely shifted.

Maybe because you slept with the man, Carly.

Was that really it? She didn't think so. And this baby would link them forever.

Forever.

If someone had told her a year ago that she would be connected to Adem for the rest of her life, she would have said they were crazy.

She hadn't chosen this path, but now that she was here, she was going to make the best of it. So she walked over to the hamper, just as a swell picked the boat up and tilted it a bit.

"Ooops!" She grabbed at the railing, only for an arm to wrap around her waist and haul her against him.

She swallowed and glanced up over her shoulder to see Adem looking down at her, a slight frown on his face. "Are you okay?"

"Just didn't expect the boat to shift when it did, I guess. Sorry about that. I don't think I would have fallen."

"Sea legs. You'll get them as time goes on."

She wasn't too sure of that, since they were feeling shakier by the minute. But that had nothing to do with the boat and everything to do with the man pressed against her. "Maybe I just need to sit for a second."

He led her over to one of the chairs and stood over her, the frown still in place. "Will you be okay while I go get the air moving?"

A little frisson of contentment went through her, until she thought of those pep talks about being more like her mom. Adem was not always going to be there with her. At least, not like he was right now. "I'm fine. Really."

"Okay, I'll be right back." Adem went to the front and unzipped part of the cover and almost immediately a breeze washed over her. It was luscious. Cooling and refreshing, sliding over her bare shoulders and sifting through her hair.

She tipped her head back. "Oh, that's lovely. So very good."

"Yes, it definitely is."

When she glanced up, he was standing over her, his eyes smoldering with an intensity she recognized from his apartment. Oh, God. She swallowed, trying to calm her heart, which was suddenly racing out of control. "Thank you so much for bringing me out here. I love it."

He dragged a hand through his hair before turning away and grabbing the picnic hamper. "I'm glad. Are you hungry?"

Surprisingly she was. She'd packed extra crackers just in case her morning sickness came back, but so far all was well. "I could definitely eat."

Adem quickly unpacked the basket onto a table screwed into the floor of the boat. Since the small table sat between their two chairs, it almost made it seem like an intimate dinner for two. All they lacked were candles.

Ridiculous. This wasn't some romantic meal. It was a planning session. Better if she remembered that fact.

He set out the plates and the tins of meats and cheeses and fruit. "This looks good."

"In the States fried chicken is the normal fare for picnics, but I guess I've lived in England too long. This sounded more appetizing to me."

"In Turkey it would have been different as well. But you're right. I've become accustomed to life here."

Would being with Adem become as normal as life in London? She couldn't imagine that, but unless he changed his mind, they would be spending a lot of time together outside of the clinic. Would being without Adem feel strange and foreign?

For her sake and his, she hoped not. It would not do to start thinking as if they'd been drawn together by anything other than the baby. If not for that, she would have spent one thrilling night and one naughty day with him. The odds were one of them would eventually leave the clinic and drift toward another job, taking with them the need for continued contact. It had happened with Kyle, despite his promises of them keeping in touch. Not that she wanted to since there was no longer anything binding them together.

Things were different this time, though. Even if she returned to the States at some point in her life, Adem would still be her baby's father. That was never going to change.

"What are you thinking?"

She looked at him. "About how strange it is to be sitting on a boat with you, getting ready to map out a future that I can't even envision at the moment."

"I know."

"What about your parents? Surely this isn't something you can keep from them forever." She couldn't imagine not telling her mom.

He'd said something about them being old-fashioned. "They wouldn't really expect you to marry me just because of the pregnancy?"

"They came from a culture very different from this one." He glanced over the bow as she dished out the food. "They actually didn't marry for love."

"What?" Oh, God, had they married because his mom had gotten pregnant?

"It was arranged. I know it's hard to understand how things like that can happen from a Western point of view, but there are all kinds of reasons to get married. In their case, it benefited their families."

"Wow. Are they happy?" They had two children together, after all.

"That's a complicated question. They've been together for many years. I'm not sure that constitutes happiness, but it's what they both know. I'm pretty sure my dad has had other women over the years, but I don't know that for sure."

"If that's the case, why would your mom stay?"

"She's the only one who can answer that. All I know is that I'll never follow in their footsteps."

"You're not ever going to get married?"

"I never thought there'd be a reason to."

Before now.

Had that thought just sifted through his mind like it had hers?

"But your brother married." Something about that made her incredibly sad. "What about love?"

"If there is such a thing, I haven't felt it."

Unfortunately for Carly, she was beginning to wonder if she might not be dangerously close to feeling that emotion.

"I believe in it, even though my only serious relationship didn't work out." She was surprised that her breakup hadn't tarnished that belief, but if anything it just made her aware of the need to tread with care around this man. Because the twinges she'd been feeling here and there...

Twinges? Those were more like...

No. Don't think about that right now. The only kind of love she wanted was the type that a mom had for her baby. The love that she now felt for this little kidney bean she was carrying around inside of her.

His next words interrupted her thoughts.

"Let's talk about the pregnancy. And to answer your earlier question, yes, I will probably have to tell my parents, but I'd rather do that after the baby is born."

The thought of being at home and delivering the baby without Adem in attendance made her swallow. But she had no right to expect him to eagerly offer to be there. She wasn't sure she should even want him there, but she did. And she had no idea why.

Her mom would come. Would even be her birth partner if she asked her to. But Carly wanted more.

"It's going to be pretty obvious to your brother and sister-in-law that I'm pregnant at some point. Unless you want me off the case."

"No. They both want you to deliver the baby." He blew out a breath. "I have no idea how I'm going to handle any of that."

She screwed up a measure of courage and picked up her fork. One way or another, she needed to know. "Are you even planning on being there when the baby is born? If you're not, I'd rather you tell me now."

CHAPTER SEVEN

BE THERE? WHAT did she mean?

"I've already said I want to be in the baby's life."

She shook her head and speared a bite of meat with her fork, then stabbed the tines through a piece of cheese. The movements were jerky, as if she was really unsure of his answer. "I know, but I'm not talking about that. I mean when he or she is born. Do you want to be there during labor?"

He hadn't thought that far down the road. But some little voice told him to tread carefully, that his answer was important. "Yes. Unless you don't want me there."

Her fork stopped halfway to her mouth and her eyes closed for a split second before looking at him again.

It was the right answer. He saw it in her face. "What about your parents? You said you didn't want them to know until after the baby was born."

"That might be a little tricky if you decide to have the baby in the hospital where lots of people know both of us."

"I want to have it at home. With just my mom and midwife in the room. And you, if you want to be there."

There was a little tickle of panic in the back of his

throat that he did his best to suppress. He'd told her he wanted to be there, but suddenly he wasn't sure. Maybe she didn't want him as a birth partner, though; after all, she said her mother would be there.

And if she did want that? Then there would be birthing classes to attend. Maybe even parenting classes. Together.

It doesn't mean you're marrying her, Adem. Just that you're supporting the mother of your child and ultimately your child.

"How do you feel about me meeting your mother? Before the actual birth?" If he was going to do this, he didn't want to suddenly be thrust into a room with a woman he'd never seen before and hope she didn't resent him for not marrying her daughter. He knew his mother well enough to know that would be exactly her reaction. In fact, she was going to have a hard time understanding why Adem didn't marry Carly.

"Do you want to?"

It took him a second to realize she was answering his question about her mother and not reading his thoughts about marriage. "I think it might be a good idea, don't you?"

"If you're worried about her reaction, don't. I promise you, she's supportive. Thrilled even."

"She'll have to meet me at some point, right?"

"I guess so. I'll check with her and see when a good time might be. But think about it carefully. Once we go down that path, there'll be no turning back. They'll know who you are."

"I think we're already at the point of no turning back. Don't you?"

A smile played at the corners of her mouth. "I think we've been there more than once."

All of a sudden the heat that he'd felt as he watched her enjoy the breeze a few minutes ago returned full force. So did that spark that said maybe marriage was the right answer, after all. "Yes. We have."

Their eyes met. Clashed.

Carly was the first to look away. "I, um, if you're sure about meeting my mom…"

"I am."

"Okay, I'll set it up. Your parents are eventually going to meet me too, when you tell them, right? Are they going to hate me?"

"No. They'll be disappointed with me. Not with you." And they would be. There was no mistaking that. But in the end, it was his life and he'd live it as he saw fit, just as he always had. Just as Basir lived his.

"They'll be mad because you didn't marry me?"

She'd hit the nail on the head. "Yes."

"You could just tell them you tried, but I refused. It wouldn't be a lie, since I did tell you I didn't want to marry anyone. And I don't."

That actually wasn't a bad idea, except for the fact that they would then badger Carly endlessly, trying to talk her into something neither of them wanted. "I don't think that would work. Why don't you let me deal with my parents."

"Sorry. I wasn't trying to interfere." She fiddled with the edge of her plate, making some tiny adjustment. He realized she'd taken his words the wrong way.

He reached across and touched her face, hooking his finger under her chin. "Hey. I know you're trying to help, and I appreciate it. I wasn't telling you to mind your own business. I just don't want to put you in an awkward situation. I would end up having to tell my parents to back off and leave us alone."

"It's okay. And no, I don't want you to have to do that. We've still got months. Let's give it some time."

"I agree."

With that they were able to move on to lighter topics as they ate, like baby names and what they hoped the child would be like. Carly actually wanted a combined name with influences from both of their home countries.

Adem hoped he or she would look like Carly. The way the light breeze blew her hair off her face, revealing high cheekbones and pale creamy skin. But with his darker skin and dark hair, there would probably be some kind of meeting in the middle. He smiled. He couldn't believe he was actually thinking about things like this.

"Oh, I almost forgot. The portable ultrasounds are going to be delivered next week. The manufacturer is coming over to show us the basics of how to use them. With everything that's going on, I didn't remember to tell you."

"Wow, I had no idea they'd be here this soon."

"I didn't either. I thought it would be a few more weeks. I'll let you know when they want to meet with us."

"Thank you. If I were a little further along, I would offer to be the guinea pig."

"I'm sure we have plenty of patients who'll be happy to volunteer."

"Maybe even Adeline."

"Maybe. I'll run it by her."

She finished her food and took a drink of her water. She'd brought a bottle of wine for him, she said, in case he wanted it. He'd opted for water instead, claiming he still needed to drive the boat home, which he did. But there was also something in him that wanted to keep her company. And that made him take a mental step back.

Was he playing house here?

He'd told her he didn't want a relationship, and he didn't. So what was with the intimate little boat ride? The talking about birth partners and whether he would or wouldn't be in that room when his child was born? All of this had seemed like a good idea at first. Until it didn't. Probably about the time that he realized how beautiful she looked sitting in that chair. How much he wanted to kiss her. To feel her belly at each stage of pregnancy.

These were dangerous games. Ones he had no business playing. Time to put a stop to it.

"Are you ready to head back?"

Maybe she sensed the change in mood, because she wrapped her arms around her waist and said, "Of course. Whenever you are."

Carly acted tough as nails at times, but then there were these little flashes of vulnerability that caught him off guard. And he hated when he was the one who brought them out in her.

Like just now. And when he'd told her he wanted nothing to do with marriage.

But to pretend things were different would just bring heartache of a different kind on down the road. He'd witnessed that firsthand. So, time to put things back on a more even keel.

He helped her stow away the leftovers and secured the basket. Then she helped him pull up the anchor and head back to his home marina.

Carly was quiet on the return trip, but he wasn't sure what he could say or do that would salvage the situation so he decided to let it ride. There'd be plenty of time to figure out the best way to relate to each other when he was a little further from the situation.

Hell, what he meant was a little further from her. Whenever he was around Carly, he didn't seem to be able to think straight. But he needed to figure it out and fast. Before he said something or did something there was no coming back from.

Carly got a call in the middle of the night that one of her patients was in labor. She was exhausted, having been out in the boat for five hours with Adem. An outing that had seemed to start out well, but then at some point he'd become distant, pulling out of that berth in a hurry. He'd barely spoken to her on the way home. Once she sensed the change in him, she went silent as well. They'd said a brief goodbye, and Adem had carried the picnic basket to the car for her. She'd gotten in her vehicle and left as if the hounds of hell were pursuing her. Only they weren't. Neither was Adem. And he'd made that point crystal clear.

She suddenly wasn't sure she wanted to have him meet her mom. Or be at the birth. In fact, she was rethinking a whole lot of things. On a lot of different levels.

Arriving at the house, she found the expectant mom

in bed, laboring, her husband beside her, guiding her through her breathing. Touching her. Rubbing her feet, her back—wherever she needed him to be, he was there.

She took a deep breath, trying not to picture Adem doing those things for her. Instead, she forced herself to focus on the situation at hand.

"Hi, Gloria. How are we doing?"

"Good. This feels much the same as our last two children." She gripped her husband Ned's hand. "I don't know what I'd do without him."

"She probably wouldn't be in this predicament if it weren't for me."

Carly smiled, but it wasn't real. The ache she'd had moments earlier quadrupled in size. She'd had this ideal little scenario of her own childbirth experience mapped out in her head. And it looked exactly like this one. Only Carly would be in that bed and Adem would be the one giving her encouraging little touches. Murmuring to her.

She stabbed that dream in the chest, because it wasn't going to happen. If it was anything like the way the day yesterday had ended up being, Adem would be sitting in a chair, while she lay turned away from him, trying desperately not to show him how much she needed his support.

Dammit. She didn't need it. Didn't need him. No matter what her heart might say.

Carly checked Gloria's cervix. Eight centimeters already. And the woman was still optimistic. Which wasn't the norm with a lot of mothers. At some point they usually started turning in on themselves, too caught up in what was going on inside their bodies.

But then Gloria and Ned had partnered together for two other children. They had this down to an art.

"I'm just going to get set up. Is there anything you need right now?"

"No. Just some ice cubes. But Ned has those for me."

Right on cue, he scooped up the glass and helped her pick a few out, while Carly got her instruments set up on clean towels on the bedside table.

Maybe she was going to have to swap things out and let her mom be her birthing partner, while Adem simply observed. She wasn't sure she was ready for that level of intimacy with him.

But she'd had such hope.

Was she pinning her hopes on him in other areas as well? Like being there when their child took his or her first steps? Or birthday celebrations? Special milestones?

You're not being fair, Carly. He's still getting used to things.

Just like she was. Maybe instead of just tossing him to the side, she should watch for patterns. If they repeated over and over, then she was going to have some hard choices to make. But now wasn't the time. No one thought clearly at three in the morning.

But she'd better figure out how to put her mind back on her job. For Gloria, Ned and this baby, who was about to make an appearance.

At nine centimeters and fully effaced, excitement crackled as they prepared to bring a new life into the world. Gloria was most comfortable on her side, so Carly let her guide her own delivery. As a midwife, she was there to assist and keep the mom and baby as safe as possible. And if something went sideways, she would take things to the next level. But she didn't expect that to happen in this case.

Ten centimeters. "Okay, Gloria, when you feel the urge to push, you can go ahead."

Ned had opted to stay up by his wife's head to support her and keep her morale high during the process. They made a good team. A team that obviously worked together in a lot of areas of their lives, not just this delivery.

Another thing she wouldn't have in common with Adem.

You work at the hospital with him. That should count for something.

Yes. And she'd worked together with him on Naomi's case.

But was that the same thing? No. But it was either take what they had right now, or nothing at all. There were no other options, so she should stop beating herself and Adem up over something that couldn't be helped.

"I need to push." Gloria's voice broke through her thoughts, and she stopped to put her mind on what was in front of her. Guiding her through fifteen minutes of strong contractions and pushing, the head appeared. Then a shoulder.

Carly eased the presenting shoulder out and then the other. As soon as that happened, the baby slipped out on the next push. She carried the newborn in its towel up to Gloria and Ned. "You have a little girl."

Adem had mentioned having a girl. And they'd talked about the name Derya Ann, which she'd loved as it incorporated both their cultures.

Placing the baby on Gloria's chest, skin to skin, she watched the cord as it continued to pulse.

Ned leaned down to kiss his wife's head. "She's absolutely beautiful. Just like you."

With her free hand, Gloria reached up to pull him back down to her. "She's both of us. We made this beautiful treasure."

Carly's fingers touched her own belly. What Gloria said was true. This couple's new baby wasn't one person or the other. She was both of them. A melding of two identities and genes, and in their case…love.

There was a saying that two out of three wasn't bad. And together she and Adem had made the tiny form that was now nestled safely inside of her.

Their baby.

Why did she keep second-guessing everything? Because she and Adem were nothing like Gloria and Ned. Nothing about the situation made her feel secure, and it bothered her that she even needed that. She was a grown woman who had loved and lost and very nearly lov—

Stop. Just stop.

"Ned, the cord has stopped pulsing—do you want to cut it?"

"Yes, please."

Handing him the surgical scissors, she clamped close to the baby's belly and showed him where to cut. It was sliced through in a second and looked perfect. Just like the newborn.

A half hour later the baby was snug and safe, and Carly had completed the documents that recorded the birth and cleaned up her instruments.

"I'm going to go so you can get acquainted with your

little one." The couple's other two children had slept through the birth, so they wouldn't meet their new sister until tomorrow.

Gloria reached for her, gripping her hand. "Thank you so much for coming. We couldn't have done it without you."

"I loved being here. I'm glad everything went so well." She smiled at the baby, who was already nursing. "I'll see myself out. Call me if you have any questions or concerns."

"We will. Thank you again."

Carly left the house and climbed into her car. Now that the rush of adrenaline had worn off, she was flat tired. Exhausted, in fact.

She drove to the first traffic light, only to have it turn red just before she arrived. All she wanted was to get home and climb in bed. She was due at the clinic in three short hours. If it weren't for Adem, she would have called to see if someone could cover for her for a couple of hours, but the sonogram machines were due to arrive this morning, and she really didn't want him to know she'd been out this late at night. Although that was ridiculous. He was just as apt to get a middle-of-the-night call from the hospital asking him to come look at a head trauma.

Resting her hands on the top of the steering wheel, she waited for the light. When it turned green she started through the intersection. From the corner of her eye she saw a movement and slammed on her brakes, but not soon enough to avoid the vehicle that hit full force against the side of her car. She felt herself spinning, head whipping around to the side, her foot still pressed hard against the brake. Her hand went to her stomach as she finally came to a jerking stop. She sat there for what seemed like an eternity, feeling a warm trickle down the side of her right temple.

She reached over to unbuckle the seat belt and then realized with horror that she hadn't pushed the bottom section down her hips as far as she should have, and that in keeping her from crashing through her windshield, her body had lunged against the belt with terrific force.

A sense of nausea built in her chest, and she leaned sideways, vomiting onto the seat. The street was eerily silent and there was no sound from anyone in the other car. Were they hurt? Wiping the back of her hand across her mouth, she reached over to try to find her cell phone, thankfully locating it immediately.

Oh, God, her baby. How hard had she hit that seat belt? Hard enough that her chest hurt from the impact.

She glanced at the screen and saw her last call was from Adem, telling her about the sonogram machines arriving tomorrow. Without thinking, she pushed the button and listened to two rings before her muddled head realized she should be calling emergency services, not Adem. She hung up and dialed the number that everyone knew by heart. In a shaky voice she told them her location and that there was another vehicle, but it was somewhere behind her and she couldn't see...

"Stay in your vehicle. Help is en route."

She lifted her hand to her head to find the source of the bleeding. Something on her temple stung. Maybe she'd hit her head.

The phone buzzed again, and thinking it was the dispatcher calling back she answered, only to hear a sleepy masculine voice. "Carly? Did you try to call me?"

"I... I..." Hearing his voice suddenly made a wall of emotion erupt, and she gave a half-sob.

"Where are you?" His voice sharpened as if he'd suddenly come fully awake.

"At an intersection." She tried to find a sign, but her eyes hurt. "I don't know which one. I had a delivery tonight. A baby girl, like ours." No, wait. She didn't know if it was a girl.

A sense of sleep was starting to take over again, only this didn't quite feel like the normal tiredness she'd had earlier.

"Carly!" His voice made her blink.

"...was an accident. I think...an ambulance."

"Where was your patient? Give me the address."

"Mmm...just want to sleep."

"No! Tell me where you are."

She tried to open her mouth to tell him, but nothing came out. Then doing what she'd longed to do ever since she left Gloria and Ned's house, she laid her head back against the seat, closing her eyes. She still heard Adem's voice off in the distance, but it was growing fainter and fainter as her hand dropped to the seat beside her.

With a sigh, her pain melted away along with her fear and she gave in to the wave that was closing over her head.

Derya Ann. Sleep well, baby.

CHAPTER EIGHT

ADEM SKIDDED INTO the Queen Victoria and practically sprinted past the admissions desk in the A&E, ignoring the shocked eyes of the staff members, some of whom knew him. All he knew was that Carly had been in a car accident, the other driver getting off with barely a scratch, although he was flaming drunk. The man had run a traffic light.

Dammit.

Of course Adem wasn't on Carly's list of emergency contacts, so he was going in there as a doctor and not as the father of her child. He was told she'd hit her head, bringing back eerie memories of the child he'd fought so hard to save but had ultimately lost.

At four in the morning, the hospital was quieter than during normal operating hours, so at the first shut exam room door, he knocked and then peeked in. There she was. Dane Hampton, one of the other neurosurgeons, was with her.

"How is she?"

The man's head tilted when he saw him. "Adem? I didn't know you were on duty tonight."

And here came the explanations, none of which he

had. "It's complicated. She works at the clinic. How is she?"

"I think she may have a slight concussion. We were about to take her to X-ray and make sure nothing else is broken."

"She's pregnant." The words came out before he could stop them. But since Carly hadn't shared the news with anyone other than her mother, he wanted to make sure they knew that before doing radiographs.

Dane glanced at a computer screen. "I see no record of that. Are you sure?"

"Yes. Like I said, she works at the clinic." He swallowed hard. "She told me."

"Confirmed? Or suspected?"

Actually, Adem didn't know if she'd had another pregnancy test done, or if she'd stopped at the one. "She's pretty sure."

"Okay. How far along, do you know?"

"Not far." Let's see, today would make almost four weeks.

Dane made a sound in his throat. "She's got bruising from the seat belt on her chest and across her abdomen."

Her abdomen?

He swore. Was the baby okay? Hell, none of that mattered right now. All he was concerned about was Carly.

"Has she regained consciousness?"

"Not yet. I pulled her records. She was out on a call, had just left the location."

At four in the morning? No, the call would have come earlier. But she had to be exhausted.

"Any sign of anything else going on?"

"Her pupils are normal and reactive. Blood pressure and temp are normal. As far as I can tell, she just conked her head."

Almost as soon as he said it, Carly's eyes fluttered and then opened, trailing around the room. He went up to the bed and looked down at her, ignoring the need to take her hand. "Hey. How are you feeling?"

"The baby?"

"I'm sure the baby is fine." The last thing he wanted to do was scare her.

"Hmm…" Her eyes closed for a second before re-opening. "We still haven't thought of a boy's name yet."

Dane's glance sharpened, coming to rest on him. He nodded toward the back of the room. When Adem followed him, he said, "Is there something I should know?"

It wasn't up to him to tell the other doctor anything. That was Carly's decision.

"Like I said, it's complicated. I just want to make sure she's okay." He would figure out all of the other stuff later. No need to tell the other man that they'd slept together but were not in a relationship, even though he knew Dane wasn't a gossip.

"That's what I'm trying to do. But if you have any personal involvement with this…*patient*…then you need to take a step back and let me handle this."

Dane was right. He knew he was. But man, turning Carly over to him was not an easy pill to swallow. "I know."

"Let me finish examining her, and then I'll come out and let you know. But thanks for telling me about the pregnancy. I've called her mother. She's on her way in."

Great. So much for setting up a time to meet her. It looked like fate had taken that out of both of their hands.

"Thanks." He hesitated. "If you could keep this between us for now, I would appreciate it."

"As long as Carly doesn't tell me something untoward happened between you, then what happens between staff members is their business, not mine. I met my wife at this hospital." He said it with a smile.

Little did the man know that he and Carly weren't getting married. Or engaged. Nor anything that remotely looked like the joining of two lives.

Hadn't that already happened, though?

"I'll be in my office."

"Okay, I'll see about having her ultrasounded. If she's three or four weeks out, we should be able to see the gestational sac at least. But we probably won't know the effect on the pregnancy for at least a couple of days. If she miscarries, it'll be somewhere in that time frame."

Trudging to his office was hard. But he couldn't demand to be there with her. He'd already closed the door on anything that smacked of commitment.

How about saying he wanted to be a part of the baby's life? Didn't that constitute commitment?

Not in the eyes of the hospital or the law. Carly was the only one who could give permission for him to know anything.

And that sucked. Big-time.

Once she was well enough, he was going to ask to be included on her emergency contact list. If she hadn't called him, he wouldn't have even known she was in an accident until after he arrived at work and realized she was missing. He didn't like that.

What if she'd been killed?

Or her brain had started swelling?

He closed his eyes, pinching the bridge of his nose between his fingers to stop the tension headache that was gathering.

And if she didn't want him on that list? He really had no right to demand to be notified, even though the baby was his.

It wasn't just the baby. He genuinely cared what happened to her.

Dammit. If he wanted to meet her mother, maybe he should go to the waiting room instead of hiding out in his office. With that thought in mind, he started to get up from his chair, only to have his mobile ring.

Thank God.

He answered. "Carly. Are you okay? The baby?"

A female voice who was definitely not Carly answered. "This is Madelaine Eliston, Carly's mom. She asked me to call you. Are you…?"

The voice trailed away. "Her baby's father? Yes."

"I see. She talked about wanting to introduce us. Can we meet?"

This wasn't exactly how he'd imagined this going down. Hell, he'd tried not to imagine it at all, but here it was. It made him realize that he probably wasn't going to be able to keep this from his parents for long, and that the idea of trying wasn't a good thing. Carly was handling all of this much better than he was.

"Is she still being examined?"

"Yes, they're doing an ultrasound right now. I'm in the waiting room. Do you want to come here?"

He certainly didn't want her coming to his office.

Not after what had happened in here. "Yes, I'll be right down."

Heading down the lift back to the ground floor, he made his way to the spot where Carly's mom was waiting for him. He definitely wasn't skidding down any halls like he had half an hour earlier. Really, all he wanted to do right now was find out how Carly was. Whether the ultrasound showed anything they could make any sense out of.

He recognized her right away. With red hair and a calm demeanor, she looked very much like her daughter. "Mrs. Eliston?"

"You're Mr. Kepler?"

"Yes, but call me Adem, please."

"I want you to know that I'm very happy for Carly. And she's thrilled."

"Thank you. I'm pretty happy as well."

He was. The accident had focused his thoughts, helped him put his priorities in order.

And if it were too late?

Hell, everything had to be okay. To lose the baby now...

He decided to ask. "Have you heard anything more?"

"Carly has a wicked headache, but the other doctor told me that's pretty normal with a concussion. I can't believe a drunk driver hit her. When will people learn?"

"Unfortunately not soon enough."

A doctor was headed their way, but it wasn't Dane this time. It was the same obstetrician that had consulted with him on Naomi's case. Raphael Dubois.

He glanced at Adem and then at Madelaine. "Are you Carly's mother?"

"I am."

He frowned slightly. "I thought Dane was doing her neurological workup."

"He is. I'm here as a friend of the family." He didn't know what else to say, and the slight tightening of Madelaine's mouth said she wasn't sure she liked the title he'd given himself. But it was too late now.

"Well, we did the ultrasound, and there is definitely a gestational sac there. We're hoping the trauma from the seat belt hasn't shaken things up too much and that the baby stays put. I take it she wants to continue with the pregnancy?"

"Yes." Madelaine said the word before he could get it out, and a good thing because Raphael might start wondering how Adem—a "friend of the family"—would know that Carly wanted her pregnancy to continue.

"Okay, good. Mr. Hampton would like her admitted for observation until tomorrow. Then she needs about a week off to make sure there are no ill effects from the concussion. Are you okay with that? Can Carly come and stay with you for a couple of days?"

That thought suddenly didn't sit well with him. He wasn't sure why, other than he wanted Carly home with him. Where he could keep an eye on her and the baby.

"Yes, of course."

"Great. As soon as we get her settled in a room, you can both go in and see her."

"Thank you."

Left alone once again, Madelaine smiled at him. "She said you're a very nice man, and I believe that."

Did she? Well, Adem wasn't too sure of that right now. "Thanks. She's a wonderful woman."

"Yes, she is. I don't know how all of this came about, but she believes you want what's best for the baby."

"I do, without a doubt."

"That's good to know. Do you also want what's best for Carly? Someone once walked out on her at a very difficult time in her life. I don't want to see her hurt like that again."

By the fiancé she'd told him about? He thought he wanted what was best for all of them. But did he really? Or was he more concerned with his own comfort and trying to change his life as little as possible?

If that was true, then he would not be as good a man as Carly believed. But he had no idea how he should view her. As someone he'd shared a few passionate hours with? Or something more?

Damn. He didn't know. All he knew was that she had somehow got under his skin in a way that no one else had. And it worried him. Made him wonder if all of his plans for his life were about to implode in his face. All of those lectures to himself about not becoming like his dad...

Madelaine was still waiting for an answer to her question. "I'd like to think I want what's best for her. I care about her."

That much was true. Would always be true.

She studied his face for several long seconds before saying, "That's all I needed to hear. Thank you." She then came over and gave him a quick hug, which made him wince.

She probably shouldn't thank him quite yet. He was still very capable of doing something that would hurt Carly, even unintentionally. But he was starting to think more and more that maybe he shouldn't have been so quick to dismiss the idea of marriage. Instead, he'd given a knee-jerk response that he might come to regret.

A nurse came over. "You can see Carly now. It looks like she might have quite a shiner by morning."

She was going to have a black eye? His chest tightened as he thought of how lucky she was that that was all she would have. She could have been killed. Or received a traumatic injury from which she might never recover.

She could still lose the baby.

No. He was not going to think along those lines. Especially knowing what he did about the removal of her ovary and the possibility that she might not be able to get pregnant again, if something happened to the second one.

"I'll let you go in first," he said to Madelaine.

"I think we should both go in. So that she knows we've met and that we're not at each other's throats."

"Did you think we would be?"

"*I* didn't." She laughed. "But Carly gave me a stiff warning, telling me to be nice."

Madelaine had the air of someone who was almost always nice. But he'd bet like any parent she could come down hard on someone who brought harm to their child. Wasn't that why she'd asked him if he had Carly's best interests at heart?

Of course it was. It was probably not so much a question as a reminder.

"Well, she'll be happy to know that you've been a lot nicer than you should have been."

She smiled again, and he found more hints of her

daughter in her facial expressions. "I don't think I have. Carly seems happy about what's happened, and that's enough for me. She respects you a lot. Even before any of this happened. She said you were doing good work in the community. And she was very excited about the ultrasound machines."

She'd talked to her mum about him? No two families could have been more different. He very rarely shared any information about his work life with his folks. Nor did they ask. His dad didn't, anyway, other than to ask if he was doing okay for himself.

"I'm happy about those machines as well. I think it'll make the clinic even more self-sufficient."

"Carly thinks so too." She motioned toward the hall-way. "Shall we go see her?"

Carly looked past her aching head to see her mother and Adem coming into the room.

"Hi." She was a little nervous that they were here together. This wasn't quite the way she'd envisioned doing these introductions. Especially since her brain seemed a little sluggish right now.

Her mom came over and kissed her cheek. "We were both worried."

"I was a little worried myself." Her voice seemed to come from a distance as she tried to focus.

Adem hadn't said anything yet, and she licked her lips. They hadn't been able to tell her with any certainty that the pregnancy would remain viable. And if she miscarried?

Well, he would have no reason to stick around. No reason to go on boating trips or sit in the park with her.

And she found that bothered her. Very, very much. She just wasn't sure why, although her head was busy trying to work something out.

There was no way to know how he would react, unless it happened. And God, she did not want to lose this baby. Not after everything that had happened.

Derya Ann, please still be in there.

She was going to be devastated if she lost it to something so very stupid like a car accident. If she'd just looked a third time before starting across that intersection...

"The other driver. Was he hurt?"

Her mother made a scoffing sound. "Not a bit. It doesn't seem fair, does it? He was drunk and ran a red light, and then gets to walk away without a scratch."

"I'm glad he's okay."

Her mom gripped her hand. "So, the doctor says you have a concussion, but that you should be fine."

"I know. He came in and talked to me. I'm surprised my hard head couldn't take a little tap like that."

"It was more than a little tap, sweetheart. Your car is totaled."

Adem still hadn't said anything, and she was getting even more nervous. Maybe it was because her mom was here. She could be a little intimidating when she wanted to. That came part and parcel with being a single mom and having to make all the decisions herself. Some of that had rubbed off on Carly as well.

Had she said something to Adem that he hadn't liked?

She'd warned her to be nice to him. And honestly,

Adem wasn't a hothouse flower. He was very capable of standing up for himself.

She couldn't stand it any longer. She was going to make him say something. "Adem, when did you get here?"

He slowly walked toward the bed. "You hung up on me after saying you'd been in an accident, so I had no idea where you were. The only thing I could think of doing was coming here."

There was something strained in his voice. A tiny thread of what she'd heard on the night when his patient had taken a turn for the worse. He was worried.

About the baby?

Well, she'd been worried too.

But it wasn't just that. What she saw in his face was different.

"Hey. I'm okay." The urge to hold her hand out for him to take swept over her, but with her mom standing right there, she didn't think he would appreciate it.

As if reading her mind, her mom leaned down and kissed her on the cheek. "I'll let you guys talk for a few minutes while I see if I can find some decent coffee in this place."

Carly smiled. "I'm glad you came."

"You're my world, sweetheart. I wouldn't want to be anywhere else."

"I know." Her mom loved her more than she could possibly deserve. She would do anything for them.

"I'll be back in about fifteen minutes."

She guessed that was her mom's way of warning her to do whatever talking they had to do in that time frame. Or maybe she was worried about coming in and finding them kissing. Or worse.

Not much chance of that with the way she was feeling. Her head really did hurt.

But probably not as bad as Naomi's had.

Her mom was out the door and Carly turned her attention back to Adem, trying to find a smile. "I never did get to try that Turkish coffee you promised me."

He didn't say anything nor did he smile, and as the seconds stretched toward minutes, she began to worry.

"You didn't tell me where you were." Those were the first real words out of his mouth.

"I'm sorry, Adem. I was confused. I'd been thinking about other things on the drive home and was on autopilot. It was late, and I was already sleepy, so I think that combined with the accident just knocked me for a loop."

He did what she'd wanted to do: threaded his fingers through hers. "Are you really okay?"

"I am. I just want the baby to be okay as well. If something happens to her…"

This time he did smile, and it lit up her world. "So you're doing it as well."

"Doing what as well?"

"Thinking of the baby as a she."

She giggled, then put a hand to her head. "Ugh. Laughing hurts. But yes. I'm already thinking of her as Derya Ann. We really do need to come up with a boy's name at some point, just so they both have equal time."

"We could always change Derya to Derrin, if the baby turns out to be a boy."

"I don't like Derrin. At all."

He squeezed her hand. "Okay. No Derrin. Dexter?"

"No."

"Let's talk about that later." He went and grabbed a chair that was folded against the wall and pulled it up to the bed. "You were on a call?"

She stiffened. "Yes. It's my job."

"I wasn't criticizing you. I know how much your patients mean to you. I just want to make sure that you call those in so they can get added to the log. What if you'd been knocked unconscious and hadn't been able to call anyone? It would help me know where to look."

It would help *him* know where to look?

That simple sentence struck a chord in her. He really had been worried. About her, and not just the baby.

"Yes, Mr. Administrator, I logged the call. I also called Emergency Services, so they also knew where to look. And my car is even equipped with that nifty little voice response system that I can use to call for help and has a tracker on it. It wasn't very likely that I would have lain in the middle of the street for very long. Someone would have come across the accident and called it in."

"Okay, I'll give you that." He paused. "I want to ask you something."

"Go ahead."

"Your mother asked if I had your best interests at heart."

She licked her lips. "She's my mom, she has to ask questions like that."

"Well, she's right. If you ever feel I don't, I would like you to tell me."

"Yeah, I'm not going to do that. No one knows my best interests but me. I'm like my mom that way. I've learned to look out for myself and tend to value my independence. So even if you think you know…maybe you don't… Or wait." She shook her head. "Ask me that again when my head doesn't feel like it's been stuffed with cotton."

"Sorry. You're right. We'll save that for later. How about this? Mr. Hampton thinks you should stay at someone's house for a week. He was looking at your mum when he said it, but what do you think about… coming home with me?"

"What? No, that would be a terrible idea."

He let go of her hand, and she realized her head injury really was affecting her. "I mean, it would be terrible because we've seen what happens when I come to your apartment. 'Tours' tend to happen. Tours that result in…" She rubbed her hand on her belly, wincing when she hit a sore spot.

"Are you okay?"

"Mmm…yes, it's just where the seat belt caught me." She swallowed, remembering something. "I should have put it lower on my abdomen, but I was tired and wanted to get home. I won't make that mistake again."

"Okay, so no coming to live with me…unless…" He hesitated. "Would you live with me if we were married?"

"But we're not."

He leaned forward, eyes fastened to hers. "Carly, we could be."

There was a strange intensity in his voice that pulled at something deep inside of her. A kernel of longing that horrified her. He didn't love her. This was about the baby. Nothing more. Nothing less. Like she'd told him a few minutes ago, no one knew her best interests but her. And after her broken engagement, she'd become an expert at self-preservation. And that warning light had just switched itself on.

She swallowed. "No. We couldn't."

"We get along well, we work well together." He attempted a smile. "We agree on a girl's name."

Could he hear himself right now? He sounded like what he'd said about his parents...about their reasons for getting married. That it had been for every reason except the right one: love.

There was no way. She wanted no part of that. Despite her achy head, it was the one thing she knew.

So she said very, very clearly, "No, Adem. I do not want to marry you. Not now. Not ever."

Carly's chest suddenly felt crammed full of the coils he'd put in Naomi's head, and they were slowly cutting off the blood supply to her heart. She was never marrying anyone for reasons other than love. And not just any love. It had to be the kind that flowed in both directions. It was the only way to remain viable, just like the baby nestled in her womb needed a two-way exchange of nutrients. One without the other... Well, that never ended well. She couldn't live without that.

Not even for Adem.

Her mom swept into the room just as he opened his mouth to say something more. Carly was glad. Glad she wasn't going to have to listen to him present her with yet another argument. One that might sound logical to everyone except for her. Besides, it wouldn't matter. Nothing was going to change her mind.

Nothing.

She smiled as her mom talked about what her orchestra would be playing at the next concert a few weeks from now and how she'd love for Adem to come and hear them. But Carly didn't care about concerts. Or anything else. What she did care about was the bleak look that had suddenly appeared in Adem's eyes. A look she didn't understand, but that filled her with foreboding.

He should be rejoicing that he'd dodged that particular bullet yet again, but he didn't look that way. He looked almost…lost.

No, that wasn't right. It had to be her concussion interfering with her thoughts again. The man didn't love her. He'd told her once that he didn't even believe love existed, or something to that effect. So what had brought that offer on?

His brother and his wife? His parents?

No, she had a feeling it was because he wanted to keep an eye on her…make sure nothing else happened that would possibly endanger his baby.

No. Not his baby. *Their* baby.

She had to make sure she kept emphasizing that point, so he didn't start thinking he could make decisions she disagreed with. Like marrying him.

Although he'd suggested, not insisted.

Was there a difference?

She was pretty sure there was.

But she couldn't ask him, because he was getting up, smiling a smile that looked as fake as all get-out. "I have an appointment this morning that I need to go to. But I'll check in on you later. Call me if you need me."

"Okay." She wasn't going to call him for anything. But she wouldn't say that in front of her mom, who would read way more into the words than she should. "See you later. Thanks for checking on me."

"Not a problem."

Except she felt like it was. Only she had no idea what that problem was. Or why. But now wasn't the time to ask him. She could do that later, when he did come to check on her.

Except Adem didn't come later. Nor did he call to see how she was doing. She chalked it up to his being busy and went home the next day with her mom, just like they'd planned. There would be plenty of time to talk later. They could then hammer out what they'd talked about, even if last night was kind of a blur. One thing she did remember, though, was that Adem had asked her to marry him. And she'd been fixated on two-way flows and why marriage between them could never work, because that love would only flow in one direction. From her. To him.

Her mind seized, grabbing that thought and tearing it apart until a stunning realization overtook her.

She loved the man. Had probably loved him from the time she'd asked him to leave the restaurant with her. She just hadn't recognized it for what it was.

And so his proposal should have made her heart sing, should make her want to jump up and shout it from the rooftops, but it hadn't.

Because it had come from a place of duty. Of following in the path that his parents had paved.

In the end she'd turned him down. Not because she wanted to. But because his offer of marriage had seemed to come for all the wrong reasons.

But what if it hadn't? What if his reasons hadn't been wrong at all?

Maybe she needed to sit down and think about what it all meant. To put some kind of brakes on a train that had been running away for far too long. And she knew exactly where she could start.

CHAPTER NINE

SHE'D TURNED HIM DOWN.

Adem sat in his office at the clinic, two portable ultrasound machines at the ready. The tech was coming to demonstrate them this afternoon, and Carly wouldn't be here for it. She was still at her mum's house, would be for another couple of days. He'd decided not to call her, since he'd got the rundown on her condition from Raphael. As far as they knew the pregnancy was still viable, and since she hadn't contacted him either, maybe it was true.

Maybe the woman was just so horrified by what he'd asked that she couldn't bring herself to look at him. After all, what was it that she'd said?

I do not want to marry you. Not now. Not ever.

She'd seen right through his request, and she'd been right to turn him down. So very right.

The words had just appeared on his tongue out of nowhere and out they'd come. She'd once told him she wouldn't settle for anything other than love. And he'd once told her he'd never felt that particular emotion, wasn't sure if he even believed in it.

So how was it that he was sitting here, wondering

why he felt like he'd been run over by a truck and left for dead?

Maybe because the one emotion he'd never believed in—never thought he was capable of feeling—had reached around and grabbed him by the throat. It couldn't be real. It had to be something to do with the baby.

Except he couldn't for the life of him figure out how he could mix up the two. When Carly was in that accident he'd panicked when her voice had begun fading away, and it had had nothing to do with the baby. That worry had been all about Carly.

Maybe that had been part of the tragedy of his parents. Maybe one of them had learned to love and one of them hadn't. How torturous of a union would that be to love someone and never have it returned?

It wouldn't be fair to him and it definitely wouldn't be fair to Carly. He was not condemning her to that kind of existence, even if she had agreed to his crazy proposition.

So what did he do about it? How did they work together and not either come to resent being thrown together time and time again or fall back into the pattern of sleeping together, knowing it was going no further than that?

Carly's mom had asked him if he had her best interests at heart.

His phone rang and he glanced to see it was his brother. Damn. He did not want to talk to Basir right now. But it might be important.

Answering the call, he leaned back in his office chair, staring at the new machines. "Hello?"

"Adem, what the hell is going on?"

He'd never heard Basir raise his voice. Ever. But right now there was an anger in his tone that was impossible to mistake. "What are you talking about?"

"Our midwife is leaving."

He sat forward in a rush. "She what?"

"I just got off the phone with her. She said she'd decided to transfer out of the clinic to the Queen Victoria and that she was notifying her patients that she'd only be available to those who would be having their babies there."

Carly loved being a community midwife. She'd told him that time and time again, had told him how much good the Victoria Clinic was doing in the surrounding neighborhoods. So what on earth would possess her to...

He had. He and his stupid proposal. Hadn't he just been sitting here thinking about how hard it was going to be to keep working together?

Evidently Carly had decided it wasn't just hard...it was impossible.

So she was quitting?

"Honestly, Basir, this is the first I've heard about it. Carly was in an accident a few days ago and was pretty shaken up. I'll talk to her and see—"

"She also said she was pregnant and that our due dates were going to be a little over a month apart."

And it was time to confess. At least to his brother. "The baby is mine."

"Excuse me?"

"I'm the father of Carly's baby."

"But—"

"Exactly. We haven't told anyone, and maybe that has

something to do with all of this. I asked her to marry me, and she turned me down."

"Why would she do that?"

"I wasn't sure at the time. But I think I'm coming to understand her reasons."

"Wow, Adem. I had no idea." There was a pause. "Do you love her?"

At least there was one member of their family who understood what was truly important.

No, make that two. Because his brother had just hit the nail on the head. He loved the woman.

"Hell. I think I do. But I'm pretty sure I've screwed everything up." He dragged a hand through his hair. "I'll talk to her, but I can't make any promises."

"Then don't. Just talk to her." There was a pause. "Let's make this generation of Keplers different from the last and learn to lead with our hearts."

"I don't know if I can do that."

"Yes. You can. You just don't know if you will."

With that, Basir hung up the phone, leaving Adem staring off into the distance.

His brother was right. He could. But he wasn't sure if he would. Or if he should. But what he could do was take away Carly's reasons for leaving the clinic by doing something he'd mentioned to her right after she'd discovered she was pregnant. She'd been vehemently opposed at the time, but now she might find herself relieved. Hadn't he said that no one person was irreplaceable?

So he was faced with one of the hardest decisions he'd ever made. Do what was in Carly's best interest. Or his own.

The answer to that seemed pretty damned simple and yet so damned hard. But what choice did he have?

None, if he wanted to do the right thing.

Taking a deep breath, he picked up the phone and dialed her number.

Carly listened to the voice mail for the third time, unable to believe her ears. Adem was going to resign?

Basir had to have told him about their phone conversation. She should have called Adem first, but she hadn't wanted him to try to talk her out of transferring to the hospital.

But to say he was going to quit so that she didn't have to?

God. She should have answered that call. But she'd been a mess. And now, unfortunately, he'd beaten her to the punch. She hadn't yet turned her paperwork in for the transfer; she'd wanted to notify her patients first. Maybe she'd been putting off the inevitable for as long as possible. But if she did it now, then they might both wind up at the hospital, working together all over again, in a huge dose of irony.

Her head was completely better, no residual headache, and her pregnancy was still going strong, thank God. Both were things to rejoice over. She hadn't seen Adem, but after the way they'd left things, she wasn't surprised that he hadn't tried to call her. Until now.

He'd probably felt as awkward as she did. But now that she was well enough to contemplate going into his office and setting things straight—to put them back the way they'd been before the accident—she found she might be too late.

He said he was going to make it official at the next hospital board meeting, but that until then he would do as much of his work as possible at his office at the hospital, so she wouldn't have to see him.

Wouldn't have to see him?

Why? Why? Why?

The thought of him being gone forever pecked at her insides, turning them into a war zone, even though she'd been the one who'd originally planned on leaving.

That last sentence of his voice mail had been a joke. *Things at the clinic will continue just like usual.*

No. No, they wouldn't.

A thin stream of anger bubbled up inside of her. He was being ridiculous. Her thoughts whirled back to almost a month ago when she'd first told him about her pregnancy. He'd thought about resigning then, but she thought she'd talked him out of it. And now they were back where they started. All because he'd asked her to marry him.

Love had to flow both ways to be viable.

Hadn't he said he would never get married, that he didn't want to live like his parents did? He wasn't even willing to *pretend*.

He'd had a strange intensity in his voice after the accident when he'd talked about marriage. One that hadn't been there in his earlier discussions.

Her heart picked up the pace. After she'd told him she would never, ever marry him, he acted strangely. She remembered thinking that she would have to talk to him once she was better to figure out how to get them back to the place they were before. And then he'd left the room, saying he would check on her later. But he hadn't. She actually hadn't heard from him again, until that phone call, which she now found odd. More than odd.

He'd been so worried about her when she was fading from consciousness in that car, and then again at the hospital.

And then he'd asked her to marry him.

Carly...we could be.

The way he'd looked at her. The way he'd said it.

Had he really meant it? As something more than what his parents had?

He'd never said love, had never even hinted that that's what was behind the proposal.

But what if it was? What if it really did flow both ways?

She mulled those words over in her mind. She knew he cared about her. Her mom told her that he'd used that exact wording when they'd spoken together in the waiting room.

But what about love?

Her head came up, the emotionless tones from Adem's voice mail forgotten. Why had she been so fervent in her rejection of what he'd asked her.

Because she didn't want to marry if it wasn't for love.

But... What. If. It. Was?

Adem had told her he'd never felt love. Didn't even believe in the emotion. But what if that had changed?

She loved him. But could he possibly...by some stretch of the imagination...?

Her thoughts whirled back through a hundred different images. Herself with her hands against that glass window. In the park, telling him about the baby, and how his face had changed when he realized he was going to be a father. On the boat laughing over silly baby names. In the hospital as he stood over her, concern and…fear…on his face. The urgency behind his offer of marriage.

That's why his proposal had seemed so horrifying to her. And why she'd ultimately decided to leave the clinic. She'd wanted him to love her. Wanted that marriage proposal to come out of the right place.

Maybe it had.

Maybe that's why he was suddenly so ready to leave the clinic so that she didn't have to. Sacrificing himself for her, in the same way she'd been ready to do for him.

She swallowed hard. Could it be that easy? And that impossibly hard?

So what did she do? Just let things remain like they were? Let Adem leave the clinic for her?

Hell, no.

The man had made her fall in love with him, despite her best attempts at thwarting Cupid's barrage of arrows. The least he could do was stand there and tell her what she meant to him. What *they* meant to him, because she and the baby were kind of a package deal at the moment.

She just had to somehow confront him where he couldn't get up and run away. Or resign. Where he would have to sit and tell her exactly what she did or didn't mean to him.

And she thought she knew the perfect place.

All she had to do was get a little help from a certain brainy cellist, who'd already laid the perfect foundation for what Carly had in mind.

CHAPTER TEN

ADEM DIDN'T KNOW why he was here.

Shepherd Hall was built to impress, with white marble columns and polished steps that led up to the huge venue. It was where countless concerts and musicals took place.

Standing at the base of the stairs with people streaming around him, he hesitated, ticket in hand.

Carly's mom had called him and reissued her invitation—the one she'd given at the hospital—asking him to attend her orchestra's first concert of the season. Had kept him on the phone until he promised to come.

Maybe she didn't know that he would soon be gone from the clinic, or that he and Carly hadn't spoken since that last day at the hospital.

He could have refused to attend. It had been on the tip of his tongue to say he had other plans, but something had made him accept the complimentary ticket. Maybe the faint hope that he would catch a glimpse of Carly somewhere in the crowded theater. She said she always attended her mother's first concert of the season.

Find her among all these people? Not likely.

Damn. He loved her. And the baby. It seemed like

that should have solved all of his problems. Instead, it seemed to have compounded them.

Unless he tried again. Unless he sat down with Carly and had a long talk. They'd tried on the boat. And he'd tried at the hospital. But their connections just kept getting crossed.

So why not try to uncross them. He hadn't exactly bared his soul during his ridiculous proposal. Instead, he'd made it sound like something out of his father's playbook instead of his own.

Basir's suggestion that this generation should get off to a fresh start made sense. And was part of the reason he'd agreed to come.

And if Carly really was here somewhere? Well, he would never find her...unless...

Moving out of the line of people surging up the steps, he pulled his phone out of the pocket of his tuxedo and found her in his contact list. Just as he started to dial the number a hand linked through his arm.

He glanced to the side, ready with an apology, when green eyes met his.

"Carly?"

With her red hair piled on top of her head, and dark sultry liner beneath her lashes, she was almost unrecognizable. And that dress...

Damn. It wasn't the navy blue she'd been carrying all those weeks ago at the hospital. This was raven black and devastating to the senses, the gathered bodice hugging her form like a glove, before billowing out into a soft cloud of fabric. She was stunning. Sophisticated. The very picture of the woman he'd imagined didn't exist, once upon a time. A woman who'd shown him just how much fun she could have, taking him on a ride to a distant land. Where things were different from how he'd believed them to be.

"Hello, Adem. I see you have a ticket too."

Was this real? Or had he somehow conjured her up?

"Yes. Compliments of your mother."

A passing thought slid through his head, and he grabbed it. "Do you think she's playing matchmaker?"

"Nope. My mom would never do that." Her fingers tightened on his arm. "But I might."

She sounded like that siren who'd once caused him to abandon his dinner just to hold her in his arms. The siren who'd comforted him when he'd been in a pit of despair.

The siren who now carried his child.

And he hoped to God he understood what she was saying.

"You're playing matchmaker?"

"I am. Interested?"

He cupped her face in his hands and stared down at her. Yes, he saw the playful temptress in there, but he also saw hints of a vulnerable woman trying to find her way through this thing called life.

That was okay. Because right now, he was a vulnerable man, trying to do the same.

"I am interested. More than you can imagine actually. But I have one condition."

She frowned. "What's that?"

"That there are no more games, and that you tell me exactly how you feel about me."

Her frown disappeared, and a slow smile appeared.

"That's easy. Very easy. I love you." She wrapped her arms around his waist. "I have a condition of my own."

"Okay…"

"I want you to tear up whatever resignation letter you might be drafting."

"Done. How about if neither one of us leaves the clinic?"

"But I don't want to cause problems if people—"

He silenced her with a kiss. "There are husband and wife doctor teams at hospitals everywhere. Why not a surgeon/midwife team. It seems we worked pretty well together once upon a time." His thumbs stroked her jawline, glorying when he felt her shiver. "And before you say anything, that's not why I asked you to marry me that day in your hospital room. I loved you then. I didn't know it at the time, but I was desperate to get you to say yes. And so I spouted off a reason that seemed rational at the time, but in doing so, I left off the most important reason of all. The only one worth saying yes to: love."

He pressed his forehead to hers, wondering if Carly's mum really had read his thoughts that day at the hospital. "Carolyn Eliston. Will you marry me? For love, this time?"

Carly stood on her tiptoes, pressing her cheek to his. "Yes. Oh yes. But only for love."

The meeting of lips was long and luscious and full of all things good and honest and real. When he pulled back she was breathless and smiling. And damn if she didn't glow.

Well, that was okay, because he was walking on air.

"Shall we go in and watch the orchestra?"

"Yes. And then afterward we can go back to your place."

Adem laughed and then wrapped his arm around her waist as they walked up the steps. "You read my mind. You'll be happy to know that I've revamped my tour program to include several new and exciting stops."

As they found their seats and the sound of the symphony swirled around them in the intimacy of the dark theater, Adem proceeded to whisper them to her, one sexy destination at a time.

EPILOGUE

ADEM TOLD HIS parents the news a few days later as she stood beside him in support, fingers linked together. He'd told her more about his folks' strained relationship, telling her that he wanted his marriage to Carly to be completely different. If anything, it made her love him even more.

His father's forbidding frown gave way to a softer look as he listened as Adem explained how much he loved Carly and how important it was to both of them that they start off their marriage knowing they had each other's support and love.

"So I am to be a grandfather twice? Both you *and* Basir?"

"Yes. Both of us."

Adem's mom glanced at her husband. "Isn't this great news, Selim?"

"Yes. It is."

And the strangest thing happened. Selim's arm slid around his wife's waist, making her eyes widen for a second before she turned back to the front, a slight smile playing at her lips.

Adem leaned down and kissed Carly's temple in a

display that was far more open than that of his parents, but from what he'd told her, even something as simple as an arm around a waist was a major departure from what the pair had shared before.

Maybe this was a new start for everyone. Carly hoped so. And whether things changed permanently for Adem's parents or not, all she knew was that she was never going back to the life she'd had before.

Oh, she intended to stay independent, but the moments of loneliness she'd had before were gone. She knew that she and her baby were both loved for who they were.

And Carly intended to take nothing for granted. She was going to enjoy every minute she got to spend with the man she loved.

And she knew that Adem had vowed to do the same. They were getting married. The sooner, the better.

Not because they had to, but because they loved each other.

And that love was enough to carry them through for the rest of their lives.

* * * * *

MILLS & BOON

Coming next month

A FLING TO STEAL HER HEART
Sue MacKay

Raphael let himself into the house and stopped. Paint fumes hit him. A foreign lightness in the hall made him gape. Wow. What a difference. Should've done it years ago. Except there'd been no motivation before. Izzy had changed everything.

She stood at the bottom of the stairs, dressed in over-large paint-spattered overalls with a roller in one hand and a wide grin on her face. A paint smear streaked across her cheek. Cute. Sexy. 'What do you think?'

I think I want to kiss that spot.

His stomach crunched, his blood hummed.

I think I want to kiss your soft lips and taste you.

Forget humming. There was a torrent in his veins. He was over waiting, being patient, giving her time. He had to do something about his feelings for her.

Dragging his eyes away from the sight that had him in melt-down, he looked around at the white with a hint of grey walls, woodwork, ceiling, and felt his mouth lifting into a smile that grew and grew. 'Amazing. Who'd have believed getting rid of that magenta could make such a difference. This hall is twice the size it was when I went to work this morning.'

'That's a relief.' She placed the roller in the clean tray.

'You were worried I wouldn't like it?' He stepped closer, put his keys and phone on the bottom stair and stood there watching the varying emotions flitting through her beautiful old-wood-coloured eyes.

'Not really.' Her teeth nibbling her lip told him otherwise.

He had to force himself not to reach over and place a finger on her lips to stop her action. 'Why wouldn't I? It was me who bought the paint two years ago.'

Izzy shifted her weight from one foot to the other, then lifted her head enough to lock those eyes on his. 'I worried I've overstepped the mark by doing this without telling you what I was up to.'

Izzy never worried about upsetting him. Carrying on with whatever she thought best was a trademark of their friendship, always had been, and was one of the reasons he adored her. Something was off centre here, and it frustrated him not knowing what that was. 'Relax. I'm more than happy with what you've done. In fact, I'm blown away.' He waved a hand at his new hall. 'This is amazing. It fires me up to get on with doing up the rest of the house.'

He hadn't noticed the tension in her shoulders until they softened, and a smile touched those lips. 'Thank you, Isabella.'

Her eyes widened and she glanced away, came back to lock eyes with him again. The tip of her tongue appeared at the corner of her mouth. 'Phew.'

Raphael could not stop himself. He reached out, placed his hands on her arms and drew her closer. 'Again, thanks. By doing this you've starting turning my house into a home and up until now I hadn't realised how important it is if I'm to continue living here and become ensconced in a London lifestyle, not just working at the hospital every available hour.'

She was shaking under his hands.

His thumbs smoothed circles on her arms. 'Izzy.'

Her breasts rose, stilled, dropped again. 'Rafe.'

Afterwards he didn't remember moving, couldn't recall anything but his mouth on hers at last. Soft. Sweet. Isabella. Strong, tough Izzy. Returning his kiss. Returning his kiss!

Continue reading
A FLING TO STEAL HER HEART
Sue MacKay

Available next month
www.millsandboon.co.uk

COMING SOON!

We really hope you enjoyed reading this book. If you're looking for more romance, be sure to head to the shops when new books are available on

Thursday 20th March

To see which titles are coming soon, please visit
millsandboon.co.uk/nextmonth

LET'S TALK

Romance

For exclusive extracts, competitions
and special offers, find us online: